A Kiss in the Dark
A Novel

Mary R. Butler

To Elicia Burroghs
Thanks for your support!
You're a great person!

Love

10/7/06

GOT Publishing

A Green Olive Tree Publication

Published by

Green Olive Tree Publishing
P.O. BOX 337
Barnesville, GA 30204-0337
http://www.got-publishing.com

ISBN-13 978-0-9636963-5-9
ISBN-10 0-9636963-5-1

LCCN 2006930087

This book is a work of fiction. Names, characters, places and incidents are products of the author's imagination or are used fictitiously. Any resemblance to actual events or locales or persons, living or dead, is entirely coincidental.

First Printing

Cover designed by Pattie Sullivan

Holy Scripture taken from the
Bible, New International Version®.
Copyright © 1973, 1978, 1984
International Bible Society.
Used by permission of Zondervan.
All rights reserved.

In memory of my parents, Willie and Thelma
&
Dedicated to my loving and supportive husband, Michael

"The tongue has the power of life and death, and those who love it will eat its fruit." Proverbs 18:21

Book One

Chapter 1

1989

It was late Saturday evening when ten-year-old Travis Malcolm and Billy Ray rode their new bikes to the Silver Rock State Park. Riding proved difficult as the two boys held onto their fishing rods, stopping every now and then to readjust their load.

"Don't lose our bait," Billy warned Travis.

Travis pulled the knapsack's shoulder strap from his arms and looked inside the bag. Satisfied that the can of worms was still in place, he closed the bag and put it back on his shoulders. "Everything's okay," he said, putting his foot on the pedal. "Let's go."

Billy looked at his watch. "Yeah. It's getting late; and I want to catch something before Mattie sends my old man looking for me. He's been getting on my nerves since Mama died."

"Yeah, I know." Travis nodded his head. "It's a shame your mama had to leave you like that."

"Leave?" Billy glanced at Travis. "She didn't leave. She died." Billy looked up toward the sky.

He became silent and he reflected on one particular Sunday, when Edna, his mother, had taken him to their church, "Lilly of the Valley Church." It wasn't a large church, but it was clean and comfortable. The preacher stood in the ordinary, simple pulpit and declared, "Jesus is the Way, the Truth and the Life!"

"Yes sir!" came the reply and it swept spontaneously through the congregation.

"He's the only way!" one of the church deaconesses shouted.

1

The organist began to play.

Someone in the back of the church shouted, "Hallelujah! Praise the Lord!"

The preacher grabbed his white handkerchief from the podium and wiped his sweaty face, before shouting, "Christ called the twelve together, these twelve were closer to the Lord. But there were other disciples. The first twelve paved the way. He called the twelve to follow him, and they stopped whatever they were doing and followed him. Church this morning I'm asking, are you ready to surrender everything including your life to follow Jesus? We're in a battle for the souls of individuals. What value do we place upon a soul? What's God value of souls? He sent his Son Jesus to die for us. We have no excuse. Jesus told the disciples to go to the house of Israel. Don't take anything with you because you'll learn how to depend on me."

"Yeeesss!" A middle-age woman shouted from the front row.

"Speak Holy Ghost," another woman sitting behind the middle-age woman shouted.

"Ministry has to be the heart, not just getting paid." Pastor Nicholson wiped his face and stepped from behind the podium and walked closer to the edge of the steps leading down to the congregation.

"Yes! Yes!" A man shouted from the back of the congregation.

"God said I'm not going to show you any tangible reward, I'm going to see if you're committed to me without the reward. The reward will come; it might be here on earth or in Heaven. Church, listen, I'm asking you this morning to ask yourself, am I still committed as I once was? Am I still willing to put my life on the line for souls? Have we become ingrown? Is it about people's souls or about us? The word of God transforms lives and the power of God backs it up. Our thing is do we want Jesus now? Do you want Jesus?" Pastor Nicholson's voice boomed throughout the church.

"Yes sir!" half of the congregation leaped to their feet.

"Jesus is the Light of the world. He's the King of kings and the Lord of lords. He's the Bread that came down from Heaven. He's the Resurrection, the Truth and the Life. He's the God that heals us! Don't shout me down now, can I get an Amen?" Pastor Nicholson shouted.

"Amen!" The people cried out.

"Thank you Jeesssus!" an older man stood up raising his hands high above his head, rocking back and forth.

"Hallelujah!" Billy's mother shouted as she raised her left hand in the air. "Thank you sweet Jesus!" Tears began to roll swiftly down her pretty round face. Then she bent over and whispered in Billy's ear. "Remember, Son," she said wiping her tears with her handkerchief, "Jesus is the answer to everything. He loves you and no matter what you do in life, you can't stop him from loving you. He's full of grace, mercy and compassion. Remember, He loves you."

Those words had meant something to him then, but now they lingered in the cold grave with his mother. She had been ill, and if Jesus was the answer, why didn't He help her?

"My dad said she's in Heaven." Travis said, ignoring Billy's silence. Billy didn't answer. "Billy!" Travis shouted, breaking Billy's focus on his mother.

"Huh?" Billy frowned looking at Travis.

"My daddy said your mother is in Heaven." Travis answered in a frustrated tone. He didn't like repeating himself.

Billy shrugged his shoulders. "I guess. I don't know if there really is a Heaven."

"You don't believe there's a Heaven? That's stupid. Everyone knows there's a Heaven." Travis said, disturbed by his friend's comment.

"How do you know there's a Heaven?" Billy scolded.

"Because Mama and Daddy said there's one. Reverend Simon talks about it every Sunday at church." Travis said defiantly challenging his friend to get out of this one.

"Okay, smart-aleck, since you know so much, why did God take my mama?"

Billy knew Travis had challenged him and he wasn't the one to back down from a good challenge.

"Maybe God didn't take your mama." Travis walked his bike around Billy. "Maybe she asked God to."

"That's crazy. Why would she want to do a thing like that?"

"I don't know," Travis said dismissing the question with a gesture of his hand. "C'mon let's go fishing before it gets dark."

"Yeah. Lead the way. I'm with you," Billy said, as he rode behind

Travis.

****

"Where is that son of yours, Darrell? I swear, that boy's gonna make me leave this house," Mattie warned Darrell Ray, pointing a long, bony finger at him. "I asked him to take out the garbage. Would you please take out the garbage? I begged him, but look." She pointed at the overrun, stuffed garbage can. "You need to make that child mind me."

"I'll take it out." Darrell picked up the can, but Mattie grabbed it from him.

"No-o-o, you ain't gonna take it out. That no-good son of yours is gonna take it out. I mean that." She returned the garbage can to its place, and then put both hands on her hips. "I'm tired of that boy. I should have never let you talk me into moving in here with you after your wife died last year."

"Don't talk like that," Darrell said, trying to hug Mattie. She pushed him away.

"Now, don't you be in here trying to give me none of your sour loving. You're gonna have to do somethin' 'bout that son of yours. It's either gonna be him or me. And another thing. Don't you think I don't see you walking around this house looking at Edna's old pictures? You're gonna have to get her out of your mind. I'm with you now, not your sanctified wife." She looked at the garbage and frowned. "By the way things look, I ain't gonna be here long, either." She stormed out of the kitchen.

"Mattie, don't talk like that." Darrell followed her to the living room. "When Billy comes home, I'll deal with him." He glanced at Edna's large portrait over the fireplace mantle. "Those pictures of Edna don't mean a thing to me."

"Yeah? Is that right?" Mattie rolled her eyes over the large portrait of Edna hanging over the fireplace.

"Yeah," he replied.

"Well, if the pictures of your wife don't mean nothing to you, then get rid of them. All my friends think I'm crazy living in here with you, and all Edna's pictures hanging on the walls." She put her hands on her bony hips. "I must be crazy for letting them stay up for so long. I'm the laughing stock of Silver Rock," she said, as she sat on the sofa.

"I'll take them down, if that's what you want." He sat beside her.

"That's what I want." She crossed her arms.

Darrell stood up from the sofa, walked into the kitchen, then back into the living room with a large trash bag. He began taking Edna's pictures off the wall.

"See? I'm taking them down," he said, as he busied himself with the task.

"Good. We got one thing settled," she said, as she watched Darrell take the pictures from the wall. "And don't let that boy of yours talk you into putting them back up again."

"No. It's about time he gets his mama out of his head." Darrell looked back at Mattie. "I should have done this a long time ago."

"That's what's the matter with him. Y'all let that child have his way too much. Edna was always babying that boy."

"Edna couldn't help it. Billy was her only child and—"

"Don't try to get soft with me, Darrell Ray, or you'll find yourself sleeping on the sofa." She looked at her watch, and then glanced out the window. "I thought I heard you tell him to be back before dark."

"I did." Darrell put the bag down and looked out the window.

"Don't you think you better go and find the spoiled brat?"

"He's with Travis. They'll be all right." He resumed taking the pictures down.

"Those pictures can wait. I want Mr. Billy in this house to take out that garbage. He's gonna learn to mind me, if nothing else."

"Come on, Mattie. He'll take out the trash when he gets here. I'll see to that." He stopped taking the pictures down, walked over to the sofa, and sat beside her. "I'll see that he minds you from now on."

"How are you gonna do that?"

"If I've got to take my belt off, I will."

"A lot of good that's gonna do. That boy is getting too big for you to handle with a belt. What he needs is a hickory stick or an extension cord." She rolled her eyes at Darrell, and cocked her head to one side. "Just like my mama used to whip my sister, Urla Mae, and me."

"If that's what it's going to take to get him to mind you. Then I'll use those things, too." He leaned closer to her to kiss her, but she pushed his face away, pushed herself up from the sofa, and walked towards the bedroom. She turned her head and looked at him "Don't start nothing you can't finish. If you can't put fear in your son, don't come knocking at my door tonight," she said as she slammed the door.

* * * * * * * * * *

The two boys were having so much fun that dark came upon them before they realized it. Travis caught less fish than Billy, and Billy wasted no time reminding him of that fact.

"Aah, you're just lucky," Travis grinned.

"What's luck got to do with it? I'm a better fisherman than you, that's all," he laughed.

"You better be glad that it's getting dark, or I'd out fish you, and you know it."

"I can out-fish you any old day. Talking about dark. You're crazy. Fish don't know that it's dark."

"These fish do," Travis laughed.

"That's crazy," Billy laughed.

"Don't you think we better be getting back? You know how angry your stepmother gets." Travis looked seriously at Billy.

He hated when Mattie stared at him all mean and stuff. She'd look at him evil-like and had a way of making him feel uncomfortable. He didn't know how Billy could stand to live in the same house with her. She disliked Billy, and Billy didn't hide the fact that it was mutual. Billy's father, Darrell Ray, seemed too nice to have a woman like that. She always told him what to do, no matter how miserable the task. Travis felt sorry for Billy's father, but more so for Billy. To lose a mother and then have to get used to a total stranger like Mattie. Travis thought it wasn't fair.

"Travis!" Billy yelled. "Don't you hear me?"

"What?" Travis turned and looked at Billy. "What are you shouting for?"

"I was talking to you and you weren't paying me any mind."

"What did you say?"

"I said don't be calling Mattie my stepmother. She and my father aren't married. I can't stand the woman. I don't see what he sees in her, anyway."

"Me, neither," Travis laughed. "You see how she eats?"

"Oink, oink!" Both boys laughed.

"C'mon, we better get going. It's dark. I'm sure my parents are probably worrying now." Travis picked up his rod and took his three small fish from the lake.

"Yeah." Billy followed suit. He took his six large fish from the water and held them up again for Travis to see.

"Aah, go away." Travis swatted his hand at Billy.

"Don't be mad 'cause I caught bigger and more fish than you," he grinned. Both boys put their fish inside the smelly knapsack.

"I hope Daddy cooks these tonight," Travis said, putting the knapsack on his back.

"I don't care if my daddy doesn't cook mine. I want him to see how many I caught."

"Would Mattie clean them?" Travis watched Billy. Both boys shook their head and said, "Naww!" They laughed as they rode away from the lake through the park.

The streets lights lit the way for Travis and Billy, as they rode their bikes down the noisy street full of children, playing red light-green light. They could see people sitting on their porches trying to keep cool. Travis scanned one of the houses, and saw Dora Echols kissing Harvey Freeman in front of the window again. It seemed like it was her favorite spot, as if she wanted to be seen.

The street smelled familiar, as Travis and Billy pedaled their bikes. It smelled like home. Travis was happy he lived on the same street as his friend. He and Billy had lived across from each other since kindergarten. He knew Billy well and looked up to him, even though they were the same age. Billy had problems with Mattie and Darrell, but he knew that Billy could take care of himself.

"We're here," Travis said, stopping his bike in his driveway. "Do you want to come in?" he asked, as he took Billy's fish out of the knapsack.

"No, I'd better be getting home myself," he said, reaching for the fish. Billy turned his bike into his drive. "I'll talk to you tomorrow. See ya," Billy shouted at Travis and pedaled up the driveway.

"Okay." Travis parked his bike under the carport and went inside.
Billy parked his bike and walked inside the house.

"Where have you been, Billy?" Darrell asked him as he walked into the house. "You got Mattie mad at me about nothing, all 'cause you want to go running all over the place. Didn't she ask you to take out the trash? Why didn't you take it out?"

Darrell grabbed him before he had a chance to defend himself. "I'm going to teach you a lesson. I'm going to soften that hard head of yours."

"I…" Billy choked on his words.

Darrell grabbed a brown extension cord from the sofa. He released Billy, and hit him repeatedly with it. Billy stood there silently without flinching.

Mattie walked quickly out of the bedroom with a big smile on her face; she sat down on the chair near the window. She wanted a ringside seat.

Darrell hit Billy again and again with the extension cord, but he just stood there as big red welts developed. "Boy, you're going to mind Mattie. You hear me?" Darrell said to Billy, who stood like a statue.

What's the matter with him? He ain't even hollering. Mattie paused and appeared to be thinking. She put one finger up and said, "I know. He's trying you, that's it. That boy is full of the devil. Beat it out of him, Darrell!" She sat back on the chair, happy that Billy was getting what he deserved. "That's all that child needs is a good beating."

"I hate you! I hate you! I hate you!" Billy spoke the words to Darrell all too softly, and then screamed, "I HATE YOU!" before running out of the house.

"See? I told you. That boy is full of the devil."

Billy threw the fish down on the front porch. He was holding them when Darrell had begun to beat him with the extension cord. He hopped on his bike.

"Hey, Billy! Where are you going?" Travis shouted across the street.

Billy didn't answer.

"Hey, Billy! Don't you hear me?" Travis said, walking across the street.

Billy ignored Travis and rushed passed him, speeding down the driveway.

"Wait!" Travis yelled at Billy. He hurried back to his house, jumped on his bike, and took off behind Billy. "Hey, wait up!" he shouted, trying to catch up with his friend.

Billy led Travis back to the semi-dark park near the lake. He jumped off his bike and ran out toward the water. Travis leaped from his bike before making a complete stop, and ran off behind him.

"What are you doing?" he asked, now standing beside Billy. "Why did you take off like that? Didn't you hear me?" He tried to catch his breath, as the words tumbled out of his mouth.

"Leave me alone!" Billy responded.

"I won't leave you alone. What's the matter with you?"

"Nothing's the matter," he replied.

Under the glow of the park's light that stood a few feet away from the boys, Travis could see big red marks on Billy's arms and a sharp reddish mark on the side of his face. "What happened to you?" he asked, looking at the welts.

"Nothing happened." Billy turned his back to Travis. "Just leave me alone."

"I can't leave you by yourself. Who knows what could happen to you out here?" He looked around the park. "Besides, you're my best friend, and best friends don't leave best friends when they're hurting."

"Who said I'm hurting?" Billy turned facing him.

"What are those marks?" He pointed at Billy's arms and face.

"Nothing."

"How can they be nothing when I'm looking at them?" Travis asked.

"I want you to go home. I didn't ask you to follow me out here."

"I know. I came because, like I said, I don't want to see you hurt."

Billy walked away from Travis, but Travis stopped him. Billy pushed himself away from Travis' grasp, mounted his bike, and rode away. Travis hurried to his bike, followed him out the park and back onto the road.

"I'm not riding all over town with you," Travis shouted. "You're going to have to tell me sooner or later."

"Go home, then!" Billy shouted at Travis. "Go home!"

"I'm not going anywhere, until you tell me what's the matter with you."

"I'm not telling you anything."

Travis sped up behind him. Seeing that he was close enough to him, he rammed his bike into Billy's rear tire. Billy's bike skidded and sent him crashing to the hard pavement.

"Why'd you do that?" Billy sat up on the road and watched Travis. He rubbed his hand. "I'm going to get you!" He stood up and rushed towards Travis.

Travis leaped off his bike and braced himself for the impact. Billy ran into Travis, and both boys hit the pavement. They rolled around on the road, then onto the grass beside the road. The two boys huffed and puffed, as they tried to hold one another down.

"Give up?" Billy shouted to Travis, as he straddled him, pinning Travis' hands to the ground.

"No. Get off of me!" Travis shouted back. Travis kicked and kicked, trying to get Billy off of him.

"Say 'uncle'," Billy teased him.

"I'm not saying that." He tried wiggling himself free. "I'm going to get you! Get off me!"

"Say 'uncle'."

"No!" Travis mustered all of his strength and kicked wildly on the ground, until Billy couldn't constrain him any longer. They rolled across the grass again. This time, Travis ended up on top.

Travis looked down, examining the scrapes on his arms and hands. "Look what you did. I'm going to get you for this."

"Get in line," Billy replied, pushing the other boy off. "My daddy did."

"What are you talking about?" Travis sat up, his anger melted into concern.

"Those little scratches on you aren't nothing compared to what I got." He sat closer to Travis. "See these welts on me? Well, my daddy decided to give me a whipping for not taking the trash out like Mattie told me."

"He hit you?"

"Beat me, more like it."

"For not taking out the trash?"

"Mattie told him that she had asked me to take it out, but I didn't want to mind her or something like that. Before I knew what was happening, he jumped on me with a cord."

"What did you do?"

"I wanted him to feel bad. So I refused to cry for him, or for Mattie."

"You stood there without crying?" Travis pictured Billy getting beat by his father and showing no emotion. "That made them mad, huh?"

"I hope so." Billy watched Travis.

"You want to stay at my house tonight?" Travis asked, looking around in the dark. "I didn't tell anyone that I was leaving. I know my father is looking for me. He was meeting me outside to help me clean my fish. That's what I was doing when I saw you, setting up a place with newspaper."

"I don't think my daddy will let me stay at your house tonight."

"I'll ask my father to ask him."

"I don't think that's going to work, either." Billy's tone was dismal.

"Why?"

"Mattie. That's why."

"Oh. Yeah." Travis sounded dismal.

"I'm glad you came."

"Huh?" Travis sounded surprised.

"I'm glad you're my friend." Billy stood up and extended his hand to Travis to help his friend up. Travis took his arm and hoisted himself to his feet. "Sorry for jumping on you like that," Billy said.

"It's okay. What are friends for if they can't fight each other every once in a while?" Travis stood beside Billy, grinning.

"Don't you get any ideas," Billy laughed. "C'mon let's go. I'm in enough trouble as it is."

"Me, too."

The two boys hopped on their bikes and rode home without talking, each lost in their own thoughts.

* * * * * * * * * *

"Well, what did Mr. Malcolm say?" Mattie asked Darrell, as soon as he walked into the house.

"He hadn't seen Billy. But Travis is missing, too." He walked into the house, holding a string of fish, "I guess he caught these." He held them up for Mattie to see.

"Get those smelly, nasty things out of here!" Mattie yelled. "I don't want that mess in my house."

"They're just fish, Mattie. The boy caught them. I think I should clean them."

He walked into the kitchen with the fish. "Where's my sharp knife?"

"If you're gonna clean them, carry them outdoors. Don't be stinking up my house!" She walked into the kitchen. "Here's the knife." She reached in the food pantry door, retrieved the knife from the empty coffee canister, and handed it to him.

He carried the knife, fish, and newspaper out on the back porch. Afterward, he brought the cleaned fish back inside and washed them in the sink. Darrell put the fish in a freezer bag with some salt, placed them in the chest freezer, and shuffled over to the sofa and sat down.

"Oh, no, Mister. You ain't sittin' on my chair smelling like fish. You need to take a shower, and put on some clean clothes."

Darrell sighed, stood up, and stomped into the bathroom to take a shower. When he returned, clean and freshly showered, he sat down on the sofa beside her. "Are you satisfied, now?"

"Yeah. I swear we'd be sitting in an outhouse if it wasn't for me to keep things clean around here."

"It's not that bad."

"Bad enough." She got up to change the TV station. "You still ain't told me what Mr. Malcolm said." Mattie assumed her position on the sofa beside him.

"He said Travis should have been outside waiting for him to clean his fish, but when he got out there, Travis was gone. He's mad at his boy, too, running off and not telling him or his mother."

"That Travis Malcolm and Billy are up to no good. I hate to see that boy from 'cross the street come over to this house. His eyes are too shifty for me. My mama said shifty-eyed people steal." She took Darrell's arm and placed it around her shoulders. "But that's all right. You did give that boy a beatin', and that's good in my book."

"I didn't beat him enough. I should have run outside behind him and beat his black behind on the street. That's what I should have done. Then, he wouldn't have you and me sitting in here worrying about him now."

"That child's gonna be all right. Anybody full of the devil is always all right. You know that."

"It's like you said, I need to start beating that child more. Beat the devil out of him, and see how he likes that."

"Don't beat him tonight. Wait until tomorrow and get him. Tonight, I got plans for you and me." She got up and turned off the TV. She beckoned him with her finger.

"Are you coming to bed?" she asked, walking to the bedroom.

Darrell Ray stood up and followed Mattie into the bedroom. He shut the door behind them.

Billy peeped inside the house. When he saw the coast was clear, he crept through the unlocked front door and tiptoed into his bedroom. He didn't turn on the lights. He got in bed fully dressed, in case he needed to make a run for it later on that night.

Meanwhile, Travis' father sent him to bed without any dinner. He lay in his bed and thought about the events of that evening. Travis had respect for Billy's father, but now he didn't know what to think. He knew Billy's father missed his wife, because he had heard Mr. Ray and his father talking one night in the den. He thought he had heard Mr. Ray cry softly in the room. He couldn't really make it out. He had pressed his ear closer to the door, before his mother caught him eavesdropping on the two men. She had scolded him and made him go to bed. Angry with her, he jerked away from her. She whacked him for his rebellious attitude. That really made him angry, but he humbled himself and walked away from her to his bedroom.

As he lay in the dark room, he wondered if Billy was getting another beating from his father. He felt sorry for Billy, but Billy didn't like any one to feel that way for him. Now he was at home in his own bed and could feel sorry for Billy as much as he wanted to. He thought about his parents and compared them to Billy's father. He knew he had the better deal.

As he continued to lie there, he no longer heard the sound of children. The sounds were replaced by barking dogs in the distance. He tried to sleep, but it eluded him as he tossed from one side of the bed to the other. He was glad that his father didn't beat him the way Billy's father had beat Billy tonight. He was glad that it was Billy's mother that had died and not his own. Travis didn't want to think that way, and hated the fact that Billy's mother had died, but he was still happy that it wasn't his mother. He felt ashamed for being happy that both of his parents were alive, and he sure was glad that Mattie was not his stepmother. *Billy had to put up with a beating from his father and with a stepmother like Mattie.* Life wasn't fair. Surprised, Travis felt warm tears roll swiftly from the corner of his eyes. He quickly wiped them. He was glad that Billy wasn't around to see him crying like a little girl. It would be all he needed, to be taunted by Billy the rest of the summer.

Silence finally blanketed the small town of Silver Rock. He could no longer hear the barking dogs. Travis looked at the clock on the nightstand. Time had slipped away. Soon it would be light, and he hadn't slept a wink. He pulled the covers up to his head and turned away from the clock. He thought about Billy and the fish. Then he began to count fish, "One fish, two fish, three, fish, four..." He drifted off to sleep.

* * * * * * * * * *

"Hey, sir," Travis said, hesitantly, watching Mr. Ray. He didn't know what to say, or even how to say it, if he did. But Mr. Ray looked at him and nodded his head.

"I guess you're looking for Billy?"

"Yes, sir," Travis said, as he stood in front of the screen door.

"I don't know whether I ought to let you see him today or not, seeing that you two caused trouble for me last night." He frowned, and then looked through the screen at Travis. "Yeah, I reckon I ought to keep Mr. Billy in today, since he wants to think that he's all grown and stuff, running away from here last night."

"But, ..."

"And you're in it with him. I can't believe that your daddy let you out of the house this morning." He looked across the street at Travis' house. "No, I'll teach my boy a lesson; even though, your father let you get away with murder. No, Billy won't be coming out today." He started to close the door.

"Who's that?" Mattie asked, coming to the door. "Oh, it's the other one. What do you want!" she snapped, as she glanced down the hallway toward Billy's room and shouted so he could hear her. "If

Billy is here, he's not coming out to play today, nor tomorrow. So you better high-tail it on out of here."

Travis saw the look on Mattie's face and knew he didn't have a chance to see Billy today, nor would he see his friend ever again, if Mattie had her way. She was out to punish anyone and everyone who had contact with Billy.

"Would you please tell him I dropped by?" he asked Billy's father, then turned to leave.

"He knows that you're here," Mattie said. Then she stormed away from the door.

"Billy! You better be up!" she shouted at Billy's closed bedroom door.

"I think you'd better leave," Mr. Ray said, as he closed the front door.

Travis stood on Billy's porch, and fear gripped his heart. He didn't like the look on Mr. Ray's face. He seemed confused, and something in his eyes was very wrong. He really didn't know what to think. He was only ten years old, but he would never forget that look.

Travis walked off the porch, taking two steps at a time. He leaped down to the sidewalk, then looked back at the house and shook his head. As he walked away from the house, he heard someone calling him. He glanced at the left side of the house and saw Billy.

"Psst," he hissed at Travis, peeping from behind the large hedge. "Shhh," Billy warned so he wouldn't alert anyone. He pointed to the front of the house.

Travis nodded his head and looked back at Billy's house to see if anyone was looking. The coast was clear. He ran quickly to the bush.

"What are you doing back here?"

"What do you think?" Billy whispered. "I'm trying to stay away from Darrell and Mattie." He looked passed Travis, watching for Mattie or Darrell to run out of the house looking for him.

"Yeah, I know what you mean. Your father looked pretty upset, and your mama—"

"She's not my mama!" He angrily interrupted. "I told you not to call her that again."

"Okay. Okay. I'm sorry. I didn't mean to call her that."

"It's all right. I know you didn't mean to. I'm just mad at Darrell."

Travis closely watched Billy. He had never heard Billy refer to his father as Darrell before. It sounded strange coming from his lips. If Travis were to call his father Adam, it would upset his father something terrible.

"What are you going to do? You can't stay behind this bush all day."

"Maybe I'll run away."

"That's a good idea." He smiled. "Then I can run away with you."

"We can run away tonight."

"Yeah, while everyone is asleep."

"I'm glad we're friends," Billy said. He gave Travis a high-five.

"Me, too," Travis gave him one back. "I know. Let's be more than friends. We can be brothers."

"How?"

"We can be blood brothers. I saw it done on TV. We cut our thumb and join them together while they bleed. Then we're brothers," Travis said, excitedly fishing inside his pants pocket for a small penknife his father had given him last year for his birthday.

"That's all we have to do? Cut ourselves?

"That's all."

"Okay. Let me see your knife." Billy took the knife and examined it. He turned it around in the palms of his hands. "Are you ready?" He pulled the small blade out.

"Wait," Travis said, putting his hand on the knife to keep Billy from cutting himself. "I saw in a movie that cowboys put the knife in the fire to clean it. Maybe we should, too." He looked around him. "Where are we going to get fire?"

"There's some matches in the kitchen drawer that Mattie keeps for lighting the stove."

"But how are you going to get them?"

"I don't know."

"I got it." Travis snapped his fingers. "My father keeps a box of matches in the bathroom medicine cabinet. He likes to read and smoke his pipe when he's in there. Go down to the lake, and I'll meet you there."

"How? My bike is in the front yard."

"Give me a second," Travis replied. He walked casual and

unsuspicious to the front yard. He glanced at Billy's front porch to see if anyone was watching. He waved his hand at Billy to signal that the coast was clear. Billy sneaked from behind the hedge and crawled on his knees to the front yard, keeping out of sight of his father and Mattie. He jumped on his bike and quickly rode down the driveway.

Twenty minutes later, Travis sped up to the lake. Billy was sitting underneath a shade tree. He didn't turn to face Travis, as he stopped and jumped off his bike. Travis didn't know what to think. He wondered if Billy was afraid to be recognized by someone, or that someone would go back and tell his father his whereabouts. Travis felt a tinge of pain for his friend's ordeal, as he walked quickly to Billy with the box of matches. He also felt a sting of pride as he thought of what those matches would help him accomplish. In a matter of minutes, his best friend would be his brother.

"Hey, I got them!" he hollered at Billy. Pulling the matches from under his shirt, he held them up for Billy to see.

"Good." Billy turned to face Travis. "Did you have any problems getting them?"

"It was easy." Travis sat down beside Billy.

"Let's do it. You're not afraid are you?" Billy looked at Travis.

"Who's afraid? It was my idea. Remember?"

Travis took the penknife from his pocket while Billy struck the match. Travis held the penknife over the small flame, the way he saw the cowboys do in the movies. Billy blew out the fire and the two boys spit on their thumb, wiping them on their shirts. Travis touched the blade to make sure that it wasn't hot. Travis pressed the small blade to his thumb and made a little incision. Drops of blood popped out. Then, Billy took the blade and did likewise. Blood welled from the tiny cut he'd made and it dripped onto his pants.

"It didn't hurt much." Travis was the first to speak. He held his thumb towards Billy's.

"It was all right," Billy said, as he took his thumb and put it to Travis' thumb and the two boys smeared their blood together.

"Will you be my blood brother?" Travis stared into Billy eyes as he asked the question.

"That sounds silly," Billy laughed.

"It's the way they did it on TV. You have to ask one another to be brothers, or it won't count."

"Okay. Yes. I'll be your brother."

"Good. Now you have to ask me the same thing."

Billy laughed, but Travis looked at him seriously. "Okay, Okay. Would you please be my brother?" Billy tried not to laugh again.

"Yes. I'll be your brother. It's done." Travis stood up, "Now, we are brothers through blood and by blood." He took two band-aids from his pocket, and wrapped one around his thumb. He handed the other to Billy.

Billy took the band-aid and stood up beside him. "Brothers through and through," he said, as he wrapped the band-aid strip around his thumb, too.

Travis hugged Billy, but he pushed him away. "What are you doing?

"I was giving my brother a hug."

"We're brothers, not sisters," Billy said. "And don't you hug me again."

"I won't," Travis replied.

"See that you don't." Billy pushed Travis' head, and then took off running.

Travis raced behind him, "I'm going to catch you! You can't outrun me!"

Billy stopped to catch his breath. He shouted to Travis who was far behind him. "Look who's talking? You can't even out fish me. How are you going to outrun me?"

"Easy," Travis said, breathless. "Wait and see. I'm going to beat you one of these days."

"Yeah. Right."

The two boys ran up and down the park near the lake for an hour, until finally they were too tired to run another step. They both collapsed onto the grass. They lay there, silently staring up at the clouds, as the clouds took on different shapes and sizes. One cloud reminded Travis of a man feeding peanuts to an elephant. It looked as if the clouds were drawing pictures for the two boys. The clouds took on ordinary likenesses of people, animals and things. Billy was the first to break the silence.

"I wonder if God lies down like us and stares at the clouds."

"He's already up there in the clouds. So, how can He?"

"I don't know. Maybe He has some clouds up there in Heaven."

"I thought you said that you don't believe in Heaven."

"I didn't say I didn't believe. I said I didn't know," Billy replied and closed his eyes. "I got to believe that my mama is up there. So that makes me want to believe." He opened his eyes. "Do you believe?"

"What? In Heaven? Yeah, I believe. My daddy says there's one. Reverend Simon said there's a Heaven. My mother believes there's one. And you say there has to be one 'cause of your mother," Travis replied. "Wouldn't it be super if we saw God looking at some clouds, too?"

"That's not going to happen." Billy pulled himself up off the ground.

"And why not?" Travis asked, as he also rose from the ground.

"Because, I said so," Billy said, and pushed Travis' head again and then took off running through the park.

Chapter 2

"*L*ook what Daddy bought his little girl!" Eddie Mitchell handed eight-year old Adrienne a book of fairy tales. He stooped down and held out his arms as Adrienne dashed happily into them.

"For me?" She planted kisses on his face. "Oh, Daddy, thanks!" She continued to kiss her father. Eddie Mitchell almost fell backward from laughter, as his daughter thrilled with delight of the little book.

"Now, now, let your old man up," Eddie said as he moved to stand. "I have a present for both of my girls." He stood and towered over Adrienne. "Where's your mother?"

"She's in the kitchen, cooking," Adrienne replied, turning pages of the book. "Oh, I love fairy tales with happy endings!" She ran toward the kitchen holding up the book in front of her, "Mama, look what Daddy brought me!" She stuck the book in front of her mother.

"That's great, dear," Donna said, as she put the lid back on the pot.

"He got you something, too," she eagerly said.

Eddie walked into the kitchen, and seeing Donna, he grinned and planted a romantic kiss on her lips. She responded to the heat of the kiss. Adrienne giggled at her parents, and then hurried out of the kitchen to her bedroom. She couldn't wait to get started on her book.

"How's my girl?" Eddie asked, looking at Donna.

"Your girl's all right, now that you're home."

He kissed her again, but this time a little longer than the first. It had been a long time since they had been together, and she cherished these moments when he was finally back, and all his attention centered on her.

"How was your trip?" she asked, hoping it would be the last for the year.

"It was one that I'll never forget, and it will be one that you won't forget, either," he added.

"How is that?" She raised her brows.

"Before I tell you the news, first let me give my best girl this." He reached inside his jacket pocket and pulled out a small black box. "I thought since we're already married and have a beautiful daughter you might as well wear this ring," he grinned, handing her the box.

"Eddie Mitchell, what have you done?" She opened the box and gasped. "Oh, darling, it's beautiful!" she cried out, quickly taking the tear shaped, one-and-a-half carat solitaire, white gold ring from the box.

"Yes, it'd better be beautiful, because it represents you and how much I love you."

She gazed at the ring, and then gave it to Eddie. He kneeled on one knee. He took her hand. "Mrs. Mitchell, would you please wear my ring of undying love and affection?" he asked, as he slid the ring on her finger.

"Yes," she said breathless, watching him.

"Now, you're officially married and belong to me," he said, as he rose. "And I want to make sure that all the other men see it, and know that you're private property," he grinned, admiring her.

"Darling, you were on a roll, until you declared that I was private property," she laughed. "But that's okay. 'Cause I love you, too."

"Good, 'cause I was afraid that you were going to tell me that I couldn't eat here tonight," he laughed, opening the pot on the stove.

"You stay out of that." She put her hand on his, pushing until the lid set back on the pot. "I've cooked your favorite."

"Chinese-pork-fried- rice?"

"No."

"Let me see," he sniffed the air. "It smells like veal pot roast."

"No, it does not," she laughed.

"Then what?"

"It's your favorite."

"Those are my favorites."

"It's Italian pork chops with herbs, and potato-spinach casserole," she laughed. "I don't know how you got veal out of that."

"Me, either, but Italian pork chops, and potato-spinach are my favorites."

"You're full of it," she laughed.

"I'll take that, as long as I'm full with you. When do we eat?"

"Go and wash up. I've set the table, and I'll call you in a little while." She put her hands on her hips and smiled at him. "And tell Adrienne to come and help me."

"I'm at your command," he said, as he walked out of the room. "Adrienne!" he yelled. "Your mama wants you to come and help with dinner."

"I'm reading my book," Adrienne shouted back.

"Put that book down, young lady, and help your mama. You have plenty of time to read your book."

"But?"

"No buts." Eddie stuck his head inside Adrienne's bedroom door. "Do what I say, and you won't get into any trouble. Do you understand me, young lady?" He waited for an answer.

Adrienne put down the book and slowly rose from the floor. She didn't want to make her father lose patience with her, because sometimes he would lose patience on her behind, as he put it. It was no use getting in trouble now, especially when he was home. He made it so much easier than her mother, because her mother worried too much. When he was home, Eddie would take her to the park, so she could play with her friends. He sometimes camped out with her in their living room. There were times he would let her invite some of her friends for sleepovers.

"Yes sir," she replied, and walked past her father.

"That's my little girl," he smiled.

Chapter 3

"That boy is set on not minding you, or me," Mattie, said as she opened the door to Billy's bedroom and seeing that it was empty. "I'm leaving this house today. Right now!" she shouted at Darrell. "What's the use of whipping that boy when he gets up and does the same thing that you whip him 'bout."

"Boys will be boys," Darrell declared. "I didn't whip Billy for leaving the house. I whipped him for not minding you."

"Whatever! I'm just tired of that child ruinin' my life with you. When are we gonna have some time to ourselves? I'm getting sick and tired of playing the mama to that son of yours, who don't appreciate nothing that we do for him. It's like I said, he's full of the devil. Devil venom is what it is." She angrily paced the floor.

"I don't want to lose you, too, Mattie. You mean the world to me," Darrell said, sitting on the sofa. "I can't lose you."

"Huh! You can't lose me? Well, that is exactly what you're doing. I can't be happy in this house." She stopped pacing the floor and looked at Darrell. "Not as long as your boy is here messin' up everything."

"What do you want me to do? The boy is my son. What can I do? His mama is dead. Poor Edna, rest her soul, and he don't have nobody but us," he tried reasoning with Mattie.

"Us! I didn't bring that child into this world. He's your problem. And you best to deal with it, or lose the best piece of ass you ever had."

"Don't say nothing like that, Mattie. We can work this thing out

23

between you, the boy, and me. He can be a good child, I know."

"There ain't a good bone in that boy's body. And I don't know why I'm here with you. You might plant one of them bad seeds in me." She sat on the sofa beside him. "I don't know why I'm here."

"I asked you to live with me, that's why."

"I shouldn't have come here. Maybe it's a curse. That's probably what it is. Edna wasn't dead a week before I moved in here with you and the child."

"It's not a curse. Edna is dead. It doesn't matter how long she's been dead. What? You wanted to wait around until her body turned to dirt?" He looked at Mattie.

"No, I didn't want to wait that long. Like you said, she is dead. Ain't no use in us waiting to start our life just 'cause hers ended."

"We can have a good life." He put his hand on her knee. "Just wait, and see."

Mattie shoved his hand from her knee and wriggled her skinny body farther down the sofa, moving away from his touch. "Our life won't be worth a hill-of-beans if Billy stays in the picture. You got to get rid of him, if you want to keep this fire burning". She crossed her arms over her chest. "Yeah, don't think 'cause I gave you some last night, that I ain't gonna let you do somethin' 'bout this."

"What you want me to do?" Darrell looked hurt. "Put the boy out? Then, what kind of father will that make me?"

"One that cares 'bout his son. Look at you; you ain't in no shape to have a ten- year old boy hangin' round this house." She glared at him. "You'd be doing that boy a favor, if you just hand him over to somebody else to raise. 'Cause I ain't the one to be raising another woman's child. I ain't the one," she cocked her head to one side and looked at him.

"Who wants a boy to raise? You know of a family that I don't know anything about? People these days are having a hard time raising their own children, let alone trying to raise someone else's."

"It's easier than you think."

"How?"

"My sister Urla Mae lives in Mobile, Alabama, and I told her that me and you might be coming down to pay her a nice long visit." She looked around the house.

"Besides, I'm ready to shed Edna's ghost. This house gives me the creeps."

"Leave Billy just like that?" He searched her eyes to see if she was kidding, but Mattie looked at him seriously. Too seriously. His voice trembled with his next words, "You want me to walk out on my son? I don't think I can do that." He lowered his head. "What about Edna?"

"What 'bout her?" She stood up in front of him. "She's dead. And you'll be doing that monster of yours a favor." She crossed her arms on her chest. "Urla Mae said we could stay as long as we want to, until you find a job, that is," she uncrossed her arms. "Urla Mae says she knows a place that's hiring. An old warehouse or somethin' like that. Well, anyhow, I called her last night, while you were sleeping, and I told her that we were coming."

"What about the boy?"

"The boy. That's all I hear around here. The boy. Well, the boy can stay with Travis and them. They got enough room over there and one more mouth to feed ain't gonna hurt'em none."

"But I don't think it's right to leave Billy with someone else. Why don't we take him with us?"

"If he comes with us, we might as well stay here. What's the use going down there, if he comes with us? That don't make no sense." She paced the floor, stopped and pointed a finger at him, "I'm gonna help you make up your mind. It's either him or me. You decide." She pointed at the front door. "When I walk outta that door, I ain't comin' back, and you better believe that."

Darrell was speechless. Angry at his silence, she walked quickly into the kitchen throwing pots and pans out of the cabinets. "I'm taking everything that I brought in this house."

Darrell followed her into the small L-shaped kitchen, "Are you leaving now?"

"As soon as I get my stuff packed, and I'll get my cousin to pick it up for me, and bring it to Alabama when he can." She hurried about the place, pulling out drawers, and emptying silverware, pots and pans into trash bags.

Darrell pleaded with her, "Mattie, please don't go. I'll do anything to keep you. I need you, Mattie. You're all I got." He began to cry. "Don't leave me, Mattie." He grabbed her, squeezing her. "Please Mattie, don't do this! Don't do it! Don't do it, Mattie!" he begged, holding on to her. He pointed to the empty walls where Edna's pictures once hung. "I even took Edna's pictures down like you wanted me to."

She tried to break away from his grasp, but to no avail. He was suffocating her with his pitiful wailing, and with the strength of his arms. Mattie did all she could to wriggle free from this towering man.

"You're hurting me!" she yelled, breathless. Darrell loosened his grasp on her.

"And you can put them pictures back on the wall, as far as I'm concerned."

Darrell released her, and began to rub his hands against her arms. "I didn't mean to hurt you," he said rubbing her neck. "I can't stand the thought of you leaving me."

Mattie stepped an arm's distance away from him, in case he couldn't control himself again and this time really hurt her. "If you want me, you know what to do," she said, and walked into the bedroom, grabbing clothes out of the closet and emptying her chest-of-drawers of everything that belonged to her. She put them in trash bags.

Darrell followed her around the house. He hoped that she would change her mind, but she continued to pack.

Finally, she called her cousin, George, to pick her up. Twenty minutes later, she sat in the cab of an old blue Ford pick-up truck. Teary-eyed, Darrell sat quietly near the window, and watched her leave as the pick-up truck drove away.

Travis and Billy rode their bikes down Mulberry Street and met the blue pick-up that carried an angry looking Mattie, who looked harshly at the boys, as they stopped their bikes and watched the truck drive out of sight.

"$\mathcal{T}$he dinner hit the spot, dear," Eddie said to Donna who was still sitting at the dinner table. "I miss these home cooked meals when I'm away from home. You sure do know the way to a man's heart." He laughed, winking at Adrienne.

"That's what my mother used to say," Donna smiled, "The way to a man's heart is through his stomach."

"What's that?" Adrienne asked, looking at her mother.

"When you're older, you'll learn what it means," Eddie grinned, watching his daughter's face scrunch up, trying to figure out what her mother had said.

"Yes, darling, your day is coming when you, too, will know the way to a man's heart," Donna smiled watching Adrienne then turned her attention back to Eddie.

"You said that you had something to tell us?" She waited to see what surprise he would spring on them this time.

"What is it, Daddy? What is it?" Adrienne sang.

"I guess my two favorite girls can stand to hear some good news." He winked at them.

"Good news?" Donna's brow rose.

"Yeah, Daddy, what good news?" Adrienne sat watching her father.

"I'm no longer going to leave you alone while I go traveling over the country for Laser and Webster Technology." He sat back in his chair waiting for a response.

"What?" Donna Mitchell looked at him, confused, "Then what are you going to do?" What happened?" She spoke rapidly. "I know how much you love that job."

"Nothing happened," he assured her. "I'm tired of working my tail off for someone else to sit back and take in all the gravy. I've been working on a project of my own for some time now. I didn't tell you, 'cause I wanted to surprise you. This last trip I took, I was getting everything in order for our move." He hesitated on this last word, and watched Donna closely. He wanted to see any reaction to let him know that he had made a bad decision without discussing it with her.

"Move?" It was all she could say. The last word caught her off guard, and she knew that her husband was waiting for her approval.

"We're going to move, Daddy?" Adrienne asked. "Will there be a park for me to play in?"

"There will be a big back yard for you to play in, dear," he added. "And a huge kitchen for your mother to cook in." He glanced at Donna, hoping that she wouldn't be too upset.

"Ooh, a back yard!" Adrienne said, happily.

Donna Mitchell ignored Adrienne's burst of joy, and focused on Eddie, who now moved his chair a little closer to hers. "Okay, Eddie, I'm trying to be patient, but it's not working." Her tone was firm. An angry look formed over her face. "Please go on."

"This project that I was telling you about is an insurance company. I'm opening my own insurance business." He looked at her, and then at Adrienne. "We're business owners. Isn't that great?" His expression glowed with excitement.

"Oh!" Donna released her breath and the anger drained from her face. "Is it for real? Oh, Eddie it's wonderful! I can't believe it! You've always wanted to be your own boss." She sprang up and danced around the room, joined by a giggling Adrienne, who didn't know why her mother was so happy, but danced around the room, too.

Eddie kicked back his chair and joined them as they danced crazily and widely around the dinner table.

"I'm so happy that you're happy," he said as they went around the table one more time. "I was hoping that you'd be okay with it."

"I'd be crazy not to be all right with it!" she replied, stopping and giving him a big kiss on the lips. "But the house, where is it? Here in the city?" She kept kissing him, while   Adrienne   leaped   and danced around the table.

"No, it's not in New York," he said growing tense.

"Where?" she froze.

"In Georgia," he said, cautiously.

"Georgia? You're moving us to the south?" Donna grabbed hold of her chair and sat down in it. She shook her head, "We're moving all the way down there? What are we going to do in Georgia? That's a redneck state!" she bellowed.

"Now, dear, this is the eighties, there aren't any rednecks any more."

Adrienne, seeing that the excitement had died down, stood looking at her parents. She didn't like the way her mother was looking at her father. It was like a truck had hit her. She sat in the chair opposite them and watched. She wished a thousand times that they wouldn't argue. She hated when her mother and father fought. It made it hard for her to play. She would get punished for no reason at all. When they fought, it made her life miserable. She sat quietly by and waited.

"Don't tell me there aren't any more rednecks. There are plenty of them here in New York, and this is a northern state, so you know it's full of them in the south."

"But, honey! Okay, honey, let's say there are some in Georgia, but I talked with one of the business consultants and they said that Atlanta is the place to be for black businessmen."

"We're moving to Atlanta?" she asked, feeling a little better about this prospect.

"Not exactly," he whispered.

"Aah," she sighed.

"We're moving to a small town just outside of Atlanta. It's a great town," he explained. "It has a good school, and the houses are dirt cheap. We can get more house for the money. You can almost buy a mansion for what they're asking here for a small house! Honey, I know it comes as a shock to you, but please give it a chance."

"Darling, I'm thrilled about the business, but the move is what I need help on. You couldn't start a business here in the city?" she asked, knowing that a small beginning insurance company in a huge city had less chance of thriving than a tomato plant in a desert.

"Dear, you know I can't make it here. We can move to Georgia and start anew."

"The house is big?" She gazed at Adrienne "And Adrienne would have a big yard to play in?"

"It's huge. I wanted you to pick it out, but I didn't want to take you there and put you in a motel. So, I said the heck with it. I know the kind of house you like. I called a realtor there, and boom here we are."

"What's the name of the town?"

"Silver Rock. You're going to love it. It even has a state park with a huge lake. I can go fishing and we could have a picnic. Donna, I'm so happy, I could shout," he laughed.

"I guess it won't hurt to give it a try," she finally said. "What can go wrong in a small town? Okay, I'll give it a shot. Redneck, or not, here we come!" she shouted, playfully. She stood up. "When are we moving?"

"In two weeks. I've hired a moving company to pack our things. The only thing that we have to do is carry some clothes in our luggage and fly to Atlanta." He stood up and pretended to fly. "My little girl, come here and give your daddy a great big kiss." He winked at Adrienne. She rushed to him and planted a big giggly kiss on his cheek. Then she said, "Look, Daddy, I can fly, too!" She ran around the room with her arms out to her side and pretended to be an airplane.

Donna laughed, "You two are the silliest things I've ever seen."

"Won't you join us, and we can be three silliest things." Eddie laughed, grabbing her. He pulled her around the room with him.

"Go, Mother!" Adrienne laughed, trying to catch them.

"Good-bye New York!" Eddie sang around the room.

"Hello, Georgia!" Donna shouted.

Chapter 5

$\mathcal{T}$he two boys rushed up the street to Billy's house. Billy jumped off his bike and ran up the steps. Travis followed closely behind. Darrell sat at the window, rocking back and forth as he stared blankly out of it. Billy stopped and motioned Travis to do the same. Travis stopped dead in his tracks and watched Billy's father rock slowly back and forth like a rocking chair. The scene pricked Travis' flesh and goose bumps ran up and down his arms. It was uncanny to see Mr. Ray rock back and forth unaware of his surroundings, just sitting there staring out the window.

Travis was the first to break the silence. "What's wrong with him?"

"I don't know," whispered Billy.

"What are we going to do?" Travis didn't want to see Mr. Ray in that kind of condition. It reminded him of a picture that he saw one night on a rerun of "Twilight Zone."

"I don't know," Billy said, as he walked up to his father. "Daddy, are you okay?" He moved closer so that he could get a good look at him. There was no answer.

"Daddy?" Billy said again, and kneeled in front of him. He put his small hands on his father's hand but Darrell didn't make a sound.

"Daddy, you're scaring me," he said and looked at Travis, "Help me."

Travis walked slowly to the father and son. He wasn't in any hurry to get there. He was afraid the show on "Twilight Zone" might come alive in Billy's living room.

"What do you want me to do?" Travis asked, kneeling beside Billy.

"I want you to help me move him to the sofa."

"How are we going to do that?"

"I'll pull his arms and you can sort of push him a little bit."

"What if he gets mad?"

"He's not going to get mad. Stop asking stupid questions and help me. On the count of three, I'm going to pull and you're going to push."

"Okay, but I'm not stupid."

"I didn't call you stupid. I said stop asking me stupid questions. Now, are you ready?"

"No, I'm not ready."

"Stop stalling."

"I'm not doing that either, but come on, let's do this and get it over with."

"Ready," Billy said, ignoring Travis' reply. "On the count of three. One, two, three." The two boys pulled and pushed on Darrell but he wouldn't budge.

"What are we going to do now?" Travis asked watching Billy.

"It's that Mattie. She did something. I know she did."

"Mattie?" Darrell blinked his eyes and looked at Billy. "Mattie's here?"

"No, she's not here," Billy, explained. "Mattie's gone."

"She's gone? Where did she go?" Darrell asked, staring at Billy.

Billy looked around the room for the first time since he walked in a few minutes ago. He saw piles of garbage bags on the floor. He saw Mattie's old oil lamp and a pair of her white tennis shoes on the floor near the bags. Then, it dawned on him that Mattie was gone for good. He looked at Travis, and Travis could see the fear in his eyes as he watched Billy look around the room, then again at him.

"I don't think you should have told him," Travis said, wondering what drove Mattie out of the house. He knew whatever it had to be, Billy's name was stamped on it.

"I have to," he stated. "I have to help him." He squeezed Darrell's hands. "Look at him. How can I not tell him the truth?"

Travis nodded his head.

"Daddy," he said slowly, "Daddy, Mattie's gone. I don't think she's coming back. I saw her inside a pick-up truck and she's packed all of her things." He spoke softly to his father. Billy didn't want to cry. He didn't want Travis to see him acting like a wimp.

Travis watched the touching scene and it made his heart move to see his blood brother's tender side. Billy always acted tough and one that could take care of his needs and yours. He wasn't a bully but he would fight if he had to, and he had girls writing him letters in school asking him if he liked them. He knew of one particular girl that Billy liked, and he gave her a hard time by pulling her ponytail and calling her names during lunch recess on the playground. He noticed that Billy wouldn't call her bad names, not like the names he called the other girls that he didn't like. He would call, Janet Wingo. "Win and go! Go and win! Win, win, go, go! Wingo!" Janet would chase Billy around the schoolyard and he pretended to give up and allow her to catch him.

"She's gone?" Darrell focused hard on Billy, and then he looked around the room. He saw the huge pile of bags on the floor near the sofa, and then he set his gaze back out the window. "I can't make her stay. She's gone. My Mattie is gone," he whispered softly, so softly that Billy and Travis barely heard what was said.

"What are we going to do?" Travis asked Billy again. "It looks like he done lost it. We have to call somebody."

"No. My daddy's all right." He glanced back at Darrell. "He's all right. I know he is." Still Billy looked worried.

"Yeah, sure he is," Travis agreed, but knowing he wasn't all right. The far away distance showed in Darrell's eyes.

"He's got to be all right," Billy replied. For the first time, Travis saw fear swell up in Billy's eyes. Billy left Darrell Ray sitting and staring out of the window.

"Do we call the police?" Travis asked Billy, as he flopped down on the sofa beside him.

"Nope, I don't think so." Billy's tone was firm but a little shaken.

"Let's call my parents."

"I don't want to do that. I told you that he'd be all right. Let's just wait awhile. I know he's going to be all right. No girl's going to get my daddy down."

"Yeah, you're right." He shrugged his shoulders.

The two boys sat on the sofa, only leaving the room when one of them had to go to the bathroom really bad, or get something to eat or drink. Time passed slowly as the two kept their eyes on Darrell Ray, who sat gazing out the window until the sun finally settled down behind the trees. Billy turned on the lamp near the sofa. Travis rose from the chair to go home. He turned and watched Billy. Billy sat silently on the sofa as if there were a sleeping newborn baby in his presence, and he was afraid he'd wake it.

Chapter 6

$\mathcal{I}$t was four weeks later, Donna Mitchell threw the new, "Welcome" doormat on the porch in front of the door of their new home. She stood back and admired the red brick ranch house.

"Aren't you glad to be here?" Eddie asked, as he walked up behind her from the garage door. He pulled her to him and hugged her with one arm around her waist as he squeezed her playfully on her round buttock with his free hand.

"It's a dream come true." She turned to faced him, and then kissed him.

"Mmh! That's more like it," he said, as he returned the kiss. "This is what I like."

"I have more of what you like," she said, sexily.

"Well, give it to me."

"Tonight," she grinned.

"Whew! I can't wait." He released her and walked towards the front door.

"Naughty." Donna blew a kiss at him as he walked away.

Adrienne met him on her way outside. She wanted to help her mother sweep off the porch. "Hey, Daddy," she said, as she tipped up on her toes so that he could kiss her easily.

"Hey, yourself," he said, bending down to kiss her.

"That tickles," she laughed.

"My mustache tickles, huh? Well, feel this." He pressed his mustache to her face and wiggled his head.

"Stop Daddy!" she yelled, as she tried to free her face from him, but he held her closer to him. Adrienne squealed with delight. She liked the way his mustache felt against her soft skin. It reminded her of a bristled kitten that needed a bath.

"I declare, I have two kids to raise," Donna spoke, shaking her head as she watched the two of them play together.

Eddie finally released the giggling child. He patted her cheeks and winked his eye. Adrienne stood motionless. She knew what her father was about to do. She returned the wink. Suddenly, Eddie had Donna in his strong arms. He held her face up against his mustache and moved his head in a circular motion. Donna tried to push him away, but he held her too firmly.

"Stop! Stop!" Those were the only words that she could shout, as Eddie moved his head round and round with his mustache pressed against her skin. Minutes later he released the hysterical Donna. She hadn't had that much fun in awhile.

"You keep that up, Mr.," she laughed, pointing a finger at him, "and I'll see to it that you'll be sleeping on the sofa tonight."

"Oh, Daddy's going to sleep on the sofa!" Adrienne leaped around the yard. "Daddy's going to sleep on the sofa!"

"You wouldn't?" Eddie replied, grinning sheepishly at his wife.

"Yes, I would," she smiled.

Adrienne danced happily around the yard. She soon forgot the two adults as she pranced and swirled around the beautiful green yard. She was happier today than any other day that she could remember. She would be starting her new school soon, and her father said she'd meet plenty of new friends. She'd be entering third grade, and somehow she felt ten feet tall.

"Beautiful lady you wouldn't dare turn me away from your bed tonight, would you?" He looked at her with eyes that spoke more than words.

Donna laughed, "Okay, okay. But if you tickle me again with that hairy thing you have across your lips, you call a mustache, I will not relent as easily."

"That's a deal," he replied, planting a kiss on her lips.

"Wait a minute. Listen to your daughter." She gazed at Adrienne dancing in the yard.

Adrienne resumed singing loudly, "Daddy's going to sleep

on the sofa."

"What will our neighbors think? She's going to have everyone thinking that you and I don't get along."

"You're the one who started it."

"Put the blame on me, huh?" Donna pointed her slender finger at him.

Eddie walked towards his dancing daughter. "Adrienne," he called. "Adrienne," he called again, touching her shoulder.

Adrienne stopped dancing and looked up at her father. She didn't like the expression he wore on his face.

"Huh?" she said, as she stopped dancing.

"You can't be singing about Daddy sleeping on the sofa out in the front yard," he spoke softly, "People will think that your mother and I are fighting."

"But you're not fighting, are you?" she looked passed her father, and looked at Donna.

"Your mother and I were joking. Remember how we tease each other all the time? Well, that's what we were doing when you heard your mother say, I'll be sleeping on the sofa."

"Oh."

"Do you understand what I'm trying to say to you?"

"Yes, Daddy," she said, but thinking grown-ups were hard to understand.

"That's more like it," he said, as he winked his eye at her. "Don't forget to help your mother." Then, he walked away towards the house.

"Did you get it settled?" Donna asked, as he walked towards her.

"Everything's fine." He grinned and entered the house.

Adrienne ran up to Donna, "Daddy told me not to forget to help you."

"That's good, dear," Donna said. "Now, get the broom and sweep the sidewalk off for me."

"Okay." Adrienne ran and picked the broom up from the porch. She swept vigorously, thinking about her new school and the new friends she'd meet.

Four hours later, Adrienne laid snuggled in her white, canopy princess bed. White lacey frills surrounded her. Rows of Barbie dolls filled her collection on her white bookcase, and another white bookcase was filled with books of all sorts. She had a collection of Cracker Jack prizes inside a shoebox her mother had given her. A yellow rocking chair set in the corner near the window, which had a small balcony for her to sit. Pictures of lady ballerinas hung throughout the room. A white, fluffy rug covered the middle of the floor. A white, five drawer chest, and matching dresser adorned the beautiful room.

A fluffy yellow, Barbie bed spread and comforter with a matching pillow sham and bed skirt created an elegant look.

"Are you asleep, Muffin?" Her daddy always called her that when he thought she was asleep. He nicknamed her that a year ago. She used to sneak blueberry muffins late at night up to her room and hide them to eat later. One night when he was making his nightly round, locking up the house and checking to see if everything was fine, he checked in on her. He caught her sneaking a blueberry muffin from underneath her bed. So her name became "Muffin," only at night.

She heard her father but didn't reply. She closed her eyes pretending to be asleep. She liked how he called her Muffin but she liked being called his little girl more. It made her feel special.

"Good night, my little girl," he said, closing the door. "Sweet dreams."

"Good..." she caught herself. But he was gone. "Good night, Daddy," she whispered. Adrienne slid herself down comfortably in the bed. Soon she was fast asleep.

Chapter 7

"*J* have to go Billy," Darrell said, looking at the boy. "I have to go. Please understand."

"Take me with you. Daddy, please take me with you," he begged.

"I can't do that." Darrell Ray crossed the floor in front of him. "It won't work with you there." He glanced at the floor. "It just won't work."

"But what's going to happen to me?" Billy looked around the living room. "I got to go with you. You need me to take care of you."

"Everything is arranged. You know that. I thought you'd like the idea of staying over at the Malcolm's."

"I'll run away! I swear!" Billy spoke with contempt.

"For what?" Darrell stood directly in front of Billy's. "What's that going to solve? Tell me."

"You're leaving, and what's that going to solve?" Billy threw the answer back at him.

"Mattie was right. The devil has you hooked, hog tied, and collared."

"That old bat doesn't know what she's talking about!" Billy stared hard at his father. "I can't believe you're going to leave me just like that!" He snapped his fingers. "Only three weeks ago, you were sitting around the house like a zombie." Billy moved some distance away from his father. "But when old Mattie calls, you go running off to her like a crazy man."

"You leave Mattie out of this. The only thing that woman tried to do for you was to be good to you, but you wouldn't let her. So you keep her name out of this."

"What did she do for you? Play your wife?" Billy spoke the words before he could stop it.

"How dare you to talk to me like that!" Darrell said harshly. He slapped Billy's face hard.

Billy rubbed his face and shouted, "How dare you take her side against me, your own flesh and blood."

"What flesh? What blood? All I see standing in front of me is a boy that I didn't want. But I did right by Edna; I didn't want any seed of mine to be called a bastard son. I never loved you like my father didn't love—," he stopped in mid-sentence. "Anyhow, you were just one more mouth to feed. I wanted no other connection. And I feel sorry for any child that's going to come through you! To have a daddy that can't love them. That's what we are, boy. Loveless! The men in our generation can't love their children the way they need to be loved. Your children will know it just like you know it now."

"Liar!" Billy screamed.

"I love Mattie more than you. What does that tell you?"

"Liar! Liar! You're a liar!" Billy swung at Darrell. Darrell held him off. "I hate you! I hate you!" Billy landed a few punches on his father.

"Listen to that bad seed flowing through your veins, manifesting itself." Darrell laughed.

"I'll kill you! Just wait! I'll kill you!" Billy screamed, swinging widely at Darrell.

"I thought I could love you. I tried to, but how can you love something that you rejected all of its natural born life?" Darrell struggled with Billy. "If only I could turn back the clock of time, then I wouldn't have to deal with you now."

"I hate you!" Billy continued to scream. "I hate your guts!"

"Well, hate me then. I want you to hate me. I want your children to feel that same hatred that you have for me right now. C'mon show me your hatred!" Darrell grinned at him.

"I'm going to get you for this. Wait and see." Tears flooded Billy's eyes, as he fought helplessly at the figure in front of him.

"When will that be?" He looked at him, but kept him from landing any more punches. "I never want to see you again. In my heart, Edna aborted you ten years ago."

"Shut uuuuppp!" Billy screamed, collapsing to the floor.

"What's going on in here?" Mr. Malcolm asked, as he entered the house without knocking, with Travis at his side.

"Nothing, the boy needed a little wake-up call."

Mr. Malcolm rushed over to the collapsed child on the floor. He kneeled down beside him. "What is it Billy?" he asked, glancing up at Darrell, who stood blankly staring at the two of them. "What's the matter?" Mr. Malcolm held the crying child in his arms. "It's going to be all right." He turned to Darrell. "I heard both of you screaming clear across the street. What's this all about?" he asked, looking from father to son.

Travis sat on the sofa. He couldn't believe what he saw. Tears poured out of his friend. He didn't like the way Billy looked. He knew that Mr. Ray had said or done something to make Billy act in such a way that brought tears. Billy was not the one for tears or anything else he considered girly.

"Nothing. The boy's just tired," Darrell said, looking at Billy. "That's all."

"But I heard screaming, and the child is very upset." Mr. Malcolm didn't believe him. He shook his head and asked Billy again," What's the matter, son?"

Billy didn't want Mr. Malcolm, or Travis to know that his father didn't want him. So he had blurted the words out, "I'm just tired." He wiped the tears with the back of his hand. He wanted to erase all signs that he had been crying, as he gazed angrily at Darrell.

"The boy's going to be all right," Darrell said, nodding his head. "I hope you can take him in tonight? I promised Mattie I'd be catching the next Greyhound out of Silver Rock first thing tonight."

Mr. Malcolm rose from the floor, helping Billy to his feet. He held on to the boy. He still didn't believe a word that the child's father said. "You're leaving tonight? Why so soon? I thought at least you'd see to the boy's first day back at school from the summer."

"I talked with Mattie today. She said if I wanted that job that her sister is holding for me, I better get on down there as soon as possible." Darrell put on a sad expression. "I hope this won't inconvenience you and Mrs. Malcolm, but the sooner I leave, the sooner I can send for Billy." He looked at Billy, and then turned his eyes quickly away from him.

"It's no inconvenience. I told you we'd be glad to take Billy into our home until you get settled in Mobile. He's practically my son." Mr. Malcolm glanced downward at Billy who was still in his arms.

"Good. Then it's settled. I'll come for the boy the first chance I get." Billy knew he was lying.

"He's not coming back for me," Billy's voice was barely audible.

"Huh? What's that?" Mr. Malcolm asked, looking at Billy.

"The child is tired," Darrell said, rolling his eyes at Billy.

"Yeah. I'm tired. Can we go now?" Billy asked, walking past Darrell, toward the door.

"What about your things?" Mr. Malcolm said, as he watched the child go toward the door.

"I don't have nothing here, anymore," he said, and walked out the door, not looking back.

Travis jumped up from the sofa, and followed him outside.

"Get his clothes together," Mr. Malcolm told Darrell, "and I'll pick them up later." Mr. Malcolm walked out the door behind the two boys.

Once out on the porch, Mr. Malcolm put his arms around Billy and Travis, "Well, what do you say we do tonight?"

"I don't know." Travis looked at Billy. He knew that his friend was hurting, and the last thing he wanted was to pretend that he wasn't. Daddy can be so inconsiderate at times, he thought.

"Mr. Malcolm, if it's all right with you, I rather go to bed." Billy gazed at Mr. Malcolm, hoping that he didn't make him angry.

"Okay. I'll let you boys turn in early tonight, and tomorrow, we'll play it by ear," he said, as they entered his house. Mrs. Malcolm met them in the foyer.

"Well," she said, "what was all the commotion over there?" Then she noticed Billy, and regretted that she had asked the question.

"Nothing, dear. But look who's here. Darrell said that he had to leave tonight."

"Tonight? Why so soon?" she asked, looking worried.

"Something about a job waiting for him in Alabama. Anyhow, he seemed to be anxious about leaving." He looked back at the two boys. "Travis, why don't you take Billy to your room, so he can settle down?"

"Yes, sir," Travis said. He and Billy walked up the stairs to Travis' bedroom.

Mr. Malcolm waited to hear Travis close his bedroom door, before continuing with his conversation. "I didn't want to say anything in front of Billy, but I believe Darrell is about to abandon his own son."

"What! Should we call the police?"

"No, we can't do that. If he's planning on doing that, then the boy would be better off with us. I hate to think of strangers raising him. Next week is the first day of school. Let's keep quiet for the boy's sake."

"Maybe you're right. I hate to think that anyone can walk out on his or her family. Poor thing. First, his mama died, and now his daddy's leaving. I hope he'll be happy with us." Mrs. Malcolm sighed.

"I hope so too, dear," Mr. Malcolm said, glancing up the stairway. "I hope to God that I'm wrong about Darrell."

"Time will tell." Mrs. Malcolm said, as she put her hand on his shoulder, "In the mean time, we'll give him the love that he needs."

"Thanks honey," He kissed her lightly on her rosy cheek, and took her hand, "I don't know what I'd do without you."

"The same here," she replied, and started up the stairs. "I'm tired. It's been a long day."

"Yeah. First thing tomorrow morning, we have to clean the junk out of the extra room for Billy."

"What about a bed?"

"We can move his bed over here."

"That's right. I forgot," she laughed. "I guess I'm not used to having three men in the house."

"It's going to be good," he said, as they entered their bedroom. He turned on the light, and closed the door.

* * * * * * * * * *

"Are you sure that you're going to be all right?" Travis asked Billy, after they entered the bedroom.

"I'll be okay," he replied, "but you just wait and see. I'm going to get back at Darrell if it's the last thing that I do." The statement rolled smoothly off his tongue.

"What did he do? We heard you and him shouting all the way over here. My mother didn't want my father to get involved, but he said that he had to do something, or it would drive him crazy." Travis sat on the bed looking at Billy.

Billy sat on the bed next to him, and he shrugged his shoulder. "I hate him," he said, staring at the wall across the room. "I wish he was dead."

"How can you say that about your daddy?" Travis said, surprised that his friend would say such a thing, even though his father had given him a hard time. But it wasn't any way to talk about your blood.

"He's already dead," came the reply.

"What did he do?"

Billy looked at Travis and waited a second before answering. He wanted to make sure that he could trust his friend. Just because they were blood brothers didn't make him trustworthy, but Travis' loyalty to Billy's friendship overrode the fear of mistrust.

"Okay, here goes." Billy glanced at the closed door; then he turned and watched Travis. "Darrell said that he never wanted me. He wished I wasn't born. He hates me." Anger began to rise in Billy, and tears surfaced, but he blinked them back and spoke again, "He said any children that I have, I'm going to hate them, too."

"He hates you? No, he's lying. I saw how he treated you. He was good to you."

"He tried to love me, but he said it wasn't any use." He looked angrily at Travis, "I wish I was never born."

"Don't say that." Travis started to put his arm around him.

Billy pushed him away. "Don't touch me." He moved down to the foot of the bed. "I'm not a sissy. You don't have to feel sorry for me."

"Sorry," Travis said, watching Billy move some distance from him. "It's only a reflex. Daddy always puts his arms around me when I'm feeling bad."

"I'm not feeling bad, so don't put your arms around me."

"Okay, I won't." Travis stood up. "Yuck, what's all the talk about children? We're too young to have children." Travis walked to the dresser and glanced at Billy. "You know what grownups do to get them, don't you?"

"Yeah," Billy nodded.

"Ooh, I hate to think about it." He glanced at his closed door, watching out for his father. "It's so nasty."

"All grownups do it," Billy replied. "Like your daddy and mother."

"I can't picture my parents doing a thing like that. It makes me sick just thinking about it."

"Well, they do." Billy lay down on the bed. "One day, so will you."

"I'm never doing a thing like that."

"When you're older like my..." he hesitated, "like your daddy, then you'll do it, and like it."

"You're going to like it?" Travis watched him closely.

"I don't know," he stared up at the ceiling. "I heard Mattie and Darrell —" He stopped for a moment, and then proceeded with his statement, "Anyway they seemed to like it."

"I'm not going to have a girlfriend, so I don't have to like it." Travis lay on the floor beside his bed, and stared at the ceiling, too.

"Whether I like doing it, or not," Billy spoke, as if he were the only one in the room, "I'm going to have plenty of girlfriends, and I'm going to do every last one of them. Then Darrell's going to see that I don't need him, 'cause I'll have thousands of girlfriends who want me." His voice rose to an angry tone. "He'll see. I don't need him. When I have all the girls, then I wouldn't need anybody. I'll show him and I'll show Jesus, too." The memories of his mother's words filled his mind, anger rose in him as he pushed the words from his thoughts. "Yeah, I'll show them. Jesus loves me, mph! I'll show Jesus he can stop loving me, too." Billy closed his eyes. He felt increasing satisfaction. He pushed the thought of his mother, his father and Jesus totally from his mind. A thin smile spread across his lips.

Travis thought of what Billy said about all his girlfriends, and he didn't want his friend to think that he was abnormal, so he decided that he would have a girlfriend or two of his own, and he'd make sure Jesus didn't love him, either. "I take back what I said. I'm going to have a girlfriend, and she's going to want me, too." He closed his eyes. "And Jesus is not going to love me, either."

The two boys lay quietly in the room, each thinking about their future, and the girlfriends they were going to have, until soon they both were drifting off to dreamland.

* * * * * * * * * *

One week later, after Darrell had abandoned him to live with the Malcolm's, Billy sat quietly on the church pew staring at Pastor Simon. Billy took one look at Pastor Simon and decided right then and there, he didn't care for the man. He had no particular reason for disliking him. He dressed nicely, he had spoken kindly to Billy as he walked into the sanctuary, and his voice carried loud and clear over the loudspeaker. Travis would have labeled him cool, but everything was cool with Travis.

Billy closed his eyes and imagined he was at the park fishing. He wished he had gotten on his bike earlier that morning and rode out to the park, then, he wouldn't be sitting in church with Travis' family now.

The Malcolm's didn't attend the same church as the Rays. The Malcolm's church was huge and elegant looking. Six big, bright chandeliers filled the place. Burgundy carpet covered the church sanctuary and foyer. Bright colored pine pews adorned the sanctuary. Green plant decorations covered the pulpit area. A huge wood podium stood in the pulpit. Seven upholstered burgundy armchairs set behind the podium. These seats were for the pastor and ministers. A large choir section was located behind the burgundy armchairs.

The mass choir was wearing gold and purple robes; they sat attentive to Pastor Simon. Pastor Simon voice bellowed through the loudspeaker, "If you want to live right, then friend, you're in the right place!"

"Amen," several men and women shouted.

"Thank you Lord," Deacon Smith shouted from the rear of the church.

"Whatever God require we ought to be responding to that. God said whatever I need to have a place of abode, sanctuary, these are the things I need to have. I Peter. 2:5 You also as living stones are being built up a spiritual house, a holy priesthood, to offer up spiritual sacrifices acceptable to God through Jesus Christ," Pastor Simon's voice boomed through the congregation.

"Yes-suh!" A man leaped to his feet excitedly waving his hand toward the pulpit.

"Preach it, Pastor," another man shouted near the pulpit.

"God had called us with a holy calling. He called you to holiness. Now that you're holy, you have a heavenly calling, now consider. . . Jesus is also our Apostle, but He is also our High Priest. He oversees the confession that we make. The confession of our faith. We can't live up to our confession without assistance. This Jesus makes interception on our behalf. Christ intercepts our weakness and when he offered it to God, it is exactly what God requires."

"That's right," people leaped from their seats shouting. "He's our interceptor."

"Praise the Lord," one of the older mothers said on the front row.

"Yes-sir, I don't know about you all, but I'm depending on the High Priest to offer up to God on my behalf. The help of the Holy Spirit of what I'm incapable to offer up on my own," Pastor Simon stopped and looked around the congregation, before continuing. "I don't know about you all, but I need Jesus!"

"C'mon now, preach." A young minister grinned from the sideline.

"Yes-suh!" A group of men on the front row pew said in unison.

"Thank you Lord," an older lady shouted from behind Billy's pew.

Billy opened his eyes and scanned the sanctuary. He saw some people standing with their hands raised, talking to God. He looked at Travis' father and mother, even though they were younger, they stood with their hands raised talking to God.

"Yeah, if you want to know the truth, you have found it, right here in Harvest for Souls Church," Pastor Simon walked away from the podium and stood in front of the congregation. He put his hand behind his ear, and held a white handkerchief from the same hand. "I said if you *want* to know Jesus, Yes-sir, you're in the right house! Can I get an Amen?"

"Amen," The people yelled.

"I said, try Jesus, He's our High Priest. He's the Bright and Morning Star. Try Him in the evening time and try Him in the morning. You can try Him at noonday," Pastor Simon song the last statement. "I said try the Looorrrd."

"Praise the Lord." Everyone shouted jumping to his or her feet.

Billy couldn't hear himself think.

Travis sat quietly beside Billy. He nudged him with his elbow, getting his attention.

"Huh?" Billy asked frowning at Travis.

"Are you okay?" Travis asked, concerned about his friend. Billy had been acting strange all morning.

Billy ignoring the question closed his eyes again wishing the pastor would disappear into thin air. But the more he wished the pastor would disappear, the more Pastor Simon preached.

Chapter 8

$\mathcal{J}$t was exactly two weeks later, at Silver Rock Elementary playground, during lunch recess, Travis and Billy saw her. Adrienne Mitchell, playing *run and catch* with the other girls in her grade, along with two of the school's nerdy fourth grade boys. Both boys couldn't take their eyes off her. They watched her as she ran and giggled while the two boys played tug of war over her. One of the boys had her by one hand, and the other had her by the other hand.

"Who's that?" Billy asked Travis.

"I don't know." Travis said, not once taking his eyes off of her. He liked the way she moved her head when she laughed, and the funny little giggling sounds that bubbled from deep inside of her was like music to his ears.

"Who's that girl over there dressed in white?" Billy asked Vincent, a boy who had been playing softball with them occasionally during recess. He pointed over to Adrienne's group.

"Who?" Vincent scanned the group, and saw who Billy was asking about. "Oh, her. I think her name is Adrienne...somebody. I'm not sure," he replied. Then, Vincent called Roy, one of the nerds who was holding onto her. Roy glanced over at them.

Vincent beckoned him to come over with a motion of his hand. Roy let go of the giggling Adrienne and ran over to see what Vincent wanted.

"Who's that girl?" Vincent asked.

"Which one?" Roy said, and then glanced at Travis, and Billy.

"The one in white," Billy said.

49

"That's Adrienne Mitchell. She's new. Her parents are from New York," he said all in one breath.

"What's she doing down here?' Travis asked.

"They moved," Roy said.

"From New York?" Vincent was amazed. "Who wants to leave New York for Georgia?"

"I guess they did. They're here," Roy, said.

"What grade is she in?" Billy asked.

"She's in my class."

"What class is that?" Travis glanced at Roy.

"You know I'm in the third grade," Roy snapped at Travis. "Don't play like you don't know."

"She's in third grade, huh?" Billy said, as he scanned the group watching Adrienne disappeared behind the overcrowded monkey bar.

"Why do y'all want to know so much about Adrienne?" Roy asked, watching them.

"We just want to know, that's all," Vincent said, as he tried to stare Roy down.

"What's it to you?" Billy said, moving in closer to Roy.

"Yeah, you don't ask us questions. We ask you," Travis said, stepping up beside Billy.

"Sorry I asked." Roy sounded nervous. "I have to go now." He looked back, but the group of children he had been playing with was nowhere in sight.

"I think you'd better go, too," Billy bended forward, coming nose to nose with Roy.

Roy didn't wait to reply. He ran from them and soon disappeared to among the crowd of children on the playground.

"Look how fast that chicken ran," Vincent laughed.

Both boys laughed and agreed that Roy was not only a nerd, but a nerdy chicken at that.

"I'll be seeing you two tomorrow," Vincent said, as he left Travis and Billy standing alone.

"See you tomorrow," Travis said.

"Bye," Billy replied.

The bell rang for the end of recess. The children found their perspective teacher and started walking back inside the school building. That's when Travis and Billy saw her again. Billy ran up behind her and shouted, "Adrienne Mitchell, choo, choo, train. Adrienne Mitchell's got a funny bang."

The song and the mischievous boy caught her by surprise. She didn't like the way he made fun of her hair bangs. She liked her hairstyle. Her mom said it made her look all grown up, and now this boy teased her about it. She tried to ignore him, but he kept repeating the song, until finally she ran behind him to ask him to stop, but Billy ran quickly down the hallway, with an angry Adrienne behind him. Travis stood there as he watched the two run inside the building. His heart seemed to be caught in his throat. Butterflies flew inside his stomach. If there was such a thing as love at first sight, then Travis was in love.

"There is a way that seems right to a man, but in the end it leads to death."
Proverb 14:12

Book Two

Chapter 9

Present

"*W*hat's wrong with you, Billy?" Travis Malcolm asked. "Marrying Adrienne after all the low-down stuff you've been doing behind her back? I know you've been cheating on her with her best friend, Janet Wingo, and I see how you've been eyeballing her mother. That's real low. What? You two got something going on that I don't know about?" Travis asked. Travis had never understood how Billy Ray could be so unfeeling toward women yet still have them flock around him the way they did. "Why are you marrying her, anyway?"

"She's a virgin."

As if that explained everything. Not a word of love had been mentioned. "So? There are virgins still out there somewhere. That doesn't tell me a thing. Just how do you know she is?"

"I've been dating her since high school. I couldn't get in her bed then, and I can't now." He leaned back in the soft black leather recliner, "Besides, she's like a prize to me, something I've been waiting on for a long time, and now I'm about to have it. It feels good! Anyway, I think I love her. She's a love trophy," he grinned.

"You think you love her, and then say she's a love trophy? Love and trophy shouldn't be used in the same sentence regarding the woman you're going to marry. Love should be the only reason that you're marrying. Your motives are off, man." He watched Billy; his eyes showed disbelief of what he just heard from his best friend's mouth. "Your motives are all wrong," he repeated, trying to shed some light on his friend's irrational decision. "What about Donna Mitchell? What part does she play in your game?"

"What about Donna?" he laughed. "She's soon to be my mother-in-law, that's all."

"That isn't what I've been seeing. She's been flirting with you pretty hard, and I don't see you trying to discourage her. I saw you making eye contact with her, and I don't like the looks that passed between you."

"Who are you, my lawyer? Am I on the witness stand?" He looked at Travis, "Oh, so you're a preacher, now? Don't let that little holy book go to your head. Get a life, and butt out of mine! Case closed," Billy growled. He pushed himself up from the recliner to get a beer from the wet bar. "Want a cold one?" Billy laughed, "Yeah, I forgot you don't drink. Man, a Christian life must be a drag."

"Funny." Travis watched Billy and knew it would do no good to talk to him now. Whenever Billy said, 'Case closed,' that's it as far as he was concerned. No ifs, ands, or buts about it.

When Billy returned to the sunken living room of his two-story executive home, a can of cold beer in his hand, he resumed his position in the recliner.

"You still got the rings?"

"Of course," Travis said, amazed that Billy actually wanted to go through the trophy-prize wedding. "Man, I just hope you know what you're doing."

Billy leaned back in his chair and laughed, "Believe me, friend, I know exactly what I'm doing. I like Adrienne, and I know she loves me, because she tells me often enough and wants me to be the only one to take a ride in her pink convertible."

Trying not to laugh, Travis looked at Billy and shook his head, "C'mon, that doesn't sound like the Adrienne I know."

"I added a little spice to the last statement," Billy laughed.

Travis looked at his watch and stood up. "We'd better go if we want to get to the rehearsal on time."

"You go on ahead. I'll meet you there."

Travis gazed at his best pal since elementary school, and even though he saw a cool, handsome, mature man, Billy continued to be that same boy on the inside. Maybe that was why he still preferred being called Billy instead of the more mature Bill or William.

"I thought we were riding to the rehearsal together?" Travis asked.

"That's where you're wrong, partner," Billy replied. "I've got some last minute things to do."

"Like cutting some corner?" Travis eyed him suspiciously.

"Call it what you like."

"On the night before your wedding?"

"Is that a special day?"

"Man, I give up!" Travis threw his arms up in the air. "Who's the unlucky young lady?"

"I promised the lucky Sheila that I'd drop by there tonight. I'm going to see what she wants, and then I'll join you all shortly. Tell Adrienne I had some errands to run, will you?" Billy asked, moving from the recliner and getting his keys and another can of beer. "Sure you don't want one?" He held up the can.

"I'm sure," Travis said, walking to the door. "I'll tell Adrienne something, but you better get there." His tone held a note of warning. Lord, forgive me, he thought. He disliked covering up for Billy, but what could he do. Billy was his best friend and best friends watched one another back's.

"I'll be there. It's my wedding rehearsal. What kind of jerk do you think I am?"

He laughed, walking Travis out the door.

* * * * * * * * * *

Adrienne Mitchell looked at herself in the full-length mirror while the sales woman at the bridal boutique adjusted the train of her wedding gown. The white strapless, full-length gown had a very straight cut, giving the dress an elegant and dignified appearance. It was designed with white satin rose petals that encircled the bust, and one string of rose petals surrounded the waist, and hem. A single, diamond-like sequin was set in each rose's leaf. The matching shawl showed a rose petal embroidered at both ends. The veil was a tiara of white roses. She knew the dress would be beautiful, just from seeing it in the display window, but now that it had been altered to fit her petite frame, it became stunning. She turned from side to side, checking the fit, and then turned to look at her mother.

"Isn't it great, Mom?" Her eyes were bright.

Donna Mitchell looked at her own reflection, turning around in circles as she ran her hand over her flat stomach. The peach color of the dress she tried on brought out the creamy milk chocolate color of her complexion. "Oh, sure. It's great, honey." She looked at herself again, liking the way it fit her curves like a second skin. She whispered to her reflection in the mirror, "I wonder how Billy would like the dress. I'd loved to have that hunk of a man peel it off me."

"Mama! You didn't even look!" Adrienne's brow creased. "Can't you give me a minute of your undivided attention?"

Donna turned to her only child. "I'm sorry, honey. I just want to look perfect on your wedding day." Then she whispered under her breath, "I also want to be the one spending tomorrow night in Billy's arms." Donna grinned, "I'd give anything to change places with you, darling dear."

She looked at the straight-cut satin and Chantilly-lace wedding gown her daughter wore. "It's gorgeous, Adrienne." She cut a quick glance back to her own reflection in the mirror. "Trust me. It truly is."

Adrienne face beamed. "I'm so happy! Tomorrow night, I'll be Mrs. Adrienne LaToya Ray. Imagine! Me! Adrienne Mitchell, a married woman. Ooh, I have waited for this for so long," she smiled radiantly. "Billy Anthony Ray. It has a real nice ring to it. Don't you think?" She held up her left hand, wiggling her ring finger to show the three-carat solitaire. "Get it? Ring?" She giggled.

Donna forced a smile, then turned her back to Adrienne and looked at her reflection in the three-sided mirror. The smile suddenly vanished. Talking about Billy made her feel hot and set her heart racing. She loved the way his broad shoulders tapered to a narrow waist, lean hips, and those long, muscular legs moving seductively when he walked. His dazzling smile melted her very bones. His teeth were perfectly even, stark white against his golden brown skin, almost as if he'd had them bleached. His almond-shaped, light brown eyes made her feel naked, even when fully clothed, which sent delightful shivers over her each time he glanced in her eyes. Just think of being with him every single day and night, as Adrienne will be after tomorrow, would simply be a dream come true.

Adrienne walked up behind Donna. "You've been staring into that mirror for fifteen minutes now. Come on, Mama. What's that secret you're hiding?"

The sound of Adrienne's voice startled her, snapping her back to her senses, but the question jarred her. Her mind worked frantically for an answer, until she saw the teasing glint in Adrienne's eyes.

"Secret? Oh, I was just having a little fantasy about a man." She grinned watching her daughter's reaction, but there was none. "I'm teasing. I was recalling my wedding, when I married your father," she lied. "It was so romantic."

"Most weddings are." Adrienne smiled back. "Hurry and change. We'll have time to eat lunch together before I go to the rehearsal."

"Great idea."

* * * * * * * * * *

Travis looked at his watch. Billy was an hour late, and still hadn't made an attempt to even call. At least he should have the courtesy to call, and it wasn't like he doesn't have a cellular, he thought, glancing over at Adrienne from time to time. She looked pretty worried, with every right to be, and to make it worse, all her bridesmaids were sitting round complaining about the waiting.

Travis walked over to Adrienne and sat next to her on the pew, "Don't look so discouraged," he said. "I know Billy. The boy is a workaholic. He can't put a case file down when he starts working on it." He pulled out his cellular, and dialed the law firm.

He knew Billy wouldn't be there, but he didn't want Adrienne to know where Billy was. How could Billy do this to her? She deserved better, he thought, sliding the phone back into its clip.

"No one answered. That's a good sign that he's on his way," Travis said.

"Are you sure?" she asked.

"Positive. He and I were going over the Webb's case, and he told me to go on and to tell you that he'd be here late and don't start without him," Travis said, ignoring the conviction, and the scripture, Proverb 19:5 that came to mind, 'A false witness will not go unpunished, and he who speaks lies will not escape.'

"Well, we might have to," she said, looking at her wedding director and coordinator, Rochelle Peavy. Rochelle frowned, as she glanced at her watch, and then looked at her. "I don't think the wedding director is going to wait any longer. Billy couldn't have planned a better night to make a late grand entrance."

Travis looked at Rochelle and said. "I think you're right. Let's start. I'll stand in for Billy," he said, getting to his feet and taking her by the hands. "I can get some practice in for my wedding."

"Okay, but where is my maid of honor?" She asked. She scanned the room looking for Janet. "I swear that girl is never where she's supposed to be."

"I think I saw her going toward the ladies room. Do you want me to go and get her? You know I'm good at that sort of thing."

"No, that will be okay," she laughed, forgetting her problem for a moment.

"Now, that's more like it. C'mon, let's go and make your wedding director and your bridesmaids happy." He walked with her down the aisle to Rochelle Peavy.

"I would like to stand in for the groom, if that's possible?" he asked.

"Right now, anything is possible," Rochelle said. "The time is getting late, and we do have a wedding tomorrow," she laughed, nudging Adrienne with her elbow.

"We sure do," she replied. "Thanks, Travis. I can count on you. Seems like you're always there. Really, thanks." She tried to kiss him on the cheek, but he was too tall. He noticed what she was trying to do, and he bent forward so she could plant one on him, but his heart started pounding, and he suddenly withdrew. *Billy gets the girl. In law-school, whenever I'd asked a girl for a date, somehow she'd wind up in Billy's arms instead. Connie Weatherspoon had chosen Billy over him and he had broken her heart.*

Adrienne felt disappointed, but gave him a hug anyway, then took him by the hand. They joined the circle with Rochelle and the others in prayer. Afterward, Rochelle organized who would escort who down the aisle. Rochelle stood at the right sideline of the altar. She hummed the wedding march to start it. Adrienne stood at the back of the church and walked slowly down the red-carpeted aisle. She still didn't know where Janet had disappeared to, but they had to start without her. She finally reached the spot where Travis stood in place of Billy. It was strange to see him standing there. She noticed that Travis and Billy were slightly similar, the same height, six foot one, lean muscular body, but that's where it stopped. Travis eyes were dark brown compared to Billy's light ones. Travis had skin of a walnut brown, opposite of Billy's golden pecan complexion. His hair was dark brown like his eyes, where Billy's was light brown. He and Billy had those same dazzling white teeth. Travis was handsome, but Billy was strikingly handsome. Even though they were so much alike in some ways, they both were also as different as night and day.

"Who gives this woman away?" Rochelle asked. She pretended to be Reverend Albright. "Your father is going to say, 'I do,' then he will go and take his seat with your mother." She looked at Adrienne. "Make sure you tell him that tomorrow, and let him know that's all he says."

"I will," she answered.

"When your father sits down, then the pastor will start the ceremony." She hurried the ritual on. "Then he will say, 'Adrienne, do you take this man to be your lawful wedding husband,' and then you'll say —"

"Yes, I do," she interrupted.

"Okay then, and so on," Rochelle said. Then she turned and looked at Travis, and repeated the same thing, only to be interrupted again.

"Yes, I do," Travis said, looking down at Adrienne, and his heart caught in his throat. He fought back the urge to grab her, to kiss her, and rush out the nearby door with her, to hold her and protect her from the world and the cruelties that it had to offer. But he closed his eyes instead, and pushed back the thoughts that his heart had sent.

"Who's this marrying my woman?" Billy shouted, as he walked in the sanctuary wearing a cream-colored tailor Armani suit with a grinning Janet by his side.

Everyone looked up and saw him come down the aisle to the center of the room. Travis glanced his way and stepped backward, "I guess my time is over." He winked at Adrienne. "She's all yours, man." He stood by Billy as Rochelle started the ritual all over again.

"Sorry, I'm late, baby." Billy bent his head and kissed Adrienne.

"I'm glad you made it," she gave him a cool look, after returning the kiss.

"Where have you been?" Adrienne whispered to Janet, who now stood beside her.

Travis couldn't hear what Adrienne had whispered to Janet, but he felt pretty sure what was said from the way Janet glanced over at Billy.

* * * * * * * * * *

Billy wearing a blue silk robe took off his solid gold necklace and put it in the bottom drawer beside the bed, and then he lay on the bed, waiting for his new bride to come from the bathroom. Adrienne had been so shy when he'd wanted to undress her, wanting all the lights off, but when he'd told her he wanted to see her naked before him, she insisted she wear the gown her mother bought as a wedding gift. Although neither of them had seen it, because Donna insisted Adrienne wait until their honeymoon to open it, Billy couldn't wait to see what kind of gift sexy Donna would buy.

Adrienne slowly emerged from the bathroom, and Billy jumped off the bed, glaring at her. "I didn't know she'd do this," Adrienne told him timidly. She looked down at the long flannel nightgown, the hem to her toes, and the sleeves to her wrists, and the collar high around the throat. She'd at least thought to leave the buttons undone hoping to take some of the grandma look from it, but it hadn't worked. All she needed to complete the outfit was a pair of spectacles and her teeth in a jar by the bed! "I'm sorry, Billy."

He tried not to laugh, thinking of seeing Donna in something this ludicrous. He could understand the joke, but Adrienne looked mortified.

"Ah, baby. It's sort of cute." Never had he seen anything so homely in his life. The material was the color of old, boiled egg yolks that had turned yucky-brown, with huge red poinsettia flowers printed from head to toe.

She looked at him with tears in her eyes. "No, it isn't. It's hideous. How could she do this?"

"Everybody pulls a joke on honeymooners. Maybe someone switched the real gift. I'll be willing to bet your mother doesn't even know it." He hoped to soothe her hurt feelings.

"But who? How?" She cried and rushed back to the bathroom

to change from the ridiculous costume. Billy followed her. He stopped and stared at his new bride as she struggled with getting the monstrous gown over her head. For the first time, he saw the contours of her naked body. The smooth silkiness of Adrienne's paper-sack-brown skin lacked a single blemish. He quickly scanned her flawless body. His heart ached. It pounded violently, threatening to give him a heart attack. He touched his own chest in a vain attempt to quiet it.

"Mmmh," he said, breaking the silence and giving his wife help with the ugly gown. He stripped it off and tossed it to the floor at her feet. His eyes took in all of her petite frame. He was hypnotized by it.

Uncomfortable with her present state and her new husband's stare, she reached down and pulled the gown up around her, but he tugged it out of her hands and threw it to one side. Bashfully, she stood there with no covering to hide herself from his wanton eyes. She tried to cover herself with her hands, but Billy laughed and grabbed her. He picked up his new wife and carried her from the bathroom and to the king-size bed. He gently lowered his prize to the soft comforter.

She covered her eyes with her hands, but Billy removed them and stared down at her. "You're the most beautiful woman I've ever seen in my life. I love you more for waiting for me. I could never love another the way I love you," he whispered in her ear.

Adrienne stared up at Billy. He hadn't spoken to her this way before. It made her feel wonderful. She was happy that she had waited. He was her knight in shining armor. She would not, could not, love another man the way she loved Billy. She had been in awe with his patience toward her, and she loved the air that he breathed, which seemed to suffocate her with more love and admiration for him. She knew that she had hit the jackpot of love. She felt a swell of pride as he looked down upon her. He belonged to her. She had captured his heart, and her heart raced from his undivided attention. She vowed that she would make him the perfect wife.

His hand slowly trailed along her soft body, leaving paths of fire with every touch. He quickly shed his robe. He reached over to the nightstand and turned off the light.

* * * * * * * * * *

The Temptations oldie "Ain't Too Proud To Beg," boomed loudly through the Pink Willow Bar and Lounge, vibrating the walls. Thick clouds of smoke lingered in the air, clouding the soft colored, red, blue, green and yellow neon lights overhead. Travis sat alone at the bar and slowly sipped at his Hennessy, while he watched a couple dance seductively on the floor. He closed his eyes, swaying to the beat, imagining Adrienne sitting close to him, whispering undying love for him, softly in his ear. He smelled the freshness of her perfume; the scent of it drove him mad. He was crazy in love with her. He sniffed her brown shoulder-length hair and cupped her face in his hands. She parted her red lips.

"Getting stoned, big boy?" A hand touched his left shoulder.

Startled, he groaned, turning to the direction of the voice. A woman grinned at him, showing rotten, missing and crooked teeth with a gold plate on the upper front tooth, a lighting streak design on it.

"That's none of your..." The last word stuck in his mouth, so he took another sip of Hennessy.

She moved closer to him, deliberately rubbing her ample breasts against him.

"What do you need that fire-water for, when you got Clara here to show you a good time? And I mean a real good time."

He tried to move away from her, tipping over his glass, spilling liquor across the bar. "See what you made me do? Hey, Mac, give me another one." He held up his empty glass.

The bartender poured another shot of liquor, then walked over to wipe the bar top "Don't you think maybe you've had enough?" he asked Travis. He gave the woman a look that said, Leave the man alone, but she ignored him. He looked at Travis. "You've drunk almost half a bottle of that stuff!"

"Mac," he grinned, "who are you serving? The customers, right?" He grinned, picking up the glass. "You know it's a funny thing, Mac. I don't drink. I'm a Christian, and we don't do that sort of thing." He took a big sip and wiped his mouth with the back of his hand.

"Yeah. Leave the man alone and let him enjoy himself," she said as she sat down on the stool next to him. "Hey, mister," she said, "What's your name?"

"Travis E. Malcolm, Attorney at Law." He muttered, and then

he slowly turned away from her. The room tipped slightly around him as he adjusted himself on the barstool.

She crossed over to the other stool and sat, facing him again. She touched the tip of his nose, licking her lips. "Now, you don't want to be rude to poor Clara, do you, Travis E. Malcolm, Attorney at Law?"

"Go away, Adrienne." He closed his eyes.

"Whatever, Sugar," she said, watching him, "I sure could use me a drink right about now."

He opened his eyes, "Hey Mac, give the lady a drink," Travis said to the bartender.

"Thank you, Travis. Travis, that's a handsome name...just like you."

"What would it be?" the bartender asked her.

"Screwdriver," she answered, "and don't be stingy with the vodka."

"One Screwdriver, coming up." He walked away to make the drink. A minute later, he set it on the bar in front of her.

She sipped the drink, "Ooooh! That's good. Thanks, Travis." She moved closer, whispering it in his ear.

"No problem," he replied, draining his glass. "Hey, Mac! Give me another one."

"Okay, but this is the last one for you."

"The last one. The last one. Why does it have to be like that, Mac?" he said, closing his eyes to stop the room from swaying so much.

The bartender put the glass down before Travis. Travis picked it up and slowly sipped. The room spun slowly around him. He closed his eyes, but the room continued to dance and tilt. He reopened them, and the lights grew dimmer.

Clara put her hands on her meaty thighs, pushed her mini skirt on up a bit farther and scooted even closer to him until she was practically sitting in his lap.

"Do you want me to show you a good time?" she asked.

He looked at her. She was the most beautiful thing he had ever seen.

"Adrienne, you're so beautiful. I knew you would realize your love for me, and come to me. I love you so much it hurts," he mumbled under his breath.

Clara grinned, and asked again, "Want to let Clara show you a good time?"

"Who's Clara, Adrienne?" He looked around the spinning room. He closed his eyes and opened them slowly. "Where's Billy? I thought you were so in love with him. Why aren't you on your honeymoon, living it up? Don't come down here bothering me, getting my hopes up. I'm trying to have a drink here. Hey, Mac! Tell Adrienne to leave me alone!"

The bartender glanced down the bar at Travis. He felt sorry for men like him, who seemed to have everything going for themselves; money, the nicest cars, big, fine houses and plenty of beautiful women hot on their trails. But what do they do? They come down and drown themselves in booze, drinking until they throw their guts up, and wind up going home with women like Clara. "Aah," he said aloud to himself. "Why am I concerned, anyway? What has he done for me, but give me a hard time and boss me around like he owns the joint or something," he said. He turned his back on Travis and waited on another customer.

"Are you ready to go, baby?" Clara took him by the hand, but he pulled away from her and yelled, "Leave me alone, Adrienne! Why do you want me now? I'm angry with you! I saw how you kissed Billy and enjoyed it. Leave me alone! I'm not going anywhere with you!" He crashed to the floor.

The bartender rushed over from behind the bar and tried to help Travis to his feet.

Clara tried to help, but the bartender warned her, "Leave the man alone. You see that he's too drunk to go home with you." He lightly slapped Travis on the cheek. "C'mon buddy, get up. I'm going to call you a cab. You're in no condition to drive," he said, finally getting Travis to his feet.

"Mind your own business," Clara said, as she tried to wrestle Travis from the hands of the bartender.

"This is my business," he snapped. "Get out!"

He walked Travis to a booth to sit down.

"You don't tell me to get out! I'm a customer, too!"

"Okay, since you're a customer, buy something."

"I don't have any money."

"No money? Then get out. You're not a buying customer."

"Is this how you treat women 'round this messy place? Don't worry. I won't step foot back in here again!" She grabbed her purse from the bar top and headed for the door.

"I hope you don't!" he shouted after her.

* * * * * * * * * *

"The wedding was beautiful, Ms. Donna," Janet Wingo said as she helped Donna and Eddie Mitchell take some of the last minute wedding gifts to their car. "I can't believe my best friend finally got married." Janet put the small packages into the Mitchell's tan Lincoln.

"Yes. It was wonderful," Donna smiled. She looked at her husband, "Don't you think so, Eddie?" she asked.

"Well, I think you outdid yourself this time, honey. Everything was great." He kissed her on the cheek and set a large box down in the backseat. "And our daughter couldn't have married a better man."

"I can vouch for that," Donna smiled, and then said softly, "Who's more perfect than Billy?"

"Huh?" Eddie glanced back at Donna.

"What?" she asked.

"I thought you said something?" Eddie asked without taking his eyes off his wife.

"I did. I said I'd vouch for that."

"I mean after that?" he asked.

"Oh that? Nothing. I was thinking out loud." She laughed and looked at Janet.

"I'm always thinking out loud, too." Janet glanced at Donna. "I guess it's a woman thing."

"Well, I guess so," Eddie said, closing the car door.

Janet looked at her watch. "It's getting late. Is there anything else you want me to do before I leave?"

"No, you can go on home. Eddie and I are going to lockup the place, and then we're out of here."

"Okay," Janet said. "And congratulations." She hugged Eddie and Donna. "Remember, you're not losing a daughter. You're gaining a son."

"Indeed, I am, thanks," Donna said, hugging her.

Janet frowned at Donna's statement. She looked at her and wondered. Could it be she has a thing for Billy? No, it can't be, she thought and dismissed it.

"Well, you take care, young lady," Eddie said looking at Janet. "And don't become a stranger in our house, just because Adrienne has moved out. You're still welcome at our home anytime."

"I'll stop by and see you all. You haven't gotten rid of me that easily," Janet said, walking to her car. "I'll be over when Adrienne and Billy get back from Hawaii. She has to finish moving her clothes and stuff."

"I don't think Adrienne is going to be in the moving mood," Eddie teased. "New bride."

"That's not funny," Donna spoke in an irritated tone.

"What are you getting so upset about?" Eddie glanced at his wife.

"I don't think you should be making fun of your daughter, that's all," she snapped, looking away from him.

"I see," he grinned, "you're having that mother-in-law jitter. It's okay, honey, you're going to make Billy a good in-law. Relax and enjoy your new son."

"Yeah. I agree with Mr. Eddie." Janet said, as she looked at Eddie Mitchell and then at Donna. "I think you all are going to be one big happy family." Janet started her car up. "I'll see you all later."

"We're right behind you," Donna and Eddie both said, walking back to the reception hall to lock up.

"Bye," she said as she drove away.

"Well, that's that. Everything is locked up." He took Donna's hand. "I'm ready to start my little honeymoon with you. It's going to be fun having the house all to ourselves."

"Yeah, like a stick in the mud," she said quietly.

"Huh? What's that?" he asked looking at Donna. "Thinking out loud again?"

"What?" She tried to look innocent.

"Well, you said something."

"I said it's going to be swell. Just the two of us," she lied.

"I'm glad you see it that way," he smiled, opening the car door for her.

"Uh-huh," she replied getting into the car, turning her head so

Eddie wouldn't see the frown on her face.

He closed the car door, quickly ran around to the other side, and slid behind the wheel. "Yeah, we're going to have some fun now," he said as he drove out of the parking lot.

Chapter 10

*A*drienne stood staring out the big picture window. She could see the white sandy beach, and the huge blue waves of the ocean left her breathless. The sunlight beamed warmly through the window. Small particles of dust danced in the rays of light, ascending and descending visibly in front of her.

As she watched the tiny particles dance, she thought about last night, and a smile appeared on her lovely face. She thought about the way Billy made her feel. Their bodies had met and melted together in unison. She had discovered a paradise that she didn't know existed before. Words couldn't explain the spell that had captivated her. All the books on making love couldn't adequately explain what she had experienced with Billy during the first week of their honeymoon.

He was so gentle, guiding her into a world unknown, and she wanted every part that belonged to her. Lost in thought, she didn't hear Billy as he entered the room.

"A penny for your thoughts," he said, standing behind her. He hugged her, planting small kisses on the nape of her smooth neck.

Adrienne shivered from the thrill that his kisses brought. She smiled staring at the ocean. "I was thinking about last night," she answered.

"And..." he urged, waiting for her to go on.

"And I want you to make love to me again," she said, turning her face toward him.

"Are you sure you were a virgin?" He laughed, picking her up in his arms and moving away from the window. He put her down gently on the king-size bed.

"You know I was," she said sweetly. "You were the first."

"Just teasing. I checked," he winked at her, removing her terry cloth robe. He caressed her, his soft lips tickling the hollow of her throat, his warm hands trailing fire up and down the length of her body.

"Wait! Wait!" she gasped, then getting up from the bed and grabbing her robe. "I need to freshen up a little." She rushed into the bathroom and closed the door and locked it.

"Hurry back," he shouted. "You know, it's against the law to keep your husband waiting!" he stated.

"When did that become a law?" She unlocked the door and poked her head out.

"Just now," he grinned.

"Ooh, you ain't right," she laughed, closing and locking the door again.

"Might not be, but I'm ready," he said, reaching for the remote control and flipping on the TV. He scanned the channels, finding the SuperStation. The Atlanta Braves were playing and were up by two in the bottom of the eighth inning.

He jumped from the bed and poured himself a glass of brandy. He walked back to the bed, sat down, and sipped his drink. He resumed his position on the bed and watched the Braves go into the ninth inning.

"Hurry," he shouted at the closed door. "What are you doing in there?" He heard the shower running. "Great." He gave up. "Okay, take your time. I have the brandy to keep me company." He looked at his glass.

Finally, Adrienne emerged from the bathroom. Steam billowed behind her as she stepped back into the air-conditioned room. She had a big fluffy towel wrapped around her.

"Drop the towel," Billy warned her.

"Wait until I get in bed first," she stated, "then I'll slip out of it."

"Drop the towel and walk slowly to me. I want to see all that I'm getting," he added.

"Do I have to?" she asked, embarrassed even at the suggestion.

"You don't have to do anything," he said.

"Good." Her tone revealed her relief.

Billy rose up from the bed and walked to her. He pulled the towel from her and threw it across the room. He left her standing there, quickly returning to the bed to watch her.

She slowly moved toward him, more embarrassed now than she had been all week. She could see his eyes staring, seeming to burn with desire.

"Now, that's more like it," he said, grabbing her and throwing her gently on the bed. "This is the way I like it." He kissed every inch of her body with passion, leaving trails of burning fire with every kiss.

Adrienne thought the whole world around her had folded in and crumbled, as she lay breathless beneath her husband. This new experience had brought out another side of her that she didn't know existed. Who would have thought I'd be feeling and acting this way? I waited so long to have a husband, and then children. My dreams are coming true. And babies by this man will be beautiful, she thought, watching him through half-closed eyes as intense heat from his kisses flared through her body. I'm going to name our first son Billy Jr., BJ for short. I'll name our first daughter Billie. We'll have dozens, maybe hundreds, she sighed, knowing she was thinking foolishly. Maybe I'll settle for four or five, or possibility six. But no matter how many or how few, I waited so long, and now it's really real. I've dreamed, I've wished, I've thought of this day for years.

Billy stopped and gazed at her, before continuing, he asked "Another penny for your thoughts?"

"I was thinking about us." She smiled dreamily up into his handsome face.

"That's good," he mumbled resuming his kisses.

"And our children." She sang the last words out.

"Children!" He stopped, sliding his body off of her and lay beside her.

"Our children," she replied.

"Children! C'mon, Adrienne! You know how I feel about that," he said, playfully nibbling her ear, his arms going around her.

Adrienne wriggled her ear free from his grasp and sat up in the bed, "No, I don't know how you feel about that," she said pulling the cover over her and putting her arms across her chest.

"So it's like that now, huh?" He rolled over to the side of the bed and sat on the edge.

"This is our honeymoon. Can this thing wait?" he rose from the bed and looked at her.

"How can our children wait?" she cried, getting up. She walked around the bed to stand beside him, staring up at him.

"C'mon, let's stop this now and get back to loving," he said, trying to put his arms around her.

"No, Billy!" she shouted as she fought her way from his arms, scrambling from his reach. "I have the right to know why you're taking such an obstinate stand on this!" She stared at him.

"I don't like children. I don't want any, plain and simple."

"What! You never once discussed this with me. I thought we were in agreement about having children."

"That's where you're wrong, Adrienne. I told you I never wanted any children, now or ever," he said.

"I didn't know you were serious about it. I thought it was just macho talk, one of those things men go through. Are you afraid of the responsibility?" she asked, growing more impatient by the minute.

"Responsibility is my last concern. I told you, I don't like children. It's no secret." He said. "C'mon, let's stop talking before one of us says something the other doesn't like."

"Too late for that," she said. "I wish I knew how strongly you felt about this."

Billy lay back on the bed and stared at her angrily, "Would it have made any difference if I had told you?" he asked. "Would you have refused to marry me?"

The question jarred her. She stared at him and couldn't answer it. All her life she had dreamed of marrying and having children to call her own. She never thought she would have one without the other.

Tears flowed down her smooth face. She felt isolated, lonely, tricked, and deceived. She suddenly grew angry and glared at him, "I'm going home!" she cried.

"What? You're not going anywhere! I won't let you leave me, Adrienne." He scrambled off the bed, trying to reason with her. "This is our honeymoon."

She moved away from him, and then she opened the closet door and took her clothes off the racks. She dressed quickly in a pair of faded jeans, a large white shirt and a pair of sandals. She unzipped her traveling suitcases and started throwing clothes in them.

"Please, don't do this, Adrienne," he pleaded with her.

She reached for the telephone and dialed the front desk, requesting a bellboy to come and pick up her things. She grabbed her single case and walked to the suite door.

"Let's talk about this," he said, blocking the door.

"I don't want to talk to you, Billy. Please get out of my way."

"Please," he said, wanting to talk some sense into her. He could see that she was determined to have her way. "C'mon, baby, stay." He grabbed her, pulling her closer. "We can work this thing out. Trust me."

"Are you going to give me children?" she watched his expression.

"I didn't say that. But we can work out our differences."

"I don't want to work out any difference. I want to have your baby," she said, pushing away from his arms.

"I won't give you that." He turned his back toward her.

"Why not?" She stood, waiting for an answer. A hard lump formed at the base of her throat. Silence filled the air. "I see." Tears swiftly erupted, flowing down her cheeks. Quickly, she ran blindly out the room and down the hallway, bumping into the bellboy.

"S'cuse me, ma'am," he said, catching her to restore her balance.

"Excuse me," she wiped the tears. "My bags are in there, 511." She pointed at the suite, and then ran down the hall.

"Are you alright?" he called after her.

"I'm okay," he heard her say. "But would you please hurry and get my bags? I have to catch a flight back to Atlanta." She hurried down the hall to the elevator.

$\mathcal{O}$n the sixth floor of Ray's and Malcolm's law firm, Destiny's Child's "Survivor" played softly in the background, as Travis sat behind his oak desk dictating a letter to his secretary, when the phone intercom on his desk buzzed. His secretary watched him suspiciously. The other secretaries in the outward office knew he was dictating a letter to her. Who had the nerve to interrupt him in the middle of it? He had made this one thing clear to his secretary and all the others, including the receptionist at the front desk. When he informed them that he didn't want to be disturbed, then that was exactly what he wanted. Reluctantly, he picked up the receiver.

"Yeah, this had better be good." He barked.

"I'm sorry, Mr. Malcolm. I didn't know what to do. Everyone is gone for lunch and there's a strange looking old man sitting out here staring at Mr. Ray's office door. I asked him if I could help, but he just shook his head and said it's hopeless. Sir, I didn't want to bother you, but I didn't know what else to do. Would you come out for a second to see what he wants? Really. He does frighten me," she whispered, into the phone, her tone holding a note of panic.

He sat back in the chair and waved at his secretary to take a break before replying to the caller. "Okay, Ms. Garcia. I'm sure the man is just passing the time. That's probably all it is, but I'll come right out. Just give me a second." He hung up the telephone, and stepped from behind his desk. "I'll be right back," he told his secretary. "It seems like someone has Ms. Garcia spooked." He opened the door and walked out to the outer office.

He walked to the reception desk where Ms. Garcia was sitting staring at the old man who sat at the chair looking back at her. Upon seeing Travis, the man became quite nervous. Travis could see why the man had frightened Yareli Garcia. He looked as if he hadn't had a shave in weeks. His beard was long and straggly, which reminded Travis of the goat man, who had a long white beard and used to come looking for empty cans in his neighborhood when he was a boy. His clothing was ragged, and his facial features had a tired and withdrawn appearance. Death seemed ready to knock on the old man's front door. It reminded Travis of a saying his mother used when he was a boy, "Chile, I got one foot in the grave and another on a banana peel." But there was something in the old man's eyes that sent a stir, more of a chill, through Travis' body.

"May I help you, sir?" Travis walked toward the man, extending his hand.

The man lowered his head and mumbled something under his breath, but Travis couldn't hear what the old man said.

"Are you lost?" Travis tried to get the man to talk, but he just kept his head lowered, raising his eyes up just enough to see Travis, and then slowly lowering them again.

A familiar feeling embraced him, and a chill swept down Travis' spine again, and an overwhelming feeling crept over him. Where had he seen those eyes before? Travis turned to Yareli, nodded his head, mouthing the words to dial 911.

The old man suddenly brushed past Travis, walking to the entrance door. Travis strolled quickly behind him and touched the man's shoulder. "Wait, don't leave."

"Must go," the old man said. He opened the door and rushed out without lifting his head, nor looking back.

Travis glanced at Yareli and stepped out into the hall. He heard the old man shout to someone to go back. He saw a shadow of a figure quickly stepped into the elevator and held the door open for the old man. The old man dashed into the elevator, and the door closed. Travis raced to the elevator while chill spread through him. Then he pushed the down arrow button to the second one. When the door finally opened, Adrienne rushed out, and upon seeing Travis, collapsed into his arms, crying.

"Adrienne!" He was caught off guard. "I'm surprised to see you!" He held her close. "Where's Billy?"

"Oh, Travis, I could die!"

Travis glanced at the elevator door that the old man had gotten on, and then he looked down at Adrienne. She seemed helpless, and more beautiful than ever, even with black mascara running down her cheeks. He wanted to kiss her. He held her closer and brushed the tears from her eyes with gentle fingers.

"C'mon now. It can't be that bad."

"Worse," she cried into his shirt.

"Shhh, c'mon, let's go inside, and you can tell me all about it. We don't want any of our neighbors in the building to know your business." He took out his handkerchief and wiped her face. "There isn't any use in letting my secretary and Yareli know your distress. Remember you're supposed to be the happy bride." Travis led her inside the office.

"Yareli, quickly, call 911," he said, "and cancel that call before the cops shows up. I don't want any of them angry with us." He ordered, and took Adrienne's arm and led her inside his office.

"Yes sir," she replied, picking the phone up from its cradle. She dialed 911.

"Ms. King, I'll get back with you later today concerning the letter. Please hold all of my calls."

"Yes, sir." She stood up and smiled at him, and then she looked at Adrienne, who tried her best to hide her distressed state, but to no avail.

Travis watched his secretary eyeing Adrienne suspiciously before leaving the two of them alone. He knew the woman had caught the scent of the runaway bride, but he could count on Ms. King's secrecy.

He led Adrienne to the beautifully crafted brown leather sofa opposite his desk, and sat down beside her, brushing a stray strand of hair from her face. "What happened out there?"

Near tears again, trying to be brave, she replied, "Billy is acting ridiculous!"

Travis had heard all sorts of descriptions concerning Billy, but never one implying ridiculous. He laughed. She looked unappreciatively at him. "I'm sorry, Adrienne. Now, what were you saying?"

Tossing her purse to the side she got up to pace the floor, both arms across her chest. "Everything was fine...until," her voice trailed, then, "Travis, you know how I feel about children?"

Travis nodded.

"When you, Billy and I used to double date, I talked about it all the time. And you remember Billy used to make jokes about it? He kept telling us that children weren't in his forecast. We all laughed and thought nothing of it. And afterward," she hurried the words along. "When we were alone, I would bring it up again. Sometimes Billy would change the subject, and there were times when he acted unconcerned about it. I brushed it off, thinking he was just being Billy." Fresh tears sprung up in her eyes. She blinked to stop them, but it didn't work.

The tears slowly slid down her face. "Oh, Travis, I don't know what to do." She stopped pacing the floor to look at him.

Travis wanted to take her in his arms and soothe the hurt away. He stood up and took her hands, led her back to the sofa, and they both sat down.

"Now, I want you to calm down," he said. Travis squeezed her hands, reassuring her to go on with what she was saying. Adrienne smiled tightly at him; she leaned over and kissed his cheek. The smell of her minted breath and the smoothness of those luscious lips as they pressed against his skin sent an electrical charge through his body. At that particular moment, he was afraid to be with her. Please, help me Lord, the request raced through his mind. Suddenly dropping her hands, he stood up and quickly walked to his desk. He wanted some distance between them before he'd do what his mind kept tempting him to do. Better safe than sorry, he thought. He couldn't trust himself with her. He wouldn't be responsible for his actions.

She sensed something was wrong. She went and stood in front of his desk. He watched her. Adrienne, if only you knew the feelings you give me when I'm near you. If only you knew how much I love you and want to be with you for the rest of our lives. I'd love you and never let you go.

"Did I do anything wrong?" she asked, not really fully understanding what happened.

"No, you didn't do anything." He stared at her, looking for any clue that would tell him she felt the same about him as he did about her.

"Good. The way you jumped off the sofa, I thought . . . Well, I didn't know what to think." She frowned and sat in the chair in front of Travis' desk. She crossed her legs.

Travis didn't dare look at her legs. Enough was enough, and he had had his share of enough. Besides, why give the devil gasoline to throw on the fire?

"Please, Adrienne, finish telling me what you started to earlier."

She rose from her chair, only to sit down again. She crossed her legs again and resumed where she had left off. "Billy and I were making...." Embarrassed, she lowered her head. "Billy and I had a huge argument. Anyway, Billy told me that he didn't want any children. I can't believe that he doesn't want to have any, but that's what he said. And when I asked him why, he wouldn't answer my question. So I left, and here I am."

"Are you sure that he's so set against having children? Maybe you misunderstood him."

"No. He told me plain and clear that he didn't like them, and he didn't want them," she replied. "And, I don't know what I'm going to do."

"Do nothing. Go home, and when he arrives, let me know. I'll see what's going on with my buddy."

Suddenly, a loud commotion made itself heard in the outer office, and Travis' door suddenly flung open. Sheila Stone, a white middle-aged blonde waltzed in with an angry Ms. King at her heels. "I'm sorry, Mr. Malcolm, but Yareli and I tried to keep her out of here. And everyone else is still at lunch."

"All I want is Billy's hotel number," she snarled at Ms. King.

Travis walked quickly from behind his desk. "That'll be all, Ms. King. I'll take care of it." He grabbed Sheila roughly by the arm and walked her quickly toward the door. "Excuse me," he nodded at Adrienne.

"Thank you, sir," Ms. King said and rolled her eyes at Sheila, before stepping out the door.

Travis held tightly to Sheila's arm as they both walked out the door behind Ms. King. He closed the door behind them, then let go of Sheila's arm, "You have a lot of nerve to come barging into my office," his tone was firm. "How dare you?"

"How dare you!" she replied, rubbing her arm. Big red welts began to develop.

She glanced at Ms King and Yareli and added, "And, what are you two looking at?"

The two women turned up their nose and rolled their eyes toward the ceiling, and turned their back to Shelia.

Travis raked his hand through his hair and sighed, "Okay. I was a little hard on you in there." He looked at her arm where his hand had been only a second ago. "If I hurt you, I didn't mean to."

"Yeah, right." She flipped her long blonde hair off her shoulder.

"I mean that. Look. Billy is not here. You know that. He's on his honeymoon. So why are you here?" He took her arm again, but gently this time, and they walked into Billy's office. He closed the door. He didn't want Adrienne to hear anything the other woman in her husband's life had to say.

"I want Billy's hotel name, or his number. I called his cell phone number, but I keep getting his recorder."

"Can that wait?"

"No. I need to tell him something. It's important that he knows." she said, as she stood facing Travis.

"What is so important that it can't wait?" He gazed at her, watching her lips spread in a triumph smile. He didn't like the look.

"I think I'm pregnant."

"No, this can't be happening!" The news caught him so off guard that he fell into the nearest chair.

He looked up at Sheila. Bad vibes sang in every nerve in him. He thought about Billy, and then Adrienne. The news would crush her. Finally, he asked, "Are you sure?"

"I missed my period."

"That doesn't mean anything," he replied, hoping it's just a delay.

"Eight weeks," she flounced into the chair opposite him.

"That long?"

"Yeah."

"But who knows these things? Right? Perhaps your body going

through the life change thing."

"I'm too young for that."

"I heard some women start as early as twenty-five. And you have to be more than thirty."

"Don't you worry about my age! Just give me his number, so I can reach him."

Travis rose, becoming impatient with her. "I can't do that. The man is on his honeymoon. And I can't have you calling him and upsetting everybody. See a doctor first, and then go from there."

"Screw you! But if that's what it's going to take, so be it." She opened the door and stormed out, slamming it behind her.

"Whoever said that you were a lady needs their head examined," he shouted at the closed door. He sank back into his chair and sat there for what seemed like hours. It couldn't be possible. Shelia is having Billy's baby. The thought gnawed at his guts. It couldn't be, and then why not? The man was sleeping with every woman that wasn't a nun. "Oh, Heavenly Father," Travis, closed his eyes, and prayed. "Oh, Lord, please don't let this be real. It'd destroy, Adrienne. And, please save my friend, Billy. He has too many women in his life. Help him Lord, please help him, and reveal to him he doesn't have to live like this. And please forgive me. I know I haven't been doing the right thing when it comes to Billy. But Billy's my friend. Lord, please understand, Billy needs me. In Jesus name. Amen."

Travis pulled his electronic address book from his pocket. He then pulled out his cell phone and dialed Billy's hotel number.

"Room 511," he said to the hotel desk clerk.

"That room is empty, sir," the man answered into the receiver. "Mr. Ray checked out yesterday."

"Thank you."

He next dialed Billy's cell phone. There was no answer, only the recorder. He flipped his cell phone closed and held it in his hand. He looked at his watch and let his head fall back against the oversized chair. It had been a day of emotionally charged events, one after another, all in the speed of a matter of minutes. It had started with the old man. Thinking about the old man sent a new chill flowing through his veins. What was it about the old man that sent such a cold, icy, feeling through him?

Travis closed his eyes, "Lord, reveal the old man to me."

"Hey, your secretary told me that you were in here," Adrienne said, walking into the office. "What are you doing in here? I thought you had run away with the Blonde."

Travis got up and walked toward her, extending his arm and taking her hand. "It's been a long day, and it's only one thirty. C'mon. Let me drive you home."

She hesitated and looked at him, "Okay, but what did she want with Billy?"

"She's a crazy client of his, and you know how people can be. When they want to see their lawyer, there's no stopping them." He hadn't told a complete lie. Sheila actually was a client of Billy's. They walked out of Billy's office.

"Ms. King, I'm going to take Mrs. Ray home. Who else is on my schedule for today?" he asked.

"Mr. Michael Webb, at 2:30," she said, looking at him and then at Adrienne. "Do you want me to cancel it, sir?"

"Yes. I'm going home, after I drop off Mrs. Ray, I'll see you tomorrow. You two be good now. When the other two ladies get back from their lunch, I want you all to go home early and get some rest." He winked at Yareli.

"Thank you! You don't have to tell us twice!" They laughed, watching Travis go into his office to retrieve his suit jacket and Adrienne's purse. A few minutes later, Travis and Adrienne walked out of the office door to the elevator.

"I'm sorry if I interrupted you," Adrienne said as they stepped into the elevator. "I can call a cab."

"Me? Stay here? I don't think so. I don't want to get my secretaries upset with me, after telling them they could go home early. Besides, taking a cab to Silver Rock will cost an arm and a leg. I need to get out of Atlanta and put on my thinking cap, anyway." They took the elevator to the lobby floor and walked across the street to the parking garage. They got into Travis' dark green Lexus and drove onto the busy Atlanta street.

* * * * * * * * * *

Silver Rock was like driving into any other small town in the south. On the right side of the highway upon entering the city, a square blue sign that read "Welcome to the City of Silver Rock. Population fifty-five thousand," greeted visitors. Huge orchards of pecan trees decorated the background as far as you could see. Expensive houses took over the scenery where the pecan orchards stopped. Small ponds dotted part of the landscape for many of the homes. There were cattle around some of the ponds in the distance. Farther up the road, new apartments shared land with a new subdivision. Development made way for other new subdivisions and town homes. BP, and several other stations, was getting new face changes. Silver Rock's small medical center, "Rock Arrow," was under renovation as well, a new wing and emergency room being added to the modest clinic. Silver Rock was being spruced up. Long, black London-style poles stood at each intersection, extending a long limb out over the streets, replacing the traditional streetlights. The old, red brick courthouse was getting new white shutters at each of it huge reflecting windows. For the physically challenged, there were smoother ramps with black painted rails that ran up to the different doors of the courthouse. The police department and its rundown jail had moved from the old landmark on Indian Springs Street to a new, larger jail built on Arrow Point Drive. The three grocery stores in town and the department stores had been swept up in the vision of the city and were under renovation as well.

Travis turned his car onto Fairfield Lane, an elegant, less new subdivision with huge traditional-style homes; two-story red brick homes with huge white columns and white round balconies at the second floor off the master bedroom lined the quiet street. Travis turned into Billy's driveway and killed the motor. He jumped out of the car running around the front end, and then he opened the door for Adrienne. She got out and followed Travis to her new home. Adrienne used the key Billy had given her earlier to move some of her clothes and furniture there. She unlocked the door. Once inside, they both relaxed.

"I'm glad to be back," Adrienne said to break the silence. She glanced around the room, without really seeing it. "But I never thought I'd be on my honeymoon without my husband."

"Billy will be here sooner than you think." He sat down on the sofa. He wondered what insanity could possibly be going through

Billy's mind. "I know I would," he muttered, leaning back onto the sofa.

"I don't know. He seemed pretty mad," she said, and curled up beside Travis. "I hope you're right."

Travis' dark eyes looked down at her, and he put his arm around her, causing her to rest her head on his hard shoulder. He gently ran his hand through her hair. Old familiar feelings stirred in his heart. The scent of her perfume assailed his nostrils, and he massaged the nape of her neck with a soft touch.

The intimacy sent a sensuous pleasure shooting through her. She was bothered by his touch, but she didn't know why. Was it the insanity of Billy's actions, or could she be bothered by the pure enjoyment of Travis' touch? Travis continued to rub the back of her neck with gentle strokes.

"I love you," he whispered, and lowered his head closer to hers. Then, he kissed her.

She liked the taste of his lips, and she closed her eyes and returned his sweet-tasting kisses, with a fervor that surprised her. Then, Billy's face suddenly flashed into her mind. "No..." she tried to talk, but she was captivated by Travis' kisses. Oh, so you're like that, huh? She heard Billy sarcastically whisper in her thoughts. Cheating on me with my best friend? Some wife you turned out to be! She pushed away from Travis' grasp. "No!" she shouted. "We can't do this." She said, jumping up from the sofa, her hands covered her face. "What are we doing? We can't do this to Billy!" She wiped her mouth bitterly with the back of her hands.

Travis eased up from the sofa and stood in front of her. His gaze met hers. "I'm sorry, Adrienne. "I shouldn't have kissed you. I don't know what came over me, but I do know one thing. I'm in love with you. I have been in love with you since the first day I saw you out on the school's playground." He stood facing her, wanting to hear her say that she loved him, too. They both stared at one another in silence, and then Adrienne's shaky voice broke the silence between them.

"You don't mean that, Travis," she replied.

"I know what I'm saying, Adrienne." He moved closer to her, but she stepped away from him, as she crossed the room, putting some distance between them.

It hurt Travis to see her move away from him. It hurt him even more to think that he had lost her forever. That was the last thing he wanted. If he couldn't have her as his wife, at least he could have her as his friend. A sinking feeling came over him. A deep, sadness that was more a physical pain than a simple emotion. It started from the pit of his stomach, and worked itself up to the center of his massive chest threaten to choke off his oxygen supply.

"We can't do this." She said weakly keeping her distance from him. Adrienne was afraid that she would give in, and she wouldn't want to face the guilt that it would cause.

"I don't want to hurt Billy anymore than you do," he said, walking closer to her. "But I can't ignore these feelings I have for you." He stopped a short distance from her. He didn't want to appear pushy. He wanted to respect her need for some space. He loved her too much, to do otherwise.

"Then, don't do this. It would kill him," she said. "You're my husband's best friend, and you're the first real Christian I've ever met."

"It's a hard thing you're asking me, Adrienne. I can't count how many times I've prayed to the Lord about this. I want to be free from you, but I love you too much." he said, "but I'll try for your sake." He gave in, his shoulders slumping. "But there's something I must know. Didn't you feel anything for me?"

"I, I…" she was speechless, but her thoughts ran rapid. Yeah, I felt something. A surge. A spark. Hidden feelings bottled up on the inside. Feelings that shouldn't be there. These feelings should be reserved for Billy. No one else. But she held her peace.

"Tell me you felt something for me," he said. "Tell me, Adrienne!" he pleaded.

"Tell you what?" Billy asked, as he strolled through the front door. He looked at Adrienne, and dropped his overnight bags on the floor beside the black recliner. "I thought you'd be here. Yeah, tell Travis why you ran out on me! Go ahead. Tell him how you made a big scene and ran out of the hotel," he demanded, unaware of the tension between the two.

"Billy." Adrienne stared at him. She lowered her head, but raised it again. "I shouldn't have come here."

"Don't be silly. This is your home," Billy reminded her. "Where else would you go?"

"You made it back, huh?" Travis said before Billy could put two and two together.

"My flight came in this afternoon." He turned and looked at Travis for the first time. "I called the office. But no one answered the phone. I guess they all went out to lunch."

"No, I told them to go home for the rest of the day."

"Why did you do that, man?" Billy asked.

"It was kind of a slow day and beside I wanted Adrienne to get home safe without being robbed of a fortune."

"Thanks, man," he said, putting his hand out to Travis. "Thanks for taking care of her."

"My pleasure," Travis shook Billy's hand. "I think I'll be leaving now and let you two straighten out whatever it is that you need to straighten out." He glanced at Adrienne with a quizzical look and questioned her with his eyes, and then he walked to the door, opened it and stepped outside. Billy followed him, leaving the door open wide.

"Did she tell you?" Billy asked, leading Travis down the driveway.

"What?" Travis answered.

"The reason she abandoned me in Hawaii?"

"She said something about you not wanting any children."

"I can't understand why she's acting this way. She knew this."

"Maybe she didn't really know, or want to know," Travis said, looking beyond Billy. He could still see Adrienne. She stood at the front door staring at them.

"I don't know," Billy dragged the words out. "I've been telling her since I asked her to marry me last year. You'd think she'd have gotten it in her head by now."

"Sometimes, when a man talks to a woman, he needs to understand that she can't hear what he's really saying, because love has blinded her to his imperfections." Travis said, turning his attention back to Billy. "Go and talk to her, but this time talk with your heart, not words." He walked to his car. Billy followed him.

"Maybe you're right. But anyhow, I don't want any

children, whether she's blinded by love or not."

"Have you ever told her about your father?" Travis said.

"About Darrell?" Billy frowned.

"Who else am I talking about?" Travis said as he leaned against his Lexus.

"I can't tell her about him." Billy glanced toward the house. "He's dead, as far as I'm concerned."

"Maybe she needs to know."

"Know what? How my old man walked out on me seventeen years ago? Why does she need to know that?" he asked, shaking his head. "Sometimes, I can't figure you out, Travis."

"Yeah. How your father left you, and how you came to live with me, and how my father took you in and treated you like his own son." Travis understood Billy's shame, but he wanted Billy to be honest with Adrienne. He wanted her to be happy with Billy, even though he ached for her to be his wife instead.

"That's easy for you to say. Until you wear my shoes, you can't relate to my problems. Man, whoever left you? Who? When you answer that, then you can relate to my pain, and the anger that I have for Darrell."

"Who was there for you?" Travis asked. "Wasn't my family there for you?"

"That's just it. It's been your family, and not mine." Billy snapped.

"You had a problem with that?" Travis asked, watching Billy with dark angry eyes.

"No. Look, Travis, I have a great deal of gratitude for your parents. They took me in, fed me, gave me a good home, and educated me. I have a lot of love for them. And they taught me one thing, to continue to press on, no matter what."

"I'm glad to hear that." Travis' tone softened.

"Do you really know why I became a lawyer, Travis?" Billy asked.

"I thought you wanted what I wanted," Travis answered. He'd always assumed that his influence had had a hand in Billy's decision to go into law, but apparently he had been wrong all these years. Travis became quiet. He wanted to hear what his friend had to say.

"I became a lawyer so that I could find Darrell, and put him away. When I used to sit in the dorm room studying, I daydreamed about

Darrell and others like him. I wanted to put all of them away. I used to see Darrell in my mind, begging me to set him free from the cage that I had him in." Billy smiled. "That's the reason I worked hard and studied night and day. I wanted him to see that I didn't need him then, and I sure as hell don't need him now."

"The years of studying were only for your father?"

"For him and everyone like him." Billy glanced at Travis. "What? Are you surprised? Of all the people that I used to hang out with, you should have been the one who knew my plans better than anyone."

"I thought we were…"

"Shhh!" He interrupted Travis. "You don't have to say it. I know what you thought. And you're right. We're more than friends. But I didn't go into law just to be with you."

Travis was disappointed. He'd always seen Billy and himself as the Three Musketeers, minus one.

"Do you remember the last thing I told you that my father said to me?" Billy asked.

Travis nodded his head.

"He told me he hated my guts, and I would hate my own children. You don't know how it feels when you know your father wished you had died in your mother's womb. But to hear your flesh and blood talk that way can make a boy sick, and when that boy becomes a man, it can eat away at his guts, and leave an empty shell filling itself with hate until it is so full that the very hate could kill a man if he ever came into your reach. The old man was right, if he had the same feelings then that I have for him now. He can't love me, and I won't be able to love my own."

"What logic is there in that?" Travis asked.

"Logic? Have you listened to a word I've said? My father hates me. For that I don't need logic. I need Darrell to feel what I felt as a small boy. The torture I had to endure knowing that my own father abandoned me. The many questions I asked myself when I cried myself to sleep every night, wondering what did I do that was so wrong that it drove my old man away from my presence. How can I be responsible for a child, when the blood of my father courses through my veins?" Billy's tone was firm. He watched Travis for any sign of recrimination.

Travis chose his next words carefully. He learned that there wasn't any use in arguing with his best friend, when Billy had made up his mind about something.

"You'll find out if there's any truth to this hate-child-love thing sooner than you think."

"Huh?" Billy frowned. "What are you talking about?"

"Man, we need to talk," Travis said, opening his car door. He looked toward Billy's house, disappointed to see that Adrienne had closed the door. "Get in the car," Travis said as he got behind the wheel.

"What's this about, man?" he asked, and looked back at his house. Then, Billy slid in on the passenger side.

Travis started up the Lexus, and then maneuvered the car past Billy's sporty black Mercedes. The Lexus eased up Fairfield Lane. The ride was a quiet one. Billy sat snug in his seat as Travis turned off Fairfield Lane onto a busy four-way intersection, and then onto Highway 52. Highway 52 was a long narrow black top paved road. Old abandoned houses dotted up and down the narrow road. There was an old torn down clubhouse sitting next to a desolate parking lot. The parking lot was covered with tall weeds and timothy grass. The scene looked despondent, and dispirited. Travis drove past the gloomy site.

Finally, he turned off a little dirt road that led into Silver Rock State Park. The park had changed a lot in the last seventeen years. Where it used to have an old wooden-wheeled mill, redirecting a small part of the river into a narrow channel that fed into the lake, it was now a Historical Landmark. A gristmill had been turned into a museum and a small souvenir store. Travis parked his car in view of the lake. He turned the engine off. Even though it wasn't yet dark, the chorus noise of crickets chirping could be heard. Old memories washed over Travis as he stared out onto the lake. In his mind, he saw Billy holding up a string of fish with a big, silly grin spread across his face. There was something else that tried to surface, but he couldn't put his finger on it, yet. He didn't turn and face Billy. He closed his eyes and took a deep breath, then exhaled slowly. He opened his eyes, but he kept looking straight ahead.

"I saw Sheila today," Travis said, still avoiding looking at his

Mary R. Butler

friend.

"So, what else is new?" Billy asked, shrugging.

"She thinks she's pregnant." Travis knew this bit of news would send Billy reeling.

"Pregnant?" Billy shouted, and leaned his head back onto the headrest. He closed his eyes before speaking. "Who's the father?" he asked.

"She said it's yours," Travis replied, finally looking at Billy.

Billy grunted. "And you believe that whore?" He shook his head, "Do you know what kind of woman Sheila is? She's a lying—"

Travis interrupted, "Whether she's a liar, or not, she's pointing the finger at you. Man, I told you to leave her alone, that she was trouble. As always, you wouldn't listen. Now, you have this thing hanging over you."

"She's a gold digger!" Billy absently touched the gold necklace hidden beneath his white Polo shirt. He motioned for Travis to put down the window on his side. He needed some air. Travis turned the key in the ignition, hit a button on his door, and Billy's window sank into the door. He turned the key again cutting off the power.

Silence filled the car. Travis eased back on the headrest, while Billy thought through his predicament.

"Did she say she was pregnant, or does she think she is?" Billy asked as if searching for the quickest way out of his dilemma.

Travis opened his eyes and lifted his head from the headrest. "She thinks she's pregnant," he replied.

"Good," Billy answered. "So it's not a definite."

"Okay, it's not definite, but what if she really is? She mentioned she hadn't had a period in weeks. We can't rule that out. If she's pregnant then you have to come up with a plan. You don't want Adrienne to find out that another woman is having your baby. Another woman having the very thing that separated you two from what should have been a perfect honeymoon. That'll go over big."

"I need a drink," Billy said in a tone that was too low for the normally outspoken man.

"That makes the two of us," Travis said.

"Women! What was she thinking? She said she was on the pill. Man, un-umm, I know what she's trying to do. She's trying to stay in my life, but it's not going to work." Billy opened the car door, and stepped outside. He walked toward the path where the lake began.

Travis stepped out of the car and followed him. "You need to talk to her." He hated to be the bearer of bad news, but Travis couldn't help thinking that maybe Billy had it coming, especially considering he liked to walk on the wild side of life.

"Yeah. You're right. I need to talk to her right away. No one is going to give birth to a child of mine!" He scanned the lake without really seeing it. "No one!"

"She might not be pregnant. Then you won't have anything to concern yourself about," Travis said, trying to ease Billy's troubled mind. He watched small waves ripple across the huge man-made lake. Fishing was good there. Travis watched three young boys sitting on a bank of the lake. Two had their lines in the water, while the third one fidgeted with his bait. The third boy looked to be younger than the other two boys. The oldest two boys reminded him of himself and Billy at that age.

"Yeah, but I'm not taking that chance, remember?" Billy said. He walked back to Travis' Lexus. He looked at his watch, and frowned, "It's getting late. Would you drive me by Sheila's house?" he asked, getting back into the car.

"Sure," Travis said, and jumped behind the steering wheel. He started the car and drove out of the park.

Chapter 12

*A*drienne opened the door for Janet. She called her to come over when Billy and Travis had left out the driveway. She felt lonely and needed someone to talk to. She could still feel the sweet taste of Travis' kiss. Adrienne was afraid that the incident had brought out some hidden monster that was buried deep down inside her. She had to admit she really liked the way he kissed. But she had to remember that she belonged to another man. But the thought of Travis sharing his true feelings for her frightfully overwhelmed her, yet at the same time, thrilled her.

"When I answered the phone, I couldn't believe it was you. What are you doing back? I thought you all weren't due back until next Friday? Where is Billy?" Janet glanced around the living room.

"He left with Travis. I don't know where they went." Adrienne paced the floor, and then she stopped and waved for Janet to have a seat. Janet sat on the sofa. Adrienne stood near the sofa, and tears rolled down her cheeks.

"What's the matter?" Janet asked, suddenly getting up and rushing to Adrienne.

She wrapped her arms around her. "What's the matter with you?"

"Oh, Janet, everything has gone wrong." She eased herself from Janet grasp, and sat on the sofa. Janet sat beside her. "Billy and I had a fight in Hawaii. I caught the first flight out. I wanted to get away," she sobbed.

"No kidding! You ran out on your honeymoon?" Janet tried to sound sad by the event, but a wicked smile spread across her face.

"We had a terrible fight. I had to do something. I was so upset with Billy that I couldn't stand to stay in the same room with him any longer."

"Did you fly back together?"

"No. He must have caught a flight right after mine, 'cause he came home about an hour ago."

"Do your parents know that you're back?" she asked.

"No. I don't want them to be worried. You know how they are?"

"Yes. I do know," Janet replied, and then asked, "What's so bad 'bout your fight that would cut off your honeymoon?" She asked as she pretended to be concerned.

"It's a long story," Adrienne said, as she lowered her head and shook it slowly. Then raised it back and looked at Janet.

"Shoot!" Janet said, crossing her hands in her lap. "I'm listening."

"It all started when I mentioned children," Adrienne said, sorrowfully. "But Billy doesn't want any."

"Children? Why do you want children now? You're newlywed. There's a plenty of time for that."

"Time? I wished that was all there is to it. Then, I would have hope. Billy doesn't want children at all!" Adrienne sobbed.

"Oh, that?" Janet brushed a strand of hair away from her face.

"He's doesn't want any, Janet. My husband doesn't want my babies."

"Sure he does," Janet said, not really wanting to see Adrienne carrying Billy's baby. "He'd be a fool not to."

"He used to tell me all the time that he doesn't like children. Really, I thought he was joking with me all that time. Until the other night. Janet, you know how much I adore children and want some of my own?"

"Things will work out," Janet said. She smiled, hoping Adrienne couldn't see the slyness in her smile. "You just keep pushing at him. He'll come around." Yeah, she thought. Right to me.

"I hope so," Adrienne answered.

"You'll see." Janet stood up from the sofa. "Look, you go on upstairs and take a long hot bath and get a little rest. Take a nap. When you wake up, I guarantee everything's going to be a whole lot better."

"But what about Billy? He'll probably be home soon."

"I'll stay here until Billy and Travis get back. I'll keep him entertained until you wake up. I promise." Janet was eager to get Adrienne upstairs and out of the way.

Adrienne pushed herself up from the sofa. "You're right. I'm tired. I need to get out of these clothes." She looked down at herself. "Good thing I moved my stuff over here or I wouldn't have anything to put on." She walked up the stairs. She stopped a few steps up and glanced back at Janet. "Thanks for staying. You're a real friend."

"No problem," she said as she watched Adrienne go on up the stairs. "No problem at all." She smiled to herself.

Chapter 13

"**C**ome over here and let me see you!" Sheila sat on the sofa, pulling Darrell Ray down beside her. "It has been a long time since I saw you last."

"It has been a while," Darrell said, in a whispery tone. "I can't believe how grown up you are. Time sure does fly by," he mumbled, with a distant stare. "Too quick."

"Yes. The last time I saw you, I was knee high to a grasshopper," she laughed, making him feel comfortable.

"Yeah, you were a little bitty ol' thing. I remember your grandmamma, Ms Lucille. She was a nice woman, God rest her soul. Do you remember those mornings when she used to bring you by the factory to see Addie?"

"Do I! It used to make Mama mad when she saw Grandmamma walking in there dragging me behind her."

"I guess Addie worked those long hours and Ms. Lucille made sure that you saw her, so you wouldn't forget how your own mother looked." He laughed, then continued to talk. "Me and the guys at the factory used to talk about you behind your folks' back. We didn't want those women mad at us for picking on you. You had those big brown eyes like a baby doe staring scared into a pair of headlights. Those long spaghetti legs kept tripping you up. You were a funny sight to see. Skinny as a rail. All morning long, you would sit near Addie, watching us work, while she kept you filled up on Cokes and honey buns. Oh, you were something else! I guess those honey buns caught up with you, just look at yourself. All grown-up, and your body has filled out in all the right places. If the guys could see you now, they wouldn't recognize you."

Sheila Stone let her head fall back as she roared with laughter. "Mr. Ray, is that the reason you didn't know me at the bus station this morning?"

"That's why I didn't recognize you until you called my name. When I saw you, I said to myself, now, that can't be Ms. Lucille's granddaughter?"

"Yes, it's me," she laughed, "I'm glad you decided to come after you got my invitation. Mama told me how hard it was to track you down. She found the last letter you wrote her. It was posted-marked Jackson, Tennessee. It's a good thing she found that letter, or we wouldn't have known where to find you."

"Yeah, I did a lot of traveling after things didn't work out for me in Mobile. Mattie had ran off to New Orleans with another man, and left me high and dry at her sister's house. Urla Mae wasn't too kind to me after Mattie left. So I figured it was high time for me to leave. I worked a lot of odd jobs here and there, trying to make ends meet. I was lucky to get Addie's mail. My former landlord came into the store one day where I hung out when I'm looking for work. She came up to me and handed me Addie's letter. She told me she thought it was important, coming all the way from Mobile. I have to be honest with you. At first, I had second thoughts about coming here." He glanced around the room. He looked tired and worn out. "But I was happy to get your letter," he replied.

"I'm glad you decided to come. I remember Mama telling me about your son. How the welfare people took him from you after your wife died."

Darrell stared at her for what seemed like eternity before speaking, "That's not exactly what happened," he said, slowly, as tears rolled down his cheeks.

"Do you want to talk about it?" Sheila asked, taking the old man's hands into hers. She patted his hands, reassuring him that he could trust her with his story.

Once again Darrell glanced around the room and then he looked at her. "Do you have anything to drink? I'm awful thirsty."

"I have a bottle of Scotch. Will that do?"

"Anything to calm my nerves," he chuckled softly.

"One Scotch on the Rocks coming up." She got up to pour the drink. "It'll only be a minute. Hold that thought, I'll be right back." She left the living room and went into the kitchen.

"I can wait," he grinned. "I don't have anywhere else to go," leaning back on the sofa.

A few minutes later, she returned to the living room, holding two tumblers of Scotch. She gave one to Darrell, and returned to her place on the sofa beside him. She sipped on the Scotch, "Mmmh! That hits the spot." She stopped sipping on her drink and announced, "Let's make a toast."

The old man held up his tumbler, "To what?"

"To you and your return home."

"To me and my return home," Darrell repeated, touching his tumbler against hers then bringing the tumbler to his mouth.

Sheila stopped him from taking a sip from the cup. "No! Wait!" she squealed. "Let's do it right!"

She held her tumbler high above her head. Darrell held his tumbler high.

"To Billy Ray and his father reunion!" Sheila cried out.

"I don't think so," he said, lowering the tumbler.

"Why not?" she asked. "You have every right to toast your son. When Billy sees you, he's going to flip. It's like a dream come true. Billy's going to owe it all to me, because I found you. What other woman have done that for him?"

"I'm not sure my boy would want to see me." The old man set the tumbler of Scotch down on the coffee table. He raised his eyes up at Sheila, "Please, don't get your hopes up."

"Mr. Ray..."

"Call me Darrell," he said.

"All right. Darrell, you couldn't help 'cause those DFACS people came and took your son away from you. They probably figured that you being a man couldn't raise a little boy by yourself. Welfare is kind of picky about that sort of thing. So, don't blame yourself for something that was out of your control. Blame the government." She picked up the tumbler of Scotch from the coffee table and handed it back to him. He pushed it away. Sheila set the cup back on the coffee table.

"I have to come straight with you, Sheila." He looked nervous. "I didn't tell the people in Mobile the truth. I didn't tell them what really happened to my boy and me. I knew they wouldn't understand."

"Understand what?" she looked confused.

"Welfare didn't take my son. I left him here...in Silver Rock."

"I don't get it."

"I walked out on my own son. I said some terrible things to him when he was a little boy. He wasn't any older than you, when I first saw you at the factory. I've been living a pure lie since the first day I set eyes on Addie, Ms. Lucille and the other people down in Mobile." He lowered his head and confessed, "When Addie wrote to me in her letter that you had moved to Silver Rock, and that you wanted to talk to me, I was nervous and excited at the same time. When she said you knew my boy, then I was really beside myself. I couldn't eat. I couldn't sleep. I just wanted to see my son. I want to see him after all these years. But I'm afraid. I'm afraid he won't feel the same about seeing me. While I was sitting on the Greyhound bus, I asked myself, what am I doing? Who was I kidding? I'll be lucky if Billy doesn't' slap the taste out of my mouth. I thought about catching the next bus back. Then something inside of me wouldn't let me do it. I have to see Billy. I have to talk with him. I want my son back." Tears surfaced at the mention of having Billy back into his life.

"Why are you telling me this?" she asked. "Now all of my plans are ruined 'cause of all the lies you been telling Mama over the years. How could you? I wasted my money sending for you!"

"No, your money wasn't wasted. It was a good charitable deed that you did. I'm thankful. I'll have a chance to make it right with my boy. This morning when you told me my boy was an attorney, I couldn't believe it, but when I saw his name up on the office door I smiled for the very first time in years. 'Cause I was so proud of my boy, he had made something of his life. And seeing Travis, I almost broke down in tears. Thank God he didn't recognize me. When I saw Travis this morning, I couldn't believe how good he looked." Tears swelled up in the old man's eyes again. "The last time I saw Travis was the last time I saw Billy. Standing in the same room close to Travis today brought back a lot of memories of my son."

"What, oh no, I can't allow you to stay here after this! I'm driving you back to Atlanta right away and putting you on the next bus out of here!" She stood up, and walked the floor. "You have to go now! You'll only complicate my plans."

"I can't leave my boy again," he stood facing her.

"Leave! You left years ago! Do you think Billy is going to let you back into his life that easy? I have news for you! I don't think so!"

"That's a chance I have to take."

"What you did to him is something that is not easily forgotten! Billy will never forget what you did!"

"I have to make him understand."

"How?" she laughed. "Mr. Ray this is not a movie, something that you can turn on and off at your will. This is real!"

"Do you want to keep him for yourself?" he asked, in a trembling tone.

"That was the plan until you spoiled it with your lies. Yes. I had it all worked out. Billy would see you, and he'd be happy that his dear old dad is back in his life after all these years. He'd see that I looked hard for you and found you homeless somewhere. Then that new wife of his would be history after Billy had seen how desperate I was to make him happy." She stood in the middle of the floor and picked up his Scotch from the coffee table. She drained the tumbler. "Now, everything is ruined 'cause of you!"

"Billy has a wife?" Darrell looked surprised. "I didn't know he had a wife. Why didn't you tell me this earlier?"

"Oh, I forgot about her. It must have slipped my mind," she grinned. "The two were married recently. But don't worry she won't be there long," she sneered.

"Billy is married?" Darrell was trying to comprehend all what Sheila was saying.

"For now," she said, turning her back to Darrell. "Get your things; I'm taking you back to Atlanta." She left the room to go to get her car keys.

"I'm not going to stand by and watch you plot my son's life!" he shouted.

"What are you going to do about it, old man?" she said, walking back into the living room, holding her purse and car keys. "Knowing your son the way I do, Billy probably would rather see you dead."

"I'll do anything to stop you from ruining my son's marriage." He walked closer to her.

"You? Humph! I don't think so." She pointed her finger at him.

"I'll stop you."

"What can you do? You don't have a dime to your name! Look around you Pop! You're standing in my apartment! Broke! And you say you're going to stop me. You don't have enough money to hitch a ride out of Silver Rock! And you're going to stop me? Get out of my house foolish old man!"

"Okay, I'm leaving! But I warn you if you so much as touch a hair on my boy's head, I'll be back, and you're going to wish you never knew this foolish old man!"

"I'm so scared!" she laughed. "Now get out!" She yelled.

"So much as touch a hair on my boy's head," he pointed his finger and shot her an angry look before walking out of the front door.

"Don't you threaten me Pop!" she shouted at the closed door.

Stepping out into the evening sun, he put his hands into his tattered jean pockets and made his way out of the apartment complex.

* * * * * * * * * *

Cascade Crest Apartments stood on the south of town over the railroad track and across from the Silver Rock Police Department. The apartments were not much to see, they were plain and in need of repair. Travis parked his car at Sheila's apartment building, and then he and Billy got out of the car.

Heavy aroma of southern fried chicken seeped through the window crevices of the ground apartment underneath Shelia's. The strong fragrance reminded Travis of his hunger pangs. He hadn't eaten at all, not even a candy bar. He inhaled the aroma as he followed Billy up the two flights of stairs to Sheila's apartment. Billy knocked on Shelia's door. They could hear movement coming from inside. Then the door opened.

"Billy!" she screeched, holding the door wider for him to enter. "I thought you were in Hawaii? I was at your office this morning! Did Travis tell you? I can't believe you're here!" Billy walked past her leaving Travis standing in the doorway. "Oh, Travis?" she said, surprised to see him.

Travis knew he was the last person Sheila wanted to see. He smiled and asked, "May I come in?"

"Sure. Yes. C'mon in," she said, stepping back to let Travis in. "Have a seat," she spoke, closing the door. "Billy I'm so glad to see you," her face glowed looking at him. "How was she?" She whispered in Billy's ear. "Is she better than me?" she asked, allowing her lips to slide smoothly off of his ears as they made there way to the side of his neck. She bit his neck softly pulling his skin between her lips.

"Stop that!" he demanded pushing her away from him.

"Why? What's wrong?" she asked innocently.

"I didn't come to socialize," Billy said. "I stopped by to hear this news you have for me."

"What are you talking about?" Sheila asked, "C'mon, let's go into the kitchen. Do you want anything to drink? I have some beer in the fridge." She walked into the kitchen.

"You know what I'm talking about, Sheila!" Billy said leaving Travis in the living room and walked into the kitchen. "It's not going to work."

Travis could hear the refrigerator door open and close.

Travis knew Billy wasn't' the one to play cat and mouse games with Sheila. He was going to catch her in her own little trap. Travis sat on the sofa. He scanned the living room. It was small, and not well furnished. An old blue faded Oriental rug lay in the middle of the floor. A scratched, cigarette-burned, coffee-stained, table sat on the rug, dividing the worn flower printed love seat from the brown wing back chair. A large oil painting of Elvis hung on the wall behind the love seat. Two-brass flowerpot stands overflowing with green plastic flowery vines, stood in different corners of the room. Cigarette butts filled the glass square ashtray on the coffee table. The smell of musk mixed with Scotch saturated the room.

"Talking about our baby?"

"Yeah, that!" he said calmly. "I want to know the truth." He walked closer to her. "Are you pregnant? And if so, who's the father?" he asked in a firm, but soft tone.

"That's not the way to ask a woman if she's having your baby." Sheila smiled coyly and moved away from him, and stood at the other end of the table and added, "I know you can ask me better than that?"

"I didn't come here to fight with you, Sheila. Please, tell me, are you pregnant, and am I the father of your baby? That's all I want to know."

"What if I am? Does it matter? Will it break some rules with you or something?"

"Sheila, would you please give me a straight answer?" he asked, walking slowly around the table toward her. Then he stopped. He didn't want to frighten her. Calmly, he asked again, "I want to know, are you carrying my child?" He made no attempt to get closer to her. "I know we can work this problem out." He reached into his back pocket and pulled out his wallet and removed six hundred dollars from it. He slapped the money down on the table. "Here, this should take care of everything. And if this is not enough, let me know. You know, you can count on me?" He put his wallet back into his pocket and took a few small steps around the table to her. If Sheila didn't think much of protecting herself, then she's the fool and he won't be part of her foolish plan. What in the world was she thinking, he thought?

"Abortion?" Sheila spit the words out. "You want me to kill our child? I will not kill my baby, Billy! I can't believe that you would think of killing your own baby!" She looked horrified.

"I want what is best for you," he said. "You have your whole life in front of you. Why throw that away?" he explained.

"No, Billy, you want what is good for you! You're selfish in asking me to kill our baby! I have news for you. I'm having our baby, whether you like it, or not!" Sheila's voice rose.

"Okay, calm down. Let's forget about what I proposed for a minute. But have you considered the hurt that this would cause a lot of people? My wife for instance. Would you deliberately hurt her for what I have done?" he asked.

"So this is what it's all about. Your precious wife." She moved a few steps around the table away from Billy. "It's a little too late for that, don't you think?"

"Sheila, you can't be serious about this. Consider the consequences."

"Consequences? Billy, you should have thought about that

when you were getting in my bed late at night." Sheila said, walking around to the other end of the table, leaving a big gap between them.

"That was my biggest mistake," Billy replied.

"I didn't plan on this baby, but it is here now, and we can't do anything about it."

"There's a lot we can do," he said. "Please, Sheila reconsider my proposal. Take the money and get rid of it."

"I'm not some defenseless fool in your courtroom." She spit the words out like venom. "Let's get one thing straight! I don't care anything for your wife! She needs to know that her husband is two-timing her, with another woman that is carrying his baby."

"I'm begging you," Billy pleaded. "I've never begged a woman before in my life, but I'm begging you not to have this baby."

"No amount of begging will stop me from having your baby. I'm having the baby, Billy. I want your baby 'cause I love you. Can't you see that? With this baby growing inside of me, I'll always have a piece of you."

"If you truly love me, you would do what I asked of you," he walked around the table face to face with her. He brushed his lips up against hers and kissed her softly.

"I do love you," she whimpered almost surrendering to his spell. "That's why I have to have your baby. I want us to be a family."

"I have a family. I have Adrienne," he said, as he turned and walked away from her disgusted by her stupidity.

"That's exactly my point! You have Adrienne, and Adrienne has you! I don't have anyone, but our baby."

"There are no us, Sheila. You were just a craving I had to fill."

"I don't believe that! I know you love me, but you don't see it yet. But when the baby comes, you'll see it." She swore.

"Sheila, listen to what you're saying. What you're saying doesn't make sense," he tried to reason with her.

"No matter what you say, I'm having our baby, come hell or high water!" she shouted. "I'm having this baby!"

"Okay, if that is how you feel, I can't stop you." He turned away from her and walked out of the kitchen.

Travis jumped to his feet as Billy came around the corner into the living room. He had heard the whole conversation between Billy and

Sheila, and he had to admit, Billy was taking the news more calmly than he thought. He felt sorry for his best friend and wished that he could comfort him in this nasty situation. Perhaps, he would come back alone later tonight and try to talk some sense into Sheila. Maybe he could persuade her to change her mind. He hoped so, for Adrienne's sake.

Suddenly, Sheila's front door opened and a small gray-haired woman strolled into the living room. She wore a huge smile as she greeted Billy and Travis.

"How'ya, Billy?" her words seemed glued together. "Where's Sheila? I didn't know she had company," She glanced away from Billy and looked at Travis.

"Hi, Charlotte," Billy said. "She's in the kitchen. We're on our way out." He walked past Charlotte to the door.

"How'ya." She gazed again at Travis, as he followed Billy to the door.

"Hello," Travis mumbled.

"Is any'thang wrong?" Charlotte asked turning and looking at them at the door.

Travis spoke first, "Nothing that can't be fixed."

"Good then," she replied as Sheila rushed out of the kitchen into the living room, carrying an iron-lead pipe in her hand. "Get out of my house!" she yelled waving the iron pipe at Billy. "I'm glad I'm carrying your baby. Poor, poor, wife. What's she going to think about her big-shot lawyer now?" She sneered.

"I see y'all are in the middle of something. I'll come back later," Charlotte said, walking toward the two men.

"That's all right, Charlotte, you're part of my family."

Charlotte stood frozen, she was afraid to take another step. Sheila seemed to have gone mad.

Travis watched Sheila's wielded the iron pipe in her hand. He quickly stepped in front of Billy shielding him from any blows Sheila might carry out. "Come on Sheila," he spoke. "Put down the pipe. Hurting Billy is not going to solve anything."

Billy stepped from behind his human shield; he studied the pipe for a moment and smiled at her and shook his head, then he turned and spoke to Travis. "Man, c'mon, let's go. This whore is crazy." He said, and walked past Travis and out the door.

"Crazy? Who are you calling crazy nigger?" she shouted walking boldly toward them. The iron pipe swayed back and forth in her hand.

Travis still facing Sheila stepped slowly out the door, watching Sheila as she held the pipe in her hand, trembling uncontrollable. Wasting no time he rushed to his car, opened the door and slid behind the wheel.

Billy sat quietly in the car watching Sheila as she looked over the balcony, spitting stream of profanities at him. She waved the pipe down in front of Travis' car. "That's right! Leave!" She shouted, drawing people to their windows and peeping out of their front doors to see what the great commotion was all about.

Travis put the key in the ignition and started the car. "Man," he said as he put the car in reverse and backed out of the parking space. "What a nut!"

"Hey, you can say that again."

"Billy you brought this on yourself. I told you, your sins are going to find you out," Travis said as he drove the car out of Sheila's apartment complex.

"Tell me when did you become a preacher, huh?" Billy asked. "Man, do I look like I need a preacher? Hell no! So, I'll appreciate you keeping your sermon to yourself. Save it for someone else. Somebody who really needs it." Billy snapped.

"If that's how you feel," Travis added, hurt by Billy's statement.

"That's how I feel. The last time someone preached to me, it was at my mama's funeral. So, I say to hell with it all. Who needs it?"

"What about God?"

"What about him? He hasn't done anything for me. I'm down here busting my own butt off trying to live my life and He's up there living his," Billy replied and rested his head on the headrest and then added, "If He wants to do something for me, He knows where to find me," he snapped.

"You shouldn't talk that way," Travis answered.

"Screw you!" Billy smirked, knowing he had upset Travis. But he deserved it, Billy thought. Sitting up thinking he's so high and mighty and everybody piss smelled except his.

The ride back to Billy's house was silent. When he pulled the car up in Billy's subdivision, he saw Janet's car parked at the curb in front of Billy's house. How did she know they were back from Hawaii so soon? The last thing Billy needed was more trouble. He knew he should say something to break the silence, but what could he say? Sheila had admitted she was carrying his best friend's baby. Now, the other vulture was perched inside his house. Travis didn't bother to cut off the car; he wanted to get home and away from the drama. He needed time to think. He needed time to clear his head. Adrienne probably wouldn't talk to him again, and he couldn't blame her.

The way he had acted, he needed his head examined. Who was he kidding? He wanted her more now than the first time he saw her. Probably the kiss, he thought. He wanted to get his best friend's wife out of his head, but he couldn't. He could still feel her lips pressed against his.

"Are you coming in?" Billy asked, looking at Travis as he lay back on the headrest with his eyes closed.

"No. I'm going home," Travis said, without opening his eyes. He was afraid Billy would see his wife in them.

"So soon?" Billy said, opening the car door.

"Yeah," he replied.

"Get out of the car, man and stay for a minute."

"Look, Billy, your wife is in there waiting for you," he said, finally opening his eyes. He raised his head from the headrest to watch him. "Get rid of Janet," he said glancing in his rear view mirror at Janet's car. "You and Adrienne need this time alone to talk. Billy, you have to come clean on this one with her. Tell Adrienne everything that's going on between you and Sheila. No holds barred. Be honest. If she loves you as much as she seems to love you, then you will have her support. I can bet my life on it," Travis said, wondering how he could give good advice when he didn't follow it himself.

"I can't tell her about Shelia now. It would destroy my marriage. She must never find out about her and the other —"

"Women you have?" Travis interjected completing the sentence.

"That's not what I was going to say," Billy turned from Travis, and stepped out of the car.

"Okay. I hit below the belt. Sorry," Travis replied.

"I'll see you later," Billy said, as he closed the car door and walked to the porch.

Travis nodded at him and backed the car out of the driveway.

Billy's front door swung open and Janet stood in the doorway with a big grin spread on her face. "I've been waiting for you to come in," she said, pulling him inside the house. "I thought Travis would never leave." She kissed him. He responded to the kiss and then pushed away from her and closed the door.

"What's the matter?" she asked, raising her head to look at him.

"Nothing is the matter," he replied, "at least not anything to worry your pretty little head about," he added, and walked past her. She followed at his heel.

"I know something is bugging you."

"How can you tell something like that?" he asked, sitting in his black leather recliner, looking at her and waiting for an answer.

"The kiss," she replied, as she sat on the floor at his feet. She began to massage his legs.

"So, you're a psychologist of emotions, huh?"

"No. But I can tell when something is wrong with my man," she said looking at him and worshipping the ground he walked on.

"There's nothing the matter. Case closed," he glanced at her and then he scanned the living room. "Where is my wife?"

"If you have to know your deal old wife is upstairs sleeping," she said, disappointed that he asked about Adrienne. Then she rose and crossed over to the sofa and unzipped her jeans and pushed them down. "Let's make love here, on the sofa, like the old days."

"Not today," he said wishing she would go away.

"See. I knew you had something heavy on your mind," she said, pulling her jeans back up and sat on his lap. "What is it?" She pleaded, wrapping her arms around him. "Is it Adrienne wanting a baby? I told that girl to get children off of her mind."

He unclasped her arms from around him. He pushed himself and her up from the recliner. "I don't want to discuss it," he answered. "Go home."

"No. I won't leave this house until you tell me the truth. What's bothering you?"

"Please, go home."

"I won't go home until you tell me what's wrong. I hate to see you like this." She whined.

"Stop your whining before it wakes Adrienne."

"I love you," she replied. "I love you so much." She began to push her jeans down her legs again. "I want you so badly."

"Keep your pants on and go home," he frowned. "I don't need —" The doorbell rang cutting him off, "Who can that be?" Billy asked, looking at Janet. "Pull up your pants and keep them up," he said, before going to the door.

"Maybe Adrienne called her parents. She could have called her mother before taking her nap." She hurried pulling up her jeans and zipped them.

"Good. What I need is more company," he said sarcastically, walking to the door and opening it. Travis stood on the other side. Billy grinned and asked, "You decided to come back, huh?" He held the door shielding Janet from Travis' view.

But Travis caught a glimpse of her smoothing her jeans. No doubt she was putting them back on.

"I see you're up to your old tricks again?" Travis whispered. "I guess you haven't had enough surprises, huh?"

"Why don't you mind your own business, Travis?" Billy said staring hard at him.

"Man, what is it going to take for you to stop all of this cheating and lying to Adrienne. She deserves to be treated with respect, especially, in her own home."

"Did you come back to preach to me again? C'mon, man, you sound like you haven't done anything to make your mama ashamed of you," he grinned.

"That's not the point," Travis said, looking beyond Billy. "Where is Adrienne?"

"She's upstairs asleep."

"Then it is true that while the cat is away the mouse will play," he grinned.

"The mouse has to come out of hiding sometimes and have fun," Billy laughed softly.

"Yeah, but if he plays a little too much, then he's liable to get caught by the cat and eaten," Travis winked his eye at Billy.

Billy frowned, "Man, is there something on your mind? As you well see, I am in a bit of a hurry," he winked back at Travis.

Travis held up Billy's wallet, "I thought maybe you would be looking for this, but I see that I was wrong once again."

Billy took the wallet out of Travis' hand and put it in the front pocket of his tan Polo shirt. "Where did I drop this?"

"I saw it on my car seat. I was going to keep on driving, but I had second thoughts about it. Everybody in Silver Rock knows you shouldn't leave home without your driver's license. Not even a fine lawyer like yourself."

"Thanks, man," Billy grinned. He glanced over his shoulder to see what Janet was up to, and turned his attention back to Travis.

Travis looked at Billy and spoke softly, not wanting Janet to hear what he had to say, "Why don't you get rid of your third wheel and have a talk with your wife."

"Maybe I was discussing things with Janet," he said lowering his voice.

"Then you're talking to the wrong woman, don't you think?" Travis questioned Billy's integrity.

"It depends on the woman," Billy replied coolly.

"It's no use talking with you! You have your heart set on doing what you want. No matter who you hurt, it's okay, because, the great Attorney Ray comes out satisfied and smelling like a rose!"

"What's eating you?" Billy asked in a firm tone, but kept his voice low.

"Look," Travis threw his hands up in the air, "Tell Adrienne I'll see her later. Why don't you and Janet continue doing what it was that you two were doing before I showed up? I'll talk to you later," Travis said, as he turned from the door and walked to his car. He shook his head as he got behind the wheel of his Lexus. He backed out of the driveway, spinning the tires as he pulled off.

Billy closed the door and walked toward Janet who stood eagerly waiting for him. She held out her arms inviting him into them.

* * * * * * * * * *

Why am I concerned with his problems anyway? Travis thought. If he wants to throw away his marriage and lose everything he has worked hard for, well that's his business, he thought as he pulled up in his own driveway. Travis' home wasn't as big and fancy as Billy's, but it was home. A simple flat with one and a half baths, three bedrooms, a dining room that joined to living room, a small office and a family room with a huge plasma color television. The house also had a double car garage and a wrap-around deck. The deck is where he spent most of his time in the spring and summer. He liked sitting on the deck, soaking up the sunshine and re-thinking his day through, or reading a good book.

Travis pulled the car into the garage and got out. He unlocked his kitchen door and walked inside the house. He turned on the lights as he made his way to his office.

Dropping his briefcase on the floor he pressed the button on the answering machine. He had several calls from important clients, but nothing that couldn't wait. He removed his tie and unbuttoned his shirt as he walked into the master bedroom. He turned on the lights. Travis completely undressed. His tall, dark brown body shone flawless in the lighted bedroom. His lean muscular body resembled a dancer who had been dancing for years on stage. He walked into the shower and turned the water. Cold. He shivered as the water made contact with his skin. Thousands of chill bumps appeared over his body. The water felt good to his skin. He needed the cold shower. Maybe then he could get Adrienne out of his head.

What was the matter with him? How could he be thinking about his best friend's wife that way? No matter how much he tried to get rid of her in his mind, his heart and his lips wouldn't let go. He felt her soft lips pressed up against his. She had wanted him, too. He could feel it. The thought of Adrienne made the water seem less cold as he closed his eyes and reenacted the scene in his mind.

$\mathcal{B}$illy kissed Janet again and again, but he couldn't get himself to be interested in her. He wrapped his hand around her ample breast and it felt like a cold piece of meat in his hands. He wanted to rid himself of her. He had to see Sheila again. He had to talk some sense into her. Maybe this time she would see it his way.

"I think I better check on Adrienne," Billy said, as he pulled himself away from Janet and zipped his pants.

"Don't," she pleaded with him. "Let's finish what we've started."

"Later," he replied.

"Please, Billy, don't close me out!"

"I'm not closing anyone out. I need time to be alone. That's all." He looked at her. Her breasts began to hang down reminding him of a dog who has had too many litters. She should take better care of herself, he thought. Man, what a waste of good tits.

"Okay you win," she threw her hands up in the air and then re-buttoned her blouse and slid back into her capri jeans.

"Go home. And I'll get with you later this week. I promise." He ushered her toward the door.

"Are you sure you want me to leave?" She pulled her car keys from her jeans pocket, hoping he'd ask her to stay.

"Yes," he answered. "I want you to leave."

"Okay, but you're going to call me, right?" She pleaded, staring at him. "Call me, Billy. I'll be waiting for your call."

"Soon." He opened the door for her.

"Call me tonight," she said, trying to kiss him before she walked out of the door. But he retreated a few steps away from her putting distance between them.

"I'll call you soon," he repeated the answer.

"Promise?" she asked, standing sadly in the doorway looking at him.

"Man, I don't have time for your games," he replied. "I said I would call you. When? I don't know. Just be glad I said I am going to do it."

"Okay, I'm glad. I'll talk to you when you call. I love you," she said, and walked out of the house and got inside her car. She waved at him as he watched her pull away from the curb.

Billy closed the door and picked up his over night bag from the floor where he had placed it earlier near the recliner and walked upstairs. He went inside the huge master bedroom. Adrienne lay sleeping on the king-size bed. He walked quietly on the plush, light blue carpet. He didn't want to wake her. He opened his closet and walked inside, placing the bag on the floor. He had rows and rows of tailor-made Armani suits, and Stacy Adams shoes of all kinds; leather, suede, snakeskin, alligator, all filled the forty wall tier chrome shoe racks. He walked out of his closet and closed the door behind him.

He walked to his red cherry antique secretary desk and quietly pulled out the writing drawer. He took an expensive gold pen from the pocket of his Polo shirt, and then wrote Adrienne a note.

Adrienne, my client called. I have to make an emergency trip to Atlanta. I'll be home later tonight. Don't wait up.
Love,
Your husband Billy

He closed the drawer and put the note on the desk. He put his pen back in his shirt pocket then looked at her. She seemed to be resting peacefully. As he stood quietly looking at her, his heart stirred for her. She had married him because she loved him, but he couldn't return the kind of love she needed from him. He was the only man that ever touched her, and to Billy, that was good enough for him. His grand prize. His trophy. He touched the gold necklace underneath his Polo shirt. It felt good to his touch. He stroked the necklace as he watched her. She was beautiful. What man wouldn't want her beside him? The old grandfather clock in the hallway chimed. Billy looked at his gold Rolex. It was getting late. It would be dark soon. He quickly walked out of the room. He had an appointment with Sheila. Things were getting out of hand, out of his control. Once things were back to normal, he could breath easily again.

Chapter 15

*J*anet drove her metallic gray Nissan Altima over the speed limit as she zipped through the south side of town. So, now she was all alone. Thanks to Adrienne. The whining brat. Billy hadn't fooled her one bit. He sent her packing because Adrienne had him all upset about them damn children. Frustrated and not wanting to be alone, she took her cell phone from the seat next to her and dialed Sheila's number. She and Sheila had met last summer in Macon at the Crow's Nest. They hit it off on the dance floor partnering up to out dance two albino twins who thought they were all that. But for the last three months every time she had called her, Sheila always had something to do or somewhere to go. Janet figured Sheila didn't want to be bothered, so she had left her alone. But now, she had a yearning to see her. Maybe they would go to the Crow's Nest but not until they had fired up a couple of joints first. "Hello," Janet said. "Shelia."

"Yes."

"Hey, girl, what's up?" Janet asked.

"Nothing. Sitting here, mad as hell!"

"Mad with who?" Janet laughed.

"My old man," Sheila snapped.

"Mmph, he must be hanging low? Got you acting like this," she laughed.

"It's not funny," she scoffed. "That nigger' thinks he got rid of me. But it is not going to be that easy."

"Girl, I didn't know you like black meat. Who is this man? I want to meet him," Janet taunted getting on Shelia's last nerve.

114

"Trust me whore, you don't need to know," Sheila replied. Janet would be the last person she'd introduce to Billy.

"Oh, so it's like that? I thought we were partners in crime?"

"We are if you say so," Sheila replied, and added, "Come on over. Charlotte just left. I need someone to talk to, if it's only you," Sheila said, matter-of-fact.

"I'm almost there now."

"I'll talk to you when you get here. I want to free my line."

"That man ain't going to call you," Janet laughed.

"I'm not thinking about him."

"Yeah, right," Janet laughed.

"Listen, get your black ass off of my phone tying up my line. I don't have call waiting. I'm not rich like some of my friends." Sheila hung up the phone before Janet could say another word.

"Cunt," Janet said to the dead phone.

Janet arrived at Sheila's apartment complex in no time. It would be getting dark soon as she hurried up the steps and knocked on Sheila's door. Sheila opened the door letting her in.

"Ooh, you look terrible!" Janet pronounced as she sat on the sofa looking at Sheila. A frown appeared across her face.

"Humph! You don't look too hot yourself," she snapped, sitting on the sofa too. She picked up her lighter and cigarettes from the coffee table and lit one. She blew several small rings in the air, and threw the lighter and cigarette pack back on the coffee table.

"I know you have something else to smoke? Beside cigarettes. I want to see some naked men humping and hear some bells ringing."

"I'm sorry, but I don't have anything to give you. And anyway why do you always come over here begging me for my stuff. Want you start bringing some sometime. I'm tired of you smoking up my stuff." Sheila frowned.

"Well, if that's the way you feel about it. You can keep your miserable joint."

"I will."

"I see that man really got you uptight. If it is not too much to ask, what's going on with you and this mystery man?" Janet asked tired of Sheila's attitude.

"A plenty," she inhaled the cigarette again and blew the smoke toward Janet. She drew on the cigarette again and exhaled. "I love him till it hurts right here," she pounced her chest over her heart. And to think I lied about carrying his baby so we could be together as a family. But what does he do? He throws six hundred dollars on the damn table and tells me to kill it." Sheila pulls the money out of her bra and waves it in front of Janet. "I ought to take this money and burn it up," she declared taking her cigarette and holding it near the money.

"Girl, that's a lot of money you're talking about burning. If you don't want it, let me have it. I'll show you what to do with it." Janet pushed herself up from the sofa, and added, "This man must be pretty special? 'Cause girl you got the down home blues." Janet threw her hands up to give Sheila a high-five. Sheila didn't respond. "Oh, so you're going to leave me hanging like that?" She laughed, "Umm-mmm, you're sprung!"

"Go to hell!" Sheila said and crushed her cigarette butt into the ashtray. "You don't know what you're talking about," she declared staring at the money.

"All I know is you got some serious issues." Janet laughed and held up one finger, "But hold that thought, because I got to pee." She rushed down the hall to the bathroom to relieve herself.

"Make sure you wash your nasty hands before you come out of there, if you're planning on smoking my stuff. I don't need your dirty hands all over it." Sheila said it loudly for Janet to hear.

"I thought you said you didn't have any?" Janet replied, leaving just enough crack in the bathroom's door to communicate with Sheila.

"I don't when it comes to you."

"Hey girl, don't cop an attitude with me. I'm not the one you're angry at, remember?" She said and flushed the toilet.

"It may as well be you, y'all both black and right now I'm upset with all the black folks in the world."

"I got to meet this brother who got your nose open. He sounds like he's got it going on," Janet said turning on the water to wash her hands.

"You better believe it girl."

"What's his name?" Janet asked.

"I'm not going to tell you that."

"What? You're afraid I'll steal him?"

"I'm not worrying about you stealing nobody from me," Sheila sneered.

"Well, what's his name if you're not afraid?" Janet wiped her hands on the towel hanging on the rack.

"Girl, I'm not telling you," she replied.

"Yeah, you're afraid of me all right," she laughed, tossing the towel back on the rack and opened the door.

"I know I'm going to regret telling you but if you must know his name is Billy."

"Billy?" Janet said standing in the bathroom door. "Billy who?"

"Billy Ray," she said, as she folded the money in her hand.

"Billy Ray, the attorney?" Janet asked, suddenly feeling nauseas. She retreated a few steps back into the bathroom and looked into the bathroom's mirror at her reflection.

"Yeah, the one and only."

"You're messing with Billy?"

"Do you know him?" She sounded puzzled.

"Kind of," Janet answered slowly still staring into the mirror.

"What does that mean?"

"I met him once through a friend," she replied growing with anger. But said nothing. She wanted to hear more of what Sheila had to say about Billy.

"A friend, huh? Well keep your hands off! He's mine!" Sheila warned.

"And how do you figure that?" Janet demanded.

"I'm having his baby."

"Pretending to have his child, remember?" She said sarcastically.

"He doesn't know that. And when and if he does find out it'd be too late. Because I'm counting on being with child by that time." She had it all planned.

Janet couldn't visualize Sheila and Billy making love it made her sick to her stomach. Her blood began to boil, as she pressed down hard on the sink basin. Janet knuckles seemed to push themselves up through her skin, her countenance darkened.

"I should have been his wife, anyway," Sheila remarked. "I'd know how to treat that kind of a man right. Billy is the type of guy that'd grow tired of a dull woman by his side. He needs a live wire like me," she added.

Feeling betrayed by Billy, Janet's heart ached and she wondered how could he have done this to her? To have another woman on the side to keep him satisfied. She would have been better off if he had just taken her heart and stomped it. She trusted him and this is how he repaid her. She didn't try to stop him when he had married Adrienne. She didn't even mind sharing him with her. In her heart she always felt that she was his second wife. A spot reserved for Adrienne and her only. But now Billy had brought in an outsider. A third party to mess things up. As tears rolled down Janet's face, she could still hear Sheila bragging on how she'd trap Billy.

Something snapped inside of her and she couldn't take listening to Sheila any longer plotting to steal Billy away from her. She wouldn't have an outsider coming in and steal him right from under her nose. It was Sheila that had Billy upset. He wouldn't make love to her because Sheila had told him about the baby. "That low-down little witch," Janet mumbled under her breath. "I'll kill her," she added, rushing out of the bathroom and down the hall to Sheila.

"Shut-up!" she yelled at Sheila.

"What?" Sheila tried to stand to her feet but slipped back onto the sofa.

"Just shut-up!" Janet yelled continually.

"Girl, what's wrong—,"

"Billy is mine," Janet interjected.

"Girl, now I know you're crazy!" Sheila rose to her feet.

Janet blinded by rage saw the lead pipe leaning against the living room wall beside the sofa where Sheila stood. She grabbed the pipe, and swung it hitting Sheila above her left eye. The impact knocked her off of her feet as she slumped back onto the sofa. Blood splattered the wall and the surrounding area and oozed down Sheila's face. Sheila lay lifeless. Her eyes stared at the ceiling.

"Now look what you made me do," she said, looking at Sheila. "I told you to shut-up. But you wouldn't listen!" She wiped the spots of blood off her hands and onto her already bloodstained blouse. Retreating to the bathroom she snatched the towel she used only minutes ago from the rack and wiped the lead pipe with it.

Wrapping the towel around the pipe she carried it back into the living room and laid it on the floor beside the sofa. Then she hurried into Sheila's bedroom and opened her closet. She found a Mike Vicks' jersey and slipped it on. She looked at herself in the mirror checking for any sign of blood. Seeing none, she strolled back into the living room turned off the lights and peeped out the window. Janet, seeing no one outside, grabbed the towel from the floor and quickly made her way to her car and slid behind the steering wheel.

She was in her car driving out of the apartment complex when she spotted Billy's Mercedes turning into the apartment entrance. She snatched her cell phone from the passenger side and dialed 911. The dispatcher picked up on the first ring. "Silver Rock Police Department," the dispatcher said.

"I would like to report a crime," Janet said.

"Are you calling from that address?" the dispatcher asked.

"No. The address is apartment J110 Cascade Crest," she answered.

"May I have your name please?"

Janet didn't answer. Instead she switched off her cell phone and tossed it back on the passenger seat. "Let me see you get yourself out of this, lover boy," she said scornfully, and then drove out of the complex.

* * * * * * * * * *

It was getting dark when Billy stepped his foot outside his car and walked up the long flight of stairs leading to Sheila's apartment. He wished she'd move to the ground level. But shrugged his shoulders after thinking this would be the last time he'd have to deal with her and her long flight of stairs. Sheila had become a risk and it was a risk he didn't care to take. Standing outside her apartment door he knocked, there was no answer. Billy fished in his pants pocket for the key she had given him. He pushed the key into the lock, but the door opened freely. "Sheila," he said, pushing the door open a little wider, so he could walk in. "Why are the lights off?" he asked, flipping the light switch. The living room lit up. "So, you're here," he said, as he closed the front door. Billy walked closer to her and what he saw next was horrifying and sickening. Sheila lay on the sofa, blood covered most of her face and part of it looked like it had been caved-in.

"Who did this to you?" he asked, checking her wrist and neck for a pulse. But couldn't find any. "Man, who could have done this?" Then fear suddenly gripped him when he realized the killer could still possibly be in the apartment. Billy saw the lead pipe beside the sofa and he picked it up and walked nervously through the apartment. "I have a weapon," he yelled, walking through the apartment and found it empty. Feeling a little audacious he walked back to where Sheila lay on the sofa. He stared at the lifeless body of the woman who had shared his bed. It had only been a couple of hours when he last seen her alive. Now, she lay on the sofa dead never to experience life again.

Watching her like that Billy grew weak, his knees buckled from underneath him and he slid to the floor beside her. He looked blankly at the pipe in his hands.

Even though the air-conditioner blasted cold air, beads of sweat begin to pour down his face. "I'm sorry Mama," he moaned, closing his eyes and resting his head against the sofa edge. "Man, I'm sorry; I didn't want you to die," he said, seeing his mother lying in her coffin. She looked younger, more beautiful lying there smiling up at him. The funeral director, a tall lean man dressed in black closed the coffin door on his mother. He screamed, "She can't breathe, open the door. Mama can't breathe in there like that!" He screamed, leaping from the church pew reaching at the coffin trying to open it. But the man dressed in black rushed to him pulling him away. Away from his Mama forever. He swung violently at the man while his father rushed to his side and carried him out of the church.

His mother couldn't breath, he remembered. He just wanted her to breath and they wouldn't let her. A tear rolled down his face then another one followed and another one after that. Billy wiped them away and sat there for what seemed like hours until he heard loud sounds at the door. Someone was knocking breaking his focus on his mother. He looked around the living room puzzled, "What am I doing here? He asked himself. The knock continued. "What? Who is it?" He asked as he rose to his feet, still holding the lead pipe in his hands.

The door suddenly burst open and two police officers rushed inside the room with their guns aimed at him. "Freeze! Lay down your weapon," The young officer shouted. Billy dropped the lead pipe. "Put your hands behind your head and walk away from the weapon!" The officer shouted again. Billy clasped his hands behind his head and moved away from the lead pipe. "Now, get on your knees," the young officer commanded. Billy dropped to his knees. The second police officer rushed over and handcuffed him.

As he was being handcuffed the young officer carefully picked up the lead pipe and then examined the body. "She's dead," he replied to the other officer. "I'll call Detective Wright."

The officer pulled Billy up and read him his rights. "You have the right to remain—"

"I didn't kill her," Billy interjected, and surprised they were arresting him. He wanted to feel the gold necklace around his neck. He thought he would then wake up from this nightmare.

Chapter 16

*D*etective Money Wright walked inside Sheila's apartment and spoke to a couple of police officers who were sealing the crime scene and dusting for prints. He looked coolly at Billy. He whispered something into one of the police officer's ear. The police officer laughed. Billy had some dealing with Detective Wright the first year out of law school. He knew the man was hard. People in the small town have connived, schemed and played a lot of cruel games on one another, but no one dared to cross Detective Wright. It was a known fact that he'd rather shoot you than to bring you in. Every since he had joined the Silver Rock Police Department crime dropped significantly earning him the Detective of the Year Award at the precinct four times in a row. He was handsome, smart and quick on his feet.

Detective Wright pulled the white handkerchief from his jacket pocket, and rubbed his forehead. He had been to dozens of crime scenes, and each one had its own flavor and always seemed to top the others. But this one was unlike the others. Its flavor just didn't add up. A Caucasian female dead, and a well-known attorney caught on the scene. It didn't make any sense to him at all. He looked at Sheila's body and then walked over to Billy. "What happened?" he asked.

Billy absorbed in his thoughts stood blankly watching the detective. Detective Wright asked again, "What happened here?"

"Huh, oh, what? I don't know," Billy finally blurted the words out.

"You don't know? Get him out of my sight," Detective Wright

said to the young officer.

"Okay, fellow, you heard him, let's go," the young police officer said, grabbing Billy under his arm and led him out of the apartment to the squad car.

The young police officer opened the car door and held Billy's head down as Billy climbed into the backseat of the car. He closed the door. Billy looked out the side rear window. The place was now crowded with people from all over the complex. They were watching and pointing at him through the window. The young police officer got into the car, and backed out of the parking space.

He plopped his head back on the leather car seat and closed his eyes, but the handcuffs wouldn't let him rest. He tried to adjust his hands to relieve the pressure caused by them, but they squeezed tightly, pinching his wrist.

Uncomfortable with the handcuffs, he closed his eyes again, but the image of the murdered Sheila kept rising in his memory. He saw Sheila's lifeless, bloodstained face staring up at him. It was a scene he would never forget. He fought back the unpleasant feeling that washed over him. How could anyone be so cruel? Who could have done such a gruesome crime? The questions flooded his mind. He admitted Sheila deserved to be put in her place, but not like this. The scene played in his mind over and over. Who would want to kill Sheila? It was obvious the lead pipe was the murder weapon. Why? It all seemed unreal to him. But someone had snuffed the life out of Sheila with the pipe.

The pipe. Man, he had picked up the pipe. How could he have been so stupid? Didn't years of law-school teach him any better than to go around picking up murder weapons? The police wouldn't have any doubt now believing he's the murderer after witnessing him with the pipe. Suddenly, things didn't look so good.

Slowly, he inhaled and exhaled; his life had changed within two weeks of his marriage. It had been a downward turmoil. The fight he had with Adrienne in Hawaii. The news that Sheila was carrying his baby, and now her cruel death.

The squad car pulled up in the back of Silver Rock County Jail. Billy opened his eyes. The police officer helped Billy out of the car and led him inside the police station. He took him to the processing room and unlocked the handcuffs from his wrists. Billy felt relieved as the handcuffs came off after being wrapped around them like a vise. But the freedom lasted only for a moment as the police officer commanded Billy to stretch his arms out in front of him. He handcuffed him again. He led Billy to an old wood square desk. He nodded for Billy to sit in the chair on the side of the desk. Billy did as indicated.

"What's your name?" The police officer asked.

"Billy," he replied.

"Your full name?" The police officer raised his brow.

"William Anthony Ray."

"Your address."

Billy gave it.

"Telephone."

Billy gave that as well.

"Your social security number?"

Again, Billy complied.

The police officer finished the writing process and stood up, motioning for Billy to get to his feet. He unlocked the handcuffs and led Billy to the finger print table. After he was fingerprinted, the police officer took his photo. He then handed him a large brown envelope and commanded him to take everything out of his pockets and put it inside the envelope. Billy did as instructed, then took off his gold Rolex and glanced at it. It had been exactly an hour since he first arrived at the police precinct; he added it to the contents. He unfastened the gold necklace around his neck and looked at it before putting it in.

Then the police officer took the brown envelope from Billy and led him to the interview room.

Detective Wright stood behind the one way mirror observing Billy before entering the room.

"Mr. Ray," I'm Detective Wright.

Billy nodded at the detective.

"I'm going to ask you a few questions about the deceased lady."

"I can't help you," Billy said in a firm tone.

"Mr. Ray, cooperate with me. It'd make things a lot easier," Detective Wright said, in a mild tone.

"If you're going to ask me who killed her? I don't know."

"Yes. I want to know what happen in that apartment," he said looking hard at Billy.

"As I told you once, I don't know," Billy held his ground.

"Did you kill her?" Detective Wright asked the question without taking his eyes off Billy.

Billy hesitated before answering the question, "No, I didn't. She was dead when I arrived at her apartment. Man, I'm in the dark as much as you are," Billy said trying to convince the detective he had nothing to do with the Sheila's death.

"I have police witnesses who saw you with the pipe."

"Man, I made a mistake. I wasn't thinking clearly. I picked it up to protect myself.

"To protect yourself?" Detective Wright asked a frown spread across his face.

"Yes. I thought whoever killed her might still be inside. So, I picked up the pipe to protect myself. It was a stupid thing to do," Billy said as he tried to reenact the scene in his mind.

"You were recently married, huh?" Detective asked.

"Yes."

"Your wife's name?"

"Adrienne," Billy paused, "Adrienne Ray."

"Your wife's maiden name?"

"Mitchell," Billy said.

"Why were you at the victim's apartment?"

"I had to ask her something."

"Something like what?"

"I know my rights," Billy shot an angry look at the detective. "I want my attorney."

"I'm only asking you a few routine questions." Detective Wright said. "It's no need for a lawyer."

"Well, am I free to go?"

"No."

"Then I won't answer anymore of your questions."

"The victim, was she a client?" Detective Wright asked, ignoring Billy's statement and watched him closely. Billy was a clever lawyer. Billy refused to answer the question. He stared at Detective Wright.

"Know what I think?" Detective Wright leaned closer to Billy. "I think she was your lover and you killed her. Y'all had a lover spat. She wanted more, but you wanted to break it off. She wouldn't give in so easily. She threatened to tell your wife. You had to stop her. So, you saw the lead pipe, and you saw your chance to get rid of her. You picked up the pipe and bashed her head in," he dramatized the event. "You probably would have gotten away with it, too if we hadn't received the phone call."

"What call? I don't know what you're talking about," Billy replied. "I didn't kill her."

"Yes, you killed her, alright."

The door to the interview room opened. An older police officer entered the room. He signaled the detective getting his attention. Detective Wright walked away from Billy to the officer.

"What you got for me?" Detective Wright asked.

"We just got a call from the crime lab; the lead pipe is the murder weapon. They found trace of blood on it. The blood belongs to the victim. They ran our perpetrator fingerprints and got a match."

"Bingo," Detective Wright sang. He walked back to Billy.

"Mr. Ray, you're under arrest for the murder of Sheila Stone."

"I told you I didn't kill her!" he exclaimed.

The officer who had processed him entered the room. He took Billy's upper arm and led him out of the room. He took Billy to a small room across from the interview room to a square wood desk, and pointed at the telephone.

"You can make one phone call."

Billy picked up the telephone and dialed Travis' number, but he got his voice mail instead. He left a message, "Travis, man, you're not going to believe this. Someone killed Sheila and I'm being arrested for her murder. Get down here as soon as you hear this. I'm at the county jail. I didn't do it man. Believe me. I didn't do it," he said then hung-up the telephone.

The police officer led Billy away from the room and turned him over to Hattie, one of the female officers who was in charge of carrying inmates to their cell. She grasped Billy gently by his arm and led him down a long corridor and to a cell.

"Why didn't you call me?" she asked Billy, as she purposefully walked slowly.

"I've been busy," he replied smoothly, trying to avoid a confrontation between them.

"Your loss," Hattie said as she unlocked his cell door. She nudged him inside and unlocked the handcuffs and pressed close against him. "You don't know what you're missing," she said brushing her lips lightly against his and stepping away. She walked out of the cell and locked it. "I'll be seeing you," she said softly and blew him a kiss before walking away.

"Hey, Billy Ray, man what'cha doin' here? What a big shot lawyer like you doin' in jail?" An inmate across his cell named James asked.

Billy recognized James Talton immediately; they had been in the same grade in high school. They both had high ambitions until James started using drugs and went a separate direction. He looked older, more like fifty-seven than twenty-seven.

"James," Billy grinned glad to see him. "Man, where have you been?" he asked, forgetting his troubles.

"I've been around," James replied.

"Man, I haven't seen you since I left home for college," Billy stated.

"Cause I've been livin' in Florida, but they had too many hurricanes down there for me. So, one morning I woke up in Tennessee and it was full of preachers. Then I moved to Ohio and was doing good for a while. Until this girl that I was livin' with started acting crazy. I had to leave there runnin' 'cause walking was too slow. That chick was crazy!" James laughed.

"What was her problem?" Billy asked.

"She wanted to quit her job so she could lay around the house with me all day," he laughed. "I wasn't having that. Wasn't no need in both of us not working. Somebody had to pay the bills."

"Man, that's cold," Billy, laughed.

"Cold or not she knew I couldn't work."

"Why's that?" Billy asked, curiously.

"How is a drug addict gonna work? I told that woman from the beginning that I was a drug addict. But she still wanted me." James's eyes twinkled when he laughed.

"She knew then, huh?" Billy grinned.

"Yeah, she knew. Anyway, what are you in here for?"

"Who's that?" Another male voice shouted from down the cell unit. "I hope that ain't who you say it is. 'Cause I have a bone to pick with a man named Billy Ray. He's been messing 'round with my woman."

"Man, shut up. Don't nobody want that ugly woman I saw you hanging out with down at the club," James shouted.

"Don't be talking about my woman like that," the man said angrily. "If you know what's good for you, you'll keep your mouth shut and stay out of this. This is between Billy and me," he shouted."

"Man, shut your big mouth. You can't get that ugly woman of yours to visit you. So tell me how in the world are you going to get even with somebody? What you need to do is get yourself out of here. Getting on my nerves. Yeah, I hear you in your bunk crying like a baby at night." James laughed, including Billy.

"Shut up!" He rushed to the cell door. "Shut up! Shut up!" He viciously shouted, and then just as suddenly, he quieted down.

"That's more like it," James said. "Shut up and suck your thumb and go to sleep you little baby."

"Who is that?" Billy asked.

"Leroy. Don't mind him, he's crazy. And this here is," he pointed to a figure lying quietly underneath a sheet on the bunk next to his. "I don't know his name as of yet. They just brought him in a couple of hours ago. You still didn't tell me what you're in here for," James replied, waiting to hear Billy's reason.

"Technicality."

"Technicality what?" James looked at Billy. "C'mon, you mean to tell me you were arrested for someone else's blunder?"

"I didn't do it," Billy answered.

"That's what we all say," James laughed

"I didn't do it," he said.

"What is it that you didn't do?" James asked.

"It doesn't matter. I didn't do it," Billy repeated himself.

"Just for good time sake," James spoke seriously. "What is it that you didn't do?"

Billy knew James wasn't going to let him have any peace until he found out why he was locked up, so he answered, "They think I murdered this female." He stared at James. "But like I said. I didn't have anything to do with it."

"So they're picking on you for nothing?" James sat on the edge of his bunk. He looked hard at Billy.

"That's exactly what they're doing," Billy answered.

"Shoot, if you didn't do it. Then who?" James added.

"I don't know, man," Billy shook his head. "I don't know." The question jarred him. He wished he knew who had killed her.

"Are you going to defend yourself?" James asked, breaking Billy's focus away from Sheila.

"What's that?" Billy asked, looking at James.

"I said who's defending you? Are you going to defend yourself?" James asked.

"No," he replied.

"Then who?" James asked.

"Travis. He's a good attorney. I want him to handle my case."

"Your friend, Travis? I remember him. Shoot, you better get somebody you don't know that well. 'Cause believe me, your friends will mess you up. I never did deal with my friends or my family. Friends and family are worst than foes. They'll smile in your face, eat you alive, spit you out, and ask you how you are doing?" he laughed.

"I can trust Travis. He'd always been there for me," Billy said. He sat down on the bunk.

No one had given any attention to the man in James' cell lying underneath the bed sheet. They didn't notice when he had shed the sheet and sat on the side of his bunk listening to their conversation. The man looked out of his cell at Billy nervously.

"Who did you k...kill?" James asked.

"I didn't kill anyone. I found her," Billy lowered his eyes to the floor. He didn't want to remember how Sheila had looked lying on the sofa with her head bashed in.

"Did you know her?" James inquired.

"Yeah, Sheila."

"Sheila?" James frowned, "Sheila who?"

"Sheila Stone," Billy answered. He looked at James.

"Sheila Stone. Man, I know that woman. Shoot. She's dead?" James rose from his bunk. "It's too bad 'cause I thinking about dropping in on her when I get out of this place. I wonder who killed her?"

"I don't know," Billy replied.

"Too bad, because she was a *mighty good piece* if you know what I mean?" James winked, and stated as a-matter-of-fact.

"Yeah, I know," Billy agreed, watching James think about Sheila.

Billy watched James lay back on the bunk and closed his eyes. A few minutes later he heard soft snoring sounds coming from James. The cellblock grew extremely quiet, as Billy lay on his bunk, but the thought of Sheila wouldn't allow him to lie peacefully. He pushed himself up and looked at James. He wanted to talk but James lay sound asleep. Then, he noticed the old man sitting on his bunk, staring at him. He watched the old man; not realizing it was his father.

"What's your name?" Billy asked.

Silently. The man lowered his head.

"What's your name?" Billy asked again. "The cat got your tongue?" Billy asked, remembering those words coming fro m Edna.

Darrell looked at Billy for a moment or two before answering, "Fred," he finally blurted softly. "My name is Fred." He lowered his head. Darrell was afraid Billy would recognize him.

"Well, Fred, what are you in here for?" Billy asked, really not caring for Fred's answer one way or another.

"Public drunk." Darrell muffled his voice.

"Drunk."

"That and raising Cain in the park with my old lady. She ought to be in here. She was just as drunk as I was. Women get away with everything."

"Billy laughed, "If you need a good lawyer. I'm your man."

"You're a lawyer? You don't look like a lawyer to me. What are you doing back here, then?

"A misunderstanding."

"I got myself a whole mess of misunderstanding tee-shirts in my closet at home. A rack full of them," Darrell said raising his head. "I don't mean to be nosy, but I overheard you tell the guys that someone got killed and they blame you?"

"Yeah. A woman I knew," Billy answered coolly. He glanced

at James. He wished he hadn't touched her now. The thought of him sleeping with Sheila made Billy's flesh crawl. He absent-mindedly reached for his gold necklace and rubbed the place where it used to lay against his skin. He wondered what Adrienne would think of him, now. Would she still want his children?

"A woman, huh?" Darrell said.

"Yeah, a woman."

"Did you love her?" Darrell asked.

"No."

"But you and she had a thing going, huh?" Darrell said still disguising his voice.

"I had a thing going with plenty of women. I love on them and leave them alone."

"Are you married?"

"Yes. All of two weeks."

"Whew! Been married only for two weeks and you're behind bars. What is your wife going to say? How does she look? Is she pretty?"

"I won't be in here long enough for her to say anything. Yes. She's very pretty. She reminds me a lot of my…" The name Edna was hanging at the tip of his tongue, but he dismissed it. He frowned and looked sternly at Darrell. "Why do you ask?"

"Curious. 'Cause if I had a pretty woman. I wouldn't waste my time fooling with other women."

"Fred, what do you know about anything?"

"I know a lot. I know women can trick you and make you throw away everything that means anything in the world to you."

"Sounds like you're confessing your life story," Billy laughed.

"More than you know." Darrell lowered his head. "More than you know."

"You're right about that. Women can be deceitful. Take Sheila for example," he hesitated, "wrong example," he squinted his eyes. "Take Adrienne, my wife, for a quick example. She was a virgin. Pure and untouched. But let's say she wanted to be Mrs. Ray so badly, that she kept herself pure for me. Because she knows I wouldn't have it any other way. Now, the question to ask is, did she deceive me into marrying her? Or did she like being a virgin?"

Darrell frowned as he pondered over the question. "I'm lost. I don't understand what you're saying."

"It's simple," Billy, explained the question he proposed. "Would she have stayed a virgin if she knew I'd marry her anyway?"

"I don't know. But I see what you're saying now."

"Man, that's why we have to watch every move a woman makes, and weigh everything that comes from their mouths."

"Sound like you're confessing now," Darrell grinned.

"Call it like you see it," Billy said lying back onto his bunk.

"What about your mother? She's a woman. What does she have to say about your logic on deceitful women?" Darrell asked, watching Billy closely.

"My mother?" Billy eyes scanned the ceiling. "She's dead."

"Oh. I'm sorry."

"That's all right. She died when I was a boy."

"A boy, huh? Mmh, that must had been a terrible thing for you? To lose a mother so young. Did you know her quite well?"

"Yes."

"I don't want to sound nosy or anything, but I can't stand to be cooped up in a closed place. If I don't talk to someone, I'll go crazy in here." Darrell said, trying to get Billy to talk about his past.

"Talk on," Billy suggested. He was glad he had someone to talk with besides James. Fred seemed harmless enough. He didn't know Billy from Adam.

"What was your mother's name?"

"Edna."

"I bet she was pretty and a good mother? Did you like her?"

"What kind of question is that?" Billy pulled himself up from his bunk. "Who doesn't like their mother?"

"Well, you know how some people are? They can't stand the sight of their mothers."

"Edna wasn't like that. She was a good mother. Yes, she was pretty. At least Travis, my best friend thought so." Billy laughed softly. "He used to tell have a crush on her. It's strange you asked me if I liked Edna. When she died I hated her for leaving me, but as time grew on, the hate died. Yes, I loved her. Even after all of these years, I love her."

Uncomfortable Darrell asked, "What about your father. Did you know him?"

"He's dead too."

"He's dead?"

"Yes. He died the year after my mother."

"Mmh, your life was full of tragedy. It's not often you hear a boy losing two parents back to back like that. It's a sad thing for a young boy to go through."

"It wasn't that horrible. A piece of cake. I don't care about it anyway. Man, why are you asking me all of these questions about my parents? They're dead. Case closed."

He closed his eyes. He wanted to shut out the memories of Edna and Darrell. Memories that were long dead until Fred raised them from their tomb.

"I'm sorry," Darrell whispered. "Really, I am."

Billy lay quietly upon the bunk and tried to remember Darrell's face, but Mr. Malcolm replaced the image of his father. Mr. Malcolm had become his father. He had helped him become the man he was today. Poor Mr. Malcolm took on the duty of raising another man's son. Darrell, who was in perfect health and capable of raising his own son, but refused to do so. The Malcolm's had taken him in and loved him with the same love Edna had provided before her death. In Billy's book, Darrell was long dead and forgotten. It was easier to keep him in his coffin and diminish all memories of him. Billy trembled at the thought of Darrell. He hated him, and didn't understand the pressure that gnawed at his gut. He quickly dismissed Darrell from his thoughts. The pressure eased up and Billy lay there, despising Fred for bringing up the ghosts of his past. It had been a long time since he had really thought anything about Darrell.

* * * * * * * * * *

Billy startled from his thoughts when a familiar voice rang in his ears.

"I got here as fast as I could," Travis said standing outside Billy's cell door.

"Huh?" Billy looked up.

"You look terrible," Travis said.

"Man, I'm glad to see you," Billy quickly rose from his bunk. "What took you so long?"

"I have been talking with the chief of police." Travis watched his old friend. "What happened?"

"I don't know. I went there to talk some sense into her. But when I arrived, she was dead. That's all I know," he replied.

"She was dead?" Travis looked at him.

"Don't give me that look, man. I know what you're thinking. I didn't do it. You have to believe me on this one. The woman was already dead when I arrived there." Billy raised his voice firmly, and walked away from the cell door.

"Okay, okay, calm down. We're going to get out of this somehow."

"We? I don't see you locked up back here. I shouldn't be, either. I didn't kill her. Get me out of here. I can't stand to be locked-up in this box. Get me out man."

"You know as well as I do the county operates differently from the city jail. It's going to take time, and you know it," Travis reminded him.

"Yeah, yeah, yeah," Billy waved his hand at Travis. "Just get me out of here as soon as possible. That's all I ask." He walked to the jail cell door and looked at Travis.

"It was bad, man. You should have seen it. Her head was caved in. Who could have done it?" he spoke to Travis, but looked beyond him in a daze.

"Detective Wright is going to talk with you. I'll be there when he does. Remember, stick to the facts."

Billy nodded; he liked the way Travis handled things. He took charge of his cases. Billy felt at ease. It was better for him if he had someone to represent him. He was well known in Silver Rock and had made a few enemies in town. He knew he wouldn't have a fair deal if he represented himself. Travis had a smooth reputation in Silver Rock, and people liked him. They were drawn to him. Anyway, he was too tired to fight. He wanted the nightmare to end. If only he hadn't gone back to Sheila's apartment, then he wouldn't be sitting in jail with a bunch of men snoring their heads off. He'd be at home making love to his wife, or to Janet.

"Adrienne. Have you talked with her?" Billy asked.

"No. I came right over when I received your message." Travis said, as he scanned the cells unit. "I'll go by your place when I leave here." He promised.

"Good. I don't want her to worry."

Travis looked at the cell across from Billy's. Darrell had been watching the two men since Travis came into the cell unit, but quickly lowered his head when Travis looked at him.

Travis looked at Darrell, wondering if the man was shy or just didn't like being stared at. He had seen him somewhere before. But where? Somehow, he couldn't put his finger on it.

"Oh yes, Travis, meet Fred. Fred, Travis," Billy said with the gesture of his hands.

"Nice to meet you Fred," Travis replied, still staring at Darrell and wondered where he had seen him.

"Likewise," Darrell said without looking at Travis or Billy. Darrell turned his back toward them and sat staring at the concrete wall.

The man seems odd, Travis thought. He definitely has some issues to deal with. But this wasn't the time and place to focus on someone else's personal problems. He had his friend to contend with.

"I think he's a little shy," Billy whispered to Travis.

"A little something," Travis made circle motions at his temple suggesting the man was crazy.

"Look man, get me out of here," Billy said in a serious tone.

"Okay," Travis said. "Hang in there. It's going to be all right."

"It's easy for you to say." Billy replied, "When you're not the one in here."

"Trust me, getting you out of here is my number one priority." Travis glanced at his watch.

"I know," Billy answered. "That is why I hired you as my attorney."

"It's getting late, I know Adrienne must be worried by now," Travis said.

"Yeah, it's getting late," Billy answered.

"Look, I'll see you first thing tomorrow morning," Travis said, looking at Billy. "Like I said, hang in there."

"I will," Billy replied, and walked away from the cell door. He lay on his bunk.

"I'll get you out of here fast," Travis said as he walked away from the cell and out of the cellblock's door.

Chapter 17

$\mathcal{T}$ravis pulled his car to a stop in Billy's driveway and turned off the ignition. It was late, and he didn't want to disturb any of Billy's neighbors. He opened the car door and stepped out of the car. He walked up to the porch and rang the doorbell, pressing it five or six times before Adrienne opened it.

"Hi, Travis." Adrienne rubbed her eyes. "I thought I heard the doorbell. Come on in. Is Billy with you?" she asked looking for him. She held Billy's note in her hand.

"I'm sorry to bother you, but I—"

She interrupted Travis, holding up the note, "I read Billy's message. He mentioned something about an emergency meeting in Atlanta. That's where you're coming from?"

"No. Why don't we sit down?" Travis asked.

"Why, is everything okay?" she asked and led him to the living room, and they sat on the sofa.

She wore a terry white robe and her hair was wrapped. He looked at her realizing how beautiful she looked without makeup. He wanted to kiss her, but he kept his distance. He didn't want to make the same mistake he had made earlier.

"Is this about what happened between us?" she asked, now ashamed to face him.

"No. I wish it were. It would be a lot easier," he said, trying to break the news to her as gently as possible. But how could he when the only thing he wanted to do was to hold her in his arms and make her his wife forever.

137

"Then what?"

"It's about Billy," he said, as he tried to focus on why he was there. Adrienne didn't make it easy for him, as he watched her lips pout into a sweet little form. He wanted to kiss them. A kiss in the dark wouldn't hurt anyone. No one would know except them. It would be their little secret. He imagined kissing her and making love to her as he looked silently into the distance.

"Why? What's the matter? Is Billy hurt? What is it, Travis?" Adrienne's voice rose to a higher pitch, breaking the silence.

"Stay calm." He said, putting his focus back into prospective. He patted her hands. They felt soft, and smooth. He squeezed them lightly and released them. "Billy has been arrested."

"Arrested!" She rose from the sofa. "I don't understand?" She looked confused. "How could he be arrested when he's in Atlanta meeting a client?"

"He's not in Atlanta, Adrienne," Travis replied rising from the sofa. He stood facing her.

"He's not in Atlanta?"

"He never went to Atlanta," Travis replied.

"Then where is he?" Adrienne said in a firm voice.

"He's in Silver Rock County Jail."

"In jail! For what?"

"For murder," he answered, feeling sick. He didn't want to hurt her with the bad news, but she had to know.

"Murder!" She looked bewildered. "Oh, come on, Travis. You're kidding?"

"No. I wish I were kidding—"

"Murder! Who? I don't understand!" She cut him off.

"Sheila… Sheila Stone," Travis answered.

"Who's Sheila?" Adrienne asked, in a firm tone.

"Remember. The blonde you saw at the office. She's dead, and they have arrested Billy for it."

"Yes, I remember her. She's his client, right? What does Billy have to do with her death?"

The question hammered at him, "He… he didn't have anything to do with her death." The words dropped out of his mouth.

"Then why are you saying she's dead, and he killed her?"

Adrienne said, coolly.

"She is Billy's client, but she wanted more than an attorney and client relationship." Travis chose his words carefully.

"She wanted what?" Adrienne frowned.

"She wanted Billy, but he wouldn't hear of it," Travis lied, hating the lie that spilled forth from his tongue.

"I don't believe it," she sat on the sofa and crossed her arms. "My husband killed someone?" She rolled her eyes, and cocked her head to one side, and looked at Travis. "I know what this is all about, Travis," she said, uncrossing her arms and shot him an angry look. "But it's not going to work! This is about the kiss. I know it. I can't believe you have the nerve to come into my home and deliberately lie to me about my husband! Well, today, when you asked me did I feel anything for you? I do. I feel sorry for you! And, I feel sorry for Billy, too! He loves you, and trusts you! For what? So, you can stab him in his back the first chance you get! That's very low Travis! I'm surprised at you…coming into our home with this mess! A nasty lie to destroy it! I don't want to hear anymore of your lies!" She pushed herself up. "Get out of my house!" She shouted, angrily pointing, and shaking a finger at him.

"Oh, no, Adrienne, you're wrong! I wouldn't hurt you for anything in the world," he explained. He was shocked by her outburst of accusations.

"Oh! I see. You'd spare my feelings, but forget about Billy's feelings!" She snapped.

"No, Adrienne, that's not true. I love Billy. I don't want to see him hurt, either." It pained him that she thought he'd deliberately harm Billy.

"Mmh! You've a strange way of showing it. First you kissed me, then, you tell me you're in love with me. Now, you're lying to me. Trying to break us up!" She snapped angrily.

"No!" Travis looked at her pleading with her with his eyes. "No. I don't want to break-up your marriage! Yeah, I kissed you and God knows I wish I can take it back, but I can't. I love you, don't you see?" He reasoned.

"Love! What do you know about love? After all the low-down mess you're pulling behind Billy's back." Adrienne crossed her arms over her chest.

"I do know I love you! I know it's wrong. I have prayed night after night, asking God to remove this thing from me," he answered. "I'm ashamed, as a Christian for having this covetous desire for you."

"Well, in my book, you're not ashamed enough." She moved a few steps away from him. "How dare you to come into my house, talking to me about love! I was happy that you were Billy's friend. He needs you. But you're not a friend of Billy, and nor are you a friend of mine. Get out!"

"But... but, Adrienne, you don't know what you're saying," he said, walking toward her.

"Don't touch me!" She warned. "Get out!" She shouted, angrily, and hurried to the door.

"Please, Adrienne," Travis followed her to the door.

"No. I will not listen to you, anymore! Get out!" She shouted, opening the door for him.

Two police officers stood on the other side of the door and were about to ring the doorbell when it flew open. "Is there a problem?" One of the officers asked, looking at Travis, and then Adrienne.

"Huh? What?" Adrienne responded, turning to the door and looking at the officers.

"Is everything fine, here?" The officer asked, again.

"Oh, yes. Everything's okay, now, that you all are here," she glanced scornfully at Travis. "I was asking this man to leave my home."

"Sir," the two officers looked at Travis.

"I'm leaving, Officers," Travis responded, walking past the two men.

"Yes, go!" Adrienne said, bitterly, watching Travis walk out the door. Then she turned her attention to the officers. "I'm sorry. May I help you all?" She asked, still shaken from the episode.

"We're looking for Mrs. Adrienne Ray," the officer said.

"I'm Mrs. Ray," she stated, wondering why they were looking for her.

"Mrs. Ray, may we come in, and talk, please?"

"Talk?" She hesitated. "Is there a problem?" She stepped to the side of the door, letting the officers in. She closed the door.

"Mrs. Ray, your husband, Mr. William Anthony Ray, has been arrested for the murder of Ms. Sheila Stone," the officers said, watching her reaction.

Adrienne stood speechless. The officers continued to talk, but the last word she heard was Billy had been arrested for Sheila's murder.

"Mr. Ray is at the Silver Rock County Jail," the officer said.

"I… I can't believe it," she said, in a low tone. "That's what Travis… oh, Travis," she whispered, realizing she had been wrong about Travis.

"One unit 12," the officer two-way radio jumped to life.

Officer Kinchen unhooked the radio from it clip, "One unit 12, Officer Kinchen, over."

"Unit 12 we're calling for back-up. There's a disturbance at 180 Tastee Ham Barbecue Pit, over," the radio's dispatcher voice rang through the two-way.

"Affirmative," Officer Kinchen stated. "Over," he replied, putting the radio back into it clip. "Ma'am," he nodded at Adrienne.

"Ma'am," the second officer spoke for the first time. The officers walked to the door, and opened it. "Good night," they said and walked out the door.

"Good night," she said, following the officers, and closing the door behind them.

Adrienne stood at the door lost for words, tears began to surface but she blinked them back, refusing to let them surface.

"Billy," she whispered, "what have you done?" She walked away from the door. "Awww!" She screamed, holding both hands to each side of her head. "Why? Why, Billy?" she shouted. "Whyy!" Adrienne's voice echoed through the house. "I must talk to someone! "I have to call, someone. Janet. Yeah, I'll call Janet. She knows what to do." Adrienne, picked up the telephone, and dialed Janet's number. Adrienne let the phone ring and ring before realizing Janet wasn't home.

"What now?" she said, pacing the floor. She quickly rushed upstairs to their bedroom, and grabbed her purse from her closet. She opened it, and fished out her small address book. She flipped through the pages, and found what she was looking for. She quickly dialed Travis' cell phone. Adrienne, felt terrible how she had treated Travis, and she didn't know what she'd say to him, but she didn't have time to worry about that, now. She needed him. She wanted his comfort.

"Hello," Travis answered on the second ring.

"Travis," Adrienne blurted the word out quickly. She didn't want to give herself time to think about what she was doing. She was afraid she'd hang-up the telephone.

"I'm sorry," she said, "the two policemen just left my house. They told me about Billy."

"Adrienne," Travis spoke softly. "Are you okay?" He asked.

"Yes. I guess. Ooh, Travis I'm not okay." He could hear the tremble in her voice.

"It's going to be all right," he said with assurance, and then began again. "I know Billy and he's innocent."

"Travis, I'm sorry," she whispered.

"There's no need to be sorry, Adrienne."

"But...but I'm sorry," she explained. "I should have known you wouldn't hurt Billy, or me," she replied, letting tears surface and move quickly down her face.

"You know, it's funny, after I left there, I started to think—" he said, but was interrupted by her.

"Travis, please, can you come over. I'm sorry I asked you to leave. If I have to stay alone in this house another minute, I don't know what I'd do," she said, between sobs.

"You're sure?" He asked.

"Yes."

"Okay, I'm only a few minutes away."

"Okay, I'll see you in a little while."

"Bye," he replied. The cell phone went dead.

Travis turned the Lexus around and headed back to Billy's house. He was glad she had come to her senses and recognized he wasn't the enemy she had portrayed him to be. Minutes, later, Travis pulled his car into Billy's driveway. He parked the car, and turned off the ignition. Travis opened the car's door and stepped outside. He scanned the house, before walking up to the front door. Travis rang the doorbell.

Adrienne opened the door apologizing to him, "I'm sorry, Travis," she repeated.

"I told you there's no need for you to be sorry. If the shoe was on the other foot, I'd be apprehensive as well," he replied walking through the door.

"But, I am sorry" she said, as she led him to the living room. They sat on the sofa.

"Are you sure you're okay?" Travis said, watching her.

"Yes. I'm okay, now, that you're here," she leaned closer to him. "Please, hold me," she stated. "I feel so bad."

Travis moved closer to her, and wrapped his arm around her. He rested his chin on the top of her head. "Do you feel better?" He asked.

"Yes. Much better." She muttered.

"Good."

"Thanks, Travis," she said, looking up at him. "Thanks for coming again, after all the stuff I said about you. I'm truly sorry," she tilted her face toward his and parted her lips.

"Like I said, it's okay," he whispered hoarsely, leaning his face closer to hers. His lips found hers.

"Oh, Travis, I'm so sorry." She met his kiss over and over again with driven passion.

"Mmmh." It was all he could utter as they embraced in the heat of the moment.

Adrienne surrendered in Travis' arms, as Travis untied the bathrobe, pushing it away from her. His smooth fingers trailed up and down her silky body, taunting it as they found their way to her perfect round breasts. He teased them and kissed them hungrily. He wanted her so badly that he could hear his heart pounding through his chest. Travis couldn't remember anyone or anything he had wanted so badly. He lost himself in her, and blocked out all reasons not to have her.

Then, suddenly a still small voice spoke to his spirit, reminding him of the scriptures, Proverb, 7:22, 23 and 27. 'All at once he followed her like an ox going to the slaughter, like a dear stepping into a noose till an arrow pierces his liver, like a bird darting into a snare, little knowing it will cost him his life. Her house is a highway to the grave, leading down to the chambers of death.'

The scriptures filled his mind, erasing his reasoning to have his way with her.

"Wait! We can't!" He said, grabbing her robe, trying to wrap it around her.

"No," she rebuttal, and clasped her arms around him. "What's wrong?"

"I can't do this," he answered. He unclasped her arms from around him. He pushed himself up from the sofa.

"Why not? Are you worrying about, Billy? He wasn't worrying about me when he killed that... that woman!" She cried, declining backward onto the sofa.

"It's not right what we're about to do." Travis looked at her. "Please, Lord forgive us!" Travis said aloud.

"I thought you said you loved me?" She crossed her arms over her chest.

"I do, but not like this."

"Well, how? Is there any other way?" She asked, wishing he'd drop the niceness.

"No. I'm sorry I guess I got carried away. I have to stay focused. I have to leave," he said, in one breath.

"Travis, you cant' leave me, now!" She looked bewildered.

"Adrienne, I have to leave. If I stay now, we might do something that we'll both eventually regret."

"I won't regret," she said, softly. "I won't regret this night at all."

"Adrienne," he said, ignoring her last statement. "You have to understand, I can't do this."

"Why not?"

Travis searched his mind for an answer. He knew he couldn't go against the Lord in this. He had messed up so many times in his walk with the Lord. Getting stone drunk for one thing and lying, and covering up for Billy and desiring his wife was another. But now it was going a step further, another level of sin. He glanced at Adrienne. The spark between them seemed to grow. Cool it, he thought averting his attention away from her.

"It's be...because ..." the words stuck to the roof of his mouth.

"Because of what?" Adrienne looked agitated.

"Because, it's not right." He forced the words out.

"It's not right?" She said, sarcastically. "Well, well, well, let me be the judge of what's right, and what's wrong. Was it right for

Billy to put me through this pain and humiliation, huh? He didn't care what his actions would do to me! Where is he? Sitting in jail for killing someone," the words rolled off her tongue. "He didn't think about me, or our marriage. And, here you are telling me it's not right. Well, I'm here to tell you what's not right. What's not right is Billy leaving me all alone. So, tell me, Travis, what's right to you?"

The question hammered at him, but he had to be honest with her. It wasn't any other way out.

"I'm a Christian," he answered.

"Yes, but that didn't stop you from telling me you love me." She uncrossed her arms and moved closer to the edge of the sofa.

"I was wrong for saying that to you. I'm sorry. Would you forgive me, please?"

"Forgive you for what? For expressing your love to me? There isn't anything to forgive." Adrienne leaned back on the sofa, again. "You should be asking me to forgive you for turning me on, and then pushing me away."

"Adrienne, I'm sorry."

"Sorry!"

"Yes. I'm sorry I can't give you what you want. I want you, badly, but I have to do what's right. Please try to understand." Travis eyed her for a moment before turning to leave.

"No, wait, Travis. Don't go. I'm sure we can work something out," Adrienne rose to her feet, walking toward Travis. She let her robe swing open revealing a white lace nightie.

"There's nothing to work out, Adrienne," he replied, as he turned and looked at her. Shaken by the contour and the silkiness of her body, Travis lowered his head, he was afraid she'd captivate him with her innocence. "I'll call you in the morning. Get some rest now. You'll need to look your best when you visit Billy tomorrow." He said, turning his back to her. "Good night." He opened the door and walked out.

Disturbed by Travis' coolness, and ashamed of her degrading behavior, Adrienne collapsed onto the sofa, and screamed.

* * * * * * * * * *

Travis found Pastor Johnson's home number in the telephone book. He slowly dialed the number. Pastor Johnson picked up the telephone on the first ring.

"Hello,"

"Hello, is this Pastor Johnson's resident?" Travis asked. He knew he had called the right number, but now, he wished he hadn't.

"This is Pastor Johnson. Who is this?" Pastor Johnson asked.

"Travis... Travis Malcolm," his tone was soft.

"Travis," Pastor Johnson recognized the name. "How are you?"

"I'm not so well, Pastor Johnson. I hate to bother you tonight, but I... I ..."

"It's all right," Pastor Johnson assured him. "What can I do for you, Travis?" He spoke with a sincere tone.

"Pastor, I need to speak with you concerning a matter I've been dealing with far too long."

"Yes." Pastor Johnson replied. "I'm listening."

"I've wanted this woman, Adrienne. I'm in love with her, but she's married to my friend, Billy."

"You're lusting after another man's wife? Is this what you're telling me, Son?"

"I guess you can call it that." Travis sighed in frustration. He hated to think it was pure lust he had for Adrienne, and not love.

"The Bible calls it lust," Pastor Johnson added. "So, this woman that you want badly is married, and she's married to your friend? How does she feel about this?"

"Tonight, she wanted me. We almost," Travis felt silly discussing it over the telephone. "May I come into your office and talk?" Travis said, suddenly becoming embarrassed of the phone call.

"Okay, tomorrow morning at 8:00 will be good. My staffs won't be in the office until 11:00."

"Pastor Johnson," Travis said, "Tonight, I wanted to be with her so badly. I felt like a man drowning. I wanted her more than anything."

"But she's married, and she doesn't belong to you. She belongs to her husband."

"He's in jail. They charged him with killing Shelia, his lover, tonight. Billy always had everything he wanted. He doesn't want, Adrienne. She's a prize to him." He tried to justify his feelings.

"Listen   to   yourself,   Son. You're desperate for this young lady. The feelings you're having for her is pure lust. A demon of lust, and I bind that demon in the name of Jesus." Pastor Johnson didn't hesitate binding the spirit that was operating against Travis.

"Pastor Johnson, I have to go now," Travis said, irritable, and suddenly feeling uncomfortable talking with Pastor Johnson.

"You will come by to see me, huh?"

"I'll see," Travis said, before hanging up the telephone. Travis stared at the telephone, he wanted to pull it from the wall, but he heard Pastor Johnson binding words. Suddenly, he felt peaceful. A calmness washed over him as he played Pastor Johnson's words over, and over in his mind. Sleep came easily.

Chapter 18

𝒯ravis stood outside Pastor Joseph Johnson's office for a moment before knocking. Small beads of sweat popped over his upper lip. He didn't know what had made him decide to come to the church. He had made up his mind that morning to dismiss the idea of paying Pastor Johnson a visit. However, after his cup of coffee, Adrienne had filled his mind with all sorts of unpleasant thoughts. He needed someone who was on higher level with God, to pray for him. Pastor Johnson had proved himself to be an authentic man of God. Travis had fallen in love with Pastor Johnson and the church after his first visit. He became part of "Sword and Shield Church," that very same day.

Pastor Johnson had been speaking on "The suffering of Jesus, and how we too, who desire to follow Jesus and to live holy will suffer." The sermon had connected within Travis' spirit. He had wanted to know more about Jesus' sufferings, and the suffering of His saints.

Travis knocked lightly on the door. A few seconds later, Pastor Johnson opened the door. "Travis. Good morning. I'm glad you could make it," Pastor Johnson smiled, clutching Travis' hand, shaking it, vigorously. "Come on in," he released Travis' hand and led Travis to a chair near the side of his desk. "After our little talk last night, I didn't think you were coming," Pastor Johnson gave a soft laugh.

"Well, after I talked with you, I didn't think I was coming, either, but I'm here. You're right; I've been a careless jerk, when it came to Adrienne." Travis leaned back into the chair.

"I'd never call you a jerk," Pastor Johnson smiled, pulling his chair from his desk; he sat in the chair and faced Travis.

"No, Pastor, you didn't have too. I'm calling myself that. I was being a jerk for another man's wife."

"Son, you're a man. When you gave your life to Christ, it didn't stop you from looking at women, but it gave you a warning to run. It gave you the discernment never to get yourself caught in a compromising situation. The enemy knows your weakness and believe me, he'll try to play on it. But God knows us better than the enemy, and God has given us an escape from the enemy."

"But...but I have been in love with this girl since elementary school." Travis explained.

"And, you don't think the devil knows that? He has been building up a wall against you. A stronghold to keep you in bondage, and a snare to keep you trapped. That is the devil's ministry, to destroy God's people. Luke chapter twenty-two, verses thirty-one, and thirty-two, and the Lord said, 'Simon, Simon! Indeed Satan has asked for you, that he may sift you as wheat. But I have prayed for you...that your faith should not fail; and when you have returned to Me, strengthen your brethren.'" Pastor Johnson leaned back in his chair. "If the enemy had the nerve to ask about Peter, what makes you think he won't ask about you? He hates to see God's children grow in holiness. He'd rather destroy us before we grow in our walk with the Lord. Oh, yeah, he's all right when we're lukewarm for the Lord. I tell the congregation all the time, the devil likes lukewarm saints. They make his job easier. He can rest under a shade tree sipping slowly on a full glass of ice cold lemonade, because he knows we're not going anywhere with our walk with the Lord. He knows we refuse to grow with Christ, and that we are spiritually handicapped, too caught up in ourselves to help anybody. But as soon as we make a stand, divorce ourselves, and desire growth and holiness, he throws away his glass of lemonade, and rushes towards us like a mad bull trying to keep his strongholds in place in our lives. Do you hear what I'm saying? Got to hear this. But, the word of God, and the blood of Jesus Christ, delivered us from his attacks. Last night, he tried to sift you like he wanted to do Peter, but the blood of Jesus, and the Spirit of the living God, reminded you who you were in Christ. He made a way of escape for you. Praise the Lord."

"Pastor Johnson, I admit I haven't been a saint. There are times when I didn't acknowledge God or my actions. I just wanted what I wanted without any regard to anyone else's feelings." His tone was low and soft.

"Then, your prayer should be asking God to kill your flesh."

"Kill my flesh? What kind of prayer is that?" Travis looked confused.

"It's the flesh that keeps us desiring the wrong things. The flesh is full of worldly thinking. It keeps us alive to the things of the world. Carnal minded thinking. We have to read the word of God everyday to renew our minds. We have a spirit on the inside of us, and we have to feed our spirit-man just like we feed our flesh. We have to feed our spirit-man everyday on the word of God. Because our spirit keeps us alive to the things of God. Galatians chapter five, verse sixteen, tells us "to walk in the Spirit, and you shall not fulfill the lust of the flesh." Pastor Johnson sat up in his chair. "Son, when we become born again, our spirit is awake to God. Your flesh stays flesh, but your spirit becomes born again reconciled to God. That's why Christ said, 'We must be born again.' This means to die to old self. What is born of the flesh is flesh, and that which born of the spirit is spirit. John chapter four, verse twenty-four, Christ tells us, 'God is Spirit, and those who worship Him must worship in spirit and truth.'"

Travis glanced at the clock on Pastor Johnson's desk; he had an appointment with Billy that morning. He wondered would Adrienne visit Billy. He sure hoped so, for Billy's sake.

"You have somewhere else to go?" Pastor Johnson asked, glancing at the clock.

"I have to see Billy this morning," Travis replied. "I spoke briefly of him to you last night on the phone."

"Yes, I remember, your friend, Billy. Well, I won't keep you," Pastor Johnson stood up.

"Thank you, Pastor," Travis rose to his feet. "I'm glad you had time to see me."

"Remember, Son, you did the right thing last night by running away from the young lady's house. Don't let the enemy tell you that you were stupid. You did the right thing by honoring God. This is warfare. It's a war going on in the spiritual realm. We enlisted in that war when we asked Jesus to be our Lord and our Savior. Let us pray." Pastor Johnson clutched Travis' hands, and they bowed their head in prayer.

He began. "Oh, Lord, please, help Travis to grow in his walk with You. Lord give him the desire to want more of You. Lord, teach him to die to his flesh. Give him a desire for holiness. Father, help him to love You with all his strength, mind, body and soul. Lord also delivery this troubled young lady, and grant her peace to face the things that has been thrown at her. But most of all I pray for this young lady and her husband's salvation. And, the young man, Billy, help him, Lord. Father, you know what happened to the young woman that was killed. Lord if Billy is innocent of this crime reveal it, and deliver him. Thank you, Lord. It's in the matchless name of Jesus. Amen." Pastor Johnson released Travis' hands.

"Thanks again," Travis said averting his eyes away from Pastor Johnson. He stepped away from the chair.

"Lord you receive the thanks," Pastor Johnson replied walking away from his desk. "I'll be seeing you in church, Sunday?" Pastor Johnson said, walking Travis to the door.

"I'll be here," Travis, answered, as he shook Pastor Johnson's hand and walked out of the office.

Pastor Johnson stood outside his door watching Travis as he walked from his sight. "Lord, keep him," he said, before walking back into his office, and closing the door.

Travis composed himself behind the steering wheel and started the car. He glanced back at the church before pulling out of the parking lot.

Chapter 19

*A*drienne watched Billy as he and a jail guard entered the visitor room. She rushed to him with open arms. Billy took her arms and held them for a moment. Then he wrapped his arms around her waist. He kissed her. She felt good in his arms. He missed her. He wanted to make love to her as he looked into her eyes, kissing her again.

"I miss you," he whispered in her ear. "I want to make love to you right now."

"We have to talk." She replied, responding coolly to his kiss, and thinking about last night in Travis' arms.

"I don't want to let you go," he held her tightly. "Let me hold you for a little while longer. We can talk, later," he said, as his lips trailed up, and down her neck.

"No, Billy," she pushed herself from his arms. "We must talk, now. Who's Sheila?" She stepped away from his grasp, as she crossed her arms over her chest, looking at him.

"What's this?" He asked, watching her.

"Billy, don't patronize me. You know exactly what I'm talking about. Why did you do it? The woman was your lover, wasn't she? Why did you kill her? What were you thinking? You can get away with something like this? I can't believe you... you did this crazy thing, and not once did you consider me or our marriage!" She shot him an angry look with her eyes. "What am I suppose to do, now?"

The questions didn't surprise him. He had rehearsed for this moment; he eyed her before turning his back to her.

"Look at me," she sneered, forming her small fist into a ball, punching him. "Answer me."

Billy turned facing her, retreating a step backward, "What do you want from me, Adrienne? Do you want me to say she was my lover? Is that it? Well, Adrienne, I have news for you. She wasn't my lover. Is that what you want to hear, huh? That's what you want to hear? Sheila wasn't my lover, Adrienne. She was a client. Strictly business. Nothing else." He walked a few steps toward her. "Did I kill her? No. Adrienne, you know me better than that. You of all people know I'm not capable of doing a thing like that."

"I hope not," she softened.

"It hurt me to think that you'd think such a thing about me," he sounded hurt. "To answer your other question, yes, Sheila wanted me badly baby, but I told her there couldn't be anything between us. Because I already have a woman I'm in love with." Billy walked closer to her. "That woman is you, baby. I'm in love with you, my wife."

"Are you sure you two weren't lovers?" She watched Billy closely. She looked for any tell-tell sign that he had been cheating on her. But there was none.

"Adrienne, are you listening to me? I'm in love with you. There's no one else. There has never been another woman in my life. You're the only one. Trust me, baby," he explained, seizing her waist. "I love you, and only you." His lips covered hers, melting all the anxiety, and anger she had stored up against him. Adrienne returned his kiss with an uncontrollable passion.

"Your problem is that you worry to much, baby," he whispered in her ear, breaking the kiss, but holding her tightly in his arms.

"I worry about you. I guess I let what they're saying about you in the paper this morning upset me."

"Don't believe half of the things you read in the papers, Adrienne. Some reporters have a way of making lies sound like the truth."

"You're right. I shouldn't depend on the paper. I'm glad we had this talk. Last night when the policemen came by the house to inform me you were in jail, I really lost it. I wasn't myself," she replied. "This thing hit me pretty hard."

"I'm sorry, Adrienne," he said, releasing her.

"I believe you, Billy," she whispered, reaching for his hand. But he pulled his hand away from her. "What's the matter?" She asked, concerned with his sudden demeanor.

"There isn't anything wrong, baby. I'm sorry I'm putting you through this. You don't deserve it. I hate to see you like this."

"Like what?"

"Worrying about me. But you don't have to. I'm going to be out of here, soon."

"Billy," she touched his shoulder.

"Yes," he answered, as he took her in his arms again. She felt soft in his arms.

"I trust you, and I believe in you." She said, looking up into his eyes.

"I'm happy to hear you say that," he kissed her. "I don't know what I'd do if I thought you didn't believe in me."

"I truly believe in you, and I love you from the bottom of my heart."

"Thanks. I needed to hear you say that," Billy said holding her closer, and burying his face into hers.

* * * * * * * * * *

"Mrs. Ray," Detective Wright called after Adrienne. "I would like to speak with you for a moment, ma'am?" He asked, catching up with her. "I'm Detective Wright, working on your husband's case. "How is Mr. Ray, today, ma'am?"

"He's okay, I suppose," she replied, pacing her steps.

"Ma'am, I hate to bother you, but I need to ask you some questions about your husband."

"Detective," she quickly glanced at him, and paced her steps even more. "I don't have anything to say to you about my husband. Would you please excuse me, but I'm in a hurry."

"Ma'am, I hate to bother you seeing you're in hurry, but it won't take too much of your time." He added quickly.

"I told you I don't have anything to say about my husband." They walked out of the precinct. She stopped walking, and faced the detective. She looked him up, and down slowly, before replying, "Detective, my husband is innocent. He's not at all capable of doing the hideous thing that you all have accused him of. Good day,

Detective," she quickly walked away.

"Mrs. Ray, I'm terribly sorry to bother you, but madam, it might clear some things up for him, and for you. You might get to know the real Billy." He spoke, catching up to her.

"What do you mean, Detective?" She asked and stopped staring at him. The statement hammered at her.

"It might clear some things up about what the papers are saying about your husband," he added, knowing he had hooked her.

"The papers print nothing but lies."

"Ma'am, you don't believe that."

"Detective, what do you know about my beliefs?

"I believe you're an intelligent young woman, who wants to know the truth about her husband." He picked the right words to reel her in.

"So, you have the truth about Billy?" She asked, wondering what this detective knew that she didn't all ready know.

"May I meet with you tomorrow?" He asked.

"I'm busy," she replied.

"Okay, the day after," he asked.

"Busy," she answered.

"Mrs. Ray, I'd love to meet with you. Believe me you won't be disappointed."

She watched the detective curiously; she wanted to hear what he had to say about Billy. "Okay, Detective. Next Wednesday at three o'clock."

"Thank you, Mrs. Ray." He smiled.

"Do you know where I live?" She asked, glancing at her watch.

"Yes ma'am. I'll be there at three. Thank you, ma'am, I've wasted too much of your time already. See you next week." He replied, happily walking back into the precinct.

* * * * * * * * * *

Travis pulled into the Silver Rock County jail parking lot. He cut off the engine, and lay his head on the seat rest. He closed his eyes, and thought about what Pastor Johnson had said. He had to die to his flesh. It sounded weird, until it made sense. He couldn't explain it. But it made a whole lot of sense to him. He opened his eyes, and stepped from the car. He pressed the door lock on his key ring and walked quickly into the precinct.

"Good evening," he said to the officers at the front desk.

"Good evening," the officers replied.

Travis wrote his name and the time on the check-in, checkout list at the front desk. He walked to the jail entry and flashed his identification card at the glass window to one of the three officers behind the large windowpane. One of the officers pressed the metal security button, releasing the door. The iron door clanked. Travis seized the heavy door and pulled and walked through it.

He walked to Billy's cellblock. Billy lay on the bunk staring at the ceiling. His hands wrapped behind his neck. He had handled the situation with Adrienne quite well. She hadn't suspected a thing after his brilliant performance. He should have been an actor, he thought. A smile tugged at the corners of his mouth.

"Hey," Travis broke Billy's concentration.

"Man, I thought I'd never say this, but I'm glad to see you," Billy rose from his bunk. "Have you found out anything?"

"No, not yet. But hang in there. I'm going to see can I get you bail," he said.

"Good," Billy looked around his cell. "Another night in this place, and I'd be out of my mind."

"When I leave here, I'm stopping by Detective Wright's office. I want to check your file."

"Good. How is it out there?" Billy asked.

"Okay." Travis answered, lowering his eyes. He was ashamed to face Billy, especially after last night.

"Adrienne came by to see me, today."

"I'm glad to hear that. How was she?" Travis asked, wondering what she had told Billy.

"She says she's okay, but I have a feeling she's not okay."

"It's expected under the circumstance," Travis explained.

"Yeah, man, but I have to get out of here. She didn't look too well."

"You'll be out of here before you know it. Don't get to familiar with this place," Travis stated.

"Don't worry about that. I won't," Billy grinned.

"I'm glad to see your spirit's up." Travis glanced at Billy.

"Yeah. Me too." Billy leaned closer to the bars. "Travis, thanks, man. Thanks for believing in me."

"What are friends for?" Travis replied. "Listen, you hang in there. I'll be back once I meet with the district attorney about bail, okay?" Travis said, putting his hand through the bars.

"Thanks," Billy said, clutching Travis' hand.

"Anytime," he replied, removing his hand from Billy's.

"Take care of Adrienne," Billy requested.

Travis pondered over the statement before answering, "You know I will," he said, walking away from the cellblock.

* * * * * * * * * *

"I'm glad you're here, Detective," Travis said, walking into Detective Wright's office. "I want to see Billy's files." He said, as he stood in front of Detective Wright's desk.

"Attorney Malcolm, how are you?" Detective Wright said in a cheerful tone.

"I'm good," Travis cut the greeting short.

"The files are right here on my desk. I was looking over them, just before you walked in." Detective Wright closed the folder, and rose to his feet, walking from behind his desk.

"You can sit at my desk and go over the file. I have to make a quick run. You'll find everything is in order." He walked toward the door. "Oh, and by the way. I have an interview with Mrs. Ray, next Wednesday," he said.

"You can't interview the suspect's wife!" Travis proclaimed.

"If the wife agrees to talk with me. I can. I spoke with Mrs. Ray, today. She agreed to talk with me."

"How low can you get?" The words breathed hotly from Travis' mouth.

"I'm a detective. I'm doing my job." He said, turning his back on Travis. He walked out of his office.

* * * * * * * * * *

An hour later, Travis slid behind the wheel of his car, pulled out his cell phone and dialed Adrienne's telephone number. He was about to hang up, before hearing Adrienne voice come over the air.

"Hi, Adrienne," he spoke closely into the mouthpiece.

"Yes," she replied.

"Good evening. I... ah, ah," he searched for the right words.

"What is it, Travis?" She asked, coldly. He had hurt her by rejecting her, and she wouldn't make it easy for him.

"I saw Billy today. He told me you came by. I'm glad you did," he said, feeling the tension over the line.

"Why shouldn't I visit him? We are married, or have you forgotten?" She snapped.

"No, Adrienne, I haven't forgotten," he replied.

"Good. Because last night, I thought maybe you had forgotten I was married to your best friend," she said sarcastically.

"Adrienne, about last night, I'm sorry. I shouldn't have led you on —"

"Led me on!" She cut him off.

"Yes. I feel responsible for last night. I shouldn't have allowed myself to kiss you. I should have known better." He tried to explain.

"I'm a grown woman, Travis. I can be responsible for myself. Two consenting adults kissed last night, and we both wanted it."

"I can vouch for that," he spoke softly, listening to her silky voice.

"Travis I know you wanted me, badly, but I wanted you even the more," she whispered into the telephone. "I wanted you to make love to me, even now, I want that."

"I can't do that, Adrienne. I can't ever do that." Travis laid his head on the headrest, and closed his eyes.

"Then, why do you call me to torture me?" She snapped.

"I call to see if you were all right?" He replied, opening his eyes, and raising his head from the headrest.

"Yes. I'm all right!" She said, coolly. "I'm as all right as I'm ever going to be!"

"Good." Travis muttered.

"Humph," Adrienne grumbled.

Travis ignored her little quirt, "I talked to Detective Wright today, and he told me you had agreed to meet with him."

"Yes."

"Why would you want to do a thing like that, Adrienne? It's not good. You have the right to call this meeting off."

"I also have the right to see him."

"Yes, if that's what you want."

"That's what I want."

"Okay, Adrienne, I can't stop you... but please let me be there when you meet with him." Travis couldn't figure out what was going on in Adrienne's head. What ever it was, he didn't like it.

"Why do you want to be there?"

"I want to be there, so I can—"

"So I won't say anything stupid? Is that it?" She interjected.

"No. I want to be there for you. Detective Wright can be mean, hard, and unpredictable."

"You make the man out to be a monster."

"He's not a monster, but his tactics are questionable."

"Suit yourself. If you want to be here, it's okay with me. He's meeting me here, next Wednesday, at three o' clock."

"Thanks, Adrienne."

"Don't mention it," she said, coolly, hanging up the telephone.

Travis held the telephone in his hand a few seconds before putting it away. She was hurt, and he could hear it in her voice. He had hurt her, and there wasn't anything to be done about it. He put the cell phone into its clip, and turned the key in the ignition, the car leaped to life. Travis pulled out of Silver Rock County Jail's parking lot.

Chapter 20

*B*illy sat across from Detective Wright, five days had passed but it seemed like an eternity as the detective slowly sipped his hot, black, coffee. He stared hard at Billy. Billy didn't like his look. Wright was muscular, stood six-six, his skin a dark chocolate. Billy felt sure that if one would cut into Wright's body you'd fine dark chocolate to the bone. Wright was handsome with fine features. He had a good grade of thick, black, wavy hair. He had high cheekbones. He reminded Billy of a Cherokee chief in one of his western history books in college. He could have easily been drafted for a model on the cover of a western romance novel. Wright's eyes were dark and they matched his complexion.

Billy cleared his throat. "Where's my attorney?" he asked. He dared not allow Wright to put fear in him, as he watched the detective with a firm expression.

"He's not here," Wright replied setting the coffee on the table. He pulled out a chair and placed his foot on it. He looked at Billy and shook his head, then picked up his cup of coffee and took another sip.

"He's not here, then why am I here?" Billy asked. He didn't like the detective's strategy. "I answered your questions already," Billy reminded him.

"I wasn't satisfied." Wright set the cup of coffee on the table.

"I want my lawyer," Billy leaned against the table.

"Stop being a rich brat," Wright replied, leaning closer to Billy.

"I know my rights," Billy said.

"Look, I know you're a fancy tail attorney with plenty of money to spend. Chicks digging you on every side, begging you to do them, but that don't mean anything to me. That's clear? To me, you're a regular, low-life, punk like the rest of the scum out on the street." His tone was harsh. He picked up his coffee without taking his eyes off of Billy.

Billy rubbed the place where his gold necklace should have been. Wright looked at him and frowned. Billy quickly put his hand on the table, and then he sat back in the chair and watched Wright.

"That's more like it," Wright said. He set the cup of coffee on the table.

"What's your full name?" He asked as he took his foot off the chair.

"William Anthony Ray," Billy replied, giving the detective what he was there for.

"What's your occupation?"

"At...at," he paused and stared hard at Detective Wright, "Attorney."

"Did you kill Sheila Stone?"

"No!"

"But you were caught with the murder weapon." He leaned against the table.

"I told you why I had the pipe in my hand."

Detective Wright picked up the cup of coffee and drained the remainder of it, then threw the Styrofoam cup into the wastebasket behind him. This was going to be a hard interview. One of those interviews he didn't like or care to participate in. But the job had to be done. "Yeah, but tell me again?" Detective Wright asked.

"I was protecting myself."

Detective Wright wasn't buying Billy's story. He squinted his eyes and frowned. "Just admit you killed her. Yes, we've established that you and the victim were lovers. But what would drive a man to kill his lover? You thought you had it made, huh? A wife at home to keep the home fire burning and a mistress across town to keep your blood boiling." He put his foot back on the chair and added, "Do you have any kids somewhere?" he asked looking suspiciously.

"I told you I didn't kill Sheila. And no I don't have any children."

"Did your wife suspect anything going on between you and Ms. Stone?" Detective Wright ignored Billy's statement as he leaned closer toward him.

"My wife didn't have anything to do with this crime." Billy grumbled, glaring at the Detective.

"You're quite sure of yourself, Mr. Ray," Detective Wright bit the bottom of his lip, and eyed Billy with a mean look.

"I know Adrienne didn't kill Sheila." Billy stared at the detective.

"And ..." the detective waited for Billy reply.

"She was home, sleep when I left to go over and speak with Sheila." Billy said, and then added, "I didn't kill her, either," Billy reared back in his seat.

"What was your reason for wanting to talk with her?" Detective Wright asked.

"I want my attorney," Billy replied.

"Mr. Ray, someone killed Ms. Stone, and right now all of the evidence is pointing at you. I'm going to get to the bottom of this case, and I'm going to nail that someone if it's the last thing I do."

Billy stared silent at the detective. He wished he would get to the bottom of the case and find Sheila's killer. She didn't deserve to die like that, he thought remembering how Sheila looked lying on the sofa.

Travis rushed into the interview room. He frowned at Detective Wright. The detective raised his right brow and gave Travis a slight, quick look-over. He had been caught interrogating the perpetrator without the proper procedures. But what the heck he thought. He was a crime fighter.

"Why are you speaking with my client?" Travis demanded to know, his tone firm. He hated it when detectives went behind attorneys' backs hoping to get confessions. He turned his back to the detective and looked at Billy. He loved Billy like a brother, and it hurt to see how the headlines of Silver Rock Tribune made him out to be a criminal.

"I'll leave the two of you alone," Wright moved his foot from the chair; he pushed the chair under the table, and walked to the door.

"I'll speak to my client in the room across the hall, if that's okay with you?"

"Suit yourself," Wright shrugged his shoulders as he walked toward the door. "Oh, and one other thing, don't forget I have an interview with Mrs. Ray, tomorrow," Detective Wright added, as he walked out of the interview room.

"He has an interview with, Adrienne?" Billy asked, staring hard at Travis.

"She agreed to meet with him," Travis said as he grabbed the door and held it open. Then, he and Billy walked out and entered the room across the hall. The room was small, but private. A square table sat in the center of the room with a telephone on top.

"Man, I've been in here for a week." Billy looked at Travis. "Why is it taking you so long to get me out of here?"

"The judge turned down your bail. He's afraid you'll skip the country."

"Man, that's ridiculous."

"I know you won't do a foolish thing like that. But that's what they're afraid of. They're afraid you'd get your money and run." Travis looked hard at Billy. "I'm trying my best to get them to make a deal with me. But they're not biting."

"Man, give me credit. Who do they think I am?" He turned his back on Travis. "I can't stay in here another day. I'm losing my mind in here." He turned to Travis and walked closer to him. "I have to get out of here for Adrienne's sake. She hates me," he pounded his fist on the table near Travis. "She hasn't visited me since last week. I tried to call her, but the answering service keeps intercepting my calls. I'm afraid all of this is taking a toll on her," he looked at Travis.

"I'll watch after her," Travis promised. "What you need to do is concentrate on getting out of here."

"You are right," Billy smiled. He put out his hand. "I'm glad you're here."

Travis grabbed Billy's hand and shook it. "I'm happy to be here. Just hold on a little longer, you're going to win this."

"I hope you're right."

"I am right."

"Who do you think killed her?" Billy asked, as he sat on the table. There weren't any chairs in the room.

That question had kept Travis awake for many nights, and it always led back to zero. The crime lab had swept over Sheila's apartment with a fine-tooth comb. They had more than a dozen fingerprints, and they were working around the clock to get a match for each of the prints.

"I don't know," he finally answered. He sat on the table beside Billy.

"What about the baby?" Billy whispered.

"Negative," Travis answered.

"So, she wasn't pregnant after all," Billy said as relief spread across his face.

"The autopsy didn't reveal any sign of pregnancy. That's good news for us," Travis said, trying to encourage Billy.

"Yeah, but it makes a strong motive. Detective Wright didn't say it, but he was hinting at something."

"Hinting at what?" Travis asked.

Billy jumped down from the table, "He was trying to trap me into giving him information about the baby. Don't you see it?"

"I don't understand."

"He figured if I knew about the baby, then it would be my motive for killing Sheila. The jerk." Billy rubbed the empty spot where his gold necklace used to hang.

"How could he have come up with such a bird-brain idea when there isn't a baby?"

"Charlotte Watson," Billy frowned. "Remember, how Sheila carried on about Charlotte being her baby's godmother?"

"Yeah," Travis nodded his head.

"Wright interviewed Charlotte and she told him about the baby."

"But her story is useless now."

"Yeah, but it can cause a level of damage to this case."

Travis thought about what Billy had said, and it all came into focus for him. Wright had a motive regardless of the outcome. If he could get Billy to admit he thought she was pregnant with his child, then Billy would have a strong motive for killing her. Wright was clever, Travis thought. He had heard Wright lived and breathed the law, and he wouldn't allow anyone to stand between him and it. He had heard plenty of stories about the detective, and he had no doubt that any of the stories were true.

"I have to get out of here. If Detective Wright has his way, I'll rot and die in prison."

"Don't worry, I'm working on it," Travis assured him.

"Work harder." Billy replied and added, "I hate this place."

"It's that bad, huh?"

"Man, I'd rather be in Australia wrestling crocodiles."

"I see you still have your sense of humor. That's good," Travis grinned.

"Yeah, for now," Billy replied, looking into the distance.

"Wright is interviewing Adrienne tomorrow. That is what I was coming over here to inform you of, and then Hattie told me you were in the interview room with him."

"She doesn't have to go through with it." Billy sighed in frustration.

"Yeah. But she wants to meet with him," Travis said. "I'll be there with her."

"Yeah," Billy looked distraught. "Why does she want to do that?"

"I don't know."

"I'm tired," Billy said as he walked to the steel door.

"In that case, I'll talk with you tomorrow," Travis said and walked to the door and stood beside Billy. Travis opened the door and they walked out. He walked Billy back to his cellblock. The guard unlocked the door and Billy walked inside of the cellblock without looking back at Travis. Travis watched him until he disappeared down the corridor.

Chapter 21

"*I*'m nervous," Adrienne said, as she sat on the sofa wringing her hands. "I'm so nervous; I don't know what to do with myself." She looked at Donna.

"It's going to turn out for the best," Donna tried to sound optimistic. She missed seeing Billy.

"Everything is going to turn out for the best for my girl," Eddie said, as he sat on the sofa beside her.

"I hope so, at least for my husband's sake," Adrienne said, as tears tried to surface in her eyes. "They're ruining him by printing those lies about him in the paper. I don't know who this Stone woman was, but my husband didn't have anything to do with her."

"The paper said she was his lover, dear," Donna said, glancing at Adrienne.

"What does the paper know?" Eddie jumped in. He shot Donna an angry look and turned his attention to their daughter.

"I asked Billy and Travis about that. They said it was nothing but lies. I believe them."

"Don't be so naïve, Adrienne. Travis and Billy are friends," Donna replied.

"He wouldn't lie to me," Adrienne said, remembering the kiss and how Travis had expressed his feelings for her.

"Yes, you're right, baby," Eddie said, trying to smooth over Donna's remark. "If there were any truth to this Sheila thing, I believe Travis would have told you so. Especially, seeing that he's saved."

"Give me a break," Donna rolled her eyes at Eddie.

166

Eddie ignored her. "Things are going to work out. Detective Wright is no one to be afraid of. He's like any other man that wears a uniform and a badge," Eddie reassured his daughter. "All you have to do is let your answers stay short and simple."

"Yes, dear. Whatever you do, remember don't volunteer any answer you aren't asked."

"That's right," Eddie said. "Answer only the questions he asks. Do not add anything."

"I can't believe we're having this conversation. It's a nightmare," Donna said, as she paced the floor. "Our name will be ruined in this town."

"What name is that?" Eddie said looking at Donna. "And please stop pacing the floor. It's making me nervous."

Donna stopped pacing the floor and looked at Eddie, crossing her arms over her chest. "Who would have believed our son-in-law would be sitting in jail for murder."

"He's innocent until proven guilty," Eddie reminded her.

"Someone needs to tell that to the papers," Donna said, uncrossing her arms.

"Yes, Mother is right. The papers have already tried him," Adrienne said and pushed herself up from the sofa and walked to the window to look outside. She was quietly seething over Billy's plight, and hadn't visited him in a week. However, she felt guilty by screening his calls, but Billy had hurt her, and she wouldn't let him off so easily. After the interview she'd pay him a visit. She had told Travis the interview would start at three o'clock. It was already two thirty. Detective Wright would be arriving at her house soon. A low moan escaped her as she walked back to the sofa and sat near Eddie.

"I hope Travis gets here on time," she said, as she thought about their last conversation over the telephone. Although, she hadn't wanted Travis to be at the interview, but now, she was happy she had relented.

"He will," Eddie said, putting his arms around her. She rested her head in the crook of his arm.

"I don't know about you two, but I'm starving," Donna said as she walked out of the living room to the kitchen in search for food.

"Have I told you how proud I am of you?" Eddie said to Adrienne as she rested on his arm.

"No."

"I'm so proud of you, and I'm glad that you're my daughter. A man couldn't ask for a better daughter."

"Thanks, Daddy," she replied, resting her head against his shoulders.

The two of them sat in silence wondering what would become of Billy.

The doorbell rang, breaking the silence. Adrienne looked nervously at Eddie. The sound of the ring vibrated through the house. Thousands of chill bumps ran up and down Adrienne's arms. She wished the ordeal would soon fade from her life, that Billy would be home again, and their lives would soon be back to normal.

Eddie rose from the sofa and reached down to help Adrienne. Donna suddenly appeared in the room, speechless, looking at them, holding a half eaten apple in her hand. They all stood in the room looking at each other and at the door. Finally, Eddie cleared his throat and walked slowly to the door. He opened the door as slowly as he had walked to it. Relief spread across his face after seeing Travis standing on the other side of the door. "It's okay, it's Travis," he informed the others.

"Good," Donna said relieved, then took another bite of her apple.

"Come on in," Eddie said to Travis, stepping to one side of the door. He grabbed Travis' hand and pumped it happily. Travis walked into the spacey open foyer, as Eddie closed the door behind them.

"I'm happy to see you, Travis," Adrienne said, walking up to him. "I was afraid you weren't going to make it," she added, "but I'm glad you're here now." She took Travis' arm and led him into the living room. Eddie followed them.

"Hello, Travis," Donna said, as she extended her hand out to him. "I want you to know that you almost scared the living daylights out of us."

"I didn't mean to frighten anyone," he said, releasing his arm from Adrienne. He shook Donna's hand.

"Well, I'm glad you're here. Have you talked with Billy?" she asked coyly.

"Yes. As a matter of fact, I spoke with him yesterday," he

said, as he shot her a knowing look. The woman was twice Billy's age, and he knew she didn't have a chance in the world with Billy, but that didn't stop her from fantasizing about her son-in-law.

"How is he?" Eddie asked, watching Donna's reaction. He didn't like the fire in Donna's eyes when she asked about Billy.

"He's okay, a little tired, but he's okay," he directed his attention toward Adrienne. She was more beautiful than the last time he saw her. "How are you, Adrienne?" he asked, without taking his eyes off her.

"Tired, huh?" Eddie said, relieved his wife didn't show any interest in his question about Billy. She had turned and walked out of the living room.

"I'm doing fine now that you're here," she said.

Eddie threw an arm around Travis' shoulder. "Come on and have a seat." He led him to the leather recliner. Travis sat down. It was Billy's favorite chair.

Eddie sat on the sofa; Adrienne joined her father. "Do you know what type of questions this Detective Wright is going to ask my daughter?" he asked, staring at Travis, "I don't want my little girl upset."

"Normal routine questions," Travis answered, as he glanced at Adrienne.

"Routine, huh?" Eddie said, thinking about this particular answer.

"I hope you're right," Adrienne spoke up.

Donna walked back into the living room, peeling a banana. She looked at Travis, "There's not much in Billy's and Adrienne's kitchen, but you're welcome to what they have in there," she said, as she stuck the top part of the banana into her mouth, and offered Travis the other half.

"No, thank you," Travis smiled.

"Are you sure?" she asked, biting the banana again.

"I'll have a piece of it," Eddie suggested.

"Yeah, right. I'll get you your own banana. Do you want anything Adrienne?" she asked.

"No Mother," she said softly.

"Okay, then." She turned her back to them. "One banana coming up," she sang walking out of the room.

Travis glanced at his watch. He had only been there ten minutes, but it seemed like hours. He was relieved that Adrienne's parents were there. He didn't trust himself to be alone with her again.

The doorbell rang, sending Donna rushing back into the living room. Eddie pushed himself up from the sofa, and walked to the door, opening it.

"Hi," Detective Wright said, as he held up his identification badge that was hanging on a silver bead chain around his neck. "I'm Detective Wright."

"Hi, Mr., or Detective Wright," the words stumbled out of Eddie's mouth. "We were expecting you. Come on in," he said, as the detective stepped through the door.

Eddie closed the door and led the detective into the living room.

"Hello," Detective Wright said, as he held his hand out towards Donna. She quickly took his hand into hers and stared at him. "Hi, I'm Donna," she said. "I'm Donna Mitchell, Billy's mother-in-law. I have heard a lot of things about you. They were all good things, I assure you," she smiled seductively.

"Nice to meet you, Ms. Mitchell," he replied, releasing his hand from her grasp.

"Likewise," Donna said, checking the detective out and liking what she saw.

"That's Mrs. Mitchell," Eddie affirmed, looking sharply at Donna.

"Mrs. Mitchell," Detective Wright nodded his head at Donna.

"This is our daughter, Adrienne," Eddie introduced her and added, "Billy's wife."

"Yes, we met," Detective nodded his head at her. Adrienne started to rise from the sofa, but he stopped her. "No, don't bother to get up, Mrs. Ray." She settled back onto the sofa. He extended his hand to her. She took his large hand and shook it. His hand was so huge; it made hers seem frail and lost in his.

Travis sat quietly, watching Donna flirt with the detective. He had to admit the detective had skills, the way he brushed off Donna nice and easy.

Detective Wright looked at Travis and smiled, "I see you're here?"

"Yes," Travis said coolly. "Do you have any objection to my being here?"

"No objection," Detective Wright said roughly.

"Good," Travis said and leaned back comfortably in the chair.

"Now, that you have met everyone, please have a seat," Eddie said.

Detective Wright walked past Travis and sat on the sofa near Adrienne.

"My wife and I will leave you three alone. If you need anything, we'll be in the kitchen," Eddie said, looking at Adrienne, he nudged Donna to follow him.

"Yes, if you need us, we'll be in the kitchen," Donna said, staring at the detective before leaving the room.

Detective Wright fished inside his jacket pocket, and pulled out a small palm-size tape recorder. He turned on the recorder and set it on the coffee table. Adrienne stared nervously at the recorder and pinched her hand hoping she would wake up from this nightmare. But she knew it was all too true. Travis sensed her fears and spoke softly to her, "Adrienne, look at me," he commanded. She looked at him. "It's going to be okay. Trust me," he added.

She nodded her head and looked at the detective. "It's going to be alright, Mrs. Ray," the detective said. "I'm going to ask you a few questions about you and your husband."

"Okay," she whispered, glancing at Travis.

"Are you ready?" Detective Wright asked.

"Yes, I'm ready," she inhaled, then, exhaled.

"Good," Detective Wright said.

"What is your name?"

"Adrienne Mit..." she paused, "I meant to say, Adrienne Ray."

"Middle name?"

"I don't have one."

"What's your husband's name?"

"William Ray, but we call him Billy."

"Middle name?"

"Anthony."

"How long have you and Mr. Ray been married?"

"One month."

"How long have you known Mr. Ray?"

"Since elementary school," she replied, still nervous.

"Be specific."

"I don't know, maybe third or fourth grade."

Adrienne glanced at Travis, she was glad that he was there, and he made her feel safe from this detective and all of his questions. Her nerves settled a little as she switched her attention back to the detective.

"Do you know Ms. Sheila Stone?" he asked taking out a recent picture of Sheila when she was alive.

"No."

"Have you ever seen her before?" He handed her the picture.

"Yes."

"Where?"

"I only saw her once; she came to my husband's office."

"When was that?"

"About a week ago. I can't remember exactly, but I remember seeing her. She came to his office looking for him," she stared at the picture of Sheila, and then gave the picture back to the detective.

"Did Ms. Stone see Mr. Ray?" He set the picture on the coffee table.

"No. My husband and I were on our honeymoon."

Detective Wright was confused; he raised his brow, "Your honeymoon?"

"Yes. Mr. and Mrs. Ray honeymooned in Hawaii. She caught an earlier flight to Atlanta without Mr. Ray," Travis said without giving any more detail.

"Let me get this straight. Mr. Ray and you honeymooned in Hawaii and you caught an earlier flight to Atlanta leaving your husband behind?"

"That's correct," she answered.

"You arrived to Atlanta alone?"

"Yes."

"Where was your husband?"

"Hawaii."

"You left your husband in Hawaii?"

"Yes, we had an argument."

"What did you argue about?"

Adrienne lowered her head and raised her eyes, looking at

Travis. Travis' face was expressionless as he watched Adrienne struggling with the question. She raised her head and looked at the detective. "Because I want to have his baby. His children."

"So you want children," he grinned. "That's normal."

"Yes, one would think, but my husband doesn't want any at all," she sighed. "That's why we argued. When I saw that he was dead against having any children, I became so angry with him, and the next thing I knew, I was sitting on a plane on my way home."

"I see. Where did you go after your flight arrived in Atlanta?"

"I flagged a cab at the airport and went to my husband's law firm."

"That location?" Detective Wright asked.

She gave him the location.

"And that's where you saw Ms. Stone, at this location?"

"Yes."

"Where were you when you saw Ms. Stone?"

"I was sitting in Travis... or Mr. Malcolm's office." She replied growing tired of the questions.

"What were you doing in Mr. Malcolm's office?"

"We were talking."

"About what?"

"About the argument Billy and I had in Hawaii."

"Did you see Ms. Stone again after seeing her at your husband's office?" He asked, watching her closely.

"No," she muttered, remembering to keep the answer short and simple.

"Did you talk to Ms. Stone at your husband's office or at any other time?" Detective Wright asked, leaning toward her.

"No."

"Did you greet Ms. Stone at all when she came to your husband's office?"

"No," Adrienne clasped her hands together. "It all happened so fast. Ms. Stone barged into Mr. Malcolm's office asking for my husband."

"She asked you about your husband?"

"No. She asked Mr. Malcolm."

"Then what happened after she asked Mr. Malcolm about Mr.

Ray?"

"Mr. Malcolm led her out of his office."

"Did Mr. Malcolm close the door behind them?"

"Yes."

"Did it strike you as odd that a woman would barge into Mr. Malcolm's office and ask him about your husband?"

"Yes. It did bother me for a moment, but Mr. Malcolm explained to me what was going on."

"And what was that?" Detective Wright asked, glancing at Travis.

"He said she was one of my husband's client and sometimes clients demanded to see their lawyers."

"I see. But did you know that Ms. Stone wasn't just a client of your husband?"

"Detective, I don't know what it is that you're implying, but my husband didn't have anything to do with Ms. Stone, other than work related." She sighed in frustration.

"Mrs. Ray," he shook his head, looking at her. "Surely you must have known Ms. Stone was more to your husband than just a client. In fact, I wish it was only a client then, I wouldn't be here now bothering you." He tried to smile, but it showed weakly. "Ms. Stone was your husband's lover." He said matter of fact.

"No, that's not true." She looked at Detective Wright. "I read those lies about my husband in the papers, and I don't believe any of it." She muttered trying to keep her composure.

Detective Wright fished into his top shirt pocket and pulled out a small notepad. He flipped through the pages and stopped. He peered over the notepad and cleared his throat.

"I have a statement," he flipped through the pages, "From a Ms. Charlotte Watson, who can identify your husband, Mr. William Anthony Ray, to be Ms. Stone's lover and the father of her baby."

"What? Who? That's a lie!" she shouted, springing from the sofa. "My husband doesn't want children and he sure doesn't have any. ! I will not answer anymore of your questions!"

"The baby was a lie from the beginning," Travis shouted, pushing himself up from the recliner. He rushed to Adrienne and held her.

"According to Ms. Watson, Ms. Stone was pregnant on the day she was killed." The detective rose from the sofa. He continued to read from his notepad. "Ms. Watson saw Mr. Ray and Mr. Malcolm at Ms. Stone's apartment Friday evening on the day she was killed. There was a verbal confrontation between Mr. Ray and Ms. Stone about the unborn baby," Detective Wright drove the statement in hard.

"That's a lie," Travis released Adrienne and walked toward the detective. "The autopsy didn't reveal a pregnancy. She lied to me and to Billy about the baby," he snapped angrily.

"What?" Adrienne uttered sharply. She lied to you, and to Billy!" No. You lied to me!" How could you? You knew Billy was cheating on me all along and you kept it a secret!" She shot him an angry look. "How many others have he had and you help him hide it!" she cried hysterically.

Detective Wright tried to say something to comfort her, but she didn't want to hear anything he had to say.

"But, I..." Travis was speechless, walking to her. "I—"

"No," she screamed cutting him off, backing away from him. "Get away from me!"

Eddie and Donna ran into the living room. "What's going on in here?" Eddie asked, looking at Adrienne as she stood in the middle of the room, trembling, with tears rushing down her face. "What is it Adrienne?" he asked rushing to her side, wrapping his arms around her, and holding her tightly.

"Yes, what's this all about?" Donna looked from the detective to Travis.

Detective Wright reached down and picked up the recorder from the table. He turned it off and slipped it into his jacket pocket.

"You heard my wife," Eddie said sternly. "What's this all about? Why's my daughter so upset?" He asked looking at Detective Wright.

"Billy has been cheating on me with..." she didn't want to pronounce Sheila's name, "with the Stone woman, and she was carrying his baby." Fresh tears escaped her tear ducts and ran swiftly down her face. "And Travis knew about it. He knew Billy was cheating on me," she snapped angrily.

"Didn't I tell you," Donna smirked, "Men are always sticking together for one another. They don't care...it's just in their nature."

"We're not going to have any men bashing in here, and those 'I told you so' remarks," Eddie said, staring angrily at Donna.

"Humph!" Donna rolled her eyes at the ceiling. "See what I mean?" She directed the question to Adrienne. "About sticking together." She threw hers hands up in the air surrendering.

"I'm sorry I upset your daughter, Mr. and Mrs. Mitchell," Detective Wright said, walking past them to the door. "I didn't mean to hurt anyone, but I hope you all understand it's my job to ask questions." He opened the door. "I see you all have some talking to do, and I'll leave you with it. Good day," he added as he walked out of the door and closed it behind him.

"The nerve of that man," Donna replied, loud enough for everyone to hear. "To have the gall to come in here getting everyone upset."

Travis tried to say something, anything, but words wouldn't form. He stood speechless watching Adrienne. His heart ached inside. At that moment he wanted to crawl under a rock.

"It's going to be all right," Eddie consoled Adrienne.

Donna walked past them and sat on the sofa. She watched Travis as he stood there. An angry look appeared on her face.

"I'm sorry, Adrienne," Travis finally found the words. "I didn't mean for you to get hurt. I'm sorry I lied about Billy. I did it to protect you," he pleaded hoping she would understand.

Instead she stepped away from Eddie and angrily walked to him and slapped him hard across the face. "You're a liar! Get out of my house! You make me sick! I hate you! Get out of my sight!" she screamed, collapsing onto the floor, crying bitterly.

Eddie rushed to her side and gathered her in his arms again. "Now, now, it's going to be alright," he said.

Donna rose to her feet, and looked at Travis. "Our daughter told you to leave."

"Yeah," Eddie looked at Travis. "I think you'd better go now." He said turning his attention back to Adrienne and helping her off the floor.

"I'll show you to the door," Donna said walking swiftly to the door and opened it.

Travis slowly followed Donna to the front door. He wanted to say something to Adrienne, but thought better of it. He had already caused enough confusion. He walked out onto the porch and down the steps.

"Humph! Church folks," Donna said, underneath her breath, but loud enough for Travis to hear, and closed the door behind him.

Travis slid behind the steering wheel of his car. He sat there for what seemed like hours. Tears suddenly flowed down his handsome, face. He wiped at them with his hands, but they continued to fall heavily. He collapsed his face into his hands and cried grievously.

Chapter 22

$\mathcal{B}$illy strolled into the Silver Rock County Jail visitor's room and he smiled at the sight of Adrienne, who sat quietly, alone, at a table. She shot him a scornful look, as he sat down at the table beside her. It had been two weeks since he had seen her. She looked beautiful, dressed in a cream-colored linen pantsuit and matching pumps. She had her hair swept up in corkscrews, and she smelled like fresh cut roses.

"Hi, baby," he grinned, as he tried to kiss her, but she moved her head sideways avoiding his kiss. His lips briefly swept her smooth cheek instead. "Baby, I'm so thrilled to see you," he said, totally ignoring her icy demeanor. "I haven't seen or heard from you. Did the Detective give you a hard time with the interview? He can be rough. Stay away from him in the future." He warned her and asked, "What's going on? I haven't seen either you or Travis." His eyes held hers. "What's going on with you two? Man, I thought Detective Wright had run you all out of Silver Rock, and no one told me." A smile tugged at the corners of Billy's mouth. "When you see Travis, please tell him that a good attorney does visit his clients every once in awhile, especially if they're friends."

"Billy, how could you?" She glared at him, blurting the words out. "How could you cheat on me?" She rose from the table and crossed her hands over her chest. She looked angrily at him, disgusted by what she saw.

The question hit him like a ton of bricks. He looked at her. She reminded him of a school of piranhas attacking its victim suddenly without any warning. "What? Be serious." He rose from the table, facing her.

"Don't act dumb with me," her voice raised a higher pitch. "You know what I'm talking about."

"No, tell me what you're talking about."

"How long have you been cheating with other women, Billy?" the words flowed strongly from her mouth.

"I don't know what you're talking about." He scanned the room to see if anyone was listening to them. Then, looked back at her. "I have never cheated on you, believe me."

"Puh-leease, the papers were right about you," she said, steaming from ear to ear.

"The papers? C'mon, Adrienne, I told you don't believe the garbage they print. They're full of lies, baby. C'mon, remember who you're talking to? Me, Billy, your husband, and I'm not going to tell you a lie. Trust me."

"The papers? Duh-uh! Negro puh-leease! The papers told the truth about you!"

"Forget the papers!" He snapped angrily.

"No, you listen to me. Detective Wright already told me everything. You're a liar!" she snapped.

"He's a liar!" Billy could feel the heat rising beneath his collar.

"You're so pitiful," she declared, putting her hands on her hips. "I feel sorry for you. You can't tell the truth, even when it's staring you in your face."

"Because it's all lies, baby" his voice rose to another level. "And I can't believe you're falling for it."

"Easily," she said, retreating a few steps backward. "You have been lying to me too long, and it's easier for you to tell me a lie than to tell me the truth."

"I'm not lying, Adrienne" he said taking a few steps towards her. "Believe me."

"Billy, don't patronize me! I wasn't born yesterday! I know you had an affair with her and Lord knows who else!" She took a few steps toward him. "Even Travis admitted you had an affair with her." Her eyes teared up.

"Travis?" he looked confused.

"Yes, Travis, your buddy, confirmed Detective Wright's story." She blinked back the tears. She refused to cry. She wouldn't let Billy see her crying. She could handle this.

"Travis?" Billy tone was puzzled.

"Yes," she replied. Her word was barely audible. "You have betrayed me! I don't ever want to see you again!" She rolled her eyes.

"C'mon, Adrienne, you don't know what you're saying," he said, trying to embrace her. She pushed him away.

He ignored her anger, and moved closer to her, hoping to reason with her. He reached for her hand, but she jerked it from his reach and crossed her hands over her chest again.

"No! Leave me alone," she yelled. A jail guard walked over from across the room, and stood near them. Billy ignored the guard. He had to talk some sense into his wife. She was upset and angry and didn't mean any of the things she had said to him, he thought.

"Okay, okay, I had an affair with Sheila, but it was before I married you. Travis should have kept his mouth shut and stayed out of my business," his tone was firm.

The confession sliced like a razor, leaving a wide-open wound, bleeding through her heart. But rage began to build itself up and began to fill the open wound.

"No, I trusted you! I loved you, and I kept myself pure for you! But for what?" She uncrossed her arms from her chest. New tears threatened to surface. She blinked her eyes to hold them back, but was unsuccessful, as tears began to roll swiftly down her cheeks. She wiped her tears with the back of her hand, seething, she spoke, "For what? A husband who didn't know how to keep his pants zipped-up. Sheila was just one of them... who knows how many more you have tucked neatly under your belt?"

"Sheila was the only one, I swear on my mother's grave," he gestured an imaginary cross over his heart.

"I don't take stock in anything else that you'd tell me, because it has all been lies, even from the beginning. I want a divorce!"

"I can't do that. I can't give you a divorce. You're my wife, for better or for worse, remember?" He walked closer to her. She retreated a few steps backward away from him.

"Forget it Billy! I'm getting a divorce whether you like it or not!

You'll be hearing from my attorney!" she said. Blinded by tears, she rushed passed him and out of the visitor's room.

Billy stood there watching her flee from him. He saw a side of her she hadn't revealed before. She had struck at him like a diamond-back rattler.

"You all right?" The guard asked, looking concerned.

"Yeah, man," Billy assured him.

"She's pissed," the guard replied.

"You can say that again."

"Women," the guard smiled.

"May I go back to my cell now?" Billy asked.

"Sure?" the guard said leading Billy back to his cell.

* * * * * * * * * *

As Billy lay on his bunk, listening to the other men talk about their families and the good time they had in the free world, his mind lingered on his misfortune. He wouldn't fight Adrienne. If a divorce was what she wanted, well a divorce she's going to get, he thought rubbing the empty place where his gold necklace once hung. He was tired of Adrienne and their fights, tired of Travis, tired of Sheila's death, tired of Silver Rock County Jail, and Detective Wright. All he wanted was some peace and quiet. He wasn't even angry with Travis for opening his mouth and revealing his secret to Adrienne. Somehow, Billy figured Travis had a good noble reason for sharing confidential information with his wife.

But he had to admit he missed James and Fred. They both had gotten out of jail last week, and the cell across from his seemed empty without them. They had built sort of a bond between them. He decided he liked Fred and would look him up as soon as he was free again.

"Yeah, I'll look up Fred," he said to no one in particular, as he lay there quietly on his bunk. His focus rested on Adrienne again. He didn't like being married and dumped in the same month. If anyone was going to do any dumping, it would be him. He lay there reflecting on his life, and it had been one big roller coaster ride, one right after another. Edna dying on him and Darrell. "Darrell," he whispered the name. He hadn't really thought about Darrell since Fred had asked about him. Fred had gotten his mind to awaken the long, dead, Darrell. Suddenly, the image of Darrell flooded his memories. He hated the man. Billy closed his eyes. He tried to block the images from his mind, but they continued to dance in his head. *Darrell, what are you doing to me? I hate you! You're dead! I hate you! I hate everything about you! I hate your looks. I hate your eyes... Darrell, those eyes, wait a minute where have I seen them before?* He thought. *Those eyes... Darrell's eyes... Darrell... Fred.* The connection sent his head reeling. He leaped to his feet. His body trembled while he visualized Fred's mannerism. His smile. He compared them to Darrell as the memories of his father flooded his mind.

Can it be? He thought. He shook his head, No, it can't be. But his mind wouldn't let him rest as it raced for an answer. Could Fred possibly be Darrell, his long lost father? I must be crazy, he thought. There's no way the two men could be the same. But would he have known his father? A person knows their parents regardless of how long it has been, even after seventeen years. Billy tried to shake off the thought. No matter how hard he tried to fight against his discovery, Billy knew in his heart that Fred was none other than Darrell Ray.

Chapter 23

$\mathcal{T}$ravis fished inside his jacket pocket for the hotel key. He pushed the card into the key-slot and pulled it out, unlocking the room's door. He pushed the door open and scanned the room before walking inside. Years of law school had taught him to be cautious of his surroundings. The room looked untouched. He walked in and closed the door behind him.

He walked through the unkempt room. The first day he checked into the hotel he had made it clear at the front desk, he didn't want any cleaning done at all in his room. He was there to get away from people, and that included the hotel's maids. The bed hadn't been made-up in the one week he had been staying at the hotel. Empty beer cans, dirty cups and bottles of Hennessy cluttered the round table near the double-pane window. He checked into the hotel feeling sorry for his self. Adrienne didn't want to see him again, and he couldn't blame her. He covered for Billy for years. She had been his friend also, but he let her down with his lies. He walked to the vanity mirror, and looked at himself in the square-shaped mirror. Tired, baggy, blood-shot eyes stared back at him. Rubbing the short beard that had grown over the week, it made him look twice his age. Staring at himself in the mirror, Travis couldn't believe it was him staring wearily back.

"I haven't seen you before," he spoke to his reflection. "What's your name?" He paused, "So you're not talking, huh? I can't blame you, because you look terrible." He smiled at his reflection.

C'mon, get a grip, Travis thought. What's going to happen to Billy if you quit on him now? "Billy, huh," the word tumbled out his mouth.

What does Billy care? Billy cares only for Billy. Billy has never said to him, "Travis, I love you and I'm glad we're friends." "Hell no!" Travis spoke to his reflection. *Billy only loves Billy, and to hell with everyone else. It had always been like that. The girls at Silver Rock High thought he was cotton candy, candy apple and sugar cane rolled up in one. Women always found Billy irresistible. The women at Grander University were thrilled to be in Billy's company. They stalked him day and night, and each night he had a different woman to fill his bed.*

Travis stood at the mirror, closed his eyes and opened them again. He noticed the clean towels hanging on the towel rack. The hotel's maid left fresh towels. Thankful for the clean towels, and the maid who broke the rule, he grabbed one of the towels and stepped into the bathroom and turned on the shower. A few seconds later, he stripped out of his clothes and stepped into the shower. He closed his eyes allowing the hot, steamy water to cascade over his smooth, handsome face. The water flowed down his dark, lean, satin, muscular body. It felt good as he stood under it, the heat seemed to seep through the pores of his skin and down to his bones.

The shower had a way of relaxing him. It worked like alcohol. It had a way of erasing problems from his mind. However, after the shower, just like alcohol, the relaxation and the pleasure eventually wore off, bringing back the pain. But he had to come to grip with himself and step back into reality. He left Ms. King in charge at the office. He had to get back. He knew Billy would be wondering what had happened to him. Turning off the water, he emerged from the shower, grabbing the towel to dry himself off.

Thirty minutes later, Travis picked up his black leather luggage. He threw it on the unmade king-size bed and unzipped it. He started throwing his clothes from the drawer inside the luggage. He opened the nightstand's drawer and took out the rest of his things. The Gideon's Bible lay at the bottom of the drawer. He picked it up and ran his fingers lightly across the golden brown book. The cover reminded Travis of his first Bible. His father had given it to him when he was ten years old. He smiled, thinking about it.

It seemed like only yesterday when he and Billy had been ten years old, riding their bikes through the park, fishing on the lake, or laying lazily under the shade tree, looking at the clouds. Travis stared at the book as he continued to run his fingers smoothly across the cover.

The day after Billy had moved in with them, Travis' father had gotten the boys up early for church. Billy wanted to stay home, but Mr. Malcolm had made it clear to the two boys that everyone who stays at the Malcolm's home has to attend church every Sunday.

Travis saw the contemptuous expression creep onto Billy's face and the anger burning in his eyes at the thought of attending church on a regular basis. Only the night before, Billy told Travis that he didn't want anything to do with his own parents, church, or Jesus, and now Mr. Malcolm was shoving church and Jesus down his throat. Parents could be so unfeeling, Travis thought. He watched Billy's reaction to what his father had said. Billy showed no sign of rebelling against his gloomy future with the Malcolm's, only his eyes showed his disappointment.

Travis loved Billy. He wanted to be like him. If Billy didn't want anything to do with church or Jesus, then neither would he. What Billy didn't like, he wouldn't like. Then the very next morning, Pastor Simon kept shouting, "That if you confess with your mouth the Lord Jesus and believe in your heart that God has raised Him from the dead, you will be saved. Unless a man be born again he can not see the kingdom of God." Pastor Simon marched down from the pulpit, and stood in front of the congregation. His voice boomed through the sanctuary. "In order to see God, in order to live a righteous life, and in order to get to Heaven, you must be born again. There's no way to God except through His Son, Jesus Christ." He glared at the congregation, again. "Please come," he reached his hands out to the congregation as he spoke in a teary, but soft, firm voice.

Travis rose from his seat without a second thought of what he was about to do. He rushed to the altar and asked Jesus to be his Lord and to come into his life. Even though he was only ten years old, Travis understood what Pastor Simon was asking, and he felt good about his decision. Meanwhile, Billy had become furious, refusing to talk with Travis for weeks. Travis grew lonely without his best friend speaking to him. Mr. Malcolm noticed the change in the two boys. He settled back and watched their behavior for a week. He didn't like the cool distance that had crept into the boys' relationship. Travis and Billy were best friends, but they avoided one another like enemies. Mr. Malcolm was concerned about them. He talked with the two boys, but they both agreed there wasn't a problem between them. Mr. Malcolm didn't pursue the matter any further. Instead, he prayed to God about the boys' problem. He knew God would work it out.

Travis continued looking at the Bible in his hand, caressing the surface lightly.

Mr. Malcolm had been right. Things did work out between them after Travis had promised Billy he wouldn't read his Bible, and he wouldn't have anything to do with Jesus anymore.

"You swear?" Billy looked at Travis. "You're not going to read your Bible anymore?"

"I'm not going to read it anymore, I swear." Travis said.

"Do you cross your heart and hope to die?" Billy asked, gazing at him.

"I cross my heart and hope to die." Travis drew an imaginary cross over his chest.

"Even, if you step on a crack and broke your mama's back," Billy watched him closely for any tell-tell signs of lying.

"Yeah. Even if I step on a crack and break my mama's back."

"Remember, if you read your Bible again you're going to die and break your mama's back." Billy warned Travis.

"I'm not going to read it again. I promise," Travis said. He didn't like the idea of breaking his mama's back.

Things were going really well between them until their second year at Silver Rock High. Travis started attending "Youth on Fire for Christ" youth group every Monday night. Billy had accompanied him the first two Mondays, but refused to return after that. He had covered for Billy by lying to Mr. Malcolm week after week until their youth pastor confronted Mr. Malcolm about Billy's absences from Monday night's activity. Mr. Malcolm punished the two young men. But Billy continued to defile Mr. Malcolm's orders. Things began to go sour between the two again. Travis eased slowly away from the Monday night youth gathering to be with his best friend.

Although, there were many afflicting   trials   and   tests throughout Billy's and Travis' relationship, the really big test came when they attended Tucker University School of Law.

One Wednesday night, after attending the "New Beginning Church of God," the word of God saturated Travis, filling him with zeal.

"Man, what girl got you floating on clouds?" Billy asked, gazing hard at Travis, as he walked into their apartment.

"None," Travis laughed.

"Somebody's daughter got you this happy," Billy grinned. "Who is it? Is it Nickie? I told you she wants you, man. Umph, umph, umph. That girl is a firecracker," Billy laughed, sitting at his desk, going over his bank account.

"It's no one," Travis said. He didn't want Billy to find out he had been going to church.

"Get out of here. Who do you think you're fooling? Remember? I'm Billy. I know when a man has been struck by a fine woman." Billy laughed.

"Trust me. There's not a woman."

"I know it's not a man." Billy looked suspiciously at Travis.

"No. Wait a minute. I like girls." Travis frowned.

"Well, who is it, then?"

"Okay. I'll tell you… if you promise me you won't get upset."

"Okay."

"You have to promise me."

"What is this? You sound like a female." Billy shot Travis a disgusting look.

"I told you I like girls."

"I'm joking with you. Lighten-up." Billy laughed. "Man, you can't take a joke?"

"Yeah. But not that kind of joke. I don't like it."

"Okay. I won't tease you. Who is the young woman?"

"It's not a woman, it is …God." Travis answered slowly.

"I don't understand," Billy replied.

"I rededicated my life back to Jesus."

"What?" Billy voice bounced off the apartment's wall.

"I gave my life back to God."

"I don't believe this. What did you do that for?"

"I wanted to. Why can't you be happy for me? What are you afraid of? You're afraid of my being saved would contaminate you?"

"No. I'm not afraid of anything or anybody. You know that."

"Then what is it?"

"We're blood brothers. And, brothers should stick together."

"What sense does that make?" Travis replied.

After Travis' confession, Billy avoided him for months. He tried talking to Billy about his strange behavior. Billy only shrugged it off refusing to talk with him.

One particular Sunday after church, Travis walked into the apartment joyfully bellowing a song. His voice boomed through the apartment, waking up Billy, and Billy's friend, Victoria. "What can wash away my sin, nothing but the blood of Jesus?"

Billy suddenly ran out of his bedroom, naked, and angrily yelling non-stop at him.

Travis tired of Billy's tirade stood his ground against him. "What's the matter with you, Billy?"

"There's nothing the matter with me! I'm sick and tired of hearing you sing that song! If you need to sing, don't bring it in here! I'm trying to sleep!"

"My singing bothers you, Billy?"

"No." He was angry at the question and sighed in frustration.

"Right," Travis muttered under his breath.

"Man, just leave me alone," Billy rolled his eyes, and threw his hands in the air.

"No. I won't leave you alone until you and I get this thing that's going on between us, settled. Right here and right now!"

"What's wrong with y'all?" Victoria staggered sleepily into the living room, pulling her robe around her.

"Nothing!" Billy snapped.

"Yeah, there's something the matter with you all right," Travis said, walking away from Billy.

"Look who's talking? The preacher!" Billy laughed.

"Listen, Billy. I like church, and you should be happy for me, and not always putting me down about it. Do you want me to completely give up my faith to satisfy you?" Travis turned facing Billy. "Is that what you want?"

"Bull's eye." Billy clapped his hands. "The man finally gets the point."

"I think—" Victoria began to say.

"Stay out of this," Billy warned her. "And who told you that you could think."

"Going to church, and reading the Bible shouldn't bother you, Billy." He glared hard at his friend. "We are grown men, now. We're no longer boys. You need to wake-up, and get with the program. Times are changing, or have you noticed?" He gazed at Billy. "It won't hurt you to go to church, sometimes."

"See, this is what I'm talking about. Now you want me to go to church. Save it because I'm not going. And I don't need your preaching, or your sarcastic remarks."

"You need my preaching more than you think." Travis glanced at Victoria. "It will do your soul some good." He looked at Billy.

"What I do with Victoria is none of your business! If it bothers you that she and I are sleeping together, making out, making love, getting right down to it, doing the nasty, then leave!" Billy stood toe to toe with Travis, shaking and pointing a finger at him.

"Don't worry. I will," Travis replied, brushing aside Billy's finger.

"There's the door." Billy retreated a few steps backwards and pointed.

"I know where the door is," Travis said, walking to it.

"You two are acting crazy!" Victoria yelled. "Billy, Travis, you two are best friends, and you two shouldn't be—"

"I told you to stay out of this!" Billy cut her off. "If he's going to preach to me, he needs to leave. I don't have time for his craziness!" Billy shouted, and then stormed angrily out of the living room into his bedroom, slamming the door behind him.

"Billy!" Victoria ran behind him.

* * * * * * * * * *

Travis sat on the bed holding the Bible in his hands. He opened it and turned to his favorite chapter, Matthew sixteen, verses twenty-six and twenty-seven. 'What good will it be for a man if he gains the whole world, yet forfeits his soul? Or what can a man give in exchange for his soul?' And the last verse, 'For the Son of Man is going to come in his Father's glory with his angels, and then he will reward each person according to what he has done.'

He read the passage several times allowing the words of God to minister to him. He looked around the room at the empty liquor bottles, and thought about what Pastor Johnson had said. "Die to your flesh, and ask the Lord to give you a desire to live right." Travis' eyes filled with tears. They swiftly rolled down his handsome face. He felt a tug at his heart. He wanted to live right. Travis fell to his knees in prayer.

"Dear Heavenly Father, I've sinned against You. Father forgive me for making my walk with You a mockery. I have followed the path of unrighteousness. I've compromised my lifestyle in order to gain a friend. Please, forgive me for putting Billy before You. And, I repent for drinking. I'll never touch another can of beer or bottle of Hennessey, or any other liquor for as long as I live. Lord, please forgive me for wanting Billy's wife. Pastor Johnson was right. I have a demon of lust. Please deliver me, and please forgive me for lying to her, and for hurting her with my lies. Lord, I repent of my sins. I dedicate my life back to You. Thank you, Lord, for forgiving me, and for loving me the way you do. In Jesus' name. Amen."

Trail of tears ran smoothly down his handsome face onto the unmade bed. He pushed himself up. He stood there surrendering himself to the presence of the Lord. Jesus spoke First John 1:9 to his heart. 'If we confess our sins, he is faithful and just and will forgive us our sins and purify us from all unrighteousness.' The word of God was loud and clear. Travis embraced the word that the Lord had spoken. He allowed Jesus to fill him with His word. Then the Lord spoke again, John 14:27, 'Peace I leave with you; my peace I give you. I do not give to you as the world gives. Do not let your hearts be troubled and do not be afraid.'

"Lord, please fill me with Your Spirit." Travis asked, sincerely. He waited patiently for the Lord. He raised his hands, surrendering to the Lord. Then suddenly, Travis' left hip began to move as if it was dislodging from its socket. He tried to stand, but the room began to tilt. He scanned the room as it swayed slowly around him. Travis fell onto the bed, intoxicated. "How can this be?" Travis said aloud. "I hadn't had anything to drink today. He lay on the bed yielding to the intoxicating feeling. He felt a warmness rise from the pit of his stomach. Peace saturated him as he lay across the bed, rivers of tears fell from him. His left hip stopped moving and peace swallowed him like a river. He was in Heaven.

Chapter 24

"*W*hat's the matter with you, gal?" Janet's mother, Mae Ella Wingo, frowned, as she stood eyeing Janet sitting on the flower print sofa, flipping nervously through a Jet magazine.

"Nothing's the matter with me, Mama," Janet exhaled, and lowered her head into the book.

"You may as well tell me, 'cause you know I'm going to find out, sooner, or later," Mae Ella assured her daughter.

"I told you, nothing is wrong." Janet cut her reply short, avoiding her mother's eyes.

"There's somethin' bothering you," Mae Ella said in one long southern draw. "You're hiding somethin' from your po' old mama."

"I told you there's nothing bothering me." Janet closed the magazine, and tossed it beside her. "I'm tired. That's all," she grumbled, crossing her left arm across her chest, and rested her right arm on the back of it, and cupped her chin in her hand.

"Child, you can say what you wanna. I know when somethin' the matter. That's what wrong with people today. Got somethin' to hide. People ain't friendly these days, 'cause they tryin' to keep all of their problems hidden. They are too proud to ask for help. And I'd never thought you would be like those kinds of people. If you don't want to tell me what's the matter with you, then suit yourself." Mae Ella grabbed the broom and began sweeping the kitchen floor.

"Humph," was all Janet could say.

"You can 'humph' me all you wanna. I don't care 'bout that." Mae Ella stopped sweeping, and leaned against the kitchen's counter. "I've been watching you now for weeks, and you act like a nervous cat in a yard full of mad dogs. Strange, you ain't one time mentioned your little town, Silver Rock. The way you're always carryin' on about that town…making it seem like I missed somethin'. And, I ain't had to beg you to stay here longer with me," Mae Ella squeezed her fingers around the broom handle, as she began sweeping the floor again.

"Mama, I told you I had some vacation time coming up, and I want to use all of my days. If I don't use them, I'd wind up losing them. I've worked too hard to lose my vacation time." Janet folded both arms across her chest.

"Are you sure?" Mae Ella said, sweeping the trash in a small pile.

"Positive." Janet rose to her feet. "Let me help you with that." Janet got the dustpan and held it to the trash pile. Mae Ella swept the trash into the dustpan.

Janet tossed the trash into the trashcan.

"I hope so," Mae Ella said, putting the broom back in its place.

"Mama, I won't lie to you. Have you ever known me to lie to you? You raised me better than that." Janet gave Mae Ella a soft hug.

Mae Ella eyed Janet, but kept silent.

"What are we eating tonight? I'm starved." Janet charged to the fridge, scanning the shelves, pretending not to notice her mother's stare.

"Leftover," Mae Ella said, turning on the oven.

"Ugh, leftover, again," Janet scrunched her nose up.

"Yeah, again." Mae Ella said, walking toward Janet. "Hand me that casserole outta' there."

"I hate leftover hash brown casserole." Janet made a face.

"If you can think of somethin' better, and plannin' on cookin', then be my guest." Mae Ella took the casserole from Janet, and put it in the oven.

"Casserole it is then," Janet sauntered back into the small living room and regained her position back on the sofa. She hated cooking.

"We'll be eating soon," Mae Ella joined her daughter on the sofa.

"Good, anything would do right about now." Janet tried to sound enthused but failed terribly at it.

"How's your friend?" Mae Ella pretended not to notice her daughter's shaky voice.

"Who?"

"Your girlfriend, in Silver Rock. The Mitchell girl."

"Oh, her." Janet didn't want to talk about Adrienne or anyone else associated with Silver Rock.

"Yeah, her." Mae Ella said sarcastically.

"Adrienne, she's okay, I guess," Janet replied, picking up the magazine, again.

"Okay, you guess? What? Y'all don't talk no mo'?" Mae Ella frowned squinting her eyes.

"We talk."

"Good. You made it seem like y'all wasn't talkin' or somethin'," Mae Ella rested her head on the sofa.

"Well, we don't talk that much," Janet lied.

"Huh, why's that?" She raised her head from the sofa, looking at Janet.

"I don't know. Maybe her new husband don't want her hanging out with single women."

"But y'all been friends since as long as I can remember," Mae Ella frowned, glancing sideways at Janet. "Surely her husband can understand that."

"She went her way, and I went mine. Simple as that." Janet flipped through the pages again.

"I don't know what to say 'bout some people." Mae Ella shook her head.

"Yeah, people act funny when they get married. They act like you're going to take their husband or something." Janet glanced at her mother.

"It's wrong for them to act like that. If y'all were best friends as children, then y'all oughta be best friends now. Whether you're married or not."

"I agree with you, Mama," Janet nodded her head.

"That boy she married. What's his name?"

"Billy."

"Yeah, Billy. That was one mannish child growing up." Mae Ella reflected back to Silver Rock. Crow feet tugged at the corners of her eyes, "I remember him, and that other little boy."

"Travis." Janet answered the question before it was asked.

"Yeah, Travis. Y'all were playing in the backyard. I think it was hide-go-seek. I walked out in the yard, and saw Travis countin'. I didn't see you or Billy. So I walked a little piece around the side of the house, and there y'all were. Billy tryin' to take off your panties. I was beyond furious. I grabbed that child, and I tried to kill that boy with my bare hands. Good thing Travis came running over there where we were and started fightin' me. If he hadn't done that, that child would be dead. I let him go, and he and Travis ran outta' my yard as fast as they could. Then I grabbed you, and I tried to beat the living day light outta' of you. Do you remember that?" Mae Ella smiled at Janet.

"Yes, I remember."

"I told you to never let that boy come near you again."

"I didn't, Mama…" Janet dragged the words out.

"And you better be glad you didn't. I didn't like him at all after that," Mae Ella closed her eyes reflecting on the particular incident.

"I was afraid to go anywhere near Billy after that beaten I got. You scared the shh …" Janet glanced at her mother, and cleared her throat remembering who she was talking to. "You scared the living day light out of me."

"Good. 'Cause, I didn't want you growing up trashy. My mama didn't raise no trash, and I wasn't 'bout too, either."

"Umm-hmm," Janet bit her lowered lip. "I know what you mean, Mama. I see them all of the time. Some women just don't have any respect for their body. It's a shame. Downright degrading how these women would give it up to everything and everybody."

"It's a shame all right," Mae Ella pushed herself up from the sofa. "The food smells ready. Let's eat." She waited for Janet. Janet rose to her feet. Mae Ella wrapped her arms around Janet's waist and they strolled into the kitchen.

Chapter 25

*A*drienne sighed, and hung up the phone in frustration. She had been calling Janet's house for over three weeks now. She had also dropped by there a few times, but there was no sign of her friend. She knew Janet should have heard the news about Billy. News traveled fast in Silver Rock, faster than the papers. So, why hadn't Janet called? The question hammered at her. It wasn't like Janet to not be there for her. If she could count on anyone's support, it was Janet. Now, after finding out about Billy's unfaithfulness, she needed her more than ever. It seemed useless talking with her mother. She had been acting cranky lately.

Adrienne needed to talk with Janet desperately, because like a time bomb she was ready to explode. She hated Billy, and Travis. They had brought feelings of shame and hurt upon her. She wished they both got what was coming to them. She wished it more so on Travis than Billy. She had trusted them, and they had let her down.

Detective Wright had suspected her, also. She didn't know Sheila had existed, and wished it had stayed that a way. Then her marriage wouldn't be in this mess now. "Ah," Adrienne exhaled. "I can't stand this." Then she quickly went upstairs to her bedroom, where her suitcases and packed boxes cluttered the room, since she had decided to move back in with her parents. Her father had been thrilled about her moving back home, but her mother didn't seem to like the idea at all. Her mother thought that she should keep Billy's house after what Billy had put her through. She wasn't about to keep the house, and that was that. As for my mother, she just has to get over it, Adrienne thought. Besides, she needed to get out of the house, anyway. It reminded her too much of Billy. She had to move on with her life without Billy, if she wanted to keep her sanity.

Suddenly, a smile tugged at the corners of Adrienne's mouth. She snatched her purse from the bed, and fished through it. Finally, finding what she was looking for. Adrienne dialed Janet's mother's phone number.

"I'm sorry, but the number you're dialing is no longer in service." The recorder spoke loudly and clearly through the phone. "Ahhh!" Adrienne sighed. She dialed the information. "What city?"

"Lost Gap."

"What state?"

"Georgia."

"What listing?"

"Mae Ella Wingo."

"Hold for the number, please." The machine gave the number.

Adrienne quickly dialed the number letting the telephone ring a few moments before hanging it up. She gazed at her watch. It was five o'clock. Lost Gap was two hours away east of Silver Rock. If she left now, she would arrive no later than seven. She hurriedly packed an overnight bag. If anyone knew where Janet was, it would be Mae Ella. Janet was close to her mother. She told her everything. Adrienne wished she and her mother had a relationship like that. She picked up the phone and dialed her mother's number. Donna picked up on the first ring.

"Hello?" Adrienne heard a sexier voice on the other end.

"Hello, Mama?" Adrienne asked, not sure if it was her mother or not.

"Adrienne, oh, hi sweetie," Donna shifted back to her usual tone.

"What are you doing?"

"Sitting here waiting for your father." Donna answered.

"Where's Daddy?"

"Your father is having one of his Chick-fil-A cravings, again." Donna laughed. "So, he's driving all the way to the city to Chick-fil-A. Can you believe that man? All that way for a chicken sandwich."

"Oh, you know daddy. When he wants Chick-fil-A, he wants Chick-fil-A."

Mary R. Butler

"Yeah, how can I forget?" Donna laughed softly and added, "How are things going with your packing? I was coming over to help, but I've been so busy at the store. You understand, don't you? It's strange but your husband brought us a lot of business at the store. I swear I can't keep up with all the people we have been getting. It's terrible, but people love to be in company of bad news. It's a tragedy about Billy, and I hate to be the one to say it, but it has been good for the store."

"Well, I'm happy to see you and Daddy prospering off of my pain." She snapped.

"Now, Adrienne you don't have to get an attitude."

"I'm not getting an attitude. Just forget it." Adrienne didn't want to hear anymore of what Donna had to say. It was bad enough her mother didn't seem to care what she was going through.

"I'm sorry, Adrienne. I didn't mean to—"

"No need to apologize, Mama. I shouldn't have attacked you," she interjected.

"Okay, enough of that." Donna switched the conversation. "Are you still not speaking to Billy?"

"I don't want to hear his name," Adrienne replied in an angry tone.

"Adrienne, I swear. What are you going to do? You can't keep avoiding the man's name. Billy is your husband. And you can't expect your father and me to continue this charade. We are bound to say Billy every once in a while." She purposely said Billy twice driving her point to Adrienne.

"I know I can't keep avoiding his name. I don't want to hear it now." She explained.

"I know, Sweetie," a wicked smile developed over Donna's face. "So what are you doing? Do you want to come over? Maybe we can watch a movie."

"No. I can't. I'm going out of town."

"Out of town? Now? This time of the day?"

"Yes. I called because I wanted you and Daddy to know where I'm staying."

"Do you think that is wise?"

"Mama, I don't know, and I don't care. I need to get away for awhile."

"Why don't you come over here, we could have a nice visit?"

"No. I need to get away from here for awhile."

"Where are you going?"

"Lost Gap."

"Lost Gap. What in Heaven for?" She inhaled and then exhaled. "Isn't that where Mae Ella lives? Adrienne, that is a two-hour drive, and you are going alone? I don't think that's a good decision."

"I'll be all right. I'm hoping Janet is there."

"What! You haven't heard from that girl yet? I know I haven't seen her since the wedding."

"I hadn't seen her since this thing happened with Billy."

"No one knows where she is?"

"No one. That's why I have to go to Lost Gap."

"Can you call Mae Ella first to see has she seen her daughter?"

"I tried calling her several times, but no one answer."

"Call again."

"No. I'm just wasting time waiting here."

"Well, if you must go, be careful and give Mae Ella my love."

"I will." Adrienne glanced at her watch. She had already talked with Donna for ten minutes. If she was going to get on the road, she had to end this conversation now.

"Mama, I'll call you when I get there. I got to run."

"Okay, but be careful and drive safe."

"Tell Daddy I'll call him when I get back in town so he can help me move my stuff back home."

"I will, dear. Be careful," she said again. "And we'll see you when you get back. Bye."

"Bye Mama." Adrienne held the phone in her hand a moment before hanging up.

Then she zipped her overnight bag, grabbed her car keys and purse, and hurried downstairs and out the door.

* * * * * * * * * *

After hanging up the telephone with Adrienne, Donna flipped through the pages of her address book and found Mae Ella's telephone number. She dialed the number.

"Hello, Mae Ella?" Donna asked softly."

"Yeah," Mae Ella said cautiously, "Who is this?"

"This is Donna Mitchell, Adrienne's mother. How's everything?" She asked, being polite but really not caring at all how Mae Ella felt.

"I'm doing good," Mae Ella responded. "How's your family?"

"We are all doing great," Donna tried to sound persuasive.

"Good." Mae Ella placed her hand over the mouthpiece and whispered to Janet. "It's Adrienne's mama."

"Shhh! don't tell her that I'm here," Janet said almost leaping off of the sofa. She stared strangely at Mae Ella.

Mae Ella glanced at her daughter, but ignored her strange behavior. Something was bothering her daughter, and she wanted to know what.

"Is there anything wrong?" Mae Ella asked, removing her hand from over mouthpiece.

"No, I'm calling to let you know my daughter is on her way to your house. She's very upset about your daughter's disappearance."

"My daughter's disappearance? But she's —,"

"Nooo! Don't' tell her I'm here," Janet tried to cover the telephone mouthpiece with her hands.

"Wait a minute, please." Mae Ella snatched the telephone away from Janet and covered the mouthpiece again. "What's the matter with you child? You said everything was all right. I don't understand my own daughter." Mae Ella shook her head.

"There's nothing wrong with me. I'm on vacation and I don't want to be bothered with anyone from Silver Rock. That's all."

"What sense does that make?"

"Mama, please, don't tell her I'm here," she begged.

"I'm not going to tell her anything, but after I get offa' this phone I want you to tell me what's going on."

"There's nothing going on." Janet looked in her mother's eyes, but couldn't keep her focus.

"Are you gonna tell me or do I have to tell Mrs. Mitchell?"

"Okay," Janet sounded defeated.

"That's more like it," Mae Ella said and then returned to her conversation with Donna. "I'm sorry 'bout that. I had a little distraction. Now what were you saying?"

"I was saying it seems like Janet just disappeared and it's

gotten my daughter so worked-up that's she's on her way to see you. She is hoping Janet is with you."

"Why didn't she call first?"

"She did, but didn't get an answer."

"Oh, so that's who that was?" Mae Ella said to no one in particular.

"Huh?" Donna sounded puzzled.

"Oh, nothing," Mae Ella replied.

"Well, Adrienne is planning on dropping by there in a little while. I just wanted to call and let you know. So you can be looking out for her. I hate to think of her driving such a long way by herself." Donna added.

"I'll be watching out for her."

"Oh and ah, Mae Ella, don't tell her I called."

"I won't."

"Good. Talk to you soon," Donna said before hanging up the telephone.

Mae Ella hung up the telephone and turned to Janet, "Now, tell me what is this all about?"

"Mama I told you." Janet lay back on the sofa. She had no intention of telling her mother anything.

"Do I have to call Mrs. Mitchell back?" Mae Ella asked.

"No," Janet leaned forward.

"Well?" Mae Ella waited.

"Well what?"

"You know good and well what I'm talking 'bout."

"Okay, Mama, I hear you. Anyway, Adrienne and I had a fight." The lies quickly formed in Janet's mind and spurted out of her mouth.

"Fight?" Mae Ella frowned.

"Yes. A fight."

"About what?"

"Billy."

"Billy? What about him?

"She thought I was having an affair with her husband."

"Why would she think something like that?" Mae Ella frown deepened. "Unless you gave her a reason."

"Someone told her they saw Billy and me at the night club and that we were doing more than talking. She asked me about it and I told her it wasn't true. But she can be so stubborn, and naturally she didn't believe me."

"Why wouldn't she believe you? She's your best friend."

"Because Travis is the one who told her that lie. She thinks because he's a Christian, he can do no wrong."

"Well, he shouldn't be lying if he a Christian." Mae Ella replied and watched her daughter closely.

"Mama, stop looking at me like that. I'm telling you the truth. I swear you never believe a word I say."

"I didn't say I didn't believe you. I'm just sitting here hoping that you weren't foolish enough to be messing with someone else's husband."

"Mama, you raised me better than that. Travis made-up that lie because he likes Adrienne more than he's admitting. This is his way of getting Billy out of the picture. With Billy out of the way, he can have Adrienne all to himself."

"But why would she take Travis' word over yours?"

"Because Travis and Billy are best friends. And she believes Travis won't do anything to hurt Billy. So, if Travis said he saw us making out at the club and later leaving together. That's all she needed to hear."

"I think y'all need to talk this thing out," Mae Ella suggested.

"I tried that."

"Well, your chance is coming again."

"Why do you say that?" Janet looked out the corners of her eyes at Mae Ella.

"Adrienne is on her way here."

"She's what?" Janet jumped up from the sofa and began pacing the floor. "Why is she coming here?"

"Sit down, girl, you're makin' me nervous."

"Mama, I got to go."

"For what?"

"I can't be here when she gets here. I have to leave now."

"Janet what sense does that make?" Mae Ella leaned backward on the sofa. "Adrienne is a nice, respectful young woman. I don't think she'd come all the way down here to start a fight with you. Tell the truth, I can't see her doing all those things you're accusing her of."

"Well, those things happened Mama," angry with her mother, she rushed out of the living room to her old bedroom. She grabbed the over night bags and started throwing her clothes in them.

"Don't run from your problems, Janet," Mae Ella said, following her to her old bedroom.

"I have to," Janet said, calmly, as she continued to throw her clothes in the bags.

"Surely you and Adrienne can sit down and talk about this like two adults." Mae Ella crossed her arms over her chest.

"Mama, I told you I tried that, but Adrienne doesn't want to listen to me, and I'm tired of trying to reason with her. All she wants to do is fight, fight, fight and I'm sick and tired of fighting with her."

"I don't think she'd come all the way here and fight with you. That's a nice girl."

"Oh, Mama, you're so blind," Janet said rolling her eyes toward the ceiling.

"Well, she was nice last summer when y'all stayed the week here." Mae Ella tried to defend her reason.

"I can't believe you're that naïve, Mama."

"I'm not naïve, and I won't allow you to speak to me like that, Janet," Mae Ella said firmly.

"I'm sorry, Mama…but I was just as naïve as you are now when it came to Adrienne. She had me fooled for a long time. I was a good friend to her. She's going to miss me. But I can't keep being her friend when she keeps on accusing me of sleeping with her husband. She ought to know I won't do anything like that to her. Besides, that'd be a reflection of you Mama. Like mama, like daughter."

"But Mrs. Mitchell said that her daughter was upset and concerned about you."

"Mrs. Mitchell doesn't know anything, Mama. She cares less of what her daughter is doing. I won't be surprised if she's out cheating on Mr. Mitchell." Janet zipped her over night bags and took them outside to her car.

"That's not a nice thing to say," Mae Ella said, following her outside.

"Like I said Mama I won't be surprised. That woman has some

heavy issues to deal with," she said, and walked back inside the house. She grabbed her purse and walked back outside to her car.

"Where are you going?" Mae Ella asked, standing beside Janet's car.

"I don't know Mama. But I'll call you as soon as I can," she embraced Mae Ella. Mae Ella returned the hug and kissed her cheek.

"Do you really have to go?" Mae Ella asked.

"I have to. And Mama, Adrienne isn't what she seems. She's a big liar and loves to start trouble. You shouldn't open your door for her. All she's going to do is spread lies and get you all upset for nothing."

"I'm not worryin' about her spreading lies. I'm worrying about you. I want you to be all right."

"I'm all right, Mama. I'll call you." Janet opened the car door, and slid behind the steering wheel. She turned the key in the ignition and started the car and rolled down the window. "Bye, Mama," she said looking sadly at Mae Ella.

"Bye, baby," Mae Ella said, touching the tips of her fingers to her mouth, she blew Janet a kiss.

Janet backed the car out of the driveway. She blew her horn, and waved at her mother before driving away. Mae Ella watched the car as it vanished from her sight.

Chapter 26

$\mathcal{D}$etective Wright stepped one foot out of his car. He scanned his surroundings before placing the other foot on the ground. He eased out of the car and quickly slapped on his sunglasses before closing the door.

After composing himself, he scanned the area once more before walking toward the apartment building. The morning air was already scorching 90-degrees and rising. A hot breeze stirred against his chocolate skin, creating beads of sweat underneath. He had interviewed everyone in Sheila's apartment building, and the ones that surrounded her building. No luck. People weren't talking. They didn't want to get involved. That was the game. No questions asked. Now, as he walked to the apartment door of his last interviewee, an unction hit him. A heavy feeling of dread absorbed him. A feeling of the wrong man sitting in jail behind bars for a crime he didn't commit. He tried shaking the feeling but it wouldn't budge. It only made Billy's innocence grow stronger. But he had heard it all before. So, why was he concerned about Billy's innocence so suddenly? Billy had all the evidence stacked-up against him. The jealous lover. The beautiful wife at home. A thriving law firm in Atlanta established his power and position. He had it all going for him until it all threatened to collapse around him. Billy couldn't allow that. He worked too hard. He couldn't stand by and watch it all crumble. Billy had to eliminate the problem. But somewhere in the pit of Detective Wright's guts, this whole situation just didn't feel right. Detective Wright sensed it, something was definitely wrong.

Charlotte mentioned Sheila was arguing with Billy and holding the lead pipe hours before her death. But where were Sheila's fingerprints? He walked slowly to the apartment front door and knocked. The door immediately swung open. A short, bald middle-age man stood on the other side. He had been expecting Detective Wright.

Detective Wright grabbed his badge and held it for the man to see. "Good morning, sir, I'm Detective Wright. Silver Rock Police Department," he said, allowing the man to read the badge.

"Don't bother, Detective. I know who you are. Please come in." He ushered Detective Wright into his apartment.

"Thank you," Detective Wright said, as he stepped inside. He welcomed the cool air blasting from the air conditioner. Taking off his sunglasses he slipped them inside his suit jacket.

"May I get you something to drink?" The man asked, quickly moving into the small kitchen before Detective Wright could object. "Soda, tea, or water?"

"Water would be fine," Detective responded.

"Water? Okay." He grabbed two bottles of cold SAM'S water from inside the fridge and handed one to Detective Wright. "Please, have a seat."

"Thank you, again, Mr. —"

"Aaron Sudden," he interjected and sat in a wingback chair across from Detective Wright.

"Thanks Mr. Sudden." Detective Wright said, as he sat in the other wingback chair. He opened the bottled water. He put the bottle to his mouth and let the cool water slide gracefully down his throat. "I needed that," he admitted, setting the half-empty bottle on the floor beside his chair.

"Just call me plain old Aaron," he grinned, and twisted the top off his bottle. "What can I do for you, Detective?" He asked. An expression of concern shrouded his face. "I know why you're here. It's about Sheila. Now, that girl was nothing but trouble. She kept a flow of men going in and out over there. But I didn't know she'd get herself killed."

Detective Wright sat amazed. It was the first time since working on this case that someone was willing to talk. Aaron was ready to tell all he knew. He quickly took out his pocket size tape recorder, turned it on, and set it on the coffee table in front of them. He also pulled out his pen and notepad.

"So, you knew Ms. Sheila Stone?" Detective Wright glanced at the tape recorder.

"Who didn't know her?" Aaron lay back in his chair. "Like I said, she was trouble." A string of chuckles begin to build in the pit of his stomach and erupted into laughter as he reminisced about Sheila.

Then as if on cue, Aaron's expression became serious. "Do you think that fellow, the lawyer, did it?" Aaron leaned forward. He set the bottled water on the end table. "I'd understand if you can't talk to me about the situation. I watch enough crime stories on TV to know that too much talking can hurt a case. You know, Detective Wright, when I was a boy, I always wanted to be a cop. But all that changed when I got drafted. Vietnam, now that was a war. After that, I didn't want to touch another gun in my life or see another Vietnamese."

"Too bad. I bet we lost a good detective," Detective Wright replied, thankful Aaron wasn't shy with words.

"Detective, I get a lot of slack from the other tenants; they tell me I ought to mind my own business. I can't help 'cause I see everything going on around here. It's right out there in front of me. What am I suppose to do? Shut my eyes?" Aaron looked to Detective Wright for justification, but Detective Wright gave none.

"Whoever killed her, I hope they get the chair," Aaron said, and then added, "I liked Sheila, she was wild but a nice person. I figured she had some enemies. But none who wanted her dead."

"How long had you known Sheila?"

"A little over a year."

"Did she have any female friends?"

"Let me think," he squinted his eyes upward. There is Charlotte. They hung out a lot. She didn't have that many women friends. But that lawyer, he used to drop by late at night." Aaron looked at the ceiling and chuckled lightly.

"What's that?"

"It's funny he never stayed all night."

"What's funny about that?"

That girl was stacked. She was hooked-up in all the right places. If

Mary R. Butler

you know what I mean?" He winked at Detective Wright. The detective ignored his suggestion. Anyway, a man had to be crazy if he didn't want to hold on to that all night."

Detective Wright flipped through his notepad as he continued to ignore Aaron's comments. "I have a witness that said Ms. Stone and Mr. Ray had an argument on the day she was killed?"

"Sheila had an argument was more like it," Aaron laughed softly.

"Why's that?" Detective Wright looked at Aaron.

"I heard this loud noise outside, so I ran to my window and peeped out. I saw Mr. Ray and another guy standing in Sheila's doorway. Sheila was hollering so loud. And Mr. Ray, he just walked down the steps cool as ever. I couldn't believe how calm he was especially with Sheila yelling like that. The other guy was scared. You could see it in his face and in the way he ran down the steps. But the lawyer he had got into the car like nothing happened. While Sheila stood on the balcony looking down at them, hollering threats and swinging that pipe."

"Did you know the other man with Mr. Ray?" Detective Wright asked as he wrote in his notepad.

"No, but I have seen him over there speaking with Mr. Ray a few times late at night.

"Could you establish a time you saw Mr. Ray at Ms. Stone's apartment on the day she died?"

"It was around six o' clock. I remember popping a bag of popcorn. I was getting ready to watch, 'Everybody Loves Raymond'."

"Are you sure of the time?" Detective Wright asked.

"I'm sure it was six. That's what time Raymond comes on, and I won't miss that show for nothing in the world."

"Did you see anyone else?" Detective Wright probed further.

"There are a few guys we know around here, but they won't do a thing like that to Sheila. Wait a minute," Aaron snapped his finger, remembering something. "There was a guy. He was with Sheila earlier in the day. He was an older man. Average height. Medium complexion. He was in his late fifties or his early sixties, sporting salt and pepper hair. She got out of the car with him and they both went inside her apartment. Then about an hour or so later, I saw him leave."

"What time was this?" Detective Wright asked.

"Around four," Aaron replied.

Detective wrote the time down in his notepad, and asked, "Was he alone?"

"Yeah," Aaron answered.

"What was he wearing?"

"A pair of jeans and a big shirt."

"Was there anything different about the man or his clothes? Or something that may have stood out?"

"No, nothing I could see."

"Why didn't you come forward in the beginning with this information?" Detective Wright asked, knowing the answer already.

"I didn't want to get involved," Aaron said, in a shameful tone. "But after awhile, I thought about it. Then I knew I had to do my patriotic duty."

"Ah," Detective Wright tried to speak, but the words stuck to the roof of his mouth like peanut butter.

"You don't need to say it, Detective. I get the picture. Patriotic or not people need to get involved." Aaron smiled.

Ignoring this statement, Detective Wright proceeded with the question. "Did the man have any outstanding face features?"

"Uh, handsome if that's considered one," Aaron tried to visualize Darrell as he spoke.

"Do you remember anything else? Think." Detective Wright asked forcefully. "Sometimes, people remember more than they realize."

"Mmm," Aaron's mind raced trying to think of anything he may have missed. He shook his head, "No, I can't think of anything more about him."

"Did you see anyone else that day at Ms. Stone's apartment besides the old man and Mr. Ray?"

"Let me see. Mmmh," he snapped his finger, again. "There was a young woman. I have seen her with Sheila a couple of times. I can't believe I forgot about her. Wow, she got a body like an hourglass. Curves in all the right places. A figure that could choke a man to death," Aaron continued to talk non-stop. "She showed up at Sheila's place around eight-o-clock. I watched her get out of her car. And about twenty minutes later, I saw her run out of Sheila's apartment.

And right after that, I saw Mr. Ray drive up.

"The woman seemed disturbed about something?" Detective Wright inquired.

"Yeah, she looked scared," Aaron answered.

"How long was it between the girl leaving Sheila's apartment and the time Mr. Ray showed up?"

"Maybe two or three minutes, at the most."

Detective Wright nodded. He scribbled in his notepad.

"Do you think she may have done it?"

"I don't know," Detective Wright replied. "That's what we are trying to find out. Describe her. What did she have on?"

Aaron grabbed the water bottle from the table and put the bottle to his mouth and turned it up, producing loud gulps from his throat as he swallowed the water. The noise irritated Detective Wright, but he sat quietly waiting for more information.

Aaron set the empty bottle on the floor beside his chair. He settled comfortably in his chair. "She was medium complexion, with brown shoulder length hair. She wore a white blouse and a pair of skintight Capri jeans. I watched her go up those steps and into Sheila's apartment. I remember thinking to myself; if I had a lady like that I wouldn't mind choking to death on them pair of legs. I know I'd die a happy man for sure." Aaron winked his eye at Detective Wright, again.

"Now, if I could only find a girl whose legs would choke you to death then, I would be in business." Detective Wright couldn't help but to smile at Aaron's animated illustration.

"Then, that would be half of Silver Rock," Aaron said, seeming amused at the idea of Detective Wright looking for a girl with a great pair of legs.

"That you are right." This time it was Detective Wright's turn to chuckle and then he stated, "Now, if I only could find this young lady."

"Let me call Charlotte. If anyone knows her it'd be Charlotte." Aaron pushed himself up from his chair and picked up the phone. "If you'd give me a few seconds, I'll find the name of those pair of legs for you." Aaron dialed Charlotte's number.

"I'm not going anywhere, Aaron," Detective Wright replied.

He didn't feel comfortable calling him Aaron. But he learned in this business, you call people whatever they wanted you to call them.

"Hello, Charlotte. Good. You're home. Listen Charlotte Detective Wright is here. He wants to know the name of one of Sheila's friends." Aaron paused. "Charlotte, you know I don't know any of Sheila's friends personally. It's a young woman. Well, before you say you don't know the girl, hear me out. She's tall, medium complexion. No. Dark medium brown. Shoulder length hair. She was with you and Sheila last summer on the fourth of July. Yeah, that's the one she had on the tennis outfit? What's her name? Janet. Do you know her last name? Detective Wright needs it. I'm helping him with this case. I can't discuss it with you its police business. That's all you know is Janet? Okay, Janet is better than nothing. Listen Charlotte, find out her last name and call me back, okay? I have to go now. Take care." Aaron hung up the telephone and walked back to his chair and sat.

In the meantime, Detective Wright scribbled Janet's description in his notepad.

"Charlotte is going to work on getting Janet's last name for us," he said, watching Detective Wright write in his notepad.

"That's good. Call me as soon as you hear something," Detective Wright said, pulling out his business card. He handed it to Aaron. He took the card and placed it on the coffee table.

"I will." Then, he snapped his fingers as he remembered one small detail. "Oh, there is one thing I forgot."

"What's that?"

"She changed clothes; she was wearing a red Mike Vick's jersey when I saw her running from Shelia's apartment.

"The football player?"

"The best," Aaron smiled, glad he remembered the jersey.

"Thanks that will help my case a lot and thanks for your time," Detective Wright said, picking up the tape recorder to turn it off. He slipped it inside his suit jacket along with the pen and notepad. Then, he extended his hand out to Aaron, ending their meeting.

Aaron grasped Detective Wright's hand and shook it firmly. "I hope I helped some."

"You've helped a whole lot," Detective Wright warranted, letting go of Aaron's hand.

"I'm glad."

"Now, I better get going." He walked to the door.

Aaron followed him.

"Thanks again," Detective Wright said, and opened the door, and walked out.

"You take care," Aaron replied, standing at the door watching the detective get inside his car.

"You too," he said nodding at Aaron before closing his car door.

Chapter 27

*R*eleased from jail that morning for public drinking and disturbing the peace, Darrell sat quietly inside the bus station. "The bus to Atlanta is now boarding," the dispatcher announced from the small ticket window. Darrell rose to his feet, looking at the ticket he held in his hand. His hands trembled as he walked toward the bus. In a small way, Darrell wished Billy had recognized him. He had enjoyed the conversation between them, even though he had to pretend to be someone else. But what else could he have done? Billy had made it loud and clear that he didn't want anything to do with his father. So, in the meantime, he enjoyed his son the best way he knew how.

"Your ticket, sir," the driver said, smiling at Darrell.

"What...huh?" Darrell asked. Seeing the driver for the first time. "Oh. Yes." Darrell handed the ticket to the driver.

"Thank you, and welcome to Greyhound," the driver smiled, tearing off the ticket stub. He handed the stub back to Darrell.

"Thank you," Darrell responded, boarding the bus. Darrell slid behind the second seat and looked out the window. He watched the driver tear off the ticket and hand the ticket stubs to the line of people boarding the bus.

"Is this seat taken, Mister?" An older, heavy-set woman asked sitting comfortably on the seat before Darrell had time to reply. "My name's Agnes Reynolds. And yours?" Agnes smiled, showing big, black gums.

"Ah, Darrell," he smiled at her and suddenly looked away,

213

glancing out the window. The last thing he wanted was to get involved in a conversation with Agnes. He had too much on his mind.

"I hate taking long trips on the bus. It just wears me out, and with all this mess going on, I am too scared to fly. Boy, that September 11 day sho' 'nough changed the face of America, didn't it?" Agnes rattled on, not giving Darrell a chance to respond. "Lord knows, my heart goes out to those people who died and their families. Those po' people didn't have a piss-rat chance of surviving. What I don't get is how can somebody enroll in a flying school to learn how to fly a plane, but they don't want to learn how to land the darn thang. Wouldn't that have raised your suspicion? But I'm jus' an ol' woman. What do I know? But it sho' done changed the way Americans think. I'm too scared to open my mail these days. Scared somebody done put some of that white powder stuff in there. Now, take Bush, he doesn't play. Just like his daddy. I like him. When you come over here messing with us, Bush got something for you." Agnes laughed, glancing out the window passed Darrell. "Doggone. When are they going to get a move on? My grandchildren are expecting me in Memphis. You know, at first I had second thoughts about going. It's hot as a piss-rat this time of the year down there. Anyway, I was sitting at home out on the front porch watching Leroy acting a fool again in his front yard. Leroy is Pearl's husband. Pearl is my friend. When Leroy gets drunk he doesn't know his right foot from his left. Well, he was acting a fool out in his yard, wanting to fight the man next door. I was sitting there watching him, and I said to myself, Agnes, them is your grandkids. How many times do you get to see them? Once a year, I answered myself. Surely, you can stand to be baked a few degrees for them. So, here I am." Agnes grinned from ear to ear.

Darrell looked at her. He was amazed she still had breath to talk. She was considered what his father used to call long-winded women.

"Wanda, that's my daughter. She's another story. A pistol she is. Just like her daddy. God rest his po' soul. Wanda says I spoil her children. Say she can't do nothing with them after I'm gone. If you can't spoil your grands, then you shouldn't be grandparents...that's what I say." Agnes laughed softly and talked on. "You got any grandchildren?"   She   asked, smiling at Darrell.

"No," Darrell replied.

"Too bad. They keep you on your toes. Pearl keeps telling me, I look young for my age. I'm sixty-five. Do I look it?" Agnes turned her body sideways so Darrell could get a full look at her face.

"Ah—"

"See what I tell you?" She cut in. "You think so too. Pearl is always asking me what my secret to the fountain of youth is. I told her it was due to no smoking, no drinking, and no fooling around." She opened her purse and pulled out a small hand fan with a picture of Dr. Martin Luther King Jr., on it. She fanned herself vigorously with it. "I know these buses are welled air-conditioned, but I need a little extra help. I don't know what's wrong with me. I am well past menopause. I don't know why I'm having these hot flashes. My doctor thinks I'm crazy. I say what does he know? They're just practicing medicine. Hoping they will work. They're only a few degrees away from my mama and her home remedies. Anyway, Wanda keeps telling me, more like ordering me, to change doctors. I've been going to my doctor for more than twenty years, and she wants me to up and leave him just like that. Young people, I don't know how they're thinking. Do you?" She watched Darrell and laughed softly. "You ain't much of a talker, huh? Well, anyway, my grandchildren are making me a surprise. Lord knows too bad they weren't born first. Then it'd have saved me a whole lot of trouble. I hope they grow up and give Wanda the blues just like she gave me. I think that little gal she got now is already doing that. She better knock that child upside her head now or that child will be knocking *her* upside the head later. If you ask me, family, humph, you got to love them. Can't up and walk away, no matter how bad they are or how mean they get. You got to love them the best way you know how." Agnes said as the last person boarded the bus.

Darrell watched the driver compose himself behind the steering wheel. He took a clipboard from side of the window and wrote on it. He put the clipboard back in place. He looked in his rearview mirror and grasped the door handle to close the bus door. Darrell leaped to his feet. "Excuse me," Darrell said to Agnes, as he eased his way past her.

"Hey, where are you going?" Agnes asked, as she swirled her legs out into the aisle letting Darrell past through.

"I'm going home," Darrell replied, glancing at Agnes. "I'm going to my son."

"Oh, you didn't tell me you had a son," Agnes called out after Darrell. He glanced back at her. She touched the lady across from her. "The nerve of some people. They got you telling all of your business, and they keep everything to themselves. Do you have grandchildren?" Agnes asked the lady.

Darrell smiled at Agnes and turned his back toward her. He walked up to the bus driver. "Sir, I'd like to get off the bus."

"Are you okay?" The driver asked.

"Yeah, I'm okay. I'm going home."

"Okay," the driver said, opening the door.

"Thank you," Darrell said, stepping off the bus.

"Have a good day, sir," the driver said and closed the door. He composed himself once again before pulling away from the bus terminal.

Darrell checked his wallet. He had ten dollars left. It was all the money he had.

* * * * * * * * * *

"Welcome back, Mr. Malcolm," Ms. King said, rising to her feet. She hugged Travis, glad to see him.

"Thank you, Ms. King," Travis said, returning her hug.

"Hi, Mr. Malcolm. We're glad you're back," the other secretaries said together.

"And I'm thrilled to be back," Travis smiled.

"I don't know how we survived without you and especially now since Mr. Ray has been locked-up," Ms. King said.

"Because in my absence I left wonderful women in charge, that's how you all survived." Travis said in a genuine tone.

"Thanks Mr. Malcolm you're so kind," Ms. King replied along with the other secretaries.

"Well, I was gone for almost a week, now it's time for me to get down to business. Ms. King would you please get Mr. Ray's files?" he asked.

"Yes sir," she answered.

"Thanks," Travis said, as he walked into his office and closed the door.

Chapter 28

*L*ost Gap was a little larger than Silver Rock. It was full of historical monuments, and buildings. The main road lined with rows of antebellum homes. Weeping widows and various colored petunias graced each yard. The scenery reminded Adrienne of the 'Gone with the Wind' set. Adrienne expected to see slaves walking up from the slave's quarter to the houses to begin their everyday routine of hard labor. The homes and streets were breathtakingly beautiful. They were southern eloquent. She drove pass the homes, and turned onto Samuel C. Towns Road. She made another turn onto Box Fashion Road; this was the poorer section of town. The houses started to look run-down. Empty bottles, cans, and paper cluttered the yards. While broken-down cars set-up on car-jacks filled plenty of spaces in the yards. The place depressed Adrienne.

Finally, a few minutes passed, she pulled her car up to the Wingo's home. The yard had been freshly swept. Adrienne could see the homemade brush broom leaning against the side of the front porch. Killing the engine, she stepped out of the car, as the front door burst open, and Mae Ella ran down the steps leading to Adrienne's car.

"Oh, I'm glad you've finally made it," Mae Ella said, giving her a big bear hug, and then led her up the steps to the house.

"I'm glad to see you too," Adrienne said, cloaking her arm through Mae Ella's arm, as they strolled inside the house.

"Sit down," Mae Ella gestured toward the sofa.

"I'm so glad to finally be here," Adrienne said, sitting on the sofa.

She looked questionable at Mae Ella. "How did you know I was coming?"

"Oh, your mother called," she said and sat in the chair opposite of her.

"My mother, umph, I should have known. I wanted to surprise you, but she ruined the surprise."

Mae Ella laughed softly and said, "That's how mothers are. We worry 'bout our babies. That's what Donna was doing. She was worried about you."

"I doubt that," Adrienne pushed her nose in the air, and made a funny face.

"She does. Trust me. All mothers worry 'bout their children, and some of us show it, and some of us don't. Someday, when you have children, you'll see what I'm talkin' 'bout." Mae Ella rose to her feet, unaware she had pushed a sore button with Adrienne. "May I get you somethin' to drink or somethin' to eat?"

"No, I'm all right."

"Well, I'm happy you're here. It's not every day I get a visit from one of my daughter's friends." Mae Ella reclaimed her seat.

"To tell the truth, Ms. Wingo, I came here looking for Janet. I was hoping she was here."

"She was here." Mae Ella answered. She didn't know what else to say. How could she tell Adrienne that the mention of her coming to Lost Gap, sent Janet packing and running?

"She was here? Where's she now?" Adrienne sounded excited. "I have so much to tell her. It's not like her to leave town and not tell me."

"She left a couple hours ago."

"Oh," she sounded disappointed, "Did she say where she was going?" Adrienne asked, the excitement leaving her.

"No, she didn't. She left here in a bit of a hurry. I'm worried 'bout my child. She doesn't seem to be herself." Mae Ella glanced closely at Adrienne and said, "Adrienne."

"Yes," Adrienne replied watching Mae Ella.

"She mentioned somethin' 'bout you accusing her of going with your husband."

"Accused her of what? What does that suppose to mean?" She

looked puzzled.

"Janet said y'all don't talk anymore. I hated to hear that. I remembered how close y'all use to be."

"And we're still close friends." Adrienne protested. She was baffled by Janet's lies. What was she trying to prove by telling her mother lies? It wasn't like her to be devious and to hurt someone. So, what was her problem?

"Ms. Wingo, I don't know why Janet would straight-out and lie on me, like that. But I have never accused her of anything."

"I'm glad to hear that. I hate to see y'all friendship end. But I wonder why she lied 'bout somethin' like that? It is a mean thing to do."

"Ms. Wingo, I don't know why Janet would do a thing like that, but it's all lies. That's why I am here. I'm going through some heavy issues right now. Janet has always been the only person I could confide in. When Billy and I would get angry at one another, Janet was there. When Billy went away to college and stop calling me, Janet was there. She has been by my side through every obstacle in my life. Now, my husband sits in the county jail for murder, and no Janet." Adrienne rose to her feet, and paced the floor. "Ms. Wingo, I don't understand your daughter. I don't understand her at all. She knows I need her."

Mae Ella pushed herself up from the chair, and embraced Adrienne. Adrienne laid her head against Mae Ella's shoulder. "Po' child, I'm sorry to hear 'bout your husband. Janet didn't tell me he was in jail. She didn't make any mention of that."

"She must have known about it or read it in the papers and —"

"Maybe she left town before the papers." Mae Ella interrupted. "That has to be the reason you hadn't heard from her." Mae Ella smiled at her. "How long has your husband been locked up?"

Adrienne was thankful Mae Ella didn't question her about the murder. She couldn't live through another episode of Sheila's name. "He's been locked-up two or four weeks, I can't remember." Adrienne retreated a few steps from her. "It has been madness all the way. I learned my husband had been having an affair, and then there's something about a baby."

"Oh you po' child, I'm sorry to hear that. It must be a blow to learn such a bad thing about your husband. I'm sure if Janet knew what you were going through she would be here with you now." Mae Ella walked closer to her and lifted Adrienne's head so she could look at her. "But, I'm sure everythin' gonna work out between you and your husband," she smiled at Adrienne.

Adrienne freed herself from Mae Ella, and retreated a few steps backward. Her body shook with anger. "I don't want it to work out between us!" Adrienne snapped.

"Listen to what you're saying. Yeah, you're angry now, 'cause your husband betrayed you. It's natural for anyone to feel the way you're feeling. But once the hurt wears off, you'll feel differently 'bout it." Mae Ella reasoned with her.

"Ms. Wingo, I have already given it plenty of thought, and it is driving me crazy, to think I kept myself pure for my husband all of these years and he couldn't keep his pants up for me." Adrienne glared at her, crossing her arms over her chest.

"Child, that is how some men are raised to sow their wild oats, and while others are raised the right way. Maybe Billy fell in that first category. It's not his fault if he was raised to think like that."

"What, trained to cheat?" She threw up her hands.

"That's not what I was tryin' to say —"

"I don't believe it," Adrienne cut her off. "You're taking up for him."

"No, I'm not taking up for him. I don't want to see you make a decision about your marriage right now and throw it away."

"Too late. I have asked Billy for a divorce. My lawyer has the papers ready to be signed. Hopefully, he'll sign the papers and free me from this unfaithful relationship," she said, as she walked back to the sofa and sat on it.

Mae Ella joined her on the sofa, and replied, "I hope you'll give this a little more thought before anything gets signed."

"Ms. Wingo, no offense, but I'm finished with thinking. I want to go on with my life and besides I can't live with a man who has been unfaithful to me. Because every time I'm with him, I'll think about her, and how many others who have shared his bed. I can't live in that kind of condition. Marriage is built on trust. I don't trust Billy anymore."

"You can learn to trust him again. Marriage is also based on forgiving one another. You got to forgive that po' child." Mae Ella shot her a pleading look.

"I can't forget about what he has done to me, so how can I forgive him, huh? Answer that."

"Adrienne, have you done anything wrong in your life?"

The question sliced deeply within her, provoking her memory back to the night when Billy was arrested. She had wanted Travis to make love to her. She was so upset with Billy she wanted revenge; she wanted him to feel the pain she was feeling. Although, she had wanted revenge, there was a part of her that wanted Travis more than she'd admit. He had stirred a hidden desire deep inside her. He pushed a button hidden even from Billy. "No," she replied, as she lowered her head, afraid Mae Ella would see she was lying.

"So, you're clean?"

"I wouldn't say that," Adrienne said weakly.

"Then, what are you saying? Help me, 'cause I'm confused."

"I'm not perfect. I have done some bad stuff I'm ashamed of. But I never went all the way. I was a virgin when I married Billy. I was faithful all the way to the altar. And how does he repay me. By telling me he doesn't want any children, and he goes and gets someone else pregnant."

Mae Ella dismissed the last statement and said, "All I'm sayin' is give your marriage a chance to pull through, before you throw it out. It's an out-right shame, but people today don't take marriage seriously. It has become a business. If things don't work out, the business dissolves."

"I wish I knew where Janet was?" Adrienne abruptly changed the subject; she was tired of talking about marriage, Billy and the whole nine-yards. She wanted to rest. Two conflicting thoughts in her mind tormented her. She couldn't forgive or forget what Billy had done.

"I bet you she's at home," Mae Ella rose to her feet, shielding the disappointment. Adrienne had flicked her last words off like a fly.

"Probably," Adrienne lay back on the sofa, unaware of Mae Ella's feelings.

"I'm getting somethin' to drink. How 'bout you? I have water, and I have cold Pepsi. Which would it be?"

"Water," Adrienne replied rising from the sofa. "I want a cold glass of water," she said, and followed her to the kitchen.

Chapter 29

Billy watched Detective Wright as he casually made his way to his cell. He disliked the detective more than ever. He was like a cold sore popping up without warning. Billy clutched the cell bars hard; he squeezed the bars imagining it to be the neck of the detective. The feeling brought pure satisfaction, and a smile tugged at the corners of his mouth.

"How are things going?" Detective Wright asked. He poked his hand through the bars. Billy left him hanging. Detective Wright pulled his hand from between the bars.

Billy let go of the bars and retreated a few steps away from the detective.

"I caught you on a bad day, huh?" Detective Wright didn't give up being nice.

"What do you want, Detective?" Billy asked in a firm tone.

"I want to ask you a few questions."

"I answered your questions already, and there's nothing more to say." Billy wished the man would leave.

"I have plenty to say." Detective Wright took out his small notepad.

"Suit yourself," Billy said and turned his back on the detective.

"Why don't you just stop being a hot-head for one minute and listen to what I have to say?" The detective put away his notepad and glared angrily at Billy. Billy turned facing the detective and glared back at him. "I have news for you, Attorney Ray," Detective Wright said, and there was no turning back. "Won't you just sit down and listen and get it in that thick skull of yours that the sun doesn't rise and shine on you."

Tired of the detective's sarcasm, Billy's anger rose. He had been insulted by the detective one time too many, and now it was time to put him in his place. *How dare this cheap, imitation, alligator shoe-wearing detective speak to me like I was a loser? I am Billy Ray, and that name carries a lot of power and respect. How dare this man stand there and put me down like trash.*

Infuriated, Billy strolled to the bar cell and held on to it. He suggested Detective Wright put his attitude, his questions, and his verbal insult up in a place where the sun doesn't shine. He also proposed to the detective to go and to be affectionate with himself.

"Oh yeah!" Detective Wright voice's rose. "Let me tell you something buster."

"Buster this!" Billy flipped him the finger.

"Wait man, wait." Detective Wright calmed down. "Look, getting mad is not going to solve your problem."

"It's a start," Billy bellowed, not taking his eyes off of the detective.

"Would you please calm down, and give me a second to speak? I'm here to help you, if you give me the chance." Detective Wright let the words tumble off his tongue before Billy had a chance to stop them from flowing.

"Help me? Yeah, rrright," he said, sounding more like a player than a lawyer.

Detective Wright tried to smile, but it was lost on Billy, and added, "Just give me a chance to explain. Hear me out." He cut his eyes at Billy.

Billy hesitated; he didn't want anymore of Detective Wright's bull. However, he shot the detective a reserved look. "You have the floor." It was all he could say.

"I've been investigating this case around the clock."

"Good for you," Billy sneered, as he watched the detective's face slowly drain itself of energy. Billy watched him as every muscle in his body tightened, but he held his composure. Detective Wright was wrecking his nerves causing his pressure to rise in the pit of his guts, like a hard ball. He became weak. Taking a few steps backward, not taking his eyes off of Detective Wright, he eased himself down on the bunk.

"Are you alright?" Detective Wright asked. "You don't look so good. Do I need to call someone?"

"No, no, I'm okay," Billy uttered. The last thing he wanted was more help from this man.

"Sure about that?" Detective Wright grew concerned about Billy. This suddenly burst of caring for this man surprised him. He pretended to glance at his watch.

"I'm sure, Detective," Billy growled.

"As I was saying, regarding this case," Detective Wright changed the subject. He didn't want to set Billy off again. "I put a lot of consideration in what you kept saying about your innocence, and I hate to see a man pay for someone else's crime. If you didn't kill Ms. Stone, then who did? I have a hunch about you, and no matter how much I try to shake it off, it still stares me straight in the face."

Billy looked at Detective Wright with interest. Was he hearing this right? He thought to himself. Did the detective believe he was innocent? Humph! Surprises come in all packages.

"I talked with a witness yesterday, and he gave me some information that may clear your name."

"Why is he just now coming forth with this information?" Billy asked, as the pressure in his stomach began to back off.

"These things take time."

"Yeah, long enough for me to rot in this cell," Billy snapped, and quickly regretted it. Even though he loathed the man at least he was trying to help. He decided he wouldn't interrupt the detective anymore. He would hear what he had to say.

"On the day of Ms. Stone's death, I have a witness who saw Ms. Stone hanging out with an older man." Detective Wright pulled out his notepad again. He read the description of the man. "Do you know anyone who fits that description?" he asked. He could tell Billy was searching his memory.

"No, not at the moment," Billy replied, the pressure subsided relieving the ball in the pit of his guts.

"And, there was a young lady." Detective Wright read her description.

"Janet," Billy thought aloud.

"So you know her?"

"Huh?" Billy frowned, and focused back on Detective Wright. Janet's face flashed before his eyes.

"You know the young lady?"

"Janet." Billy rose to his feet. "Yeah, her name is Janet Wingo. What does she have to do with this?" He asked.

"Apparently, a lot. It seems our Ms. Wingo has something to hide."

"You think she killed Sheila?"

"That's my hunch," Detective Wright answered.

"Man," Billy was speechless.

"Do you know where I can find Ms. Wingo?"

"Ah, she lives across town in Union Place near the lake," he said, then remembered the address. "827 Union Hill Drive."

"Are you a praying man, Mr. Ray?" Detective Wright asked smiling through the bars.

Billy's frown deepened. "I don't believing in praying, Detective," he articulated the words sourly.

"Too bad." Detective Wright stepped away from the cell.

Billy didn't want to talk religion with the detective. As far as he was concerned, God was in Heaven doing his thing, and he was on earth doing his.

"Mr. Ray, whether you acknowledge it or not, I believe someone is praying for you. They have to be, because I had you guilty on the first day I saw you in Ms. Stone's apartment. You were guilty as hell to me then, and I can't figure out why I don't feel that way now. Usually, I'll say, 'Lock him up and throw away the key, if he didn't commit this crime, there's another crime he did commit." Detective Wright cleared his throat, scanned the cellblock, and then gazed at Billy again.

"Maybe its just good old-fashioned luck," Billy threw the statement out, hoping Detective Wright would take the bait and run with it instead of honing in on God.

"Perhaps." Detective Wright shrugged his shoulders. "Anyway, I'm going to call on Ms. Wingo, maybe she has something she wants to tell me."

"Janet can be stubborn," Billy said abruptly and knew he had spoken too fast.

"You knew her quite well, huh?" Detective Wright eyed Billy with a sheepish grin plastered across his face.

"Janet and I had some dealings, and that's all I'm willing to say on the subject."

"I understand Mr. Ray, but do keep in mind, if, and that's a really big if, if Ms. Wingo is our killer, people can point fingers and say you urged her to kill Ms. Stone. And, don't look over the fact that Ms. Wingo may agree with your accusers and name you as her accomplice," Detective Wright warned Billy of all the angles concerning the case.

"What about the old man?" he asked, refusing to accept Janet as the killer.

"Yeah, the old man. You want to know what I think? I think the old man was really pissed with Ms. Stone about something. Perhaps, she didn't take advantage of his wanting to spend some time with her."

"Maybe," Billy replied, as Darrell's face ran across his mind like a marquee. He could see his father clearly now as he flopped down on his bunk. His eyes registered on the detective.

"What is it, Mr. Ray?" Detective Wright asked.

"The old man, read his description for me again, please." A sickening feeling washed over him as he recalled the face of Darrell and that of Fred. "No, forget it for a second I thought it was someone I knew," Billy said, staring at the ceiling.

"Sure?" Detective Wright asked.

"I'm sure."

"There's isn't anything you want to tell me?" Detective asked, as he surveyed Billy lying on the bunk staring at the ceiling.

"No," he replied.

"Okay," Detective Wright paused. Billy was hiding something, and he could smell it, but what? He'd get to the bottom of it sooner or later. He preferred sooner, but he had to make the best of what he had for now, Janet. "I'll talk to you later," he said, as he turned to leave. "Oh, there's one more thing," Detective Wright said turning and facing Billy again.

"What's that?" Billy eyes bored through the detective.

"Tell me about the money." He walked back to the cell and stood in front of it.

"What money?" Billy expressed questionably.

"Mr. Ray, you are a smart attorney, and if you don't come clean with me, how can I help you?"

"I don't know what you're talking about," he said. He knew clearly what the detective was getting at. But he refused to confess that he knew about Sheila's fake pregnancy.

"Maybe this will jog your memory," Detective Wright said, pressing against the cell bars. "On the evening Ms. Stone was killed, she was clutching six hundred dollars in her hand. Do you have any ideal where she got the money?"

Billy stared at the detective for what seemed like hours before replying. Had the detective stumbled on a clue, and why didn't he notice the money in Sheila's hand when he had found her? The questions raced through his mind. "Off the record, Detective?" he asked and waited for Detective Wright to reply.

"Okay, off the record," he said looking sternly at him.

"I dropped by Sheila's house earlier that day to talk. She had been spreading some bad news about me." Billy paused for a moment, watching the detective's reaction.

"News about the baby?" Detective Wright asked.

He nodded his head slowly. "Yes, she claimed I was the father. So, Travis and I paid her a visit. She confessed she was pregnant, and I was the father. I asked her to get rid of the baby. Then, I laid six hundred dollars on the table. She became extremely upset and refused to have an abortion. I quickly left her house. I planned to visit her again later when we were alone. Maybe then I could talk some sense into her. But when I arrived at her apartment…you know the rest."

"Off the record?" he asked, and flashed Billy a weak smile.

"Off the record," Billy answered.

"Yeah, yeah," Detective said.

"Thanks man," Billy said glancing at him through the bars.

"Ah, forget it," the detective replied, shrugging his shoulders, and walking away from the cell.

"Don't be so modest, Detective!"

"Yeah, yeah." He waved his hand and walked out of the cellblock.

What was Darrell doing back in Silver Rock, and what's he trying to prove?

Where has he been all these years, and what does he want, now? These questions attacked Billy. This episode in his life has been one roller coaster ride down hill. It didn't seem real, like someone had written a book, headlined him as the main character but forgot to tell him.

* * * * * * ***

Detective Wright sat behind his small desk typing as he played the interview in his mind that he had with Aaron. Aaron mentioned Ms. Wingo acted like something or someone had frightened her when she ran out of Ms. Stone's apartment. She could have run out because she saw Ms. Stone's lifeless body crumpled on the sofa. But why didn't she scream for help or get someone's attention? Why did she run out of the victim's apartment without saying a word to anyone? The answer lies with Ms. Wingo. She was the key. He could feel it. The hunch was too strong and he knew without a shadow of a doubt that he was on the right lead. He'd bet his last dollar that she played a major role in the death of Ms. Stone. Mr. Ray and Ms. Wingo had a continued fling, and in walked Ms. Stone getting Mr. Ray's attention, initiating a love triangle. Ms. Wingo wasn't hearing that and in a passion rage, she killed her. The story was a shot in the dark, but he'd bet his life he wasn't too far off the path. Detective Wright finished typing up the affidavit and the no knock search warrant and placed the papers inside an envelope, and put the envelope inside his suit jacket. Now it was the time to visit Judge Bennett to sign the warrant. Detective Wright pushed himself up from behind his desk and strolled casually to the door and walked out.

Chapter 30

"*M*r. Malcolm you have to stop and eat," Ms. King said in a concerned tone. "You haven't stopped working since you arrived. You have to eat something." Ms. King put her head inside Travis' office.

"I'll grab a bite as soon as I finish going over Mr. Ray's files. I promise." Travis smiled at Ms. King. She had become like a mother to him, fussing over him. It reminded him of his own mother. He wondered had his parents heard the news. He knew they hadn't and wondered should he give them a call. But the thought disappeared as quickly as it had appeared. Besides, he didn't have the heart to call and upset them. He'd wait and see how things turned out. Maybe he wouldn't have to tell them at all.

"You see that you do just that," she replied. "I worry about you and Mr. Ray." Ms. King's eyes misted a little, and then she started to close the door.

"Ms. King."

"Yes?" she asked putting her head back through the door.

"Ms. King, I want to tell you how much I appreciate you, and the others. If it wasn't for you ladies, this firm wouldn't last long."

"That's a kind thing to say." Ms. King's eyes watered as she looked at Travis.

"Thank you for managing the office while I was away."

"Anytime, Mr. Malcolm," she said wiping away her tears gently with the back of her hand. "And please, get Mr. Ray off the hook because we know he's innocent."

"I'll do my best," Travis said.

"I know you will, and that's good enough for us," Ms. King said sweetly. Then, she closed the door behind her.

Travis closed his eyes and laid his head against his chair, and bounced an eraser head pencil against his chin, allowing his mind to digest what he had been studying concerning Billy's case. Everything had happened so fast that he couldn't believe it had been a month since the arrest of his best friend. And plus he hadn't seen Billy in almost a week. He had to face him and today had to be that day. Billy would be furious regarding his deficiency with the case, and who could blame him? But what could he have done? He could have done anything except run away, he thought.

Reopening his eyes, he stuffed the files inside his briefcase and pushed himself up from his chair behind his desk. He quickly put on his suit jacket, and marched out the door into the reception area. Ms. King and the other secretaries smiled as he walked toward them.

"I'm glad to see you're taking a break," Ms. King said with a twinkle in her eyes.

"Yes, we have been worried about you," another secretary proclaimed.

"Uh-huh, I thought we'd have to bust into your office and tow you out," Yareli laughed at her colorful language. But the laughter fell on death ears amongst her peers. "Well, I thought it was funny," Yareli said weakly.

"Thanks for your concern," Travis said to Yareli. "Forgive me for not laughing, but I thought it was funny, too. My problem is I've rested too much already, and it's time for me to get back to work and take care of the business at hand." He set his briefcase on the receptionist's desk. "I hope you ladies don't mind watching the office again today. I'm going to see Mr. Ray, and ladies please pray for me," he smiled imagining how upset Billy must be.

"Please, give Mr. Ray our love," Ms. King added.

"Yes, give him our love," the other secretaries chimed in.

"That, I will do," Travis replied as he picked up his briefcase. "Ladies, once again, thanks and I'll see you all tomorrow."

"We'll see you tomorrow and drive carefully," they all said at once, watching him as he walked out the door.

Once out on the street, Travis walked to his car and composed himself behind the steering wheel. For a moment he sat quietly thinking about Christ and the blood He shed for the world. Christ didn't commit any crime or wrongdoing, yet He was jailed, beat and treated like a common criminal. He was nailed to the cross. He was pierced in the side. Blood and water gushed from his pierced side and it ran down the cross washing away our sins. The same blood that took away the sins of the world can take away his best friend's sins. He had prayed for Billy more than he could count, and it didn't seem to affect him in anyway. Some people won't be saved, he thought, maybe Billy was one of those people. But the scripture, First Timothy Chapter two, verses one, three, five and six came to mind, "I urge, then, first of all, that requests, prayers, intercession and thanksgiving be made for everyone. This is good, and pleases God our Savior, who wants all men to be saved and to come to acknowledge of the truth. For there is one God and one mediator between God and men, the man Christ Jesus, who gave himself as a ransom for all men-the testimony given in its proper time."

He sat there a little while longer meditating on the scriptures. "That's it," he said. "God's desire is for all men to be saved, and why not Billy? God's desire is for Billy to be saved also." A huge smile tugged at the corners of his mouth, because it wasn't too late for his best friend. He prayed, "Father, I pray for Billy that through Your mercy and Your loving kindness, please save him. Thank You, in the name of Jesus." He started the car and pulled out of the parking lot. He engaged the CD and Michael Redman's song of worship filled the car. He bellowed the tune, "'I'm going back to the heart of worship. It's all about You. It's all about You, Jesus.'"

* * * * * * * * * *

"It sho' was nice seein' you again," Mae Ella said walking Adrienne to her car. "I thought you were going to spend the night with me."

"It was nice seeing you, too, Ms. Wingo. As much as I'd like to stay all night, I've got to get back to Silver Rock."

"I understand but be careful driving home. It's so much happening out there. It bothers me knowing you have to drive so far, alone."

"I'll be fine once I get on the interstate." Adrienne swept her hair back with the tips of her fingers.

"Yeah, things are gonna work out for you and your husband, you'll see," Mae Ella proclaimed, giving Adrienne a slight hug.

Adrienne pretended not to hear, as she returned the hug. Then she opened her car door, and tossed her purse onto the passenger seat. Facing Mae Ella again as if she hadn't spoken about her husband. "I'm going to go by Janet's house when I get back."

"Do that, I'm sure that girl is home with her feet propped up, and here we are worrying 'bout her for no reason at all." Mae Ella smiled.

"I'm sure you're right," Adrienne replied as a smile tried to tug at the corners of her mouth, but didn't quite make it. She was worried about her friend and had every right to be. Janet was acting weird; it was totally out of character to distance her self like that.

"I know I am," Mae Ella replied.

Adrienne hugged Mae Ella again. This time she hugged her more firmly and kissed her on her cheek. "I'll call you when I get home."

"Okay, baby, and don't you be upset with Janet. She's all right and like I said, I bet she's at home, 'cause where else could she be? I'm her only kin, and she hates staying in those motels. My baby loves Silver Rock and she's not gonna stay away from it too long."

"Okay," Adrienne said retreating from Mae Ella. She got into her car and started up the engine. "I'll call you when I hear from her."

"The same here," Mae Ella promised.

Adrienne closed the car door and blew Mae Ella a kiss as she pulled away from the curb. Mae Ella watched the car as it became smaller and smaller down the long stretched road. "I hope things work out," she said still looking in the direction of the car until it disappeared from her view.

* * * * * * * * * *

Kareem Bennett wasn't just an ordinary judge; he was the first African-American judge elected in Silver Rock. He worked hard proving he was the best man for the job. He stole a quick glance at his name "Judge Kareem Bennett" inscribed in gold on an oblong name plate on his desk. A smile lit across his face; he had reached his ultimate goal of becoming the first African-American judge of that town. It had been a long time coming and the wait was exhilarating.

Judge Bennett sat behind his desk looking over a case when Keron Anderson, his secretary, buzzed his intercom phone. "Judge Bennett, I'm sorry to disturb you," she said in a whispery tone into the phone, "but Detective Wright is here to see you, sir."

"Okay, Ms. Anderson, but give me a few minutes, and then send him in," he replied. He lay the file folder down and rose to his feet, and picked up his cup of coffee, and walked from behind his desk. He took a sip of the hot, steamy coffee and positioned himself on the sofa, setting his cup on the end table beside the chair. A few minutes later, Keron opened the door and stepped aside for the detective to enter the room. Leaving the two men alone, she closed the door behind her.

"Good evening, Detective Wright," Judge Bennett rose to his feet and extended his hand to the detective.

"Good evening Judge Bennett," he replied shaking the judge's hand.

"Have a seat," he said withdrawing his hand from Detective Wright. He pointed at the single chair across from him.

"Thanks." Detective Wright walked to the chair and sat down.

"What can I do for you?" he asked, sitting in his chair again.

"Judge Bennett, I have a search warrant for Ms. Janet Wingo. Sir, I have probable cause she's our killer. I believe she murdered Ms. Sheila Stone." Detective Wright took out the search warrant and handed it to Judge Bennett. Judge Bennett looked over the warrant.

"Who's Janet Wingo?"

"She was a friend of the victim. And she was seen on the day Ms. Stone was killed. A witness saw her rushing out of Ms. Stone's apartment a few minutes before Mr. Ray arrived." Detective Wright leaned forward; he watched Judge Bennett process the information, before adding, "Sir, I believe we have the wrong person locked up for killing Ms. Stone."

"Are you sure of this?" Judge Bennett frowned. The last thing he needed was a circle case. The papers would love to perpetrate the S.R. P.D. as a bunch of clowns.

"I'm positive," he answered. "Mr. Ray, he's plenty of things, but he's no killer." He clasped his hands together and folded them in front of him.

"Why is this witness just now coming   forward   with   this information?" Judge Bennett asked.

"He didn't want to get involved."

"What made him come forth now?"

"I don't know — maybe his conscience wouldn't let him sleep.

"Where does Ms. Wingo fit in all of this?"

"The jealous girlfriend."

"What brought you to that conclusion?"

"My gut instinct. I won't rest until I know for a fact Ms. Wingo isn't the killer. My witness saw her rushing from the apartment and a few minutes later, Mr. Ray shows up. She could have set him up. I don't know," he said it more to himself than to Judge Bennett.

"Why would she go through all of the trouble of setting him up? It was a risk on her part of getting caught?"

"I don't know all the small details yet, but I'll bet Ms. Wingo is our murderess." Detective Wright didn't go around betting on any and everything. But when he had a gut feeling about something, it was worth betting.

"I hope you're right Detective Wright. It doesn't look good for one of ours to be accused of murder," he was speaking of Billy. Then, he pulled a pen from his shirt pocket and signed the warrant. He gave it back to the detective. Detective Wright slipped it inside his suit jacket.

"I have a strong hunch about this case," Detective Wright said in a confidential tone. "Twenty years of fighting crime have paid off big, and besides these hunches have never failed me, yet."

"Make sure it stays that away. That's the last thing we need."

"Don't worry sir, you won't regret a thing."

"I better not." Judge Bennett's tone carried a matter-of-fact.

"You can trust me," Detective Wright said, as he pushed himself up from the chair.

****

Janet, restless, paced the small motel room, as the memory of Shelia's death loomed vividly in front of her, larger than life itself. The ashtray was overrun with dozens of half-burnt Doral's; she frowned disgustingly at them. She wasn't a smoker and detested the things. But now they had become her only friend, and besides, they did calm her wrecked nerves. "What have I done?" she asked herself, gazing around the room. "I can't go on like this. I need to tell someone what I've done." She made her way to the bed and dropped down on it. She turned on her back and stared at the ceiling. "Oh, Mama, your baby isn't so innocent anymore," she groaned moving her head from side to side. "I killed someone!" her voice rose to a high pitch tone. "I killed Sheila. Ooh, Billy what have I done to you? Please don't hate me for getting you in this mess. I love you. I did it for us. I could not stand to know you were in the arms of Sheila. I shared you with Adrienne, wasn't that enough?" She sobbed. "I did it because I love you, can't you see that? You love me I know it. It's me that you love, not Sheila or Adrienne, but me, me!"

She curled her fingers into fists and beat on the pillow before burying her head into it.

* * * * * * * * * *

Adrienne looked at the car clock; she had made good timing when she drove into Silver Rock. She had driven non-stop, ignoring the speed limit and the possibility of a ticket. The words Mae Ella spoke had occupied her mind, until they were actually making sense to her. She considered Mae Ella's wisdom, but inside she understood there wasn't any forgiveness for her husband. Anyway, if she did take him back, how would life be for them? This deception would always come between them. She had lost her trust in him, an important factor that couldn't easily be retrieved. Day by day she would grow resentful of him, and she loved him too much to allow that to happen. What am I to do? The thought plagued her as she turned left onto Fairfield Lane.

A few minutes later, she turned into her driveway and cut off the engine. She opened the door and jumped out. Once inside she rested her head against the sofa and reenacted the scene at the home of Janet's mother. Mae Ella had pleaded with her to give her marriage a second chance. But how could she, when she felt anything but forgiveness? *Women like Mae Ella were too outmoded in this day and time. Time had changed and the sooner they discovered this, the better off they'd be.* Her thoughts lingered.

A second chance, humph, a second chance hadn't crossed her mind. He had betrayed her, and she had the right to disbar herself from the marriage. Did he really love her, or did he use her to be the perfect wife for the perfect lawyer? The questions drained her. She lay on the sofa wondering did he care about her at all.

Then, the kiss she had shared with Travis sparked an interest in her own unfaithfulness. She had thoroughly enjoyed the passion between them, even though she knew she shouldn't have let it gone that far. But this was different, she thought. She hadn't gone all the way with Travis. Anyway, she was justified in the way she acted with him. Billy didn't care about their marriage so why should she? Adrienne's thoughts escapade around Billy's infidelity, and she had very good reasons why she should have cheated on him with his best friend. But she now secretly thanked Travis for keeping his head and not allowing things to get out of hand. She remembered him talking about how he couldn't do this to God. For the first time, she wondered what God was like? Whatever it was, Travis seemed to respect it. She couldn't remember Travis talking to her about God at any other time, except for that particular night.

But then Travis wasn't any better, he had lied to protect Billy for who knows how long? She should still be angry at Travis, and she tried to continue in that vein, but her heart yielded against it. She wouldn't stay angry with him long. The sound of the doorbell traveled through the house, awakening her trip down memory lane. "Who could that be?" She asked, as she rose from the sofa. She hadn't informed her parents of her arrival. As far as they were concerned, she was still in Lost Gap. The doorbell rang again. "Maybe its Janet." Adrienne put on her brightest smile and rushed to the door. She opened it, and Travis stood on the other side.

"Hi," he said, watching her but kept his mind focused on why he was there.

"Hi Travis," she replied, not knowing what to do. Should she invite him in or slam the door in his face?

"Listen Adrienne, I have to talk to you. Please, may I come in?" he asked, hoping she had a change of heart. He wanted desperately to salvage their relationship.

"I don't think it's wise for you to be here," she suggested as the feeling of betrayal started to rise again.

"C'mon, Adrienne we need to talk. Please hear me out." He stepped closer to the door, putting one foot over the threshold. He had to talk to her. Please, Lord help me, he thought.

"Hmmm." She tapped her fingernails on the surface of the door before answering, "Okay, only for a few minutes, and please be quick about it. I was in the middle of packing." She stepped aside to let him pass.

"Thanks," he said as he walked passed her into the house. Thank you Lord, the thought raced through his mind.

"Don't mention it," she said closing the door and led him into the living room. "Have a seat," she said, waiting for him to sit. He sank into Billy's favorite chair. "What's on your mind?" she asked as she sat on the sofa across from him.

"Us. I have us on my mind," he said without taking his eyes off of her.

"Us?" she looked puzzled.

"Yes, us," he repeated, and leaned forward in the chair.

"What about us?" she balked.

"Adrienne, I'm terribly sorry for leading you on. I shouldn't have kissed you, nor should I have confessed my feelings to you. Please forgive me for that. And I should have been honest with you about Billy. I should have warned you a long time ago. Please, can you find it in your heart to forgive me?" The words Travis spoke were sincere. He deeply wanted her forgiveness if nothing else. Adrienne's friendship and her forgiveness mattered strongly to him. He didn't want to lose any of that. He acted wrong with their friendship and had taken it for granted. It hurt him. It was almost like losing a family member.

"Travis, I do believe I played a role in our little...well you know what I'm trying to say." Her mouth twisted in a tight, little smile. She felt uncomfortable in the room with Travis staring at her, watching her every move.

"No, Adrienne, I knew better than to put my hands on you. I was wrong. I was only thinking about myself."

"We both were thinking about our—"

"No," he cut her off. "You're married to my best friend, and you were happy with him until your little disagreement in Hawaii. I took advantage of your pain and tried to win your love through it. I didn't care what it would have done to you or to Billy. Acquiring your heart was my top priority. I'm embarrassed to recall the thoughts I had toward you. I wanted you more than anything even life itself," he explained to her.

Her voice rose a little. "So, how do you feel now?"

"I still love you," he admitted, "but I can't allow any of my feelings toward you to take me away from my relationship with Christ. I've repented for my actions and asked God to forgive me of my sins. He has forgiven me, and I have to move on in my life. And in time I'll meet the woman God has for me." Travis spoke sincerely.

His words sank into her heart, "Uh, uh," was all she could say. She frantically searched for words but none came.

"I'm here asking you to forgive me, also." He shot her a pleading look. Perplexed, mixed emotions raced through the core of her soul. A part of her begged to give in to his plea, and another part of her pushed to flee from his presence.

"I, I, don't know what to say." She rose to her feet dumbfounded.

"Just say you'll forgive me," he replied. His words filled with hope.

"I don't know if I can forgive you, Travis," she said turning her back to him. "You did hurt me."

"I know I hurt you, and I'm truly sorry, believe me. If I could wipe out everything I've done to you, I would." Travis pushed himself up from the recliner, walking to her. He reached for her, and touched her softly as he turned her toward him and looked into her eyes. She could see tears forming in his eyes, and it tugged at her heart.

"I, uh, ooh, Travis," she whispered softly.

"Please, please forgive me," he said as tears ran smoothly down his face. "I don't want to lose our friendship. This has taught me a very valuable lesson. Be truthful at all times, no matter what." He wiped the tears away.

"I hope you truly learned a lesson from all of this." She looked at him, as her heart begin to surrender to his sincere words.

"Trust me, I did."

Reluctantly, she answered, "Okay, Travis I forgive you."

"Thank you Adrienne," he said and wrapped his arms around her. "This means a lot to me. Thank you for forgiving me."

"You're forgiven," she said, returning the hug.

"Thank you, Jesus," he whispered and released her.

* * * * * * * * * *

Mary R. Butler

Darrell stood near the trash bin outside the Quick Mart convenient store. Finding an empty beer bottle he picked it up and threw it, shattering one side of the store's window. "Now, that should do the job," he said to himself, as he waited for the store clerk to run out.

Chapter 31

$\mathcal{T}$he officer walked him down the cellblock corridor. He pressed the metal button, and the cell door opened. He led Darrell into the empty cell and unlocked his handcuffs, and walked out, leaving him alone in the cell. Darrell looked around the old familiar place; it was the same one he had been released from earlier. Darrell looked past the officer, because he wanted to see his son. But Billy was asleep on the bunk. Good, he thought, it would give him enough time to think about what he's going to say to him. Darrell sat on the bunk watching his son as he tossed and turned on his bunk. He reminded him so much of himself. Billy was an exact copy of him when he was that age. It was like looking at himself in a mirror; only the mirror was caught in a time zone. Darrell sat in the empty cell remembering how easy it was when Edna was alive, and Billy had been crazy about him. Those were the days, he thought.

"Hah!" Billy jumped, kicking his legs over the side of the bed trying to catch his breath. And clasping his hands over his face, he leaned toward the floor. Shaking all over. How his head pounded maliciously as he softly massaged the sides of his temple looking for relief.

Billy remembered the dream vividly; it had awakened him and frightened him badly. He had walked into a monstrous, colorful room filled with the best furniture, cars, and clothes money could buy. One hundred dollar bills covered the four gigantic walls, and an oversized mahogany chair sat in the middle of the room. He stood amazed at the superior of the room focusing in on its splendor, and on each item as he made his way to the oversized chair and sat in it. A broad smile tugged at the corners of his mouth, and it erupted into a full laugh. He had finally reached his goal—to be the richest man the world has seen. "Oh Man!" he shouted. "All this is mine! I'm filthy rich! Ooh money! Money! Money! Money. I'm rich! Yes, yes!" He shouted, leaping from the chair and dancing around it. "I'm rich! I'm rich! I'm rich!" he shouted happily. "Hear me world? I'm rich!" he declared, as he strolled joyfully to the money-covered walls. Pulling a hundred dollar from the wall, he rolled it into a cigar shape and pretended to smoke it. He laughed while throwing the cigar-shaped money to the floor and pulling more from the wall. He threw a handful of it in the air. He ran around the room grabbing money from the walls and throwing it in the air. Afterward, he rushed to the rows of cars. There were a variety of Rolls-Royce models everywhere. There were Rolls-Royce Corniche, Silver Spirit, Silver Spirit III, Park Ward, Silver Seraph, Silver Wraith II, Silver Shadow, Silver Shadow II, Phantom, Phantom V, Phantom VI, Silver Dawn, and even a Silver Spur II Touring Limousine. He opened the car door to the Corniche convertible and slid comfortably behind the steering wheel. He stroked the dash made of fine wood and the fine wood covering the console and waist rails. The choice wood was wonderful and pleasing to his touch. He glided his hand across the full Connolly hide upholstery and laid his head back on the headrest. He had finally arrived, and it felt great. What would he do with all his money? He would bank it and make more, he thought. But his thoughts died suddenly, as he watched in horror, as millions of worms ate themselves through the walls and began eating the money from the walls. He quickly got out of the Rolls and ran frantically to the wall in front of him, beating wildly at the worms. But the worms were untouchable. There wasn't anything he could do to stop the hungry parasites from eating his money.

Then, suddenly there was a loud explosion, and Billy turned to face the noise and saw that everything in the room had burst into flames. The cars, the clothes, the furniture and the money were gone. Fire raced across the room, surrounding him. He could feel the intensity of the heat as the flames licked wildly at him. He was a dead man as far as he was concerned. Every   dream,   hope,   and   goal came crashing down at his feet. Then, without warning fire coursed through his body causing excruciating pain. Collapsing on the floor, as the fire raced through his body creating more pain worst than the last. "Help, help me, God!" he uttered, as he closed his eyes waiting for death to devour him, in fact he welcomed it.

It was all too real, he thought holding his face in his hands rocking back and forth as sweat drenched his face. The dry ham and cheese sandwich he had eaten earlier made its way back up, causing him to leap from his bunk, throwing his head over the toilet emptying his lunch. He sat there over the toilet a little while longer before working up the nerves to abandon it. Flushing the toilet, he wiped his face with the tail of his shirt. The dream had drained him. It was all so real.

"What's your problem, buddy?" Darrell asked, looking at Billy through the cell bars.

"Huh?" He looked up, looking through the cell bars.

"It's me, Fred. I thought I would never see you again, but I'm back. Hey, what's the matter with you?" Darrell rose to his feet and walked to the cell bars. "The way you leaped up out of your sleep like you saw a ghost or something." Billy couldn't believe his eyes. Here was Fred, but it wasn't Fred trying to have small talk with him. The man who had abandoned him so long ago stood a few feet from him pretending to be someone else. Billy rose steady to his feet and walked to the cell bar.

"Where have you been?" Billy asked coolly. The question was packed with ammunition. He shot Darrell a scowling look and sarcastically asked the question again. "Where have you been hiding?"

"Hiding? Man, naw," he laughed. "I hadn't been hiding."

Billy ignored Darrell's answer and asked, "Are you from here?" Darrell didn't discern Billy's sarcastic tone or the resentment in his voice.

"No."

"Silver Rock is a nice city, man, a good place to live. What made you visit our little town, family?"

"Mmmh," he paused. "You can say that."

"Now what does that mean? You can say that. Either you have

family in town or not. Which one is it?" he became irritable. He hated Darrell.

"I had a family here once," Darrell said slowly, noticing the change in Billy's voice. He looked across the cell into Billy's eyes, and he knew his secret was out. Billy knew he was his father. "I'm sorry son," he said.

"Sorry? Sorry? That's all you have to say? I'm sorry son! Damn, I'm sorry too. I'm sorry you had me. And now you want to waltz back into my life as if nothing happened. The long lost Darrell! Listen man, my father died a long time ago and dead people don't come back, and they sure don't talk." He pushed the words through clenched teeth, not giving Darrell a chance to defend himself.

"What y'all talking about down there?" Someone shouted from down the cellblock.

"Stay out of this," Billy shouted back.

"Okay, but y'all need to shut up so I can get some sleep."

"Up yours," Billy shouted.

"Look," Darrell interjected in a pleading tone, "I know it was wrong leaving you the way I did and saying all those bad things to you. I regretted it since the day I left. I wanted to come back to get you, but I was too ashamed, so I stayed away. I knew the Malcolm's would take good care of you. Billy, I am truly sorry, and I want to make it up to you. Please let me do that?"

"What the hell are you talking about? Make up? Seventeen years wasted, and you want to make up!"

Darrell searched his son's eyes for mercy, but there was none.

"Nothing to say, huh? I thought so," he snapped. "Do you want to know something?" he smirked. "I don't need you! Never had!"

"But, but—"

"Drop dead!" Billy snapped, and turned his back toward Darrell.

Darrell's voice quivered, "I love you," as tears slowly rolled down his cheeks.

"Love!" Billy turned facing Darrell again. "Don't talk to me about love! Just get away from me old man." Billy gestured his hand at Darrell, dismissing him, and walked back to his bunk and lay with his back facing Darrell.

Travis walked into the police department filled with hope. God had answered his prayer and worked things out between them. Adrienne had forgiven him. Now it was time to face Billy. He strolled to the front desk and signed in.

"Oh, Mr. Malcolm, Detective Wright would like to have a word with you," a pretty female officer spoke behind the desk.

"He's in his office?"

"No, he's with the DA."

"The DA?" he looked puzzled.

"Yes, but he should be arriving anytime now," she assured him.

"Thank you."

"You're welcome," she smiled.

He walked to the guard window and flashed his identification card and strolled through the entrance. He had been away too long. Man, he couldn't wait for this episode of his life to blow over and for everything to return to normal. But things wouldn't be the same between him and Billy. He couldn't continue to be unequally yoked with someone. He had to cut off his partnership with Billy and find himself a new partner—someone who shared the same belief as he. One Sunday Pastor Johnson had said, "A believer must have the attitude that they're saved because they love God, and hate sin. Because the love of God won't leave any room for the position of sin. Hating sin is a life preserver. It will keep us from doing wrong, from committing sin. Loving God motivates us. God doesn't deliver us from our friends, but from our enemies. The thing that we love so much more than God is an enemy to us, and we don't want to get rid of it. Instead we bear it because it has become a friend. It hadn't made sense to him then, but at that very moment, it became crystal clear. A person's attitudes, habits, and anything else that's destroying him and keeping him away from God is an enemy. Even though it is an enemy, it has been embraced as a friend.

Travis walked through the cellblock's door. He had to end it with Billy as soon as possible. Billy would be furious, yes. But he'd bounce back in no time. This, he was sure of.

"Hey." He said, as he stood outside Billy's cell. Billy turned, facing him and shot him an angry look with his eyes.

"Man, where the hell you been?" Billy hoisted himself up from the bunk.

"I'm sorry I ran off without telling you, but I had a pretty good reason. Please don't be upset." Travis set his briefcase on the floor.

"What is this? Suddenly everyone is sorry."

"Huh?" he replied.

Billy walked toward Travis. "If I hear that word I'm sorry one more time, I'm going to kill someone for real."

"But, I am—"

"Don't say it!" he interjected.

"What's eating you? I was gone only for a few days."

"And that's too long for my attorney. What's wrong with you man? Disappearing on me like that. The case getting too hard for you?"

"Look, I said I was sorry. I wasn't myself lately. I had to get away. Surely you can understand that?"

"Forget it," he uttered and walked back to the bunk. He lay on it again.

"He's mad with me," Darrell spoke for the first time since Travis arrived.

"Huh?" Travis turned, facing the cell behind him. "What did you say?"

"Don't talk to him," Billy snapped loudly.

"He's upset with me."

"Why?" Travis eyed Darrell. Then it hit him, at first like a slow moving train. But it hit him just the same, and it hit hard as he recognized the old man from the office. A chill swept through him as he stared into Darrell's eyes. He had seen those eyes before, but where? Travis' mind flashed back when he was a boy standing on the Ray's front porch talking with Billy's father. "Mr. Ray?" Travis muttered.

Clapping his hands, Billy rose to his feet. "Bravo."

"Mr. Ray?" Travis said softly. "Ah, ah, I'm glad to see you again," he pushed his arm between the cell bars and grasped Darrell's hand.

"Thank you, Travis," he said pumping Travis' hand with joy. "It means so much to me to hear you say that."

"Why are you shaking his hand?" Billy asked disdainfully. "Have you forgotten how he abandoned me? The man doesn't deserve your kindness." The words spiraled from his mouth.

Travis ignored Billy as he released Darrell's hand. "Where have you been?" he asked excitedly, and added, "And what are you in here for?"

"Well, I've been living in Jackson, Tennessee," he answered, lowering his head. "And I'm in here because...well the first time for loitering on the town square. And I'm in here now for breaking a store window."

"Whew, how did you do that?"

"I broke it so I could be with my son, again," Darrell lifted his head making eye contact with him.

"Well, it worked," Travis smiled. "But don't worry, I'll see what I can do."

"I'm not worrying," he answered, looking beyond him and looking at Billy.

"Why didn't you say anything to me at the office?" Travis asked. He couldn't believe Billy's father had come back after all those years. It was like seeing a ghost.

"I was scared" he answered, still watching Billy.

"Oh, so you knew he was in town, and you didn't say anything about it? What a friend you turned out to be." Billy glared at Travis.

"No. He dropped by the office when you were in Hawaii. Honestly, I didn't have any idea it was your father until now."

"That is not my father," he uttered, pointing angrily at Travis.

"Edna would be proud of you son if she was alive," Darrell said, ignoring Billy's last statement.

"Leave my mother out of this!" Billy said, grabbing the cell bars. He pressed his face close between the bars. "Don't you ever mention her name again!"

"Please son, give me another chance," he said.

"Yeah, everyone deserves a second chance," Travis replied, watching Billy.

"Yeah, everyone except him." Billy snapped and walked away from the bars.

"Why not?" Travis asked.

"He doesn't deserve a second chance from me nor you. He can go to hell!" Billy sat on his bunk.

"C'mon Billy. You don't mean that?"

"Get off my back!"

"C'mon, Billy, you have to forgive your father for what he did and move on with your life."

"I have moved on with my life or haven't you noticed? Oh, I forgot, you're too busy playing this Holy Roller game until your head is stuck way up your ass!" Billy laughed wickedly.

"That's not funny," Travis frowned.

"Funny! Man, what do you know about funny? How funny was it when he allowed Mattie to treat me the way she did, huh? Was it funny when he walked out on me for her? Answer that. And was it funny when he told me he never wanted anything to do with me? I wish it was his body buried in that grave instead of my mother's." He stared fiercely at Darrell. "Now you're telling me God doesn't want this man in hell. What kind of God is that? Darrell should be in there and everyone like him."

"God is a merciful God, and he gives all of us a second chance to get it right with Him."

"I don't want to hear that, Travis. God took my mother, and He didn't stop Darrell from running away. What kind of God would let bad things happen to people, huh? Answer that. What kind of God would wipe out a child's family?"

"I don't know why your mother died, and I don't know why your father ran away with another woman, but I do know one thing, God loves you."

"Save that for your church."

"No, I'm saving it for you." Travis walked up to Billy's cell. "Stop blaming God for everything. God didn't kill your mother. She was sick, and she died. Has it ever crossed your mind that maybe God delivered your mama from her illness? And He had my family there to give you a home when your father deserted you? Do you think all these things were a surprise to God? Certainly not. He knows everything about you. There's nothing hidden from His sight. In the book of Jeremiah, He told Jeremiah, 'Before I formed you in the womb I knew you.' Billy, just like Jeremiah, God knew you before He formed you in your mother's womb. He knows everything about you, even down to the tiniest detail. God was not caught off guard when your mother died or when your father ran away. He prepared you before it all happened. But the only thing you can think of is getting even with your father, by letting him see how big of a man you have become."

"Screw you!" Billy said angrily.

"Why won't you listen?"

"Forget you," he muttered. "I don't need you!"

"What makes you think you don't need anyone?"

"Because I'm in control of my life."

"Listen to yourself. How ridiculous does that sound? Did you have control over your mother's death? Or your father's abandon - ment?"

"I was a child then, but now I'm a man, and I have control over my life!"

"What about Adrienne? Could you control her desire of not wanting to be a mother someday?"

"That doesn't count."

"Yes, it does count and so does everything else."

"I'm warning you to get off my back."

"What are you going to do?"

"I'm going to ..."

"Fire me?"

"Look, just stop talking to me about God. I don't want to hear it. Like I said, I'm in control of my life, and I don't need your God."

"You're not in control of your life or anything else as that goes. God is in control."

"Don't give me that," Billy snapped.

"It's true." Travis pressed against Billy's cell.

"Get out of my face!" Billy snapped, and lay on his bunk and stared at the ceiling.

"No, I won't get out of your face."

"Okay, stand there and do what you have to do if that makes you feel good, but I'm not listening."

"Billy no matter how you feel about God or what you say about Him, He loves you. He sent Jesus His Son to die for you. He reconciled us back to Himself through His Son." Billy ignored him. "Adam sinned against God in the garden of Eden by disobeying

God's command not to eat from the Tree of the Knowledge of Good and Evil. But Adam totally disregarded God's command and ate from the tree, anyway. That is when sin entered into the world through Adam. Because he disobeyed God's command not to eat of the tree. And that sin that Adam received progressed down through Adam's seed. This is why every man that is born through Adam's bloodline is a sinner."

"What can I do?" Darrell asked.

Travis turned, facing him and replied, "You must be born again."

"How?" he asked sincerely.

"Romans 10:9 says, 'Confess with your mouth Jesus Christ is Lord and believe in your heart God raised him from the dead and you shall be saved.'"

"I want that," Darrell replied.

"You want to be saved?" Travis asked and glanced at Billy. But Billy continued to ignore him.

"Yes, I want that." Darrell answered.

"Okay," he said, as he stood closer to Darrell's cell. He hadn't led anyone to salvation before; he didn't know exactly what to do. But he remembered how Pastor Simon had prayed that day for him. Travis stood in front of Darrell and said, "Repeat this prayer after me, and then when we're done, you can say what's on your heart to God."

"It's that simple?"

"Yes, it's that simple," he replied.

"Traitor!" Billy shouted as he rose to his feet. "He doesn't deserve to be saved. Leave him alone!" Billy scoffed.

"I can't do that Billy," he said as he began to pray.

After Darrell had received Jesus as his Lord and Savior, he also prayed. "God I don't know how to say this, but I messed up real bad with my son, and I hope things can be right with us, again." Darrell said, as he wiped his tears with the back of his hand.

"That's good." Travis said as he watched the tears flow down Darrell's face. His heart filled with compassion for him.

"Thank you," Darrell finally said.

"Ha!" Billy said loudly. "That's one prayer that won't get answered."

"Don't thank me, thank God."

"I wouldn't be too quick to thank God if I were him," Billy uttered. "Because there's no way things are going to get right between us." Billy couldn't believe Travis had chosen their relationship over Darrell. If this is the way Travis was going to act about God, then he'd find himself a new partner when things were over. There's no way he was going to share his business with a religious fanatic, and traitor.

* * * * * * * * * *

Detective Wright sat in his car outside Janet's house waiting for his back up. There was extreme calmness about the place. The house stood gravely in the shadows. The front yard was in bad need of mowing. He noticed the mailbox was stuffed with mail. A sure sign for any burglary. Looking at the search warrant, he read over the list again, and then placed the list back inside his suit jacket pocket. Tapping his fingers against the steering wheel, he began to talk to God. Now, Detective Wright didn't consider himself a God-fearing man, but he believed God was there and that was enough for him.

"God, you know, ah I don't know what I will find in this house. Hey, I don't even know why I am making such a big deal over this case. Maybe, Mr. Ray is guilty, and yeah, maybe he's not. But someone murdered that young woman and I got to find that someone. And if Ms. Wingo is that someone please let me find evidence against her. That's all I'm asking. Thanks." Detective Wright blinked his eyes and looked through the windshield at the sky and wondered had God heard him.

Chapter 32

"Mr. Ray, you're now a saved man, and every angel in Heaven is rejoicing because of that," Travis said in a joyful tone.

"I don't feel no different," Darrell replied, looking at Travis.

"Yeah, but trust me. You're saved. You're a new creature in Christ."

"Huh?" Darrell looked puzzled.

"You're a new man in Christ. The old man that you used to be is done away with, and you have become a new man. You're born again." Travis couldn't contain his joy as he looked at Darrell. Winning a soul to Christ felt great!

"Yeah, yeah, yeah." Billy watched from his bunk. He rubbed the empty place where his necklace should have been. He missed the security it brought him.

"Billy," Travis said, turning and facing him, "don't let what your father did to you in the past come between what you and he could have right now." Travis leaned against Billy's cell.

"What are you? A stranger?" Billy sat on his bunk glaring at Travis. "You prayed for someone and suddenly, you're a freaking hero! What that man done to me can't ever be erased! So, you can continue to play your all hail to the saints' role, but keep me the friggin' out! And another thing," Billy said as he walked to the cell and stood facing Travis. "Go ahead, enjoy your new buddy, but when this is over, I want you and your buddy to stay the hell away from me!"

"What does that mean?" Travis asked, staring at Billy.

"It means our partnership is dissolved!" Billy said angrily.

"You read my mind!" Travis snapped.

"Yeah? Well, that is good! Read this! When this is over our friendship is terminated, completed, finished!" Billy shouted, hitting the cell's bars and walking away.

"Good! I don't know why I went into business with you anyway. What a sap I've been!" Travis retreated a few steps backward. His body felt drained.

"You're not a sap, Travis." Darrell looked compassionately at Travis. "I'm the only sap in here. I left my son when he needed me, and I've been paying that price every day of my life."

Billy turned and faced Darrell. "Hooray for you!" he shouted. "Let's bring out the violins. The old man has been paying the price!"

"Billy, what I have to say to you, now, I know it won't matter. But I got to say what's on my heart. That night I said some bad things to you. I told you that the men in our family could never love their children. I lied. I loved you then, and I love you now. It hasn't changed. I have no excuse for my actions. I let a woman come between us." Darrell's eyes pleaded with Billy to give him another chance to prove his love.

"Let's get one thing straight old man, I don't need you!" Billy shouted. "I don't need anyone!" How could his father stand there and have the gall to look him in his face and lie? Billy didn't know how he could do it, but there's one thing he did know, Darrell was full of it.

"I love you," Darrell said, clasping his hands around the cell. He looked sadly at him. And Billy's heart grew colder. How dare this man think he can just come back to Silver Rock and think everything has been forgotten between them?

His anger seethed through his pores as he glared at Darrell. "Man, what do you know about love? Look at me! I'm a grown man, not some little schoolboy you pushed around after Edna died. You were right. You never did love me and now I can't love anything that comes from me! You did that to me!"

"Billy—" Travis said.

"No," Billy interjected. "I want him to hear, because of him, I blamed myself for not being the son he wanted. I kept asking myself, 'What's wrong with me?' You had me believing I wasn't worthy of your love! It hurt me right here!" Billy pounded his chest over his heart.

"Billy, if I could turn back the hands of time I would," Darrell replied. "Son, I messed up real bad. I had no idea it would hurt you that much. I thought with you staying with your best friend that you would get over me in a day or two." Darrell's eyes welled up with tears. He couldn't take anymore of this. He lowered his head.

"Billy, you didn't tell me." Travis stared in amazement. Sure, he knew it hurt Billy when his father ran out on him but not to this magnitude. Billy was always teasing and joking with his friends. He never once hinted how terrible it was for him.

"You were too busy being saved, remember?" Billy glared at him.

"I wish you had talked to me. You acted as if nothing had happened," Travis said.

"Man, and that's all it was, acting. When you're rejected by your own father that is all you can do. Act." Billy walked to the cell. "Hey, but I pulled it off. I proved to myself that I'm a fighter."

"Billy, it's the peace of God that sustained you." Travis looked at Billy.

"There you go again." Billy walked away from the cell and lay on his bunk. "I'm tired—if you have business with me, let it wait until tomorrow. I'll be here." Billy turned his back on Travis and Darrell.

"I love my son, really I do." Darrell choked back the tears.

"I know you love him," Travis professed.

"Yeah," Darrell shook his head slowly. "But thanks for believing in me," he said, clearing his throat and wiping his tears with the back of his hand.

"Billy will believe in you again someday. The only thing that the both of us can do now is to trust in God and pray."

"I'll do just that," he agreed.

"That's good," Travis replied. He then looked at Billy for a moment. He still loved his best friend. "Oh God, please save him," he whispered.

"Thanks," Darrell said, pushing his hand through the cell bar.

"What's this for?" Travis asked as he grasped Darrell's hand and held it.

"For being a good friend to my son."

"No need for that. Billy is like a brother to me." He affirmed the handshake and discharged Darrell's hand.

"I know son, that's why I want to thank you. Y'all have been a family to him. And, when you talk with Adam and your mother, tell them I said thanks a lot."

"My parents were happy to be there for the both of you." Travis remembered how his father took time from his busy schedule to spend time with Billy and him. Billy had been reluctant at first. Yet, he lowered his armor to enjoy the father and son outings. A broad smile spread across Travis' face as different childhood scenes played in his memory. He made a mental note in his mind to call his parents soon. They had left tons of messages on his answering machine. They must be frustrated with him by now, he thought. "I'll relate your gratitude to them. They'll be happy to hear from you." Travis said, smiling at Darrell.

"I would like to see them. Are they doing well?" Darrell asked.

"Very well. I'll tell them they must come for a visit soon. They'd be thrilled to see you."

* * * * * * * * * *

Adrienne heard the doorbell ring. She opened it and was surprised to see Detective Wright standing on the outside. "What can I do for you, Detective Wright?" she asked, reservedly.

"Mrs. Ray, I hate to bother you, but I must speak with you," he replied.

"I've told you all I know," she said, a little indignant.

"Yes, I'm aware of that, Mrs. Ray. But there's a matter that needs to be cleared up."

"What's that?"

"Do you know a Ms. Janet Wingo?"

"Yes, but what does she have to do with anything?"

"I found out that your husband and Ms. Wingo were on friendly terms."

"Janet and I are friends," she looked impatiently at the detective.

"Mrs. Ray, may I come in, please?" he asked.

"Okay, but only for a minute. I'm packing."

Oh, going somewhere?" he asked, stepping inside.

"Yeah, FYI...I'm going home." She said as she led him to the living room filled with boxes. "What is this about?" she asked, sitting on the sofa. She gestured for him to sit also.

He sat across from her and stated, "Mrs. Ray, I have cause to believe that your husband is innocent."

"You what?" she leaned forward.

"I believe Mr. Ray is innocent."

"My husband is innocent?"

"It looks that way. But we'll know more when the lab results are back."

"My husband, I meant Mr. Ray may be released from jail?" she mumbled.

"If things continue to go in his favor he could be out in no time. I'm going to the DA after I leave here and inform him of my findings."

"Thank you Detective Wright," she smiled.

"I figured you want to hear some good news. But there is another reason why I'm here. It's about Ms. Wingo."

"What about her?" she asked and settled comfortably on the sofa.

"How well did you know her?" he asked.

"I told you Detective Wright, she's my best friend."

"Do you believe your best friend is able to commit a murder?"

"What kind of talk is that? I know her well enough to know that she's not a killer."

"I have a witness who can place Ms. Wingo at the crime scene of Ms. Stone. And I also found enough evidence in Ms. Wingo's home to close this case against your husband."

"I don't believe it," she said.

"Mrs. Ray, your best friend wasn't the woman you thought she was."

"Janet is my best friend and if she knew Sheila I'd have known. She doesn't' have many friends, but the ones she does have I know them. I don't know what you're getting at, but Janet and I don't keep secrets from each other."

"Are you sure?" Detective Wright looked at her concerned. It was sad that this woman who was obviously intelligent but who didn't have the faculty to look beyond her husband's good looks and his charming personality to detect when her best friend was on the move for her husband.

"Yes, I'm sure we have no secrets."

"Well in that case I need to ask you for a favor." Detective Wright added.

"And what's that?" she replied.

"Do you know where I can find Ms. Wingo?" he asked.

"I don't know where she's at."

"Does she have any relatives?"

"Her mother, Ms. Mae Ella lives in Lost Gap, but she doesn't have a clue either."

"May I have her phone number and address, please?" he asked taking out his pen and notepad from his suit jacket's pocket.

She gave him the information and watched as he scribbled it in his notepad and then put it away.

"Thank you, Mrs. Ray," he said, as he pushed himself up from the chair.

"Detective Wright, Janet didn't kill anyone," she said, and rose to her feet.

"We'll let the evidence decide that," he said walking to the front door. "I'll be talking to you soon," he said, as he opened the door and let himself out.

She watched him as he let himself out and she thought about what he had said about Janet and secrets. Janet wouldn't keep anything from her nor would she? Doubts began to rise. No, she wouldn't. Not Janet. The doubts died as quickly as they had risen.

Seconds later she waltzed into the kitchen and poured herself a glass of orange juice. The juice was cold and felt good gliding down the back of her throat. She was thirstier than she had thought. Draining the glass, she set it on the counter and hurried upstairs. She wanted to finish packing before the moving men arrived the following day. She really didn't feel like going back to live with her parents, but she felt as if she didn't have a choice in the situation. An apartment would have been sufficient, but her father wouldn't stand for her to be alone in her condition as he put it. Her parents treated her like a child, even though she had complained to them about it hundreds of times. Her father would always remind her that she would be his little girl forever. She'd have to have a really serious talk with her father the sooner the better.

* * * * * * * * * *

The telephone rang sharply sending a piercing sound through Travis' house, jolting him from his sleep. Reaching out, he grabbed the phone without raising his head from his over-size pillow. "Hello," he said drowsily.

"Travis?" she spoke in a lively tone. "Did I wake you?"

"Adrienne?" he said, sitting up suddenly. He looked at the clock on the nightstand. It was four in the morning. Why was she calling so early? He wondered. "Is everything okay?" he asked. Travis thought about Billy and the shape he was in yesterday when he had called him a traitor and dissolved their partnership and friendship.

"Everything is okay," she sighed and then hesitated, "Have you talked with Detective Wright?" She sounded tired.

"No," he said, raking a hand through his hair.

She inhaled and then exhaled, "Well, I guess you haven't heard."

"Heard what?"

"Detective Wright was here yesterday and he believes Janet has something to do with Sheila's death."

"He what?" he scrambled out of bed.

"Detective Wright is convinced Billy is innocent."

"What else did he say?" he turned on the bedside lamp, grabbing his robe from the foot of the bed.

"He asked me a few questions about Janet."

"Wow!" was all he could say.

"Do you believe it?" she asked holding her breath and waiting for a reply.

"Anything is possible," he answered, finally. "And if he's right about this, it will clear Billy," he paced the floor.

"Good for him," she replied, she didn't know whether to be angry or to be happy for Billy. He could be getting out soon and here she was running home to Daddy.

"I saw him yesterday and I—,"

"How is he," she interjected.

"He's okay, but there is something that you need to know. Billy's father, Darrell is in town."

"His father? How can that be? He told me his father died a year after his mother."

"Believe me, he's very much alive."

"But why would he say his father is dead?"

"It's a long story, and hopefully he'll share it with you one day."

"Travis, you know Billy's story, please tell me why would he deliberately lie about a thing like that?" she didn't bother to hide the frustration in her voice.

"I wished I could Adrienne, but it's not my place to discuss Billy's business with you or anyone else. When the time is right, he'll come clean with you. I know it."

"You know I can't be with him any longer. I just know when I look at him I'll be seeing Sheila."

"That's not true. You love Billy and I really believe he feels the same way about you. You have to give your marriage a second chance. Don't make the mistake by throwing it away. God can heal your relationship with Billy."

"I don't know, Travis. Remember, he doesn't want any children, and I want them. What's the use of God keeping our relationship alive when things are rotten in the baby department?"

"God can move the heart of kings. What is your husband compared to kings of great nations? You have to trust God in this."

"Easier said than done." She uttered.

"It's easier than you think. God loves us and He's concerned about our little problems as much as our big problems."

"That's good to know because He seems so far away from me. And sometimes, I wonder if He cares," she replied.

God is so awesome that His presence covers the whole world. The entire universe."

"I've heard all of that before, Travis."

"Yeah, but have you really heard?"

The question hammered at her until she dismissed it, changing the subject all together. "Oh, Travis do you think she could have done something crazy like that?"

"I have to admit, Detective Wright must have a strong lead, or he wouldn't be wasting his time looking for her."

"I wished she would call."

"I'm going to the jail in a few hours. Would you meet me there?"

"I don't think that's a good idea," she remarked.

"Adrienne, you have to forgive him."

"I've already done that. It's the forgetting I can't do."

"He needs you."

"He was doing great without me. Besides, I'm moving back with my parents today."

"That soon, huh?"

"I think it is best for everyone."

"You two can work it out. I'll call my pastor and schedule a marriage counseling session for you."

"Forget it, it won't work."

"But, but—,'

"Bye Travis," she said, and then she hung up.

* * * * * * * * * *

The sun just began to rise as Detective Wright drove his car onto the curb of Janet's mother's house. He got out of the car and made his way to the front door and knocked on the door. After knocking for a while, Mae Ella opened the door and peeked out. "Ms. Mae Ella Wingo?" he asked as he held up his identification badge.

"Detective Wright?" she asked as she glanced at the badge.

"Yes ma'am," he answered. "I called you yesterday evening," he added.

"Yes, I remember, please come in," she said opening the door for him to come in.

"Thank you, ma'am," he said and followed her inside the house to the den.

"Have a seat while I get you something to drink."

"Don't bother, ma'am," he waved off the suggestion.

"Well, okay," she said, and sat on the love seat beside him.

"Now, what's this 'bout my daughter?" she spoke warmly.

"Ms. Wingo, do you know where I can find your daughter?"

"No, I hadn't heard from her since she left here four or five days ago.'

"So, she was here?" Detective Wright pulled out his notepad and wrote down the information.

"Yes."

"Did she tell you anything?" he asked, looking at her.

"No, she didn't tell me nothing. Maybe you want to tell me what's going on here? Has Janet done something that I should know about?" She became slightly nervous.

"Ms. Wingo, I have reason to believe your daughter murdered Ms. Stone in Silver Rock."

"What?" she leaped to her feet. "That's insane!" she yelled. Mae Ella grew faint, by Detective Wright's words. She couldn't believe what she was hearing. She walked across the room, then turned and looked at him. "No, she wouldn't do anything like that. My baby wouldn't hurt nobody."

"Ms. Wingo, I hate to bring you bad news about your daughter, but I recovered evidence in her home that points to her. I'm afraid she's the one we want for the murder of Sheila Stone."

"Who is that?" Mae Ella asked, as tears begin to run smoothly down her face.

"Ms. Stone was a friend of your daughter, and it seems as if she and your daughter were seeing the same man."

"What man?"

"C'mon, Ms. Wingo, please try to sit down," he spoke calmly.

"I want to know what man, Mr. Wright," she demanded, as she sat back on the love seat.

"Mr. Billy Ray."

"No, see that there is where you're wrong. Billy is Adrienne's husband. My daughter and that child are best friends. My baby won't ever stoop that low and do a thing like that. They are best friends."

"Ms. Wingo," Detective Wright said, and rose to his feet. "Please call me when you hear from your daughter." He gave her one of his cards.

"Detective Wright if Janet did a thing like that she wasn't in her right mind. She couldna' have done the things you're saying. Not my baby!" The tears flowed freely as she repeated, "She couldna' done those things."

"Ms. Wingo, please call me."

"I will," she promised looking up at him.

"I hope I'll be hearing from you soon," he said and walked out of the house, leaving her alone.

* * * * * * * * *

"Adrienne!" Donna's voice trailed through the house. "Yoo-hoo, Adrienne!" she called, walking into the living room and then into the kitchen.

"I'm up here!" Adrienne stood on the upstairs balcony.

"Are you finished packing?" Donna asked, walking back into the living room area and up the stairs.

"Yes, I'm finished."

"Then what are you waiting for? Your father wants you home right away. He doesn't like seeing you unhappy."

"Who said I'm unhappy? She snapped, and then returned to the bedroom.

"No one dear," she answered, standing in the bedroom's doorway. She was startled by Adrienne's outburst of anger.

"Sorry, Mother, I'm a little on the edge today." She sat on the king-size bed and tucked her feet under her.

"That's all right." Donna crossed the room and sat beside her. She looked at the bed and wondered how Billy looked lying in it. The thought of him still excited her, even though he was locked up and may never see daylight again. He still had her heart racing just the same. "How is Billy?" she asked, shyly. "Is he fighting you about the divorce?"

"No, he's not," Adrienne looked tired.

"Maybe he wants it real bad then. Because if I was a man and my wife wanted a divorce, I'll still be raising hell with her." Donna smoothed the mini dress. She liked the way it fit her and complimented her legs.

"Mother, I don't know what to do. One minute I can't stand to be in this house, and the next minute I don't want to leave this place." She glanced around the room.

"Honey, Billy cheated on you, and he killed his lover to cover it up. So, what more do you need to make-up your mind?"

"We can't blame him. Anyone could have killed Sheila." She got off of the bed. "Besides, Detective Wright is now looking for Janet."

"Janet? Why is he looking for her?" Donna looked confused.

"He said he had something on her. She might be his killer." Adrienne said with little satisfaction.

"It can't be true. That sweet child?"

"Sometimes, even sweet people can flip the switch, you know?"

"I guess you're right," Donna said and lay back on the bed, looking at the ceiling fan go round and round. "Does that thing aggravate your sinuses?"

"I don't sleep with it on."

"I thought about putting one in our bedroom." Donna rose from the bed and watched Janet brush her hair in the mirror. "But you know your father? He swears every thing messes with his sinuses." She laughed. "Come to think of it, everything does mess with his sinuses. It drives me crazy."

Adrienne ignored Donna's last statement. As far as she was concerned everything drove her mother crazy.

So, if Janet killed that girl, then Billy would be home soon? Donna's mind raced, focusing on Billy. A smile played at the corners of her mouth. *I'll get another chance to try to reel him into my bed.* The thought made her body quiver all over for wanting him. Picturing herself sharing Billy's bed made her shiver with goose bumps.

"It seems that way," she replied, putting the hairbrush on the dresser. She stepped into the walk-in closet.

"You have to leave before he gets out."

"Why?" she asked from inside the closet.

"Surely, when he gets out you don't want to be here. Trust me." She smiled wickedly.

"Mother, I'll be long gone before he gets out." She envisioned Billy walking through the front door, and being very acceptable of impregnating her.

"Well, if you ask me —,"

"I didn't ask you, Mother," she interjected from inside the closet.

"Anyway, as I was saying your father wants you to hurry home," she glanced at her watch. "Look at the time. Where in the world had it gone?"

"You have plans today?" Adrienne asked.

"I'm picking up your father's prescription." Donna answered while staring at herself in the mirror. She rubbed her hand over her flat stomach, admiring her voluptuous figure.

"Daddy's not feeling well?"

"Yes, he's alright," she turned to get a peek at her backside.

"Then why are you picking up prescription for him?"

"To keep the home fire burning," she laughed softly, turning and facing the mirror, again.

"Do you have to leave right this minute?"

"If I want to make it to the drug store before it closes." She brushed the hair away from her face and added, "I definitely won't go home without those little babies."

"Well, give Daddy my love. Tell him I'll see him later on when the movers get here. If not, I'll see him tomorrow."

"Good, so you are coming home right away. Good for you. Hopefully we'll see you later this evening," Donna said stepping into the closet. "I always said Billy had fine taste," she stood admiring the rows of expensive suits. "The man certainly has style."

"That he does." Adrienne looked around the closet admiring them, too. "Indeed, he does."

"Anyway, I'll see you later, honey," Donna said, blowing her a kiss.

"Okay, Mother," she smiled.

Alone once again, she stood with her back against the wall and slid slowly to the closet floor. What is the matter with me? Billy had hurt her and she wanted nothing else to do with him and his lies. No matter how hard she fought to hold on to the ice around her heart, it was melting. Even the anger that had once consumed her was wasting away. She loved Billy and wanted desperately to live her life with him. But the ecstasy of children danced through her head. She clasped her hands over her face and wept bitterly.

* * * * * * * * * *

Detective Wright walked into his office and his assistant met him with a big grin plastered across his face. "It's back. We got a match. The blood found on Ms. Wingo clothes matched the victim."

"Great! I never doubted it wouldn't match. Now we have to find out where she's hiding." Detective Wright felt good. Now the only thing to do was to sit back and wait for that phone call.

Chapter 33

"*H*i Mama," Janet's voice cracked through the receiver as she lay on her stomach across the unmade bed while staring down at the floor.

"Janet. Baby, where are you? I've been worried sick 'bout you. There was a detective here asking about you." Mae Ella's tone carried a mixture of fear and concern.

"Detective? Why was he asking about me?" Janet fought back the panic in her voice.

"Baby, he said he has reason to believe you killed someone back in Silver Rock."

"What? He's got me mixed up with someone else."

"He thinks you're involved," she said, staring out the living room window. Storm clouds moved rapidly across the sky, as the afternoon light grew darker. She glanced nervously at the clouds. "He found evidence in your house."

"He searched my home? He had no right to be in my house!" Janet snapped. The blood stained clothes flashed before her. She had hidden them at least she thought. Things were happening so fast she couldn't think straight. She had planned to destroy them when everything had blown over, and Billy was convicted for the murder and sitting pretty in prison.

"Baby, come home so I can help you," Mae Ella pleaded.

"Mama, you didn't fall for that, did you? They're a bunch of lies." She couldn't control the panic any longer. "They're lies I tell you! Those people are out to get me! And, you believed that mess? You never once believed anything I told you!"

"Baby I just want you to—"

Janet cut in, "It's true Mama. Remember that time when I told you how my sweater got torn at the high school dance? Did you believe me? No. You swear to this day I let some nappy head boy rip it off of me! You have never trusted me! Now you're taking that detective's side against me!"

"Janet, I'm not taking nobody's side. I want to help you. Can't you see that? I want to help you. And that detective ain't gonna give up looking." She rose to her feet propping the cordless phone between her neck and shoulder.

"He's not going to find me."

"Baby, just listen to yourself," Mae Ella urged. "Janet, if you haven't done anything wrong, then you have nothing to be worried 'bout. Why don't you just come home?"

"Okay, Mama. To prove to you I didn't do anything wrong, I'm coming home," her voice quivered. Mae Ella could hear the nervousness in her daughter's tone. Janet needed help, and she couldn't stand by and watch her destroy herself by running away.

"Wait til' we see what the storm is gonna do. You ain't got no business driving around out there now. It looks like tornado weather." Mae Ella looked out the kitchen window and knew something bad was coming. "Lord, have mercy on us," she said, for a moment forgetting Janet was on the phone line.

"I'll see you in a little while," Janet murmured.

"Huh? Did you say something?" Janet's voice broke the spell over her.

"I'll be home in a little while," she dragged the words out.

"Okay, baby. I'll see you when you get here. Bye."

"Bye Mama," Janet whispered.

Mae Ella pushed the talk button turning the phone off and walked back into the living room. Making her way into her bedroom she picked up the card Detective Wright had given her, and sat on her bed. She dialed his number.

"Detective Wright speaking," he said, answering the phone on its first ring.

"Detective Wright?" she spoke wearily into the mouthpiece.

"Yes," he answered.

"This is Mae Ella. Janet's mother."

"Ms. Wingo, how are you?" Detective Wright asked sincerely.

"I'm not doing too well," she answered.

"Oh, I see," he replied.

"I heard from Janet a few minutes ago."

"She contacted you?"

"Yes. I just finished talkin' with her. She's coming home today."

"Ms. Wingo, I know that making this call had to be the hardest thing you have ever had to do. But I appreciate you doing the right thing. I promise you I will try to help your daughter as much as I can."

"Detective Wright, I love my child, and I hate to think how she's going to be treated 'cause of this." Detective Wright remained silent as she continued to talk, "If my baby did this thing, then I want her to take full responsibility. I didn't raise my daughter to hurt anyone." She couldn't stop the tears from flowing. She wiped them with the back of her hand and added, "Detective Wright, I know that other woman is hurting for her child 'cause I'm hurting for mine. I want to do the right thing. I believe if the shoe were on the other foot, she'd do the same."

"Ms. Wingo, what you're doing is an honorable thing. If only more people were like you."

"I don't feel so honorable right about now. I'm leading my daughter into a trap." She felt terribly guilty.

"Ms. Wingo, trust me, you're doing the right thing, and I'm going to see to it that your daughter gets a fair trial."

"Thank you. I really believe that."

"Thank you, ma'am"

"What about Billy? What's going to happen to him?" she asked.

"After the DA's investigation, he'll probably go free."

"I'm glad for him."

"Yes ma'am."

"Detective Wright, it looks strange, but I am protecting my daughter."

"Yes, I know. Ma'am, you're an amazing woman, and I really mean that."

"Thank you, Detective Wright."

"I'll see you in a little while. And, thanks again."

"Take your time. There's a storm coming."

"Be seeing you, bye for now."

"Okay, bye." She hung up the phone and got up from the bed. Then, she kneeled beside it and prayed. "Lord, You're wonderful, and Your mercy endures throughout all generations. I pray for my daughter, Janet. I pray for peace on her and for all of the people she has hurt. Please, help my baby to understand that I love her. That's why I'm turning her in to Detective Wright. Lord, please help her to understand." She cried as she laid her head on the soft bed, listening to the thunder rumbling through the sky. The lighting flashed, the wind howled and the rain began to beat down upon her home.

Chapter 34

*O*pening Detective Wright's office door, Travis didn't bother to knock as he rushed inside the room. "I need to talk to you," he said angrily, standing at the detective's desk. Detective Wright raised his head, looked at Travis and covered his hand over the phone's mouthpiece. He pointed to a chair near his desk. "I'll be with you in a minute." But Travis blatantly ignored his suggestion and continued standing.

Detective Wright smiled and returned his focus back to the phone conversation. "Yes, sir," Detective Wright said, pressing the phone closer to his ear. I'd need at least two of your deputies to accompany me to the Wingo's home to make an arrest. That's right," he said, looking at his watch. "Un-huh, give me about two hours, and I'll fill you in on the details once I arrive. Thanks, Sheriff, for your help. See you soon," he said, putting the phone back on its cradle. Then he looked at Travis and said, "Mr. Malcolm, I have some good news." He gripped his hands behind his head and lay back in his chair.

"Why didn't anyone bother to inform me about what's going on with my client?" Travis demanded, not hearing a word Detective Wright had said. "I had to find out through his wife."

"Now, calm down for a second," Detective Wright frowned, releasing his hands from behind his head, "I haven't seen you to tell you anything."

"What's this about Wingo?" Travis ignored Detective Wright's last statement.

"All right, calm down. The thing is…we found some evidence in

271

Ms. Wingo's home, enough to bring charges against her."

"Evidence?" Travis raised his brow. "Janet?" He looked puzzled.

"It's all in my report."

"Janet and Sheila, they knew each other?"

"Yeah, they knew each other and they were both seeing the same man. Motive is simple, a jealous girlfriend."

"And do you believe she'd confess to that?" Travis asked.

"Who needs a confession? I've got evidence," he said, and rose to his feet and walked from behind the desk and faced Travis. "Know what I think? I think your partner would be happy to hear some good news. Why don't you run along and tell him?"

Anger flashed across Travis' face and he stood toe to toe with Detective Wright. How dare Wright dismiss him as if he were a child! He opened his mouth to give Detective Wright a piece of his mind, and tell him what he could do with his so called "run along" advice. But the Holy Spirit reminded him of what Pastor Johnson had said about giving in to anger. Travis quickly sent up a prayer in his mind. Lord, help me to stay calm. Please, set a guard over my mouth. Thank You, in Jesus name.

"Okay, Detective, I'll tell Billy the good news," he said calmly. "And, you go and get her."

Detective Wright smiled and placed his hand on Travis' shoulder, leading him to the door. "I'm sorry for that last statement. You had every right to knock my block off, but you proved to be the better man. I'll see you later." He opened the door.

"Yeah, later," Travis said, walking out of the office.

* * * * * * * * * *

"Hey, people!" Travis said, walking inside the cellblock.

"Hey," Darrell said, standing to his feet. "I'm glad you came by. Boy, I tell you I slept like a baby last night. You know, I hadn't slept like that in years. Thanks for that prayer."

"Praise the Lord." Travis smiled, looking from Darrell to Billy. Billy didn't bother to rise from his bunk nor speak. He felt betrayed by his best friend, and he wanted him to feel the sting of that betrayal.

"Hi, man," Travis said, standing at Billy's cell. Billy glared at Travis and then turned his back toward him to face the wall.

"So, you're not speaking to me, huh?" Travis asked.

"I'll speak when I find someone worth speaking to!" Billy's words sliced deep.

"Well, in that case I guess you don't mind my not sharing some important information with you."

"What kind of info?" Billy asked, turning facing Travis.

"It looks as if you might be getting out of here soon."

"What's that?" Billy rose suddenly from his bunk. "What's going on?" He asked, walking toward Travis.

"Detective Wright is bringing in a prime suspect."

"Who?" Billy was confused.

"Someone you and I both know."

"Man, I know a lot of people. C'mon, tell me who?"

"He's bringing in Janet."

"Janet. My Janet? Man, what does she have to do with this?"

"According to Detective Wright, a lot."

"That's good news," Darrell said, grinning from ear to ear.

"Yeah, it's good news, all right," he uttered looking at Billy. He wished things could be the same between them.

"You bet it is!" Billy laughed, excitedly.

"That's only the second bit of good news," Travis responded.

"What?" Billy frowned.

"The real good news is Jesus Christ," he replied, hitting a nerve as Billy shot him an angry look.

"The good news is salvation," he continued to speak, ignoring Billy's anger.

"Man, is it possible that we can have a decent conversation without you bringing God into the picture?" he snapped, rolling his eyes at Travis and Darrell.

"Don't knock anything until you have tried it," Travis responded.

"I tried it once, remember? And like before, I don't need it. What good has it done me?" Billy asked, grinning wickedly. Travis bit the corner of his lower left lip out of habit. Billy's grin deepened. Because he knew this only meant one thing. Travis' confidence was shaken, and he was lost for words.

"You toyed with it like you have toyed with everything and everyone else in your life," Travis replied. The words flowed boldly from his lips. "Believe me, when I say if you had really tried it, we wouldn't be having this conversation, now."

"So, that's it, huh?" Billy asked. "Those days when you disappeared must have been a special time for you. What was it? A holy week?" Billy laughed retreating a few steps backward. "Man, since you been back, that is all I hear, God, God, God! Talk about something else sometimes. Anything besides God." He glared at Travis as he retreated to his bunk. What was Travis' problem, anyway? He thought. The man's young, wealthy and too smart to be weighed down with this holy crap. Religion is for the poor. Everyone knows that. So, why is Travis beating his head against the wall for this God stuff? Billy was astonished. What is it that kept him talking about Jesus? What kept him seeking the unknown and embracing what he could not see? The questions hammered away inside Billy's head.

"That's exactly what it was. A holy retreat." Travis smiled. "I had an experience with God, and I can't begin to express it." Travis said in a joyous tone.

"Good for you," Billy sneered. "But do everyone in here a favor and keep the encounter to yourself." Then, he mildly regretted speaking so harshly to Travis. Maybe he was on to something. Who knows? Billy thought, remembering Edna and her words to him. "Jesus is the answer," she had told him.

"What are you afraid of Billy?" Travis asked.

"Who's afraid?" Billy got to his feet.

"Maybe you are. Maybe you're afraid of God."

"That's silly," he remarked, walking towards the cell bars. "Why should I be afraid of God?"

"That He might change you," Travis replied.

Billy's heart pounded hard. Travis hadn't spoken this boldly to him before. Who was this new creature? He looked and sounded like Travis, but this boldness didn't belong to him. Somehow he had found courage to standup to Billy, and Billy didn't care for this new and improved Travis.

"Do you believe this?" Billy asked Darrell, waiting for a reply, and forgetting the hatred for his father.

"Yeah, I do, Son. You have always bossed him around, and now he's not going to let you do that anymore." Darrell tried to soften his words. He didn't want to lose his son any further.

"Man, what do you know?" Billy scowled. "You don't know anything about me!"

"I know I love you," Darrell whispered loud enough for Billy to hear.

"Stop lying to yourself! What do you know about love?" Billy pointed his finger at Darrell and then waved him off. The last thing he wanted was to listen to his father's lies. "This God stuff has turned you into a freaking nut case. Do you want to know what you sound like? You sound like a fool!" The anger penetrated Billy's body.

"Great!" Travis beamed. "Then, I'm on the right path."

"Man, you are crazy!" Billy shouted, and his entire body shook. He walked away and lay on his bunk, staring at the ceiling.

"Billy, I've prayed that God would help you get out of this mess, if you're really innocent," Travis said, not letting him off that easy. "Do you honestly think things are going in your favor because Detective Wright likes you? If you don't open your eyes and see the hand of God working on your behalf, then you really have some big issues," he said, staring at Billy through the cell bars.

"Yeah, yeah, yeah," Billy responded nonchalantly. "If you say so!"

"I love you, Billy!" Travis abruptly changed the subject. He didn't want to push God on Billy and alienate him further.

"Whatever!" Billy replied, unruffled, and turned his back toward them again.

Travis looked sadly at him and then turned to Darrell. "Listen, I need a little time alone. I'll be back as soon as I hear from Detective Wright. And I'm going to see about getting you out of here."

"Thanks," Darrell smiled. "That would be good."

"Yeah," Travis said. "I'll see you two in a little while."

"We'll be here." Darrell wished he could say more to encourage him, but he was lost for words.

* * * * * * * * * *

The knock echoed through the house. Janet looked horribly at Mae Ella. "Are you expecting someone?" she asked, pushing herself up from the chair.

"Yeah," Mae Ella answered, and she rose to her feet.

"Who?" Janet asked, rubbing her hands together. "Don't let

anyone know I'm here, Mama," she hissed, rushing past her and into Mae Ella's bedroom.

Mae Ella walked slowly to the door, prolonging her steps as much as possible. The knock came again, but this time more firmly and repetitiously.

"Okay, okay, I'm coming," she yelled, stepping up her pace a bit. She inhaled and exhaled, knowing Detective Wright would be standing on the other side. She opened the door.

"Ms. Wingo," Detective Wright addressed Mae Ella warmly.

"Detective Wright," Mae Ella nodded slowly and stepped sideway, letting him in.

Detective Wright and a Silver Rock police officer entered the room, followed by two of Lost Gap's police officers. The officers greeted Mae Ella, and she responded with a half smile and closed the door behind them.

"Thank you again," Detective Wright said, really feeling sorry for her.

"No need to thank me, Detective Wright," she lowered her voice. "I ain't doing this for you. I'm doing it for my baby. She needs help. Lord knows she does."

"She'll get the help she—" Janet entered the room and cut off Detective Wright's sentence.

"What have you done, Mama?" She shouted and glared at Mae Ella baring her teeth. Mae Ella flinched.

The police officers rushed to her. She rolled her eyes at them, and then gave her mother a hatred look.

"Please Janet, forgive me. I'm doing this for your own good!" Mae Ella pleaded, watching her through watery eyes.

"You turned me in, Mama? You turned me in? How could you do this to me! How could you?" She screamed. "I thought you loved me, Mama? I trusted you!"

"I do love you, baby," Mae Ella walked closer to her.

"Don't you come near me!" She screamed.

"Ms. Wingo," Detective Wright spoke loudly getting Janet's attention. "Do you know why we're here?"

"Save it, I know why you're here," Janet looked at him for the first time. "You're here 'cause I killed Sheila." Then she looked at Mae

Ella and frowned. "Yeah, that's right, Mama. I killed her. I killed that little bitch!"

"Stop it!" Mae Ella interjected. "Baby, you don't know what you're saying."

"I know what I'm saying, Mama! I killed her! I killed her because she was messing with Billy. That's right, Mama. Billy loved me until that white heifer tried to take him away from me. She was going to trick him into believing she was having his baby!" She looked at the officers and said, "Do you believe that? But I stopped her! I stopped her from spreading her lies." She looked at her mother again, "Mama, you should have seen all the blood when I hit her with that pipe. Ooh, how she bled," she giggled. "Now, that cunt can't mess with my man anymore 'cause she's dead and Billy is mine!" She screamed like a wild animal, sending chills down Mae Ella's spine.

"No, Janet! You're wrong. Billy ain't your man and he's never gonna be. That man belongs to Adrienne. Billy is Adrienne's husband and not yours." Mae Ella replied, and tears rolled down her face.

"No, Mama! You're wrong! Billy always belonged to me. Even when we were in middle school. He was my lover." Janet laughed. "Mama, we made love all over your house and in your bed," she confessed and rolled her eyes at Mae Ella. But Mae Ella said nothing. "Oh, you don't have anything to say now, huh?" she shouted.

"We just got a confession," Detective Wright informed the officer. "Read Ms. Janet Wingo her rights."

The officer opened the handcuffs and placed them around Janet's wrists. "Ms. Janet Wingo, you have the right to remain silent. If you give up the right to remain silent, anything you say can be and—"

"Lord help me," Mae Ella interjected loudly as her eyes rolled back into her head, blackness enveloped her.

Book Three

Chapter 35

$\mathcal{I}$t had been exactly two months since he had been released from the county jail and good riddance to each of those suckers is what his attitude displayed on the day he walked out a free man. He slid comfortably behind the wheel of his Mercedes and touched the gold necklace with the tip of his fingers. It gave him a genuine, good feeling to have it back in his possession and he continued to stroke the necklace; a familiar sense of control rocked his body leaving him giddy and a little light-headed. He sat quietly rubbing the necklace with more frequency and feeling more in control, his mind sped back to the day when he had first come in contact with it.

Making out all night with Victoria, Travis had come in that particular morning singing, loudly. It wasn't the noise that bothered him, but the meaning of the words that the song carried. 'What can wash away my sin? Nothing but the blood of Jesus.' Hearing those words had awakened something deep inside of him and he quickly pushed Victoria away, and leaped to his feet, and rushed into the other room, yelling at Travis to cut it out or else. That's when Travis began preaching, suggesting the song would do his soul good. His soul, humph, it wasn't Travis' business thinking about his soul. His soul was his soul and he could do whatever he wanted to do with it. And if that meant screwing Victoria and the rest of the gang, so be it. It wasn't anybody's business but his own, and besides, it wasn't hurting anyone.

That day the song haunted him, leaving him feeling depressed. He had to get away, do something, anything. He had to get it out of his head. So, he jumped into his Honda and drove toward the small town that housed the University. Passing all the little shops he drove to the outskirt of town. The sun pierced into his car, dazzling the interior with its sunny rays. He spotted the stone washed building, he had seen it plenty of times, but never stop to investigate it contents. Driving up to the building, he killed the engine and laid his head against the headrest closing his eyes. The words of the song played over and over in his head. Reopening his eyes, he scanned the sign up on the building. Funny he never noticed the sign before. Billy read the sign, 'Lift Your Spirit with the Jewelry of a Lifetime.' He hastily ambled out of the car and strolled inside the building.

He strolled down three glass cases before a short middle-aged man asked could he be of service. There was one necklace that quickly caught his eye. He asked the man to let him see the necklace; he lifted it from its satin black case. Billy rubbed his fingers across its smooth surface. A funny feeling penetrated the tips of his fingers, and moved up to his hand and spread warmly through his body. He closed his hand around the necklace; it felt good in his hand.

At that moment he didn't give a care what Travis thought of him and his soul. The words of the song faded while he held the necklace, reopening and closing his hand around it intensively.

Snapping back to the present he stared at the mirror and quickly looked away realizing he had been sitting there staring at himself. He tucked the necklace safely underneath his tan polo shirt, and roared the engine to life, pressed the accelerator and the car launched forward, kicking up gravel and dust as he went racing out of the park and headed back to town.

Days earlier, he had met with Adrienne's attorney for finalizing their divorce. While locked up in jail, he had agreed to give her a divorce, but now he had second thoughts about it. He had to see her and maybe they could talk. He'd tell her he was ready to have babies with her, but reconsidered the idea as he drove into the Mitchell's subdivision. Making a left on Triple Oaks Lane and another left on Dogwood Circle, he came to Adrienne's parents' street. He turned right onto Cherry Ridge Drive and parked halfway down the street from his in-laws' home. He killed his engine and sat uneasy watching the house. He had every right to be there; after all, she was still his wife for a little while, he told himself. He touched the necklace underneath his shirt and relaxed. He laid his head against the headrest and concentrated on the house.

* * * * * * * * * *

"I missed Mr. Ray," Ms. King said, and then added, "If you ask me, coming to work is not the same, anymore."

"I know that's right." Yareli stated, and dabbed her wet eyes with tissues. "I missed his million dollar smile!"

"We do too," the other secretaries all said at once.

* * * * * * * * * *

The Silver Rock cab pulled up in Billy's driveway and Darrell stepped out. He surveyed his surrounding before handing the cabbie his fare. Luckily, Billy was the only William Ray in the phone book, he thought as he stood outside his son's home, watching the cab drive away. Seeing the cab disappear, he didn't feel so good. He stood perspiring, trembling with fear. But there was no turning back. He had to do what he had come to do. And that was to win his son back. He walked quickly to the front door before he could change his mind. After standing there a few minutes, he forced himself to ring the doorbell. No answer. So he pushed it a second time and a third until finally realizing his son wasn't home.

He walked around to the back of the house and climbed the stairs leading to the second-story deck. Beautiful patio furniture adorned the wide deck, shaded by the tall trees. Darrell sat on a plush cushiony chaise lounge and looked around and smiled. His son definitely had made his way in life. His eyes began to water; he wished he had been there to watch his son grow from an eager little boy to a successful young man.

Darrell lay back and allowed the tears to come; no one was there to see him, anyway. So, he cried and wished he hadn't given up on his son seventeen years ago.

* * * * * * * * * *

Adrienne turned into the Orchard's subdivision without noticing the black Mercedes parked a few yards from her parents' home. She drove ahead mechanically, as she pulled up in the driveway and parked her SUV and turned off the engine. She unbuckled her seatbelt, grabbed her purse, opened the door and slid out of the vehicle. Closing the door, she hit the alarm on the SUV keypad and made her way to the house. Once inside the house she kicked off her shoes, and walked into the family room where she tossed her purse on the sofa and dropped on the divan. What a morning it had been! She recalled her meeting with her lawyer. Billy had given her his home.

Billy's heart pounded wildly as he watched Adrienne get out of the SUV and strolled into the house. He watched her intently. He wanted to see her for one last time. She had been the last piece of the puzzle that fit his trail of success. Funny, Travis had called her the trophy in his showcase of trophies. Too bad our marriage didn't work. She probably still wants plenty of babies, he thought. And after their divorce is finalized, she could find a man who will meet her wishes and produce a house full. Picturing Adrienne with another man who would happily make her a mother filled his mind. The scene was bothersome and somewhat amusing. Better some other man than me, he thought and composed himself behind the steering wheel. He turned the ignition and fired up the engine.

He drove slowly past the Mitchell's home and made a U turn then left the subdivision for the last time. He had come to the conclusion the farther he was away from Silver Rock, the better for everyone. He had found a small apartment in Locust Grove, south of Silver Rock. The town was small but beautiful and a good place for someone like him to make a new start. He drove to Interstate 75 South and got on the freeway and drove another hour or so before exiting off.

The place was fascinating and breathtaking as he passed all the small shops neatly lined up in a row on one side of the street. Railroad tracks set across from the stores. He drove until he found the small duplex he was looking for. It wasn't much to look at but at least it would serve its purpose. He could stay low-keyed for a while.

Pulling his car up on the duplex's driveway he turned it off, and then got out. He opened the trunk and took out two large luggage. Carrying the luggage in both hands he stepped on the porch, and set them down, and unlocked the door to his new apartment.

"You must be our new neighbor?" A young woman asked, walking out of her door with dyed-blonde braids and blacken hair roots.

"Yes. I'm Billy...Billy Ray," he added looking at the woman and tried hard not to stare at her head.

"The name is Florence, but everybody calls me Flo," she smiled showing crooked white teeth.

"Nice to meet you, Flo," he said, picking up his luggage and turning away from her, hinting that their conversation was over. He kicked the door open with his foot.

She ignored him and pushed farther, "Where are you from?"

"Silver Rock," he answered, walking inside the duplex. She followed him inside.

"Silver Rock. Hey, that's a nice place. What'cha doing here, then? Shuck, a little hick town like this ain't the right place for someone coming out of Silver Rock." She sat on the sofa uninvited.

"It's a long story," he said watching her and wondered if all the people in town were anything like her. He set his luggage down.

"Mama," a little girl cried, standing in Billy's doorway.

"C'mon in here, Donna Lisa," Flo said and rose to her feet. "This here is my daughter, Donna Lisa."

"I figured that," he smiled at Donna Lisa. "Please excuse me, but I have to finish getting some bags out of the car." He said walking back out the door. Billy didn't want to be rude, but she was really pushing it.

"I can help," she said, grabbing Donna Lisa's hand and following him outside.

"That's okay," he quickly added, walking toward his car.

"That sho' is a nice ride," she said. "You gonna have to take me and Donna Lisa for a ride one day. I never rode in a Mercedes before."

"As you see I'm quite busy and—"

"Donna Lisa likes your car, too. Don't you, baby?" Flo interjected and kissed Donna Lisa's puffy cheek. Billy cleared his throat and was about to reply, but was cut off again by her, "Yes that sure is a pretty car, indeed," she chuckled. "You ain't hungry, are you? 'Cause Donna Lisa and I have plenty of food on the stove. Just come over and help yourself."

"No, but thank you anyway. I'm going to relax for awhile and then look at some papers I need to work on." Why was he explaining to her what he was about to do? It wasn't any concern to her what he did and did not do.

"You a contractor or something?" she asked releasing Donna Lisa's hand.

"I'm an attorney."

"A lawyer? What? You hear that Donna Lisa, we got us a lawyer living right next door." Flo said, with a big grin plastered across her face.

"Well, I hate to break off this conversation, but I'll be seeing you around," he added and walked past her and Donna Lisa.

"Okay, I'll be seeing you then. But if you get hungry like I said, I have plenty of food on the stove. Nice meeting you."

"The same here," he lied.

C'mon, Donna Lisa, let's go. Flo and Donna Lisa disappeared into their apartment.

He sighed and walked back inside his duplex and closed the door.

* * * * * * * * * *

Awaking from a deep sleep, Darrell rose from the lounge and looked around the deck and wondered where he was. Then it all came back to him. He was at his son's home. He went to the door and knocked, and there was still no answer. He walked back to the lounge and stretched out on it again. The sun was starting to settle down over the horizon. It'd be night soon. He looked up toward the sky and daydreamed that he and Billy were a family. A warm smile appeared at the corners of his mouth.

* * * * * * * * * *

"He gave you his home?" Donna asked and then frowned. "What's his motive?"

"Now, you're sounding like my attorney," she replied. "He thinks Billy gave me the house to win me back. And like I told my attorney, that'd be the day."

"A wise lawyer," Donna uttered.

"I think it wonderful," Eddie exclaimed. "Something good did come out of all of this, after all."

"Yeah, after he done embarrassed all of us," Donna said sarcastically.

"Now, honey let's don't go through that again. You know

how upset Adrienne gets when you talk about that."

"It's okay, Daddy," she assured him. "I have cried all the tears I'm going to cry. Anyway, I'm numb from all the pain."

"So, where is he planning to live?" Donna asked.

"My attorney said he's moving out of town," she answered, looking off into the distance.

"Out of town!" Eddie arched his brow.

"Where?" Donna asked.

"He didn't tell me, and I didn't ask, Mother."

"Good Lord, the man is leaving town. That's taking it a little too far, don't you agree?" Eddie asked Adrienne.

"I don't want to talk about it," she snapped and marched out of the room.

"Humph! What's wrong with her?" Donna became incensed by Adrienne's angry outburst.

"She's tired and she has been through a lot, lately," Eddie said, defending his daughter.

"Haven't we all?" Donna proclaimed angrily and stormed out of the room. He watched his wife disappear from his sight before following her.

* * * * * * * * *

The sun had set and it was well past eight o clock, the small town had shutdown for the night. Only two of the five service stations were still open. Evidence of big developers had taken over the city as new subdivisions sprouted up along the highway. Locust Grove, like Silver Rock, was a gold mine and everybody from all walks of life sought the town and the riches it had to give. Billy was glad he had chosen the town. He'd start over and become the most influential attorney Locust Grove has ever seen.

He glanced at the speed odometer and slowed the car down. The last thing he needed was a ticket, he thought and closed both hands around the steering wheel and stared into the distance as his mind turned over the events that had taken several weeks of his life.

Detective Wright wasn't a bad person once you got to know him. He had bent over backwards to prove my innocence, and I thanked him for making my case a personal one.

Trophy in a showcase. The words penetrated his thoughts. If she was only a trophy, then why did his heart feel like it would break in pieces? This was a new experience for him and it hurt. In the past, he would be the one who left them hurting...the heartbreaker. So, who was this new creature that possessed him now? His heart ached terribly. He needed to talk to someone. There wasn't anyone, he had walked out on Travis, law firm and all. Who needed a religious fanatic for a friend? He did, he thought. Who was he kidding? He missed Travis. He remembered the vow he had made with him. A vow of blood brothers. Their blood mixed together made them a family.

Another small ache started in his heart and grew into anger as he remembered the night Darrel had beaten him. But Travis was there for him and felt as badly as he had. He remembered the bad times and the good times. The good times outweighed the bad because he could always count on Travis no matter what.

He sped the car on down the highway; darkness surrounded his view as his mind focused on Janet and Sheila. How could he have been so careless? He was a counselor for God's sake. The questions jabbed away at him. The memory of Sheila's death would forever be etched in his mind. He gripped the steering wheel harder until his hands began to ache and he dared not let up. If only he could have been there to stop Janet. The episode has cost him his best friend and partner, his wife and now it threatened to rob him of his sanity. He stared straight ahead into the night.

Then, suddenly out of no where in the middle of the highway two large eyes peered at him, looking fearfully into the headlights. The deer stood blind and helpless in the path of Billy's car. Billy quickly slammed on the brakes, missing the animal only by inches as it leaped and trotted off the highway and into the woods. The Mercedes violently lurched forward and skidded to the side of the road and landed on a small patch of grass. Billy, aghast, caught his breath and peered out into the darkness to scan the small area surrounding his car. Then he examined himself for any injuries, and afterward he opened the door and jumped out leaving the door open wide. Realizing he could have been killed or badly injured, his knees buckled from under him, and he leaned against his car for support, closing his eyes. He touched the necklace.

He kept his hand on to the car to study himself while he walked around it, looking for any damages. Minutes later, he got back into his car, fired up the engine and maneuvered himself back onto the highway. A few feet in front of him there was a side road and a sign that read 'Life Rd'. A strange name for a road, he thought and wondered where it would lead. He turned onto it. The road led to a small churchyard filled with cars. His first impulse was to turn his car around and get far away from there. Instead he pulled up in the yard, killed the engine, and got out.

What am I doing? he thought, walking toward the church entrance. He could hear music coming from inside the small brick building. Back away and run, his mind screamed. But his feet had a mind of their own as he climbed the church steps. The church's door suddenly opened and a slender middle-age man smiled and grabbed his hand and pumped it freely welcoming him to Life Church. Billy forced a smile and followed the man inside.

"My name is Bob," he said, walking inside the entrance of the sanctuary.

"Ah, Billy," he said looking at Bob for a moment, and then looking at the other people inside watching him with warm friendly smiles as he and Bob walked down the aisle. Then, Bob stepped aside and allowed Billy to ease into the third pew then he sat beside him.

The preacher shouted, "God is a just, compassionate, loving God and full of mercy. He's our heavenly Father and He will never let us down. He's not anything like our earthly fathers who have, and who will sometimes let us down. For He has adopted us as sons and as daughters into His family through the blood of Jesus!" he shouted as he swept his handkerchief over his sweaty face. Billy sat erect and attentive, hearing and watching every move the preacher made until his voice faded more and more into the background of his mind.

He saw his own father letting him down and not really loving him the way he should have been loved. A father who showered all of his love on Mattie. He chose her over him and the old pain resurfaced, joining with the new. Pain that was deeply hidden inside of him. Pain that he vowed that he would never know again. So, why was he feeling this old hurt, now? Would his heart never stop breaking?

Jesus is the answer. What are you afraid of? Afraid God is going to save you and mess up your life? What can wash away your sins? Nothing but the blood of Jesus. Billy clutched both hands to the sides of his face and hunched forward in his seat.

"What's wrong?" Bob asked, leaning toward him.

Billy opened his eyes and looked around the church and people were staring at him. He looked at Bob and a single tear rolled down the corner of his eye. What's this? He thought, wiping the tear with the palm of his hand.

"It's okay," Bob whispered.

"No, it's not okay," he replied, embarrassed by it all. "I'm a man and men don't have emotions." He tried to sound convincing but he could hear the quake in his voice. Any minute now he was going to break down and cry. He knew it.

"It's okay for a man to cry," Bob explained.

"Not for me," Billy growled and pushed himself up from the pew. "I have to leave here," he said pushing past Bob. Bob jumped up and followed him out of the church.

The last thing Billy heard the preacher say as he was walking out of the sanctuary, "Don't run from your heavenly Father, but run to Him. For God so loved the world that He gave His only begotten Son that whosoever believe in Him shall not perish, but have everlasting life."

Once back in the night air, Billy rubbed the necklace. He didn't see Bob until he had placed his hand on his shoulder. "Listen," Bob said, "I don't know you, but I believe God told me to tell you that everything your mother said about Him is true. And when your father walked out on you, God didn't leave you but He watched over you, keeping you safe until the day you would accept him as your heavenly Father. God said do not put your trust in man-made things because they are useless. Your necklace is useless; it's only metal made by the hand of man. Then Bob said, 'I have called you,' said the Lord, 'do not be afraid. I'm the Lord God who created you. I call you by name because you belong to Me. When you went through deep waters and great trouble I was with you,' said the Lord. 'But listen now my servant, the Lord who made you and helps you say do not be afraid. For I have chosen you, do not fear. I will give you abundant water to quench your thirst and to moisten your parched fields. I will pour out my Spirit and My blessing on your children. They will thrive like watered grass, like willows on a riverbank.'

It was all Billy could bear as he collapsed into Bob's arms and tears ran heavily down his handsome face and he weakly asked, "What must I do?"

"Acknowledge that you are a sinner and ask God to forgive you of your sins, and confess with your mouth and believe in your heart that Jesus Christ is Lord. He died for your sins and on the third day he rose again, and now he sits at the right hand of God. Do you believe this and is this what you want?" Bob asked holding onto him.

"Yes, I believe, and yes this is what I want," Billy admitted, between tears. And Bob led him in the prayer of salvation and baptized him in the power of the Holy Ghost.

Billy felt every strain, every tension leave him, and a peace like one he never knew washed over him, consuming him totally. Bob held Billy for a few more minutes before freeing his arm from around him.

"I don't know what to say," Billy admitted.

"Just praise the Lord," Bob replied, smiling happily that God had saved another one of His children from the pits of hell.

"Praise the Lord," Billy said, and found the very same words that he once couldn't use roll freely from his mouth. Billy promised Bob he would visit the church again after they had said their good-byes.

An hour later, he got back on Interstate 75 and drove to Silver Rock. He had to see Adrienne and asked for her forgiveness. Maybe she'd grant it and give their marriage a second chance. And he'd find Travis and resume their partnership and their friendship. Then there's his father. He'd have to find him, too, and develop a relationship between them. He would try hard with the old man. Finally, he drove into the town of Silver Rock and then to the Mitchell's home.

He turned off the car and sat for a minute or two, looking at the house. He opened the car door and got out. He closed the door quietly behind him and reached for the gold necklace. He jerked it from around his neck and walked to the Mitchell's garbage can sitting at the curb, opened it, and threw the necklace inside. A heavy burden lifted from him. He looked at the necklace lying at the bottom of the garbage can and added, "I won't need you anymore. I've found someone greater and His name is Jesus." He closed the lid back over the garbage can, feeling refreshed as he marched up to the Mitchell's front door and rung the doorbell.

Donna opened the door and sneered, "What are you doing here?" she asked, eyeing him suspiciously.

"I want to see my wife," he answered.

"She doesn't want to see you," she said bitterly, and then added, "How dare you do that to us. You could have gotten any woman in your bed. But no you had to pick Adrienne's best friend." Donna shot him an angry look.

"Listen, mother-in-law, cool it," he muttered underneath his breath. He didn't want to fight with her. He just wanted to see Adrienne.

"How dare you to speak to me that way," she snapped, lowering her voice. "With all the problems you caused my daughter, and hitting the sack with Janet. Now that's low even for you!"

"Would it have been better if I had hit the sack with her mother instead of her best friend?" he asked. The words hit hard causing her to flinch, and he smiled and added, "It wasn't so bad when you were coming on to me all those years, was it? Do you want to know the reason why I didn't bother? Because, dear mother-in-law, believe it or not, even I have standards. Besides, you didn't turn me on." His words of rejection sank into her heart and the effect of them crept onto her face.

Silence fell over them, and awkwardly, Donna feeling defeated, forced a smile and stepped aside-letting Billy in.

"Have a seat in the living room, and I'll get Adrienne." Donna said, disappearing leaving Billy in the foyer alone. He strolled into the living room and sat on the sofa.

"Billy," Adrienne said standing in the living room's doorway.

"Adrienne," he said and rose to his feet.

"What are you doing here?" she asked, seeming confused and made no attempt to enter the room.

"I'm here to see you," he walked towards her.

"We have nothing to say to each other." Adrienne crossed her arms over her chest. "You made that clear when you were messing around. Especially, when you messed with Janet. How could you have done that to me?" She glared at him.

"I'm sorry," he said.

"Is that all you have to say? I'm sorry?" She frowned and gestured with her hands angrily.

"No, that's not all I have to say, Adrienne. Please, let's sit down and talk?" Billy pleaded. She rolled her eyes toward the ceiling and reluctantly gave in. She walked inside the room and sat in a chair. He sat on the sofa across from her, and for the first time he realized how much he truly loved her.

"Talk," she said coolly.

Jesus, I don't really know how to pray, but if you can find it in Your heart, please help me. This is one case I don't want to lose.

After a moment, he said, "First, I want to say, how awful I feel about hurting you. I know what I say won't erase the pain, but I'm asking you to find it in your heart to forgive me. I deeply regret hurting you and I wish I could take it all back. I've been selfish and foolish, and I have no excuse for my actions. I take the blame for what I did. And for that I'm truly, truly sorry and I do love you. Women, money and power blinded me. I needed women so I could control them, money so I could feel good about myself, and I needed power so I wouldn't have to take rejection or crap from anyone. Baby, I'm the first to admit, I screwed-up. You know it's funny," he laughed softly. "I used to get so upset with Travis because he believed in Jesus and all of that religion stuff. And tonight I realized I wasn't angry with him for his belief, but I was angry with myself for not believing. Deep down inside of me the words Travis spoke about Jesus connected with something in me. I couldn't explain it then, but now I understand it." He looked closely at her. "Tonight, I found Jesus and women, money, and power don't matter to me anymore. I don't want those things. I want you. Adrienne, for the first time in my life I'm in love. God had done this for me. Tonight, He allowed me to love Him. And now I want a chance to really *love* you." Then tears formed beneath his eyelids and they rolled down his face and he allowed them to come as he cupped his hands over his face humbling himself before God and his wife.

Strong compassion swept through her and she rushed to his side, lifting his hands from his face, she sat beside him and held his hands in hers. "I love you too, Billy. I have never stopped loving you," she kissed his hands.

He looked at her and said, "Adrienne, I want us to have a family."

"We will," she said kissing him now through her own tears. "Oh, Billy, if Jesus can turn you around, I want Him, too, and I want our children to know Him."

"Yeah, they're going to know Him. Thank you, Adrienne," he whispered, returning her kiss.

"I love you and I do forgive you," she replied. "Please, show me what must I do to be saved?"

"Let's call Travis, he knows what to do," he replied happily, as he had never been in his life. He unfastened his cell phone from the clip and dialed Travis' number.

"My mother was right," he said looking at Adrienne.

"Your mother?" she smiled.

"Yes, my mother, Edna. She told me once, 'Jesus is the answer.' And she was right," he said kissing her again. "Hey, Travis, it's me, Billy."

"So He answered and said to me: This is the word of the Lord to Zerubbabel: 'Not by might nor by power, but by My Spirit says the Lord of hosts.'"
Zechariah 4:6

Acknowledgments

First, I want to thank my Lord and Savior, Jesus Christ for gifting me with creative ideas and writing skills to do what I do.

I would like to thank my husband Michael for all of his support in my professional and personal life. He took on my chores and household responsibilities while I sat in my basement office and wrote this book.

I want to say "thank you" to my two daughters, Nicole and Danielle, who pushed me to finish writing this book.

To my loving mother who instilled Christ's love in me. She always told us to "always trust in the Lord because the Lord will make a way out of no way." Speaking of us, I want to thank my sisters and brothers who have spoiled and supported me since childhood. I would name them all but I do not have enough space to do so.

I'd like to give a grateful and sincere thank you to my spiritual mother and father, Pastors Bobby and Marye Smith, for their encouraging and prophetic word over my life and to my wonderful family at WOPW church.

I would like to send a special thank you to my other spiritual father and mother, Pastor Woodrow and Minister Francine Walker. They encouraged me in my walk with God. And special thanks to my family at ALC church.

I would also like to thank Minister Ruby Pugh, who believed in the gifts and talent God has given me.

A special thanks to all of my uncles, aunts, and cousins for their support and to all of my in-laws for their support.

And a super thanks to all of my readers.

I hope you all enjoy reading this novel as much as I have enjoyed writing it. May God bless each and every one of you. "Thanks!"

Discussion Questions

- What is the significance of the title in regards to the content of the novel?
- Did Billy commit adultery while he was married to Adrienne? What examples in the book demonstrate his adulterous acts?
- In your opinion, can adultery be forgiven in a marriage? Can unfaithfulness be forgiven in a non-marital relationship?
- Talk about the strengths and weaknesses of Billy Ray, Travis Malcolm, Adrienne Mitchell, Darrel Ray, and Janet Wingo.
- If you could create a different alternate ending, what would it be?
- What role does God play in each of the main character's lives?
- Discuss the symbolism behind Billy's necklace. Do you think this was an idol for Billy?
- What does the Bible say about marriage?
- What does the Bible way about adultery?
- What does the Bible say about sex outside of marriage?
- What does the Bible say about forgiveness?
- Is forgiveness an act of kindness or a moral requirement?